ENTANGLED WITH THE ENDUAR

TO DEFEND A BRIDE

Ra'Sa and Melisa's Standalone

DANIELA A. MERA

Western Continent
Iravida Ruins
Enduvida
Sisterhood's Enclave
Shvathemar

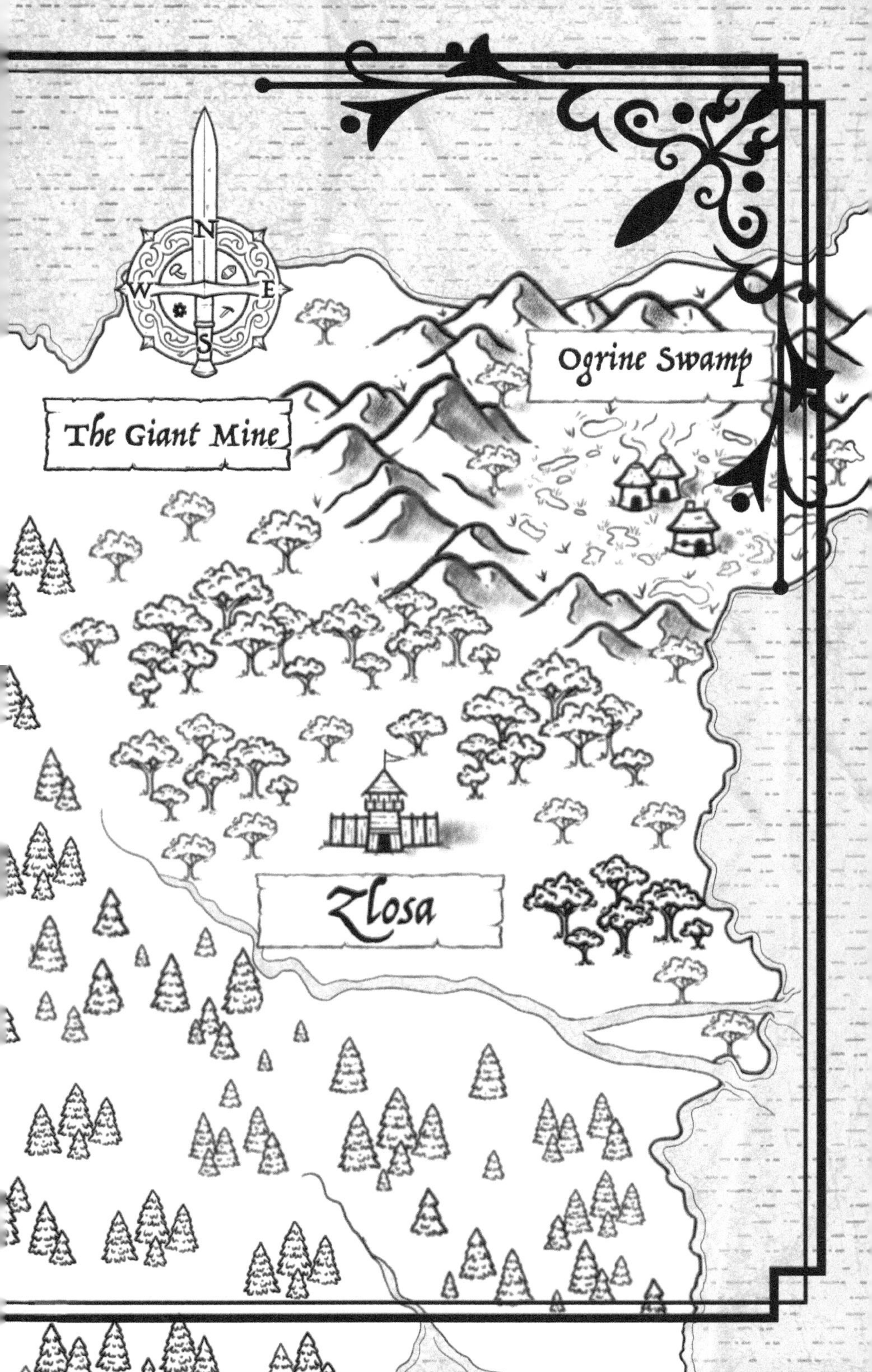
N
W
E
S
Ogrine Swamp
The Giant Mine
Zlosa

COPYRIGHT

First ebook edition October 2024

Book Cover Design by Artscandre
Book couple art by Agnieszka Gromulska @aseriaart on IG
Map by Daniela A. Mera
Book Artwork by Daniela A. Mera
Edited by Sydney Hunt
Proofread by Chelsea Barton

ASIN (ebook): B0CVR38Z33
ISBN (paperback): 978-1-960343-23-9
ISBN (hardback): 978-1-960343-25-3

SUGGESTED READING ORDER

Entangled with the Enduar is a series of interconnected stories. Some are duets, others are standalones. While you do not have to read in this order, it is recommended for maximum enjoyment. (Note that not all books are out yet. Enjoy this sneak preview!)

Teo and Estela's Duet (Completed)

1. To Steal a Bride

2. To Ignite a Flame

Ra'Sa and Melisa's Standalone (Completed)

3. To Defend a Bride

Arlet and Vann's Duet (2025)

5. To Beguile a Bride

6. To Enchant a Stone

Niht and Abi's Standalone (Spring 2026)

7. To Charm a Bride

Ulla and Thorne's Duet (2026)

8. To Trade a Bride

9. To Burn a King

Joso and Selena's Standalone (Summer 2027)

10. To Tame a Bride

Paoli and Si'Kirin's Duet (Fall 2027)

11. To Bewitch a Bride

12. To Bleed a God

PRONUNCIATION GUIDE AND LIST OF TERMS

Ceremonies

Grutaliah Bondyr (grew-tah-lee-ah bon-deer)—Mating Ceremony

Dual'moraan (do-al-more-ahn)—First Cut

Hlumrynna (hu-loom-ree-nah)—Parting Ceremony

Hlums'dor (hu-LOOMS-dore)—Travel blessing

Enduar Words:

Enduar (en-doo-are)—knowledgeable ones

Ruh'duar (ruh-doo-are)—cave-born Enduares

Hlum-scri (hu-loom-scree)—magical cards

Mihk daourn (meek dow-oor-n)—I love you

Pater (pah-ter) —Father

Mater (mah-ter)—Mother

Fihlius (fill-ee-oos)

Elvish Words:

Bláth (bl-OGH)—warm

Vaimpír (vahm-peer)—vampire *heh* (also know to the Enduares as "cold ones")

Creatures:

Cave rat - **Ruc'rad** (ruck-rad)

Cave bear - **Ruh'Glumdlor** (ruh glum-dl-ore)

Cave bat - **Ruc'ciel** (ruck-cee-el)

Crystal wraith - **Glacialmara** (glass-ee-al-mar-ah)

Glow spiders - **Aradhlum** (ah-rahd-loom)

Glow wyrms - **Wyrmhlum** (worm-loom)

Characters

GODS

Grutabela—*grew-TAH-bell-ah*

Endu—*EN-doo*
Doros—*DOOR-ose*
Nicnevin—*NIC-neh-ven*
Yde—*EE-dee*
Khuohr—*KOR*
Abhartach—OW-er-tagh

HUMANS
Estela-*es-TEL-ah*
Mikal—*Meek-AHL*
Arlet—*ARE-let*
Aitana—*ah-EE-tah-na*
Abi—*Ah-bee*
Paoli—*Pow-lee*
Melisa—*Meh-lee-sah*
Luiz—*Loo-ees*
Selena—seh-LEN-ah
Carolina—*ca-row-lee-nah*
Salma—sahl-mah
Isaraya—*ee-sah-ray-ah*

ENDUARES
Teo/Ma'Teo—*TAY-oh/mah TAY-oh*
Vann—*Van*
Liana—*LEE-an-ah*
Svanna—*sv-AH-nah*
Ulla—*OO-lah*
Iryth—*EE-rith*
Neela—*NEE-lah*
Ra'Salore—*Rah-sah-lore-eh*
Fira—*FEE-rah*
Joso—*JAW-sow*
Lothar—*LOW-thar*
Thasinia—THAS-in-EE-ah

Dyrn—*D-URN*
Velen—*VEH-lehn*
Tirin—*TEE-reen*
Niht—*night*
Faol—*fa-OHL*
Keio—*Kay-oh*
Rila—*Ree-lah*
Adra—*ad-RAH*
Urira—*oo-RYE-ah*
Si'Kirin—*sih-KEE-reen*
Ner'Feon—*ner-fey-own*
Ka'Prinn—*KAH-prin*

GIANTS
Rholker—*ROLL-ker*
Uvog—*OO-vog*
Fektir—*FEK-teer*
Marej—*mah-RESH*
Eneko—*EN-eh-co*
Hibsej—HIB-sedge
Relmos—REL-mos
Urdort—UHR-dohrt
Veklor—*VEK-lore*

ELVES
Mrath—*Mu-rah-th*
Arion—*AH-r-eye-own*
Thorne—*th-OR-n*
Ayla Daecaryn—*AY-la day-CARE-n*
Elanila—*EE-lah-nill-ah*
Farryn—*FARE-en*
Glyni—GLIH-*nee*
Lusha—*LOO-sha*
Taenya—*TAYN-ya*

WELCOME BACK TO ENDUVIDA!

Dear reader, there are many things to be said, but know that the most important of all is 'thank you.'

For those who have been with me since book one of this series, my TSABby readers, thank you for giving me the strength to finish this book.

Before we begin, I would like to set the stage with two very important points. This book can be read by itself, but it will contain spoilers for a prior duology, *To Steal a Bride* and *To Ignite a Flame.* Reading Teo and Estela's duet may make certain events in *To Defend a Bride* be more meaningful for readers.

Next, while this book is a monster romantasy about true love and overcoming the challenges of life, this book also contains serious mature content like:

- Mentions of sexual assault
- Rape
- Sexual harassment
- Forced sex work and slavery

- Slut shaming
- Mentions of traumatic childbirth
- Death
- Blood/gore
- Self harm
- Decapitation/death
- Emotional abuse
- Mentions of child abuse/neglect
- Anxiety/panic attacks
- Strong language

For on-page instances of rape, I have included in-book warnings. If you would prefer to skip the entire chapters, please do not read:

1. The prologue
2. Chapter 22
3. Chapter 36

Please take care of yourself, and remember that no book is worth your mental health and wellbeing. If you have been the victim of any of the above and have not yet recieved help, let this be your sign. You are strong. You are fierce. You are capable.

Con mucho amor,

Daniela

To everyone who didn't need to be saved, but really wished someone had done it anyway.

A Note from the Scholar's Wife

This note was found magically tacked to a weathered, slightly gray, piece of paper on Antonio Castillas's desk:

Toño,

I know you are close to unlocking the mysteries of the Enduar Reign, but found this behind your desk while cleaning. It's probably my favorite of your findings. It's half wrinkled, but I think that we should frame this one over the journal entry you sent out last week.

Con amor,

Carmen

The aforementioned poem:

In the shadows deep, where I did roam,
I was a man out of place, lost in my home.
The under mountain, cold and dim,
Left me lonely—a stranger within.

But when I set forth, far from the stone,
On a mission I hated, with her I was thrown.
In the world beyond the dark,
like a miracle, change did spark.

In my heart did bloom
a glowing cave flower, dispelling gloom.
Then small, unsure hands came into view
and my resolve softened like the sky turned from black to blue.

No longer lost, no longer lone,
With them, I've found a new life
and place to call my own.

PROLOGUE

MELISA

NOTE: This entire chapter contains a serious trigger warning.

Nearly Five Years Ago…

"I'll tell you what I tell all the first-timers. Run, and we'll tie you down."

The giant walks out of the small hut and leaves me on the icy table. Whoever arranged these godsforsaken rooms should've had the good sense to put down a bedding pad.

After Seranya died, I'd put this off as long as I could. I'd starved myself to ensure I never bled, and when drops of crimson spotted the threadbare fabric wrapped around my loins, I hid it.

Some people aren't meant to be mothers.

It's my mother's voice that echoes in my mind now. She'd made two things very clear: she hated having me, and she was sure I'd do a worse job than her.

Just didn't have the instincts.

The fur covering the hut's entrance is pushed back. I look up to see the slave entering. The man, whom I've never seen before, wears a makeshift robe crafted from the same vegetable-dyed cloth that was used to make my simple shift.

Seranya once told me that the two best parts of the breeding pens were being clean and wearing fresh clothes, but I've thus far been underwhelmed.

Once the fur flap closes, I see the man's face more clearly. He's middle-aged, and deep wrinkles are etched next to his down-turned mouth. Dark, wet hair hangs in his mahogany-black eyes.

Though the reddish undertone of his brown skin is warm, his expression is anything but. He's displeased with what he sees.

A familiar tightening in my chest starts. What could I have done in the last ten seconds that would have him so vexed?

I'm lying on the table just like the healer showed me. I've removed my undergarments and spread my hair around my head in a 'pleasing manner.' The man strides over, and his acrid sweat sours the air.

Did they just send him from the lumber yards?

"My name is Melisa," I choke out.

He doesn't respond as he reaches toward the bowl of oil. My cheeks burn in shame.

"Should we—" I clear my throat. "Can I at least know your name before we start?"

He unties the band at his midsection with his non-oiled fingers, still ignoring me, and the fabric falls open. Coarse, black hair is scattered along his chest and in a line from his navel all the way down to…

I swallow.

"Please. Your name?" I try again.

"Quiet." He lets out an exasperated sigh. "You are my third today, and I'm getting tired."

The admission hangs in the air as he begins to stroke himself. Watching causes invisible needles to prick my neck.

I look away, toward the exit, aware that they didn't make good on the promises to tie me down. I could try to run, but it takes a surprisingly short amount of time for him to prepare.

He pushes back my simple dress, exposing me fully to the air, and inserts himself unceremoniously.

It *hurts,* and I gasp.

"Fuck," he says. "This is your first year?"

Heat crawls all across my skin as I nod.

"You're a little old to just be starting."

"I'm twenty-three years old," I bite back, feeling his member stretch and tear my insides.

He lets out a satisfied sound, and I bit back my disgust. I'd been told that the act of breeding was mostly pleasurable for the man, but the evidence of such things was painful.

Was this what it was supposed to be like?

The sensation of movement deep within makes me grit my teeth. If I could be like the beasts that shed their fur after winter and shed both him and this memory, I would.

"Are you just going to lay there?" he finally asks, moving his hips backward.

My nerves mount, wrapping a band around my chest. It steals all of my breath and makes the pain worse.

Can't breathe. Can't move. Can't escape.

Looking frantically around the room, I wonder just how I am supposed to do anything with him pinning me down to this table.

He makes a frustrated noise, so I jerk my hips up. A groan slips out of him, and I freeze.

Gathering strength, I choke on another breath and do it again. It elicits the same reaction.

I choke back a sob when a fresh wave of pain radiates through my hips. Biting my lip, I look at the wooden ceiling above me. I try to pretend I am tending to the cattle or walking the forests.

I'd helped with animal husbandry, so I knew how this worked, but gods, it's so much worse than I'd imagined.

Animals are drawn to each other by their very natures. This is… this is hell.

We continue like that for a few more minutes, and then he grunts and pulls out.

Something wet and sticky slides across my thigh, and my eyes unfocus.

"That was… Well, just stay like that for a while. I'll see you again tomorrow." His hand strokes my inner thigh, and the intimacy makes bile rise up my throat.

Now, it's my turn to remain silent. I study the rotting wood above me, memorizing each knot and beam. As I do, one of those cursed tears slips out of my eye and down my temple.

Growing up, I'd fancied dozens of people. Both the boys flexing their muscles in the river, and the girls with pretty round faces and silky long hair.

As I grew, I'd wanted men—I'd wanted women—but denied myself both because I'd never wanted *this*.

When someone else plucks the strings of your life, you cannot avoid the bitter notes of their song. For the giants, we are animals. Devoid of sophisticated wants and passions.

Left to tables over beds.

The man who just rutted me haunts the back of my eyelids, and his voice sounds in my ears.

I'll see you tomorrow.

I grit my teeth, wincing.

"Not fucking likely," I whisper, forcing myself to open my eyes and look for something sharp. The examination instruments are nearby. Even though the man told me to stay on the table, I slide off. My bare feet pad against the pounded earth. I pick up a tool with the pointed edge.

I'd seen the inside of both animals and humans. I know that if I cut myself near my womb, they won't let me continue.

Pulling up my dress, I expose my lower belly and try to ignore the seed slipping down my legs. Except, it's not just seed.

It's blood.

The sight of red makes my pulse race. I can't stay here.

I can't do this.

I take the tool to my belly and slice. A sharp, searing pain rips across me, and I let out a sob.

The sound is loud enough to have one of the slaves waiting outside barge in. When she sees me, she doesn't even look surprised.

She makes an aggravated sound and grabs the tool from my hand, restraining me. The pain is radiating up my front, and I can hardly breathe. Blood is leaking down the front of my body.

"*Healer*!" she calls, and then the same giant who sent me in here enters.

He frowns and shakes his head.

"I knew we should've tied this one down," he grumbles, pushing me back onto the bed. The rope bites and scratches as I'm restrained.

He takes an agonizingly long amount of time inspecting the wound. Prodding at it. Stretching it back.

More tears stream down my face.

I'm never going to fucking cry again.

Then he grabs a needle and starts to sew my flesh together. I want to scream, to sob into the flat table beneath me. But something hardens and says, *no*.

I remain still, letting the tears crust on my cheeks.

"Will she be well enough to continue tomorrow?" another voice says—someone else who has come to watch the show.

"No. The cut is too deep," the healer responds.

Good. Now, I can only hope I don't get pregnant.

PART I

CHAPTER 1
MELISA

Present Day…

I hide in the safety of the tightly packed trees with thirty-two women—all human slaves. A few, like me, are comfort women. The rest have been taken from the breeding pens.

It's the night of the new Giant King's coronation, yet we aren't anywhere near the palace. We've come to escape the giant capital, Zlosa.

It's not going well.

"What's this?" a giant calls from the open meadow right next to the fence that keeps us all locked in. He stands with several warriors. Enormous, battle-honed conquerors, more akin to mountains than men.

They are strapped with leather armor and spears. Hair is piled high atop their head. Battle scars are on clear display across bulging chest and arm muscles.

One human is free from the cover of the trees. A queen, she calls herself, though I knew her as the High King Rholker's prisoner.

Estela of the humans and Enduares.

She's small, hardly coming up to my chin in height, but her shoulders are squared, and her back is straight despite the cold.

Though she is nothing more than a valley compared to the mountainous warriors, she glares up at them without fear. The hood of her cloak is blown back and curly brown hair escapes braids to billow in the night breeze.

She named herself our own personal hero.

I watch, holding my breath and expecting the worst. Many fancy themselves heroes, and most aren't worth their weight in lumber. People who believe themselves in a certain light—good, noble—aren't willing to do what it takes to make a difference.

"You are mistaken. The doctor sent us into the woods to search for herbs," she calls out into the inky black air. A white cloud billows in front of her. It is a normal sight in winter, but it looks like magic spilling out of her soul. "There's an outbreak of disease."

The corners of my mouth tug upward.

She's lying with such ease—perhaps not a perfect hero, after all. Just a woman doing what it takes to get out of this hell hole in one piece.

I respect that.

The giants kidnapped her over a month ago, and the new king himself assigned me to care for her. I helped her bathe, mended her clothes, and dressed her.

Slowly, we became… not *friends*. Allies, perhaps. So much so that I let her convince me to try to escape Zlosa. A death wish for any slave in ordinary conditions, but the promise of the trolls presents extraordinary circumstances.

I'm skeptical by nature, but I found her passionate confidence contagious. The way she spoke about the home of the

Trolls—Enduvida—sounded like just what I was looking for: a safe new life.

I need a new life. Fast. In a place where they don't care what I did with the giants. The promises of no slavery and men in search of women to care for were just bonuses.

"Disgusting lying, bitches. Step back," the giant calls.

I fucking hate them.

Another gust of wind almost blows back the cloak covering the costume Estela wears, which would expose her as the king's escaped pet.

A frenetic energy pulses through the air as I watch Estela. She seems as fearless as any wild animal.

"Wait!" Estela cries.

The giant warrior extends his spear and parts the black cloak that was meant to cover Estela's ridiculous diamond costume, which makes her look like a godsdamned snow pixie.

The giant's eyes gleam with surprise. He's found something very valuable indeed, and now we're all going to pay the price with blood.

"You belong to the king!" the giant roars. "Men! Find and kill the others. They're trying to escape!"

"*Maldita sea, hijo de su puta madre,*"[1] I curse in the human tongue—a rarity for me.

My stomach drops, and I look back at the other slaves.

"Stay in the trees! You'll be harder to catch," I yell.

We've barely begun to scatter when Abi, another comfort woman I'd personally invited on this death mission, screams. The space before us lights up. Bright white flashes, striking quick as lightning and making me temporarily blind. I fall against a tree.

A wet gurgle sounds from the front of the trees. When the light dims, I see the giant lying on the ground with an arrow sticking out of his neck.

My mouth falls open, and I press my hand to my mouth to silence my scream.

Several more arrows fly through the air and lodge themselves in the ground with an audible *thud*. Abi's scream is joined by nearly every woman in the group.

"Are those more giants?" a new woman shouts.

I turn back. "What giant would kill one of its own?"

The woman doesn't listen, running toward the fence that would lead us to freedom. I grab my skirt and run after her.

"Wait!" I yell, but she still ignores me.

Dodging branches, I use my hands to grab onto tree trunks and propel me forward. When I reach the spot where the copse of trees thins, I draw a deep breath.

"Please! Don't—!" I start.

One of the giant's axes swings through the air. Time slows as I watch the blade slice through her clothes, flesh, and bone as if it were nothing.

Nothing.

The bottom half of her falls to the ground, and the top half topples soon after.

There's more screaming behind me, but I fall to my knees and retch. The sparse contents of my stomach scatter in the snow.

Damn Estela, and damn my secretly optimistic heart for believing her.

We'll all die before we even meet the monstrous race that Estela claims has saved her. I need to get back to Eneko. There are girls depending on me in the slave pens. I can't die like this.

I turn back to Abi. "Get them to safety!"

She's stopped screaming, but her round, curvy face is ashy, and tears streak her cheeks. Her ample chest heaves as she looks at me with wide eyes.

"I can't—"

"You can." I take her soft, half-frozen arms in my hands, willing her to feel the confidence she doesn't have.

Her already wide eyes seem to bulge out of her sockets.

When I turn back and look up, my words evaporate like mist under the blazing sun.

Charging down the hillside, atop all manner of beasts and strange, flying creatures, is a troop of warriors. The beings I've been waiting for have skin as blue as the daylit sky, while dozens of women have different shades of fleshy tones, from black to white.

Trolls... and elves?

There are nearly as many of them as there are of us. Definitely enough to fight off the giants while we escape. It turns out Estela wasn't quite as delusional as I started to think.

Women start to gather on either side of me.

"The blue demons?" someone asks.

I turn my head and find Estela fighting off a whole godsdamned giant herself.

The beginning of a smile tugs at the corners of my mouth.

Thank you for being right, you crazy bitch.

"They sure are," I say.

Which means… the rest of my plan will have to come next. If those tall, strong blue men are really so dedicated to their women as Estela has said, then I need to pick one. And fast.

It's not hard to tell which troll has come for Estela, because he charges straight to her while she fights the giants. His blue eyes shine, brilliant, and dazzling.

Is that magic? Or bloodlust?

My gaze is drawn to the next rider who races toward us. He is tall, just like the king, and gods…

Look at those arms.

They flex as he holds onto the reins of a serpentine beast made entirely of glittering crystal.

He beckons toward us, and I start ushering the women out of the trees.

When his flying stone-like serpent comes to a halt before us, he calls, "Get on!"

I grab the nearest woman and shove her forward. He plucks her out of my arms and moves her to the elf at his flank. More women pass from his mount to the elves riding bears, enormous wolves, and deer.

We repeat this several times until only two of us are left in the forest. My mind races.

Two humans for two riders. One troll, and one elf.

Glancing over my shoulder, I see the woman has almost caught up to me. She reaches out, and I see my chance at safety flash before my eyes. So I leap forward and leave the other woman to climb onto the bear with the elf.

He catches me with ease, looking down and meeting my eyes.

In that instant, while chaos surrounds us, I know I've found what I sought.

Estela thought I was escaping Zlosa for the chance to find a mate—my 'perfect half.' It is not a husband I seek, but a safe future. If this troll is a kinder and more attractive master than Eneko was, all the better.

When the troll pulls me up in front of him, his large body cradles mine, and the sensation of invincibility settles over my skin. I allow myself to lean back. The smell of leather, incense, and stone overtakes me.

Gods. He definitely will be the one.

A noble man can be manipulated just as easily as a hedonistic one.

I slide my hand around his arm and feel the reaction behind me as he tenses. He needs to feel needed in order to get protective, so I spare a whimper.

It works.

"You are going to be all right now," he murmurs.

The sound of his voice sends a shiver down my spine. It's got a light accent that brings out the deep, rich tones of the common tongue.

A feeling deep in my gut that has always guided me begins to spread and take over. This is *right.*

"Thank you," I say to him, a touch more pathetic than I feel.

One of the giants hurls into our path. The hulking troll man carrying me is unfazed. He reaches out his arm, and the ground beneath us groans as earthen chunks fling out from under the snow.

A pointed rod of stone forms before my eyes. He conjures something akin to a sword with swirling, sharpened rocks. He then rams the giant clear through.

I scream and press against him.

"Don't look," he says, as I hear the crunch of bone. His large hand comes to cover my back.

I lean into him.

This is exactly what I was hoping for.

1. Damn you, you son of a bitch.

CHAPTER 2
RA'SA

Snow covers the world around us as we travel away from Zlosa. The sun has just begun to set along the horizon, and it's the first time I've felt like I can breathe all day.

The overworld is a torturous place, and I hadn't intended on ever spending so much time outside of the mountains. However, I had been personally chosen by King Teo to help him rescue his mate—our new human queen: Estela.

I had anticipated our bringing home a handful of humans… but thirty-four?

Enduvida is going to be a madhouse.

After I've helped set up camp, I slink away from the bustling movement. The humans whisper to each other, and the elves laugh around the fire that they now build.

It's all a strange, unwelcome assault on my senses. Trees line the area, and I lean against one, thinking.

I've never seen so many humans in one place. They're flighty and look around like lost *ruh'glumdlor* cubs, moving between tents, huddling together, and avoiding my gaze.

I never had a problem with the old custom of stealing them and helping them escape their giant masters. But when we stole Estela, I saw them as a curse on our people. Unnecessary risks.

My younger brother Tirin was a hunter, like our late father. The unmasked joy on his face when we learned that Enduares could mate with humans was almost endearing. For a full week, he spoke of nothing else.

"You can find a wife, and we can have a family again," he'd told me over and over.

He'd hung around corners, looking at the redheaded one who lives in our caves. He watched the queen with rapt attention, even before she accepted the charge to lead us.

And then he went and sacrificed his life for the humans.

For the chance for me to have a family in the future.

I loathe their presence, and to some extent, them. And yet… we need them—I need one to carry on my family line.

Arms crossed and frowning, I watch the human women whose cause my brother died for. A bitter flavor coats my tongue. They don't even know who he was.

I take in dirty black hair and too-thin bodies. I watch the swell of pregnant bellies, feeling a strange churning in my gut.

Until now, I've mostly just worked to corral the women to safety. They are all cut and bruised after evacuating from Zlosa.

They aren't unattractive—for *humans*—but none catch my eye.

When Teo found his mate, he sensed her across space and time. She had barely entered Enduvida, and she had no crystal when their mating song started.

Now that I stand on the sideline, I wait for the same thing to happen.

And yet, all is quiet.

I feel nothing.

Frustrated, I shift my position on the tree. I must feel something—*anything*.

I think of my father telling us the story of choosing my mother. When he saw her, he'd known even before the mating song started.

Perhaps it will be more like the rising of the sun on the horizon rather than a lightning bolt sent to strike me down.

The women continue to move slowly, sluggishly. Their human features are too soft. They are too weak. If they were Enduar women, they would be doing *something*. Helping with the cooking, the tending, or guarding our camps.

Perhaps it is for the best that I don't sing for one of these starving women, just as I never sang for any of the Enduar women.

I've always been too silent, too serious. Especially after the volcano. Once, I'd tried courting Neela only for her to laugh in my face.

And now even Neela's mated to a human.

My lips curl.

When I see two elves carrying a heavy pack filled with leather tents, I push off the tree to help them. Unease filters through my limbs as I walk closer and grab onto the pack.

One grins at me with her strange, sharp teeth.

"Not all of you are useless then," she says teasingly.

I ignore the elf and keep walking—she can go back to the two dozen sisters she brought with her.

After putting down the woven pack, something red moves in the corner of my eye. It's a stark contrast to the blues, greens, browns, and blinding whites.

It's the woman I carried back from Zlosa.

I stiffen as I take in her long, raven-black hair and smooth golden-brown skin. They've given her a dark cloak to cover the red dress, but it fails to cover the way her hips, soft belly, and rear curve.

My head tilts to the side as a new emotion tightens my shoulders.

"My, you are so strong," she says—not to me, though her feminine voice caresses my ear. She grins up at Niht, her hands on his biceps as he helps her off a *glacialmara*.

My fingers twitch as Niht leans in to say something to her, sliding his hand to her shoulder.

Before I know it, I walk toward them.

When I get close enough, Niht stops what he was saying, and they both turn to look at me.

The woman's smile fades, and I feel her reaction like a blow to my stomach. I am not a friendly person. I do not smile as the other men do.

"Niht," I say, still looking at the woman. "I think Teo was looking for you."

The smile returns to her face tenfold, and it's like my heart has turned into a flint. Something strikes against it, sparking glowing embers to warm my chest.

"But I—" Niht starts.

The mysterious woman in red brushes her hand over Niht's arm again, clearly still looking at me, and says, "Thank you so much for your help, Niht. I'm sure I'll see you later."

More satisfaction floods my body. The cavernous hole inside of me has only grown wider with each death of my people, but now, standing here, it shrinks.

Just a little.

Niht lets out a sigh and walks away.

Alone with the beauty, I get a closer look at the way her hair complements her pretty, oval face. The cold air makes her high cheekbones turn a rich, rosy color. A few jewels hang from her ears and around her neck. My eyes drop to her full red lips, which are still pulled back into a smile around her white, straight teeth.

I wait.

My back tenses.

No song.

I resist the urge to turn and walk away.

"My name is Melisa," she says, breaking the silence. "Thank you for carrying me last night."

Excellent, now I have to speak to her. I grimace.

"Ra'Salore," I say back.

She raises one perfectly arched eyebrow. "Your name is longer than the others."

My lips press together, and my fists tighten.

"We all used to have longer names like mine," I say, annoyed at yet another reminder how far my people have fallen.

Her head tilts to the side, and deep brown eyes, the color of dark mead, gleam in the firelight. The flecks of golden sparks near her irises are a world within themselves.

"And why are you the only one now?" she asks casually.

"I find the old ways appealing."

"Does that include eating humans?" she says with a laugh.

Her mirth makes heat spread up my neck. Though she may be beautiful—again, *for a human*—she's rude. She'd turn me down just like the others.

"That was never true. We don't eat other races."

The pretty laughter stops, and some of her easy kindness fades. Good.

"So I've heard." She reaches out and straightens the top of my leather armor.

I freeze under her touch, having never made much contact with a woman who wasn't a healer or my mother.

"Ra'Salore is charming, but I think I will call you… Ra'Sa," she says as her hand slides from my collar to my arm and lingers.

I stare down at her, emotions building and compacting like the layers of rock beneath our feet.

"That's not my name," I say and step back.

She grins and peruses my form. Her smile grows wider, and those molten eyes sparkle.

"No, but I think it fits you well. Do you have a wife?"

I frown and shake my head once.

"No?" She bats her lashes. "I'm shocked. There's no woman in your life at all?"

Is she mocking me?

"I care for my mother," I grit out.

She looks surprised and then smiles.

That's all it takes for me to straighten my shoulders, stretching the tightness, and leave. Might as well follow after Niht and find a task.

Finding King Teo near one of the supply bags doesn't take long. His mouth is turned down as he surveys all of us. Already, I can sense a speech coming on. He will be particular about the humans.

What do I care? There is nothing there for me.

“My King,” I say. “Do you need anything?”

My leader looks up at me with wild, haunted eyes.

He frowns. “What was that?”

“How can I help?”

“Oh. Hmm.” He sighs. “Could you keep watch tonight?”

I nod. “Understood.”

He’s not finished.

“Gods. It’s all just so awful.”

King Teo rakes a hand over his face, smearing a bit of soot over one of his cheeks.

Conflicting emotions war within me. On the one hand, he’s my king. He thinks of his people, and he’s the entire reason that any of us have survived this long in any semblance of a home.

On the other hand, he can be a real bastard.

He can be impulsive. Authoritative. Not to mention the insufferable favoritism he shows Lord Vann. He doesn’t realize the sway he has over others, particularly the way he was able to influence my brother.

Sure, he never asked Tirin to give up his life. But Tirin trusted him. Looked up to him.

King Teo turns back to me. “What do you think?”

I take a deep breath. “I think we did the right thing by bringing them with us.”

He nods thoughtfully.

“I hope you know how grateful I am for all you’ve done. I know you didn’t want to come,” he adds.

I chew on my lip. "I'd better go eat something and find a spot to watch the woods for the night."

He looks like he wants to say something else but thinks better of it and lets me walk away.

As I make my way through the other humans, Enduares, and Elves, someone tries to stop me. When I catch a glimpse of Niht, I freeze.

"Friend," he starts.

I yank my arm out of his grasp. "What do you want, old man?"

"Ho, peace. You are irritated. I see that now." He straightens and continues, "The woman you were speaking with—"

"What about her?" I snarl, still feeling the painful pricks of rejection, of knowing that our goddess never favors me to have a mate.

"That is one of the comfort women we've brought back. Queen Estela explained to me that she belonged to one of the giant lords."

I frown. What a vile, disgusting practice.

"Has your song begun?" he asks. "Is that why you watch her?"

Must he pour salt water over this wound? I grit my teeth and then shake my head once, eager to leave.

"Then I just want to warn you to be… careful with your expectations. She is open with me as well. It could be her nature to act interested."

Irritation builds under my skin. "Niht, we are not friends. Do not concern yourself with my *expectations*."

The old man dares to look upset, and I start to walk again.

"Ra'Salore," he starts.

I turn back and point a finger at him. “I don’t want her. We did not sing for each other. Leave me be.”

My gaze turns back to the fire where the female slaves congregate. Melisa sits with the others, combing through their hair. Her tresses are unbound, same as the other humans.

Enduares keep their hair braided and bound, only letting the strands free in front of family as children or as mates when they are grown.

I should look away from the slightly erotic scene.

The humans don’t share my customs. The raven-haired one probably doesn’t even know what this means for someone like me. But my heart stirs, and my fingers ache to braid her locks.

My eyes widen in horror. Such a strong reaction for someone I haven’t sung for. It shouldn’t happen. She’s small. Weak.

And yet, I give my Fuegorra a few more moments near the group to ensure my mate is nowhere in sight.

The silence cuts deep.

CHAPTER 3
MELISA

"We'll reach the caves tonight," one of the elves, Glyni, leans over and says. She's pretty—really stunning—with long blond hair and labor-hardened muscles. She's been friendly enough as we walk, chattering about knife skils and gossiping about people I don't know.

It's a talent of mine to appear interested in anything.

"Are you planning on coming with us?" I say with a smile, conspiratorially bumping her shoulder with mine.

She grins. "I am. A certain azure creature promised me a spot in his bed."

I laugh, and she starts to chatter about just how blue certain parts of Niht are.

Apparently, incredibly blue—like cornflowers in the elven forest. And long. Thick, like some other type of flower she doesn't bother translating into the common tongue. Not to mention capable of reaching places that could make a woman weep.

None of that matters to me. Comfort women have very few things they get to keep for themselves. When I started working for my master Eneko, I was in pain.

Pain turned to shame. Shame bred anger, making it impossible to do my duty—which meant no food. I had to temper all feelings, at least a little, so I made a rule: no orgasms. Cutting out another intense emotion helped keep my life… well, not uncomplicated, but *less* complicated.

If I wanted pleasure, I would give it to myself. I was better at it anyway.

I let Glyni go on, occasionally humming my approval and discretely scanning the group for Ra'Sa. He is the tallest of the Enduares, after the king, so it only takes me a few moments to spot him in the crowd. The strikingly handsome features make my heart beat just a little faster.

"You know, they told us to be gentle with you humans. But you're a robust thing. We'd take you back to the enclave where my people dwell if you'd like," the elf says.

A smile tugs at the corner of my mouth, causing my wind-chapped lips to crack. Two small faces appear in my thoughts. Girls back in the slave pens who depend on me.

"That's kind. But I'm afraid I came for what the human queen offered me," I say slowly.

"And what was that?"

"Safety," I say without hesitation. "Freedom. A future."

Glyni nods thoughtfully.

"I hear they're mostly men. So if you truly want to stay in those caves, I recommend you get yourself bedded and wedded before more slaves inevitably are brought back," she says.

"Rest assured, I'm working hard to do just that."

"Have any caught your eye?"

Ra'Sa.

"I'm considering my options."

Lies. It was decided when Ra'Sa swept me onto that strange, crystal snake.

"Regardless," I start. "It shouldn't take long. They are all so —"

"Intense. Yes, you get used to it. All of that attention will be focused on your sheath in no time," she says.

I press my lips together to hold back another smile. "Sheath?" I've heard a woman's sex called many things, but never anything relating to weaponry.

Glyni bites her lip, also trying to contain her mirth. She gives me a brisk nod.

"Well then, besides being long and girthy, I suppose I should ask if the Enduar *swords* are very sharp?" I tease.

Her feline eyes flick to me, green irises shining in the mid-morning light.

"They're made of the finest steel I've ever wielded."

"And should I be oiling my sheath regularly to ensure a comfortable home for the blade?"

Glyni breaks first. Secretive laughter bubbles up between us again.

Abi, another comfort woman, appears at our side. She's short, but she's a sturdy thing. Her heaving breasts wobble under the cloak as she huffs.

"What scandalous things are you whispering about now?" she says with a smile.

I throw my arm around her shoulders.

Back in Zlosa, five comfort women allied with each other. We got each other supplies, helped with hazards of the trade, and gossiped while laundering our masters' clothes.

Abi joined the group a year ago when Juan picked her. She had a rough start. If there's one thing people hate more than comfort women, it's a human foreman like Juan.

And yet, she was strong despite what the other slaves put her through. I also like her curious edge. She's genuine and open. Life in Zlosa never took away the hopes she had for a perfect life.

She was drawn to me early on because I listened to her.

Being a comfort woman is more than just laying on your back. It's about inspiring a certain air of, well, *comfort*. Around me, secrets can flow more freely. People are uninhibited from being their true selves. The trick is letting people show you who they are without returning the favor.

"We're speaking of men," I say at last, smiling. "And finding a new home in Enduvida."

"I already have a home, and it's far away from this miserable cold," Glyni says suddenly. "I just enjoy a good rut."

Abi sighs dreamily and gazes off in the direction I was just looking in.

Ra'Sa.

A part of me tenses. If she's set her eye on the troll, that could complicate things.

"I can't wait to set foot in Enduvida," Abi says.

"Do you have a little husband picked out?" Glyni says, laughing.

Abi shakes her head. "No, but I have hope."

I relax a little. Too many women invested in the same man creates issues. It's not that I don't want the other women to be safe; it's just that I want that, too.

My head swivels back, and I look at Ra'Sa once more. I know that there are more men back at the caves. But, if there's anything I've learned in the last six years, it's that I can't trade current opportunities for future ones.

I think Ra'Sa is interested in me. Thrice, I've caught him staring at me from the shadows.

He is strong, quiet, and respectful. He will do just fine. I just have to hope the nonsense with the crystals they keep mentioning doesn't ruin that.

I keep my eyes fixed on his face for a second too long when he looks directly at me. My cheeks heat, and Glyni's words echo in my mind.

All that intensity. Focused on my core.

A shiver runs up my spine. It's almost like we are back on that snake-like crystal steed for a second. I feel his phantom hand cover me, and the raging storm inside me quiets.

My core throbs.

Fuck. I think I… *want* the tall blue monster.

No, no, no, no.

I blink again, swallowing hard, trying to ease myself out of the emotion. In the last three years, I have never once let myself fall apart in front of one of the men I'm servicing.

Now is not the time to start.

Casting him a slow smile, I slow my pace until I find myself standing beside him. The look he casts me is slightly unsure.

Poor thing. He has no idea what I have in store for him.

"Ra'Sa," I say brightly.

He looks down at me, confused. It catches me off guard, and I miss the stone in the path. I let out a soft sound when I trip, and his hand reaches up and rests at the small of my back.

His hand is gentle and sizeable, but not grotesque like the palms of the giants. He's large enough to make me feel small, but not so large as to hurt.

I grin and tell myself to get a grip.

"Melisa," he grumbles after a moment.

"You left early this morning," I say.

He frowns. "Help was needed while packing up the camp."

His hand moves and brushes one strand of my hair off my shoulder. I keep a tight rein on my stuttering breath.

"I was hoping you and I would travel together again today," I say, eyeing one of the beasts they call crystal wraiths we rode yesterday.

He straightens. "We gave the *glacialmaras* we had to the pregnant humans. And one for the king and his queen."

I lean into him as I speak, so my shoulder brushes the bottom of his arm. "So chivalrous."

He pauses, then looks down at me. "Are you well? You stumble often."

Something shrivels inside of me. "I'm fine."

His hand reaches out and steadies my back once more. "Niht is nearby. I'm sure he wouldn't mind carrying you."

"I might just do that," I say roughly.

But Niht and Glyni are definitely sneaking every chance they get, and hell if I will be the uncomfortable third party with no desire to participate.

There are no other men besides Ra'Sa. Perhaps I'm rushing this, but I won't settle for an old or weak Enduar.

So, even though my cheeks heat and my heart pounds, I don't leave Ra'Sa's side.

We walk an hour, mostly in silence. I only occasionally glance at Ra'Sa. He isn't unpleasant to look at, for a nonhuman. It's as if he was hewn out of the raw earth and sculpted by a master craftsman.

When he meets Wren and Thea, will he be a monster or a friend in their eyes?

"You told me you care for your mother. I think that's lovely. What's her name?"

"Mer'Leuel."

"Very pretty."

No response.

"Are you looking for a wife among us humans?" I ask, trying to get him talking.

He shoots me a seething look and then ignores me.

I take a deep breath. There's only one thing he seems capable of responding to. So I swallow my pride and trip again.

"Melisa, you are not well. Let me seek out Niht—"

"But you are right here," I say coyly.

He lets out a long breath and slips his arms around my waist. Nothing quite compares to the way the softness of my body meets the hard lines of his. A small flame stokes itself at the bottom of my belly, and I press my legs together, uncomfortable.

"Thank you," I say.

He doesn't respond.

As more hours pass, I continue studying him, and he moves silently. I purse my lips, thinking about the best way to seduce him.

When I finally hook him, will he want kisses or for me to trail my hands over his groin and act impressed at the size?

Shortly after being taken as a comfort woman, I was grouped with a dozen other slaves for training. We were all given half a dozen paintings sewn together. They showed twenty-four sexual positions. We memorize them all before being given back to the men.

Some are more appealing than others, but for some reason, almost all of them seem interesting when applying Ra'Sa to the equation.

We follow behind all the men and women, missing most of the views when night falls around us. The evening is gentle, though, with the vast open sky twinkling with silver stars.

I've never been anywhere other than Zlosa. It's sad to miss seeing whatever bits of the world lurk in the inky blackness. But then, we crest another hill, and I ask Ra'Sa to put me down.

When I look at what awaits us, I gasp. I don't mean for it to happen, but I've never seen anything like… this.

Beneath us are two glaciers with a narrow passageway in between. Spell lights are bobbing above a thick blanket of fog that dances over the glassy, blue ice, reaching up toward us like floating waves.

For a second, something akin to fear grips me, despite the men and women disappearing into the cloud hovering near the ground. I stop on the road abruptly.

"Melisa?" It's the first thing he's said since he started carrying me here.

I don't respond immediately, transfixed by the landscape.

I take one step forward. "Sorry. It's just a little terrifying."

He smiles gently. Barely a twitch of his mouth, but it makes me feel better.

"It's also beautiful," I blurt out.

"It is," he says slowly.

When I look back up, he's not looking at the misty clouds kissing the massive ice formations. He's looking at me with his eyebrows knit together. He looks away quickly; all confusion fades until it's like it never existed.

I turn away and start walking, feeling pleased.

He follows.

My lungs slowly remember how to breathe as we move through the passage. Soon, I almost enjoy the thick, frosted air. It is salty. My mind wanders as it combines with the sounds of the ocean outside the ice chunks. The creaks and groans of ice floes help me settle back into reality.

It isn't until we emerge on the other side that I hear shouting and find three elves holding all the humans back. The clash of metal against bone is sharp and unmistakable, as is the screech that fills the air. When I reach for Ra'Sa this time, he stiffens.

"You don't like to see blood," he says, putting his arms around me again.

"No," I murmur. I tell myself that I stay in his arms because men need to feel like they can care for their women. The fact that he happens to be right here is of little consequence.

It doesn't take long for the hunters and warriors to clean up the situation and for us to be ushered on our way. At last, I see Estela near the front. She speaks with the men who saunter over from slaughtering the awful, gray-skinned beings.

"I should go help," Ra'Sa murmurs.

I look up at him and nod. "All right."

He hesitates. "Are you… well?"

"Well enough," I say.

I continue walking when another one of the trolls catches my eye and sends me a smile. I return it, then push further into the group.

He's not as big as Ra'Sa.

Abi and another friend, Paoli, join me. They excitedly speak with their hands . I just barely catch the signed words, *"hay mas hombres."*[1]

Paoli is tall and lithe, with sleek black hair and slanted eyes. Her tongue had been cut out years before, and, like Abi, she has a scar stretching across her face. It's a cruel reminder of the life before, not unlike the scars etched into my arms.

When Paoli joined our laundry group, she and Abi became fast friends—true friends—despite their differences in disposition.

Abi is sparkling wine. Paoli is aged whisky.

I look away from the women as Estela, another woman who called me friend, steps forward.

"How is everyone?" the queen calls in the human tongue.

Some of us respond weakly, others loudly, but we all gaze beyond her to the gleaming golden door leading into the mountain. Shockingly red veins swirl around the doorway, like swathes of red fabric stored within the mountain's stone.

"We're going to enter now. Though most will be sleeping, some may still come to greet us. Remember, you need not speak with anyone you don't wish to. They will be curious, not aggressive. And I will be there the entire time."

I huff a short laugh. She looks at the women as if they are less eager than their expressions. I don't see a single face that isn't at least a little excited.

Not for the first time, Estela truly looks like a queen—prim and proper and full of firm reassurance. It's not bad. I just don't know if it's necessary.

I let her have her moment as the men move about. When we start walking again, there's a palpable energy in the air—a sweet vibration that starts in the ground and moves through my boots. We fall into a line, and the hunters stand behind us, casting uneasy glances at the shadowy forest to the right.

I take a sharp breath when we approach the cave's entrance.

A thick smell of damp stone and soft sulphuric fumes hits me square in the face. A faint, rhythmic pumping sound also pounds in the back of my skull.

It's a peculiar place, to be sure, but I smile. Estela had once described golden carvings and large crystals. We haven't seen the crystals yet, but gold lines the hallways as we move down into the city.

I lose sight of Ra'Sa just as Estela stops halfway down the tunnel. She continues greeting and ushering us, but there's a hollow look to her face. When I pass by her, I take her hand.

"Well done," I murmur, drawing her out of her intense focus.

She pauses and looks at me with a broken sort of smile. She urges me forward as her mate, the king, nods at me and wraps his hand around her waist.

Just as I leave the hallway, a song begins to play around us. It feels like what a dozen cascading stars might sound like. When I move, it clings to my skin, engulfing me like water. I am disoriented as blue beings emerge from their neatly designed houses in the distance.

I'm too entranced as my head naturally tilts backward, hungry to take in every detail. Glinting surfaces cause a thrumming in my chest—something hungry for adventure wrapped up in gleaming surfaces of rich purples, blood red, springtime green, and every shade of marvelous blue. The cavern is massive—easily a hundred times larger than any Enduar, as they like to call themselves.

Up to this moment, they were still trolls to me. Ancient, lethal, eerily observant, sure. But also hunters banished deep beneath the earth to hide their bloodthirsty ways while they mine their valuable diamonds.

Now, seeing the way the crystals grow out of the rock and hearing the song of their home solidifies Estela's stories. These people are the heirs to a rich unseen legacy—one they are inviting humans to join.

For the first time in years, my eyes burn.

It feels safe here. Peaceful. Gentle. It is exactly what I was looking for.

This could be a home for my family, once I get them.

People have started swarming around me, guiding the humans away from the massive bridges and walkways that magically move by themselves. Many go directly for Teo and Estela, but I am left on the fringe.

It's time to find the man I'm meant to seduce. But before I can look for Ra'Sa, someone grabs my shoulder. A woman with red hair pulls me back.

Her skin is paler than most humans, and freckles dot her nose and cheeks. They continue all the way up to the thick, curly hair spilling out of a style arranged atop her head. When she smiles, there's a warmth that can be felt throughout my entire being.

"I'm Arlet," she says sweetly. "Welcome to Enduvida."

1. There are more men.

CHAPTER 4

RA'SA

Upon arriving in the caves, I was carted off to a meeting with the king and queen.

Goddess bless me, it was short. However, someone let another elf under the mountain. Thorne, they call him. A pretentious gnat with his nose so far up the elvish leader's ass that he can't see his precious sky.

It's put me in a foul mood, only made worse by the noise of the humans being situated for the evening. The world feels like it's spinning out of control. People pour out of Hammerhead Hall and rush past me with blankets, spell lights, buckets, and various bags filled with what appears to be clothes.

The only grace I'm granted is the gentle nighttime song that rings from the clock tower in the middle of the city—four in the morning.

Mother should still be asleep, and hopefully, I'll get to rest within the hour. My pace picks up, and I move quickly through the houses.

While many murmur a greeting or send me a kind smile, none stop to speak with me. Not even the stone benders I am charged with leading as one of the city's council members.

A small voice in the back of my mind says to me that Tirin would've come to greet me if he were still alive.

A strange emotion knots in my chest. I'd been quiet most of the trek back from Zlosa—I likely wouldn't have spoken at all if Melisa hadn't come to my side and stuck there.

Strange woman.

I push forward, ignoring the familiar twinge of pain that's become so normal in the past months. I quickly cross the distance through the residential section and arrive at the door to my mother's house.

Seeing the circular dwelling with the curved rectangular door tightens the muscles between my shoulder blades. I moved back into this house after Tirin's death, but it's still filled with a lifetime of struggle.

I grab the handle, pull it open, and step inside. The spell lights are off, but a foul smell is coming from the small kitchen.

Holding my breath, I venture into the space. A pile of pots and plates is in the small sink. I groan.

Mother doesn't like to eat with the others, but if the dishes are still dirty… I wonder if she's eaten at all since I left. My palms sweat as I hurry into her room.

The door is open, so it's easy to push inside without being heard. When I see her lying on the bed, chest rising and falling under ancient woven blankets, I relax. Then I notice a plate next to her nightstand.

Several, actually.

I let out a sigh of relief, creeping over and picking up the dirty dishes.

Svanna, the advisor who leads the miners, must've cared for her while I was gone. Making a note to thank her, I return to the kitchen and start to wash.

Luckily, Ma is only one person. It doesn't take me long to scrape away the grime and filth, but scrubbing the smell out of the bronze sink takes ages.

Just as I start wiping down the counters, I hear a soft voice whisper behind me.

"*Fihlius,*" she starts. *Son*, in Enduar.

I hum a greeting but don't stop cleaning until her hand touches my shoulder. Finally, I turn to look at her.

Mer'Leuel was a proud Enduar woman, but time has worn her down. It's chipped away at the delicate features of her once beautiful face and replaced them with loose skin. Her hair is hastily tied into a low bun, with dozens of silver strands escaping down her neck and back. Most days, I have to help her style her locks since her eyesight has faded in the last half century.

Her brown nightgown is crumpled, and the lines around her mouth pull down.

"My son. Please, *stop*," she says again, this time more firmly. She comes around and takes the scouring tool from my hand. "I will do it."

"But you didn't do it, not for a week," I say, pressing my lips together.

Her frown deepens. "If I had known you were coming, I would've cleaned."

I wave her off and lock away the frustration and embarrassment burning up my neck. "It is fine. I am glad to see you are well."

She takes a deep breath and draws me from the kitchen area to the common room. There is a long sofa and several chairs. She sits, but I glare at the spot that used to be occupied by Tirin.

"Did you already eat?" she asks.

I nod. "I grabbed a little food before visiting."

She scowls. "Did you really?"

"No."

"That's what I thought. You traveled long; you must eat," she coaxes.

I take a deep breath, gathering the strength to tell her that more humans have arrived, and I am mated to none of them. She's old and hardened by grief, but she's got a tender heart.

I just need to do it.

Someone walks past our home, chattering about the group of humans filling up at least two dozen previously unoccupied houses.

I roll my eyes, but Ma stills and looks at me.

"More humans? How many?"

It's impossible to miss the way that her countenance brightens. She knows what the humans mean to us Enduares—a chance at a new generation. Mates for everyone in our cave.

Disappointment threads through my heart, and I put away trinkets and fold blankets scattered around the sitting area.

"We rescued several dozen humans from Zlosa. More than thirty."

My mother stands, and her hand goes over her mouth as her eyes drop to my neck. She immediately sees the absence of my glowing mating marks, and her eyes dim, brows knitting together.

"I take it you didn't find a mate."

I pause. "No."

All the light in my mother's face is snuffed out as she sinks back to her sad, sullen behavior.

"If there is no song, then you are not mated."

My fists clench.

"There are more humans in Zlosa. One of them will…" I trail off.

What if none of them are my mate? And even if one was, what if they cast me off like those of my own kind?

"I am sorry, my son. But perhaps it's for the best," she says softly. "What do you know of courting a woman? There have never been enough around for you to practice with."

Her words sting. I carried Melisa and tended to her well enough. She didn't complain. When I meet the woman the goddess Grutabela has destined to be mine, I could do even more. Force myself to *be* more.

"Your lack of faith wounds me," I say sardonically.

My mother gives me a sad smile and cups my cheek.

"You know I love you. But these things take time. The stones will sing your fate when you are ready."

As she searches my eyes, she frowns. "I hope you are not so eager to find a mate for my sake. I am fine."

I reach up and grab her hand. "You are not. You haven't been. Not since Tirin's death, and not even before that. You barely move; you leave the house filthy."

She recoils from my outburst.

I place my palm over the absence of her touch. "Ma, I'm sorry. I—"

"No, don't take it back now. I know what this is. You pity me. What a poor woman I am, left alone. Well, Salore, I am alone.

My mate is dead. My daughters are dead. My son is dead, but I am not. And neither are you."

"Yes. I know. But if I find a woman—"

"Please, stop this." My mother's hands return and cup either side of my face. "I know you do this because you believe yourself the man of our home. A leader. But it's just us. You do not need to do this for me."

I grit my teeth. "I don't do it only for you; I also do it for Tirin. He died so that I might have this."

"And what do you want?"

When I don't answer, my mother shakes her head. "Your father wouldn't have wanted this, and neither would your brother. Tirin died so you could have a mate, not just suffer through what should be the most beautiful, sacred song of your lifetime."

I detest when she invokes my father. Ra'Tirsa was the greatest man I'd ever known. He served in one of the nine battalions that protected the king's treasures during the First Great War.

He taught me everything I know about being a man. Because of him, I know how to keep my head in the face of chaos. To trust myself when all others doubt me. He showed me true honor. Strength.

How can my mother think that I have cast all of those lessons to the wayside?

"Enough. It is my choice. I *am* the one who leads this family—*I am the only one left*."

My mother drops her arms and steps away from me. "So this is how it will be?"

I nod. "Yes. I will tell you when I have met the woman."

Her mouth opens, but then thinks better of her words.

"I will return tomorrow to help you clean the rest of your home," I say, brushing out of the space and gently closing the door behind me.

For a second, I stand there.

My chest goes concave. Many things pass through my mind, but mostly I ache. It's a familiar pain that has become so broad and blunt that it's hard to identify what part of my innards it pierces.

I look up at the top of Enduvida, observing the familiar inky blackness accentuated with crystals and pretty bobbles.

Things are quieter now, but my body sags against the door. It would be wise to unwind before attempting to sleep.

CHAPTER 5

MELISA

I never imagined that I'd be wandering through tunnels filled with glow-spiders, cave bears, and these trolls who call themselves Enduares, but here we are. Deep underground. Far from the sunlight that used to warm me every morning.

Shortly after arriving and being swept up in a sea of blue folk, we were fed and found places to sleep. When I didn't see Ra'Sa, I decided to continue exploring. I looked inside empty houses and around corners and found mushrooms, small beasts with glowing eyes, and no shortage of wonders.

Begrudgingly, I fully accepted that Estela had been telling the truth about this place.

Blood doesn't stain the walls, and there are hundreds of gentle monsters willing to help the humans.

I need to get Thea and Wren here as quickly as possible, ideally before their birthdays in a few weeks.

Griselda… well. I don't know if Griselda would come.

As we trekked back from Zlosa, I'd pictured myself touring Enduvida in a few hours and then making my decision. Regardless of my choice, I would leave the city. Either to go for my family, or return to hell on earth.

That plan crumbled when I saw the Enduares and elves fighting those beasts. I saw their dead bodies. They had teeth and claws.

I don't know how to fight. Navigating across terrains as brutal as the ones we crossed are for those with more worldly experience.

In the last hour, traversing through tunnels, I'd considered finally seducing Ra'Sa and asking him to take me. The worry with that option is that he will report to the Enduar king, and everyone will start asking questions about where I am going.

I don't think I'm ready to tell them about the girls yet.

Estela could be an option. She is kind and might keep my secret.

But, then again, she once confided that Enduar mates can speak to each other's mind. The lack of privacy sounds awful.

As each exit strategy proves futile, nerves congregate in my chest, and I keep exploring. Everything is beautiful in this city, from the golden metalwork to the red crystal temple in the middle of the city, pulsing with life. The houses are finer than any hut I've ever seen.

Letting my hand stretch out, I brush my fingers along the smooth stone walls. A small spider steps onto my hand. I watch it dance across my palm for a second.

I've always felt a strange kinship with creatures after working with the cattle, even grotesque ones such as spiders. Insects and beasts do not inspire fear—not when giants and men can be so much worse.

That was why I tamed Coco. She'd been a snarling, injured wolf found bleeding between the trees. I nursed her back to health, and then she helped me through some of the most gruesome moments of my life.

Unexpectedly, I find the entrance to what looks like the bathing pools. I take a deep breath and walk inside. This place has a pleasant sound, like music playing in another room.

The tune plucks out echoes of bittersweet grief, and if I try hard enough, I can feel little hands pressed against my thighs and hips, wanting to be picked up. I push those thoughts away. They have no place in my head right now.

The closer I get to the humid pool, the more I feel itchy with grime. I hate being dirty. Washing away the trek should help me sleep, and tomorrow, I can find a way back to Zlosa.

The lighting in the room is dim. It's like dozens of cool-toned candles flicker on the walls. Pretty effect, but I prefer the sunlight.

More glow lights up the end of the small cavern, and I stare at the round, glowing bulbs with delicate curly tendrils splayed across the stone walls. They bloom in clusters and remind me of twirling sea creatures.

Movement from the water draws my eyes to the pools. I look around, not expecting anyone to be here. Then I see a man, suspended in the middle of the pool, head tilted downward.

Silvery, braided hair floats behind him, and his arms are outstretched on either side. I recognize the broad shoulders and pointed ears.

Ra'Sa.

He looks like…

Oh gods, he looks like he's drowned.

Godsdamnit. I need him alive.

"Ra'Sa?" I call.

No response.

Fuck.

My chest tightens to the point of pain. I grab my cloak, untie the ribbon at my neck, and throw it to the ground along with my red dress. With nothing more than a thin slip and the loincloth tied around my hips, I dive headfirst into the water.

"Ra'Sa!" I shout. The pool is much deeper than I thought.

Large crystals shine underwater, pulsing erratically, and little bioluminescent flecks sparkle along my skin as I swim forward.

Just as I reach to grab him, he turns around, pulling his head out of the water.

"What on earth are you doing?" he demands.

I stop swimming and swish my hands back and forth to help me tread water. It doesn't work as well as I'd like, and some water gets in my mouth.

I sputter and push over to the side of the pool. "Saving you! You looked like *you had drowned*."

His hand moves gracefully, and he glides through the water with ease. A strange expression appears on his face as his eyes search me. Then those glittering blue eyes dip lower.

I look down at my breasts. They are just barely skimming the top of the water, and the cool cave air causes my nipples to harden. The thin fabric reveals just about everything.

My eyes go to my arms and wrists, and I see the notches carved in my flesh. I'm glad the water hides them because a mostly naked woman could be just what Ra'Sa needs to lose control.

The Enduar quickly snaps his gaze back up to my face.

Annnd… *nevermind.*

His face softens. "That was kind of you."

That may be the closest thing to a compliment he's ever given me. I should preen, but a part of me is confused. If he were a human or a giant, he would've come closer to me. He would've wanted to touch me. Move me to be on full display.

"Anyone would've done the same."

An awkward silence fills the air between us. A pool apart. His simple shirt clings to his blue skin as he swims even further away from me.

I'd already resigned myself to his pushing out of the pool and leaving me alone. But he finally says, "I didn't realize anyone would be here this late."

I look around the glowing areas, marveling at the glinting crystal that catches my eye deep in the water. Thea would love this.

"I didn't think anyone would be here either," I say.

He pushes off the corner of the pool, gliding through the water with expert grace. My breath hitches as he comes closer, his clothes showcasing the sinewy bulge of his muscles with perfect, glittering clarity.

When he's close enough to touch, he treads water. I sink deeper into the warmth of the pool, easing the chilly ache across my breasts.

This is the first time he's willingly stayed near me, and I don't want to waste this moment. I've never seduced a man in water, but I figure the mechanics will be the same.

One fuck to freedom.

Suddenly, a long blue tail skims across the top of the water, brushing my arm. I flinch away, not realizing what it is.

"And why are you here?" Ra'Sa asks, frowning at my reaction.

Mierda.[1]

I turn around fully, and I let my chest be visible just under the water's surface.

Come closer, I urge silently.

"I needed to bathe."

Offer to help.

He nods thoughtfully, turning around. "I will leave you then."

Something twists in my gut as he swims to the opposite edge of the pool. What did I do wrong? Is he really so unaffected?

Desperation has my heart racing. He can't leave yet. I'm supposed to be cementing this relationship.

"Wait!" I call after him.

He turns back toward me. The faint light outlines his features in a stunning, cool silver. I admire the straight line of his nose and his full, purplish lips. They purse slightly as his eyes of pure open skies meet mine.

I swallow.

Just go for it.

"Why were you here?"

Different emotions flash across his face as he considers his words. "I like the song of these pools."

Huh. How surprisingly honest.

"I don't think I hear the song." My voice is soft. "Will you show me?"

"You would… want me to stay?" he says slowly.

"Yes," I respond instantly.

His eyebrows furrow. "Do you humans not worry over others seeing you so exposed?"

I bite my lip. "We do sometimes. But I don't mind you looking."

I watch as his throat bobs and feel a sort of satisfaction.

He comes even closer than before, sparkling water rippling around us. Heat radiates off of him. It's pleasant in the warm water.

"You saw my magic on the trek here. I am what my people call a Stone Bender. I can shift most rocks—large or small—and change them. I feel them like I feel my heartbeat. I speak to them just how I speak to you now."

His tail brushes over my bare calf, and I cease listening.

I've been used and touched a thousand times. I can do this.

Reaching out, I place my hand on his chest. His pulse stutters under my touch, and then his hand envelopes mine.

He removes my hand.

"Silence remains," he mutters so quietly I can hardly hear.

"What did you say?"

His eyes snap back open. "Nothing."

"Can you change the notes in the song?"

He smiles, and it takes my breath away.

"Hold your breath and sink down until your ears are submerged."

I obey but also venture to open my eyes underwater. The beautiful blues, reds, and greens sparkle before me. Ra'Sa takes a deep breath and lets out an enormous air bubble with sweet melodies.

Sound travels differently through the water. It's fractured and distorted, but when the sound hits the crystals, they sing together.

It's a louder song than the one following me through the caves.

It… dazzles me.

It's also full of sadness and mourning. I understand such feelings, having left behind my family to come here and see if it was safe for them to follow.

My chest starts to hurt, and I push up through the water's surface before the panic can set in—no need to have an attack with this hulking, blue Enduar next to me.

Need to be alone.

I take a few deep breaths. As he exits the water, he asks, "Are you well? I didn't realize humans cannot last so long without air."

The attack, threatening to steal all my breath, doesn't subside, so I force him away. "I'm fine. Thank you."

He frowns but retreats.

I mourn his loss, wrapping my arms around my chest.

"Very well. There is usually soap left along the back wall."

I fix a practiced smile on my face and wait for him to leave.

His wet footprints across the cave floor unsettle me as I wait in the warm water.

Once he's gone, I retrieve some soap and take a long breath. He didn't seem mad.

Tomorrow, I'll kiss him. It will drive him wild and make up for… whatever this was.

All is not lost.

1. Shit.

CHAPTER 6

MELISA

This godsdamned city is enormous, and I keep getting lost. Between hundreds of unoccupied homes, bobbing lights, and dozens of smells, each different from the last, I can't find the house they gave me.

I lean against one of the doors and let out a long breath. I slept like shit, tossing and turning, dreaming of Ra'Sa drowning. After waking up the third time, drenched in sweat and convinced that Ra'Sa had died before I had enough time to inspire a passionate obsession deeper than the oceans, I decided to abandon sleep.

It's not early, not really, but most of the others are still exhausted and are nestled safely in their beds.

Walking down the streets that separate the groups of houses, I notice the tools and weapons hanging on the outside of the occupied homes. Hammers hang above collections of crystals and other contraptions I neither recognize nor know how to use. Wheels, pumps, and long, wickedly sharp blades. It's all curious. All strange.

A part of me hopes to see Ra'Sa. On the trek, I noticed he was also an early riser. I slow my pace when a few Enduares leave their homes. Some reach for their hammers, but all nod to me as they pass. The sheer muscle mass and height stretch above me, proud and strong with every step.

Some say simple greetings in the human tongue, and I answer with common language words. It's strange to see them all acting this way, as if it were normal for me to wander through their city.

I've even seen a few women. They match Enduar strength and raw allure, with skin the color of rippling ocean waves, but they don't approach.

One man shuts the door firmly behind him, and I'm disappointed yet again to see that it isn't Ra'Sa.

He's not one of the Enduares we traveled with. He's beautiful, as they all are—stronger than any human—but he's not mighty like a certain stone bender.

I cast him a slow smile. He tosses me an easy greeting.

Instead of walking past, he pauses.

"You're one of the new humans, no?"

I nod. "I am. They call me Melisa."

"Melisa. Charmed. They call me Faol." He dips his head, and a scar comes into view I hadn't noticed earlier. It's a brutal marking slashed across his face. When he pulls his head back up, curiosity sparkles in his features.

Spell lights cause his straight, thick strands of hair to shine, and his lips easily pull from frown to smile. It's a pleasant thing to behold. He inspects me as I inspect him, and for a second, I consider stepping closer—just to test the waters, however briefly.

But instead, his eyebrows furrow, and he steps away.

A strange sting pricks my chest before a hand rests on my shoulder.

"Faol. Can I help you?" Ra'Sa's voice feels like a feather-light touch sliding up my spine.

My heart jolts.

Is he softening to me?

I look up to meet Ra'Sa's eyes and smile sweetly. He smirks, and my heart sputters. The sharp angles of his soul chip away another bit of my armor, and for a glimmer of a second, I think about how I wanted to kiss him today.

Better yet, I want to ravish those sweet lips. Kissing certainly should be on the list of ways I make him fall in love with me.

The Enduar next to us, Faol, clears his throat. "Lord Ra'Salore. My apologies. She looked lost. I didn't realize—"

"All is forgiven. You should run along and see if Lord Lothar is feeling better. He was distressed after the meeting last night," Ra'Sa says gently.

Faol starts to move away, leaving us alone between the quiet homes, and I turn to look at Ra'Sa.

"Good morning. I didn't realize you attended a meeting last night," I say swiftly.

A frown pulls the corners of his mouth back down. "I didn't tell you while we were in the pools?"

I shake my head.

"I must've been distracted," he says with a smirk.

Pleasure warms my belly. I'm going to wrap him around my finger so tightly.

"I'd be happy to distract you further."

I watch the reaction spread across his face. It starts with the widening of his pupils and ends with the flaring of his nostrils. I reach out to touch him, but he catches my wrist. His grasp is firm but gentle.

"I don't know much about humans or your mating customs," he says after a moment. "But for me and my people, you seem… interested, to say the least."

I suck in a sharp breath. "Would it please you if I was interested?"

His brows draw together, and his hand slides from my wrist to my palm. “It matters little. We are not mated.”

The heated air between us goes cold, and I pull out of his grasp. “Why are you telling me this?”

“It is a kindness. If we are not mated, what is the point? I do not wish you to think I care for you when we cannot be.”

I step away from him. Estela had mentioned mates—the person some foreign god chose for you—but I didn’t realize the only way to find a future was by procuring one.

I’ve been wasting my time like a *fucking idiot*.

My chest burns.

“Do the rest of your people share this sentiment?”

“Yes.”

My cheeks go flame red. If he won’t touch me without a godsdamned matehood, and neither will any other man, then I guess I’ll have to find a mate—and fast because I need to get back.

“How do I know if one of you is my mate?” I ask, frustrated and hot.

“A song will bloom in the very air around you.”

I roll my eyes. “There’s already a song playing.”

“Yes, but this one will be different. You probably will hear it after they place a stone in your chest.”

I huff and start to walk away from him.

His footsteps sound, and he touches my arm. “Wait.”

I turn around and take a deep breath before asking, “Yes?”

“I saw them preparing breakfast. You should go.”

I bite my lip. “Go where?”

“To eat.” He looks at the enormous clock tower watching over the city, then purses his lips. "I need to meet with the other stone benders soon, but I will show you the way."

“Thank you,” I grit out.

We walk in silence, with nothing but the bustle of people passing us and the common sounds of the cave to break through my disappointment. When we arrive in a massive hall with mushrooms lining the outer walls, he pauses, and I step away.

Looking up, I see Teo and Estela cooking food like commoners. What a sight.

Ra'Sa breaks away from my side.

“Be well. We will likely see each other later,” he says abruptly, then disappears.

I purse my lips and find some other women already arriving at breakfast. I walk into their huddle, greeting them brightly. Some look frightfully pregnant.

My sympathies.

Abi and Paoli are chatting near the feasting tables, and I go to stand near them.

"Afternoon!" they all say brightly to me as I approach.

I smile and nod. “Hello, friends. Hope you all slept well.”

They share a look.

"You left before all of us. I was surprised. Hell, I could hardly slide out of bed after all the walking we did. Did your mating song call you?” Abi asks, her tone verging on excited.

Something clicks in my mind. That's what Ra'Sa had been talking about. A new strain of nerves slither through my ribs.

"I thought mating only happened with those stones in your chest," I say absently when I catch three of the other rescued slaves watching us across the pavilion. They whisper and narrow their eyes.

I frown at their reaction. Back in Zlosa, there had always been a general mistrust of comfort women. Hilarious to think that a woman who shares a man's bed also shares his ideals, but the prejudice runs strong.

It surprises me to see it here, seeing as how they wouldn't have escaped without us.

A new woman joins our conversation, and I'm happy to see not all share their sentiment.

"I heard the queen's song started before she had her stone. And someone told me Lola started to feel poorly last night when they all rushed out of their houses," the pregnant woman says while easing herself onto a bench. "Suddenly, she was too hot, and she swooned right into the arms of a tall man."

I twist my fingers, wondering if that's true. Ra'Sa is unattached. Will one of the other humans be mated to him?

Probably.

It's time to let the idea of him go.

Most of the women have washed, and all of them look much better than we did while traveling. One even looks like Seranya, with her oval face and broad lips.

A wistful memory returns, and I try to let some of the pent up feelings flow away. Life is never so bad that I can't find a way out.

I take a deep breath, straighten my shirt, and then turn to the people cooking our meal. King Teo hovers around Estela like he can't help but keep her close. It's somehow endearing, especially when he wraps his hands around her waist while she cuts.

I sit and watch for as long as possible, taking in all kinds of Enduares as they filter into the pavilion.

One with an elaborate, crystal-laden dress saunters around. I smile when I hear the crystals clink and chime with each step. She's regal. Proud. With toned arms and a rod-straight spine. This is the kind of woman you take drinking.

Then, another woman enters. This Enduar is different from all the rest, with a grey tone to her blue skin and strikingly silver hair. It's pulled up tight in a bun—meaning she's unmated—but she pulls out a set of knives for chopping and sets to work. Her quick, precise cuts are fascinating.

"I want to work with her," Abi says, breaking away from her conversation.

I smile and nod. "You probably will soon."

When a little troll girl comes to join them in their cooking, something bursts in my chest. I know her—she said hello to me the night before.

Rila.

She passes out bowls of soup, and the pavilion fills with humans and Enduares alike. Sadly, she doesn't come to speak to me today.

Instead, I focus on the human man who returned to Enduvida. He also joins us in the meal, clinging to the walls, and I watch him carefully. He looks like a lumber yard slave. While we traveled, he practically refused to look at any of us.

"Have any of you started a mating song?" I ask, turning back to the women at my table.

All of them frown, shaking their heads.

"I'm sure someone will soon," I say brightly.

"How will we ever find one if they keep separating us from the men?" grumbles a newcomer whom I don't recognize.

"Are they keeping us separate?" Abi asks.

In response, the woman lifts her spoon from her bowl and points at the entrance.

Not eating, I watch the enormous arches that lead to the feasting area. Every now and again, I see a few of the men try to enter the pavilion, presumably to get a closer look at the humans. They look at us like children look at toys—wide-eyed and somewhat hungry.

It's a stark contrast to the blatant possessiveness that Ra'Sa regards me with, but it's not unwelcome.

A few Enduares helping with the meal approach the new guests, hand them food, and send them away. The men leave, looking miserable.

Interesting.

I continue to watch until Estela walks to the front of the tables.

"*¿Todos tienen comida?*"[1] she says in the human tongue.

We all start to nod.

Estels steps forward, and I can already tell she's preparing for a lecture. Our eyes meet, and I cast her a reassuring smile when she opens her mouth.

"As you can imagine, living in a cave is not ideal for humans," she starts. "The lack of sunlight will do cruel things to your mind, skin, and soul. While leaving the cave is an option, we have had problems with vaimpír attacks. Add in the state of our relationships with the giants, and the wisest place to be is here. Luckily, we have a way for you to get sunlight."

When Estela reaches into her dress's neckline and pulls it down, I perk up. I'd seen the stone embedded in her chest many times, but now there was a curiosity surrounding it that I didn't have before.

Around me, most of the women let out confused noises, moving forward to get a better look at what they may be missing. Her action only shows about half of the actual stone, for I know that it dips down to the bottom of her breasts.

When she can't pull down her shirt further, a human man walks forward, one who had lived in Enduvida before we arrived.

He has long, black hair and the beginnings of a beard and pulls up his shirt. He's scrawny as far as slaves go. Interestingly, even a few months under the mountain hasn't improved the constant emaciation most experienced in Zlosa.

His crystal isn't the same shape as Estela's; it's more round and much more red, but I imagine it works similarly in function.

I watch with a critical eye, and a woman shouts, *"¿Qué demonios es eso?"*[2]

The beautiful older Enduar reappears, crystals still chiming, and casts a disapproving look into the crowd. I like her—she doesn't act like any of us are breakable.

When I get back, I'll have to make friends with her.

"It's called a Fuegorra, and it is our most sacred stone," the new woman calls back into the crowd. "Enduares have used these gems since the dawn of time. They extend your life, help your body heal when you are ill, and signal your mate. The insertion is not painful, I can assure you—especially since we already have several humans who wear them in their chests."

As she speaks, I notice that a few Enduar men return, waiting at the entrance. And then, the king quietly breaks away from the meal and exits.

Seeing the king walk away makes me anxious. Hearing about the underground customs doesn't excite me—not when my top priority is finding a way to back to my family.

I start to hurry out of the area and after the king, only to realize I don't know exactly where he went. I walk faster, reaching another cluster of homes, looking around frantically for the house I'd slept in.

It's nowhere to be seen.

Frustrated, the small failures of the day start to creep up on me. I think of how I didn't kiss Ra'Sa, there's no mating between us, and I'm no closer to getting back to Zlosa.

For a minute, thoughts of Griselda press in. I try not to think too much about how she treated me growing up—I was strong enough to handle it.

Some might even say I was better for it.

But now, knowing that they are alone with her is terrifying. I press a hand to my chest and then straighten.

You just didn't rest long enough.

I start looking for the small home that I share with Abi and Paoli. Sleep will do me well, and tomorrow, I will go to get my stone.

What happens if your plan fails and you are sent back to Eneko's home? What will he do if he ever sees that on you?

Gods.

I shove the thoughts away. I already braved the trek here. Hell, I escaped. I'll deal with Eneko. It won't be too hard to hide it or never lie with him again.

Besides, if the stone chooses someone for me, it might be easier than getting Ra'Sa to react to my advances like any other normal, female-preferring man. The ritual they described could do me good.

I try to consider it, but my thoughts stubbornly stray back to Ra'Sa. If I'd picked any other man, they would've been waiting for me at my bed or followed me around, ready to sweep me off my feet at a moment's notice.

But he's an Enduar, and he wants a mate.

I sigh and look around the neighborhood, suddenly realizing it looks familiar. This time, I actually find my way back to my house.

As I approach the circular, deep blue building, I see an elderly woman exit her home across the way. It seems strange that she isn't at the feast.

Pausing for a second, I decide to go to her.

She's out in the front, plucking mushrooms from pots that cover the front side of her home, but she stops when she sees me approach.

"Hello," I say.

She smiles warily. "Morning, human."

I blink at her greeting. "Are you hungry? They have food in the common area right now."

I gesture over in the direction of the hall.

"Oh, that is kind of you." She shakes her head and holds up the mushrooms in her basket. "I'm just fine, though. I don't enjoy the way they cut their mushrooms."

I smile. "Not too many humans for you?"

Her lips quirk up.

“Never too many humans.” She pauses and places some more of her fungi into a basket. "What did you say your name was?"

"I didn't. But I'm Melisa," I say.

“It was nice to meet you, Melisa. They call me Leuel.”

I nod, her name instantly ringing a bell. Ra’Sa had used the name… for his mother. A new feeling crashes over me.

I’m out of place here.

The woman seems to notice my distress.

"You best go back to what you were doing. I'll need to prepare my lunch," she says, still harvesting.

I force a smile on my face. “Of course. Enjoy.”

She smiles but doesn’t say anything more as I return to my house and walk inside.

I look around the room at the brightly textured fabrics and sit down.

Ra’Sa’s mother. It’s such a quotidian, mundane thing to see a mother outside her house, picking mushrooms. She was… kind to me.

That unsettles me deeply.

After another hour passes, staring up at the roof of my new home and memorizing the strange, gleaming material, I close my eyes and relax into the soft cushions.

1. Does everyone have food?

2. What the hell is that?

CHAPTER 7

RA'SA

At the age of sixteen, Enduares are sent deep into the caverns to perform a ceremony called the *dual'moraan*, which means "joining of stone."

For us, it's a rite of passage that marks our first days as an adult. Usually, at this time, our powers are set free. Some people will even find magic awakens in their bones—as it was for me.

Some Enduares will be given the gift of song and healing. A few will be given the gift of prophecy, like our queen and Mother Liana. Others will find themselves gifted with metal bending, as Svanna was. Even fewer will learn to bend their very bones.

Stone bending, my magic, is the most common gift, yet it has proven the most valuable time and time again. Our king, Teo, has a potent version of this magic that has kept us safe.

Thus far, few humans have exhibited magical powers, but today, all of the women we brought back from Zlosa will descend into the mountain and complete the ritual.

Though the air is charged with humans and Enduares rushing through the city, it's a bittersweet time for me.

The entire city will gather to honor these new creatures. But half a decade ago, I was the first in Enduvida to perform the ceremony.

Shortly after the volcano erupted, I had descended entirely alone.

After, Mother Liana had joined the stone to my chest, and then my mother congratulated me. Sure, there was a small feast, but everyone was still grieving.

Today, I envy these humans for the celebration I never received. I was prepared to dwell on my displeasure for the rest of the day.

That is, until a stone bender came to my home and summoned me to a meeting with King Ma'Teo. This is not a political meeting; it's also not meant to discuss strategy for another attack on the giants.

No, we are being corralled by Teo like small boys.

He lectures us on the importance of leaving the human women alone, and I tune him out, leaning against one of the walls and staring at the ceiling.

My mind has much better things to occupy my time.

"Would it please you if I was interested?" Melisa had said.

Why? Why would she care for me without a matehood?

Surely she would find Enduares strange and unattractive, just as I find her small, too soft, and...

My skin heats at the ghost of her touch. Black hair glimmering and coated in the glowing water. I see her splayed out against the other side of the pool, umber gold body floating in the water. Her breasts were round, firm, with dark brown nipples.

I'd never seen anything like it, but gods on their stony thrones, it had done something to my cock. I wanted to grab them, to draw them into my—

One of the men shifts next to me, and I straighten, discreetly adjusting the pressure in my breeches. I shouldn't think of her. Not in that manner.

Not at all, I correct. She's some other man's mate.

"I am serious as death. Do not speak to them unless they speak to you. And if, by some miracle, they come to you, do not snatch them away like common beasts," Teo admonishes.

Those around me nod, but I let out an irritated sigh. What does he know of such things? He stole his wife and started this mess.

Besides, it's not like anyone here would touch a woman without permission.

Would it please you if I was interested?

Melisa's voice invades my head once again.

As if my strange thoughts called her, the smell of fragrant roses mixed with sultry cinnamon fills my nose. It's like a forest garden grows right next to us.

But then I look to the side to see Melisa standing next to me.

My mouth parts, and she smiles.

"Good morning, Ra'Sa," she says quietly.

Without thinking, my tail brushes toward her. She grins and reaches out to brush the furry tip. I shudder at such an intimate touch, then remember myself and snap my tail back to my body.

My heart stutters in my chest. "Melisa."

Her name on my tongue feels different than before.

"What is this?" she whispers.

I roll my eyes. "Our king is treating us like infants."

She grins, and my chest hurts again.

No one has heard us yet. How anyone could miss the woman at my side, I don't know. Despite my best efforts, I can't seem to stay away from her.

When I inhale, that somewhat spiced scent sings to me, inviting me to unwrap her mysteries one by one.

I still.

What are these thoughts?

"But there are so many of them. I can count at least eight houses that must be repaired if we hope to expand with so many families," Foal, the scarred hunter, says.

Melisa leaves my side, but my eyes stay glued to her as she speaks. "If you think that a house will be enough to sway a woman into your bed, you might be right."

Half a dozen whispers break out around me, shifting from surprise and curiosity at her arrival to determination. They scheme and plot for a place to keep their new mates. Some of them whisper over women that they hope to mate with.

Melisa's name sounds once, and I turn to see one of my stone benders say, "That's the one I spoke about last night."

I give him a withering glare, but her words sink into my thoughts.

The humans just wanted... A home. Not gold or jewels.

I frown.

"Melisa, I do not know if it is wise for you to be here," Teo says wearily.

Melisa steps forward and looks him up and down. She doesn't bow—she doesn't even dip her head. She uses no honorifics, either. It's like she invites him to earn her trust.

Something about the blatant courage makes me smile. I like seeing him knocked down. Just a bit.

"I wanted to know what you were scheming about. And, believe me, I've handled worse than all of you," she says. I don't like the glint in her eye.

Teo, however, shifts his weight and crosses his arms.

"I am trying to explain why the women should be unbothered for a while."

She raises an eyebrow, still not backing down or bowing.

"Do you know where they have been?"

"My queen told me most came from the breeding pens," the king says.

"That's right. They were tied to a table, treated like chattel, and still walk among us. These women are not fragile flowers who will crumble at any man's attention. We knew what we signed up for when we met Estela outside the Zlosian Palace."

My cheeks heat, as if Melisa slapped me across the face. I'd thought them weak… but to hear what they had been through…

I'd been too harsh.

More emotions gather inside my midsection. A new thought surfaces in my mind. Something I'd been too blind to see before.

For months, I had grieved my brother. I'd blamed the humans and my king. That thinking had blinded me to the true enemies and led me to ignore my brother's vision.

He'd had a large, generous heart. He wanted a future for the Enduares and the humans.

My throat closes. I'd been selfish with his dreams.

"Not everyone seemed happy in that room with Estela," Teo says.

She shrugs, and her silky hair spills over her shoulder. "They just finally have a voice. Don't fault them for wanting to use it. But that doesn't mean they don't want to be here."

How had I not realized what a beautiful, eloquent creature Melisa is?

"Estela is a wonderful woman, but she was never in the breeding pens. They consisted of a large expanse of rooms. Women were kept in close quarters, unable to work or leave for a period of four months while their cycles, temperatures, and bodies were monitored closely for signs that it was time for them to be placed in a room with a man."

I hold my breath. The name alone gives a picture of what happened inside, but… gods. The cruelty. The injustice.

I can hardly believe what a complete ass I'd been to women who'd lived through that.

Melisa continues.

"Then, they are left there for three days. Once the man is spent, the women are returned to their beds. If they are pregnant, they are gifted a hut. Some men go along with it and become proper fathers, while others beat their women. Some forced them into any manner of painful positions.

"So that is where all of these women come from—four small walls. Sure, they are wounded, some already carry children, and they all are tired, but don't think for a second they aren't strong. They want what Estela has promised—homes, mates, families—lives where they work for what they eat and nothing more," she finishes.

Everyone is silent, but my ears ring. I was surrounded by broken humans who only wanted a semblance of peace after a storm.

Had I not been born into the storm myself? And deep down, did I not long for the same thing?

Keio steps forward. “I will gladly care for a woman with a child. I spent all of last night rearranging my things, and there is space.”

Melisa returns to my side. As her body heat leeches into mine, my muscles relax. I turn to look at her and start to say something just as Vann comes into the crowd. He nods to me, and I catch a warning in his eye.

As a fellow council member, I step away from Melisa and fall in line behind him, but not before glancing back at the woman in red who has my heart racing.

Lord Vann leans over and whispers, “There’s been a problem. Go get weapons. Meet us on the way out of the city.”

“Understood.”

I look back one more time.

CHAPTER 8
Melisa

I watch Ra'Sa leave while I stand in Hammerhead Hall, surrounded by Enduares. The other Enduar spoke to him, and then he just… left.

But not before looking back at me.

There was something vast and tortured in that look. His sky-blue eyes had turned stormy, and that unsettled me.

Did he pity me for the things I shared?

He had no way of knowing that I had once gone to the breeding pens. There was no way in heaven or hell that he knew what happened when I laid there on that table, or what I did.

I start to sweat, and my pulse quickens.

The king finishes his speech abruptly after getting the men to promise that they won't go anywhere near the gem ceremony today.

To be honest, I had dreaded putting the crystal in my chest. Despite all the obvious benefits, I wasn't sure if I wanted a mate. I just wanted a protector—someone to give me and the girls a home.

A mate feels too personal. Kind of like letting myself finish for a man.

I bite my lip as some of the attendees of King Teo's little party begin to approach. Letting out a deep breath, I smile broadly.

"You are brave, woman," one of them says. He looks at me with deep, steel-gray eyes.

I dip my head. "Well, thank you for listening."

Another, with white hair steps forward, places his fist over his chest and bows to me.

"I am called Sikur. I will look for you after the ceremony. It would be an honor to be mated to a human like you," he says.

Something twists in my gut, and I think of Ra'Sa. "My, what a compliment."

More men begin to swarm, but Niht splits through all of them.

"All right. Off to work. I'm sure Melisa doesn't want you drooling on her fresh clothes," he calls.

I grin up at the aging Enduar, noticing the lines just starting to show in the corners of his eyes.

"Thank you, Niht," I say as sincerely as possible.

He winks at me. "Always here to help a woman in need."

I laugh. "I'm sure. Give my regards to Glyni."

He smiles, and I turn to walk out of Hammerhead Hall.

"Good luck at the ceremony!" he calls after me.

Once away from the hordes of large, muscled men, I lean against one of the pillars and let out a long breath. Staying in Enduvida is the right choice.

But the Fuegorra…

I think back to Glyni's offer. I could go with her and the other elves. But it doesn't seem like a place suited for children.

You don't have to decide right now.

So, instead, I wonder where Ra'Sa has gone. The Palace? To see his mother?

It shouldn't matter. Not after what he said, but I catch sight of his silver hair and oversized shoulder, and I feel pulled from my spot.

I look around me, finding the area mostly empty, and follow behind him at a safe distance.

Another man joins Ra'Sa, and they continue on, faces stern and heads fixed on the path ahead. They pass the palace and the homes and head into the tunnel that leads out of the city.

My interest piques.

I give them a head start before hurrying along behind. My legs ache from the speed since I'm not fully healed from the trek.

The pumping sound from inside the city starts to fade, and the air grows colder and crisper.

Enduvida's entrance is wide open, and the hunters stand just outside with the Enduar King. Everyone's faces are set in grim expressions, and it doesn't take long to see why.

Quietly stepping out into the open air, into the sunlight I was starting to miss, I look down and see a dead human lying in the snow, a message carved into his chest in the common tongue.

I choke back a gasp, pressing my hand to my mouth. The blood, the color of his lips. It's… gods, it's awful.

And it seems just like something a giant would do.

Of course. Our escape isn't as harmless as I thought it would be. We aren't just left to be forgotten. The new king doesn't merely presume us dead.

High King Rholker is particular with the humans—his obsession with Estela is appalling. Eneko had a good relationship with the king. On more than one occasion, I observed his ways. I should've known that he wouldn't let any of us be at peace.

This could mean a war. How am I supposed to find a mate in the midst of all that? There isn't time.

The Enduares will need to win this conflict before it has a chance to doom us all. I've come so close to getting a new home. I need to do something to stop it.

My head spins.

When I lived with Eneko, he was accustomed to spilling the contents of his mind after rutting me. It wasn't intimacy, not really—more like another kind of release. Sexual, and then mental.

Most of the time, the information was trivial. He told me idle gossip about other foremen and frustrations with Hibsej or his sons. But sometimes, it was important. Matters of the court.

Eneko knows the king. My old master has access to information that could turn the tides of a battle.

I'd been worrying about returning to Zlosa because the road was too dangerous to travel alone, but if I offered to help the Enduares, I bet they would give me someone to travel with. A bodyguard.

My mind soars, producing one name. Ra'Sa.

Nothing changes a man's mind like close proximity to temptation.

The pieces of my plan aren't fully formed, but my gut tells me yes.

Returning to Zlosa means sacrifice. But it also means a clear path to bringing my girls to Enduvida, with its pretty houses and glowing fungi.

Hard, but it would be worth it.

And the Enduares? If I make myself useful, there is no way they would ever cast me out. Mate or no mate. I'd make sure the two little girls in Zlosa would finally be safe.

CHAPTER 9

RA'SA

When I meet up with Teo and Vann, Melisa is nowhere to be seen. It's a small mercy. She's reached into my head and twisted up my mind. Mates, pain, safety, what does it all mean?

She is not meant to be mine, but for the first time… I wish.

I *want.*

What the fuck *am I supposed to do with that?*

That is until we exit the tunnels and find a human man on the ground.

My lip curls at the writing carved into his chest:

THIS ISN'T OVER

I grimace, a few sparks of hatred reignite. The giants are our natural enemies, but the cruelty they subject to the humans is too far.

All of the remaining dregs of my ire toward humans flow out of me, like the final breath of a dying beast, just as Melisa's smell joins us.

"Trouble in paradise?" Melisa asks.

"You followed us," I growl. It was a bad idea because she doesn't like blood.

"Shouldn't you be preparing for the *dual'moraan* ceremony?" Teo says, and I cast him a wayward glance.

"I was when I spotted you hurrying out of the cave. Your wife told me I was welcome anywhere," she says, smiling and batting her lashes. Falseness drips off her tongue.

It's disrespectful to the man lying on the ground, but I imagine myself blocking the ugly scene and tasting her tongue for the first time. It would be sweet, like her smell.

"You must tell no one that this has happened," Teo says.

Her eyes narrow, and I find like her fire.

"You wish me to lie?"

"No," Teo bites out before taking a deep breath and relaxing his shoulders. "I am asking you to help maintain the peace. We are still at war with the giants. I can promise we will protect everyone inside, but right now, our actions need to be calculated. This would cause unnecessary panic."

Melisa bites her lip. "And what if I tell your wife?"

"I will tell her myself," Teo says.

Her mistrust intrigues me. It's yet another layer in the mystery of her.

"This is from the giants, yes?" she says at last.

Teo nods as she gazes back down at the corpse.

"If they wish to fight you, why don't they bring an army right away?" she asks.

Vann interjects, "Estela reported a nasty skirmish on the night of the coronation. That has likely strained lots of relationships between the giant lords. Rholker has been cut a lot of slack. It's hard to tell how much more his court will spare."

Melisa nods, looking up and meeting King Teo's eye. There's something fearful and raw buried in her gaze.

"I used to be the whore of Foreman Eneko. He's one of the few giant supervisors in the slave fields and has lots of information on Rholker. For example, his new bride is actually the sister of his first betrothed." She leans in. "Word has it he killed the first woman."

Every part of me, from the top of my head to the tip of my tail freezes. Is she offering herself again? Even the suggestion has my fists tightening and blood heating.

"I am so sorry they put you in that position," Teo says.

I scoff. That's it? He should be promising to bring down the sky itself upon the giants. Sympathy isn't enough for their crimes against her.

Melisa waves him off. "Don't be. I do what needs to be done. Which begs the question, how do you solve a problem like this? One where the giants threaten to return and lay waste to us all."

Teo drags a hand over his face. "Information and allies, so that we might make a solid plan. We have already made great strides in coming up with strategies to attack the giants with information Estela brought back."

Melisa looks doubtful.

I don't like any of this.

She's got a devious, powerful heart. I would've been proud to claim it and stop this from happening.

But I wasn't blessed with such a privilege.

"What information?" Melisa asks.

"She learned the names of several lords and some of Rholker's inner workings—like his friendliness with the *Brujas* and Elf King. It's already helped us to make a plan."

The king trails off, and his silence breeds unease. When he looks back at Melisa, I know he's considering her offer.

"Of course, the fight she started has caused complications. We need to know what those are," Teo says. "Do the giants war within themselves? How can we best help the humans? Does Rholker plan to send an army after us? Will we wake up with knives at our throats?"

Melisa nods and smooths her hand over her dress.

I frown as she does. Although it has been cleaned, it is still the same garment she wore when we brought her back from Zlosa.

How had I not noticed? It must bear the memories of a thousand awful nights. She shouldn't feel obligated to wear it anymore.

Melisa smiles. "As a comfort woman, I know many men. My master loves to talk."

"Would you share the information you've uncovered?" Teo asks.

She smiles. "I would do more than that. I would go back as your spy and dig up even more."

Blood roars in my ears.

There's no fucking way.

I step forward just as Teo says, "Absolutely not."

For once, he's made a good decision, but that does not stop the red that edges my vision.

She frowns, but it's not just displeasure. There's something under her expression—a kind of panic.

Yet another new layer I don't understand.

When we walked away from the giant capital, she was nothing but smiles and soft touches. This is the first time I've seen her composure break outside of the few moments she was confronted with violence.

Something splits my soul in half, and I find myself with equal parts anguish and confusion.

She can't do this.

"If you love women so much, you must trust us to know what is best. I can do this—if it worries you, then let me bring one of your men." She holds up a hand and points it directly at me.

Something rears its feral head inside of me and hisses. *Yes.*

It wasn't that long ago that Tirin was saying those same words to me. He asked me to trust him, to let him make his own choices. And now, here she is, asking the same.

Some might call it a coincidence.

It doesn't feel like that.

A new flood of conflicting emotions rushes through me. On the one hand, of course, she would trust me to come with her. I can protect her—*defend* her—from the giants.

On the other hand, does she know that she's asking me to watch as she returns to her old master?

What do you care? She's not your mate.

Fuck off.

"If possible, I think Ra'Sa would make a handsome human," she says.

Heat creeps up to my cheeks. I'm not used to being so easily flattered, but then again, I've never met anyone like her. I don't know what to say. What man would agree to this?

"Lord Ra'Salore detests the overworld. We will find someone else," Teo starts.

It's his refusal that makes the decision for me.

"No need to search. I would do it, My King," I say through gritted teeth.

Teo casts me a dark look. "You would volunteer to leave again? The last time you left, you hated every second of it."

I let out a bitter laugh. I will hate it all again, but that doesn't mean I don't think I should go. I need to be there.

For *her*.

"Give me one reason why you should go," he demands.

My fists curl and uncurl. "I understand I was unpleasant, but now I have experience walking the land above. Besides, she pointed at me when she asked."

Melisa smirks. "That I did. He seems good with his magic."

Teo makes a frustrated noise. "I suppose now we should figure out how we are going to hide a seven-foot Enduar with a tail."

One of the elves who has joined us in the caves, the man with short white hair, steps forward. "Pardon the intrusion."

Teo looks livid, letting out an exaggerated growl. "Anyone else hiding?"

"No need to get heated. Mrath sent me here to keep an eye on you. It seems like this delicious little human has an in with the giant lords. She's even recruited a big blue bodyguard."

Thorne grins, but I glare.

"Glyni can glamour him into a human without any problem, but it would only last a day at most. He'd need to bring some of the magic with him," Thorne continues.

My anger fades, replaced with a weariness.

Teo waits a long moment and then nods.

"Very well. It is decided." Then he looks back at Melisa. "It would likely be for the best that you don't participate in the *dual'moraan.* Sending you back with a stone in your chest could be your death."

She nods. "My thoughts exactly."

Unbidden, Melisa's dead body pops up in my mind. I desperately dash the image to pieces as a dull roar sounds in my ears.

What have I gotten myself into?

CHAPTER 10

MELISA

Ra'Sa escorts me from the entrance to the troll city. In the corner of my eye, I glimpse the other Enduares collecting the dead, carved body of a human man. I look away.

Away from death, away from the blood, away from the man who agreed to come with me.

"Melisa. I don't think—"

"Ra'Sa, I've made my choice."

"But why make *that choice?*"

I don't know if I can tell him the truth—that I must get my family. My throat aches, and I walk faster.

"Will you at least tell me if you are all right?" Ra'Sa calls after me, quickly catching up.

"That was difficult to see," I say, trying to change the subject and hoping it takes his mind off the mission.

I certainly can't stop thinking about how he'd agreed to come.

A tightness brackets his mouth, and he pauses near the end of the tunnel.

"Why not skip the ceremony since you won't be getting a gem?" he asks bitterly.

Good question.

I suppose it has something to do with my optimism… or maybe I just want to escape from the pity in his eyes.

I shake my head, "I want to see the ritual."

"Will you be all right?" He's not usually so talkative.

His tone makes me pause. When I look up, I see his usually stern gaze soften.

Why?

He told me he wanted nothing to do with me unless we were mated, which we definitely are not.

"I will be with the other women. I will be fine."

We walk the rest of the way in silence and then reach the cave, where Estela and the other women are waiting.

I admire her tightly braided hair. She no longer wears the giants' clothes. Now, she is resplendent in her Enduar silks. The gown hugs her body and trails on the ground behind her. The only thing out of place is the look of worry splashed across her features.

She shouldn't let such emotions be so apparent. Men don't like a worrier.

My thoughts walk backward, and I realize my error. She struck gold with her mate. Having King Teo means she never has to be concerned about what men prefer again.

I look back up at Ra'Sa one last time.

He's coming with me—my plan is back on.

The others haven't noticed us yet, so I kiss his hand. He's too tall for me to reach up and kiss his cheek.

His mouth parts.

"I will see you later," I say softly.

Shock gives way to confusion, and then he starts to grin.

Not just a dim smile like he has shown before; his whole face lights up. I've never seen anything like it; it stuns me just as the music in the water did.

No no no.

I give him a curt nod and join the women. Estela spots me quickly and comes over.

"You look nice with your hair piled atop your head," she says.

I reach up to touch it.

"Arlet helped me," I say. "That redhead could tame an ox's locks."

A strange look crosses Estela's face, but she smiles anyway and says, "Arlet taught me everything I know."

She only spares me a few more words before she breaks off to address the group.

"Today, you travel deep into our city to hunt for your Fuegorra. It will be placed in your chest, and once you put it in, it cannot be removed. You will be counted among the Enduar people."

The women around me buzz excitedly, but something sinks in my stomach like a stone. If I'm going back to Eneko, I must remain unaltered.

I will not have anything placed in my chest.

I will continue as I am.

Free from a mate, but disjointed from the community until my mission is complete.

The women here are content, happy even, as they call out how much they love being in the under mountain. They are right; it is a good place to live.

I pat Estela on the back when she looks scandalized over a particularly explicit joke one of the women tells—something about making babies.

"Chin up," I say to the queen. "You know, I never knew either of my parents. Here's to children knowing where they come from!"

Several of the women raise their water glasses into the air as if they were fine goblets of mead and take a long drink. No one detects my lie, and I'm content to let it be.

Just as I begin to say something else to Estela, the wise woman emerges from the ground. She is even more stunning up close. She is distinctly Enduar, from her white silver hair to her deep blue skin, but she is more otherworldly and ethereal than the others.

Perhaps it is the thousands of crystals that hang off of her dress, but I bet she could blend in with the side of the cave if she tried.

She and Estela begin to speak as Abi and Paoli walk over.

The two women grin at me.

"So," Abi says, taking hold of my arm, "What do you think?"

I smile at her as she twirls.

"You both look fucking gorgeous," I say, hinting at an old inside joke.

They both laugh, but Abi shakes her head.

"I mean about the caves. Look at what they've done for the ceremony!" She points at the glowing orbs above us.

"I like it here. It's much more beautiful than I imagined," I say.

"Agreed," Abi says. "Have you chosen someone yet?"

"Joso is very handsome," another woman says, coming over.

I recognize the name of the tall, burly hunter and frown. He'd stood near the redhead the night we arrived.

"I believe he is with Arlet."

The woman I don't know frowns. "Oh. Damn. Well, I am sure there are others."

I nod. "But not Ra'Sa."

He's still tasked with taking me to Zlosa. I require his whole, unyielding attention.

Paoli catches my eye and signs, *He is very handsome. I hope you sing soon.*

I smile and sign back, *thank you.*

Abi sighs, "I think I like Niht."

Paoli lets out a silent laugh.

"The old one?" I ask.

She shrugs. "He's charming."

I let out a laugh. "He is spending his nights with one of the elves."

"And? I can be patient," she says deviously.

Gods, these women.

I give her a quick hug and then move forward as the procession down to the crystal cavern starts. The women begin lining up, and the singing starts.

I am transported away from this world. As the wise woman swings her golden lantern back and forth, the dazzling light gives me goosebumps.

A million pinpricks on my skin wake me up as I'm handed a crystal, and I walk.

When we reach the forges, they hand out hammers. I politely decline seconds before I catch Ra'Sa's eye. It is gentle and kind.

A part of me is glad that he will take me to Zlosa. There is something so reassuring about him. He'll meet the girls as we travel back here.

I wonder if he will be as kind and reassuring to them.

As we finally reach the cavern filled with glowing red crystals, I pause. Fuegorras are everywhere.

Awe turns into excitement. I can hardly believe the shine and glow of the gems.

"Listen for your match." Liana's powerful voice fills the room. "It will sing a melody that you will recognize instantly, just as clearly as I speak to you now. Be mindful of your hammer strikes, though. The crystal you break out now will be sported on your chest till the day you die—no one wants a lopsided oval like the one Velen cut twenty years ago."

Laughter ripples through the room. I make a note to meet that man.

The women around me start to move, and jealousy builds in my gut. I will not be able to join them.

But… *Soon,* I remind myself and watch as all the others find their stone.

Unexpectedly, while standing at the back of the cave, waiting for the others to finish, a song starts up to my left.

It is a cold, bitter song. One that calls to the innermost depths of my soul.

I gasp as I move forward, reaching toward one of the crystals. This one glints brighter than all the others, and my breathing is shallow.

I shouldn't do this… But I reach toward it anyway.

As my finger brushes the gleaming crystal, something cracks open inside of me. It's no longer a faint song playing off in the distance. It is a symphony that morphs from pain and bitterness to sweetness.

Like a promise of what it could do to me.

I recoil.

Backing away from everyone, I let the flashes of light at the front of the cavern continue as I slink back out into the hallway. I wait for the others to partake in this ritual, knowing that such things are not meant for me.

I *refused them*.

The panic starts. First, with full body chills and then with nausea. I fear throwing up. Sweat collects up my back, and I press shaky hands to my mouth as my heart gallops.

If Ra'Sa were here…

I stop the thought before it can continue, swallowing the bile and closing my eyes against a wave of dizziness.

Godsdamnit, this is a full-fledged waking nightmare. I breathe in through my nose and out through my mouth.

The ritual progresses, and I wait outside until all that's left is the soreness in my body as I press myself against the cavern wall.

When a head peeks out of the cave, I straighten, pushing away all other effects lingering inside my body. I smile and approach Abi as she exits.

Her face is tear-streaked, and she grins like she's seen light for the first time. To say I'm not intrigued would be a lie, but I didn't get a stone so there is no reason in wishing. Swallowing my sourness, I take her hand.

"And? Let me see," I press.

She smiles at me and pulls down the top of her tunic. Her Fuegorra crystal sits neatly next to her heart.

My eyebrows raise.

"It's lovely." I kiss her forehead. "Well done, *amiga.*"[1]

While inspecting Paoli's gem, Estela meets my eye and frowns.

She knows I didn't reach for my gem. I see the question in her face and try to escape. Though small, she catches up to me.

"What happened?" she demands, clearly referencing my lack of crystal.

I wince. I didn't get it because I'm going back. All that work to flee Zlosa, and now I'm returning to the lion's den.

"I didn't want to do the ritual. All right?"

"Why not?"

Good *fuck*. Does she never stop?

I turn back around, glaring at her. The reason sits on the tip of my tongue, but King Teo told me not to tell his wife about anything. Not the body, or the plan—certainly not about the deal we've made.

"Why don't you ask your husband?" I push away from her.

Her eyes burn hot on my back, but I'm not ready to talk to her about leaving. I don't want her to try to talk me out of it. Her pity would be even worse.

She knew I was a comfort woman, but she doesn't know about my family. Nor will I tell her the lengths I've gone through to protect them. I'll be damned before I let her judge me.

I'm one of the first to leave the tunnels, and I don't bother looking for Ra'Sa. He would want to comfort me, but my plans for him only work if he cares for me… not the other way around.

If he holds me, I'll crack. I can't let these feelings grow. My attachment to him makes me hesitate to do what is necessary.

I can't ever do that.

When my house comes into view, I let out a sigh. It doesn't take me long to push inside and go to my bed in the back. I drop down and pull out a small pouch from my belongings.

Undoing the drawstrings, I pull out a rag doll and a necklace. The jewelry was made of Estela's wedding dress—the cord braided stone silk and pendant a golden button.

She gave it to me while I helped her dress in captivity and convinced me to come with her.

The doll… it's made of homespun fabric and has a small puff of a cottony substance for the head. The face is drawn with berry dye.

The girls made this for me so I wouldn't forget them.

I leave the necklace on the bed and hug the doll close.

I do this so Thea and Wren will never *ever* be forced into a breeding pen, or picked up by a giant in a field. They will live good, full lives for themselves. Free.

My eyes burn.

Before the tears can fall, I put the items back in their place and push the bag away. I lay down on the bed, settling in as I stare at the ceiling.

My heart weeps like an open wound. I feel shame. Regret. It would be nice to stay here a little longer, but I do not live only for myself.

Enduvida will still be here when my mission is finished. I will do my part to make sure of it.

1. Friend.

CHAPTER II
RA'SA

The Next Day…

I hardly slept last night. I should regret my decision to go to Zlosa, but I can't. I can't stop hearing Melisa's words or remembering what it felt like when she told us about the hell she'd crawled out of.

It haunts me.

So much so that I barely register the motions of the day. I hardly feel it when they take me to the elves to fix my face.

When the queen asked me to cut my hair—an act that an Enduar would only take upon the death of a mate—I gritted my teeth and thought about how human women only want roofs over their heads.

Until an hour ago, I had long hair that any Enduar would be proud of. Now, it is black and falls to my chin.

Comparison can be the thief of joy, but it can also put life into perspective. Traditions, though comforting, must fall to the wayside when so many lives are at risk. I will be a slave, and human slaves regularly cut their hair. The reasons do not matter. I must do what needs to be done.

"Use this. Keep one next to you while you sleep so the glamour will replenish every evening around midnight. Otherwise, you will wake up as blue as the day your mother birthed you, my fiendish friend," Thorne says. "If you need to call upon the magic outside of midnight, say *Blàth.*"

My mouth trips on the word as I try to repeat it, and he smiles reassuringly.

He's one of the only men in the elven resistance, and I'm convinced his leader sent him here to spy on us. I shouldn't like him.

But… he is helping us—particularly me—so I remain undecided on my loyalties.

His white hair falls in orderly curls around his face, and I eyeball the length. It's short, just as mine is now.

"Thank you," I grumble as I take the small sack of pebbles in my hand.

It is small, barely larger than my palm, and the stones inside are practically shards of rock. But the contact causes a buzzing to skitter across my skin.

Elven magic.

I wonder what my father would think about my cutting my hair and using foreign magic. Perhaps he would find it amusing. He had a seriousness about him, but he so dearly loved to laugh.

In that regard, we are different. But laughter has meant little when all that's left of our family of seven is me and my mother. The first time I laughed in years was when Melisa jumped into that pool after me.

My gaze travels over to Melisa. Queen Estela holds her close. The two of them smile at each other, and I strain my ears to hear the words pass between them, when Melisa turns her head to meet my gaze.

Until now, my heartbeat has been slow and steady, but when I look into Melisa's unflinching, golden-warm gaze, I feel like I've just spent two hours training with the stone benders.

I sweat, my muscles feel strange, and, if I still had my tail in this form, it would probably be swishing back and forth.

When she smiles, it feels like my chest might burst.

Is this matehood?

I listen closely to the air around us, waiting for the access to her mind that comes with a mate, but her thoughts are silent. No song sings to me, and no pain appears on my neck, signaling mating marks.

Melisa turns back to Estela, who hands her a few small trinkets. The glint of a red stone makes me tilt my head to the side.

Red beryl—a healing stone. It matches Melisa's dress.

My eyes catch on her deep red lips… again. The deep color makes her teeth appear even more white.

I've never seen someone wear so much red, and now I know it relates to being a comfort woman. I don't like it.

Heat creeps up my neck.

Mother Liana comes up the tunnel, interrupting my thoughts to hold out yet another pouch. This one is larger than the other.

"These are speaking stones. I have prepared as many as possible," Liana says, as I take the bag. "Only send the most important information."

While putting all of the gifts in my pack, Melisa joins my side.

"Thank you, Mother Liana," she says, her voice bright and sweet.

It's almost enough to stroke a smile out of my lips.

Almost.

I turn to look at King Teo. We've disagreed on many points within the caves before, but I begrudgingly admit that he isn't an incompetent sovereign.

Melisa would've never accepted no for his final answer. I am grateful he granted me leave to go with her.

He reaches out his hand. "Are you prepared to leave?"

I tentatively take it. "We are. Thank you for your help."

"It was nothing," he says.

Melisa gravitates to my side, and I let a few shallow breaths filled with her spiced flower scent fill my nose.

"I am prepared to leave as well. I must thank you, King Teo, for accepting my request."

Teo's mouth flattens into a harsh line. "I would've preferred other means."

I agree.

Melisa smiles. "You can thank us when the king is dead, and we are safely nestled back in Enduvida."

She says the words with certainty, but unease ripples through my body. I hold out my arm, and she takes it without hesitation.

"See you all soon!" she says cheerfully.

While I appreciate her optimism, it feels hollow.

I dip my head toward the crowd and say, "We will return as soon as possible."

We walk out of the cave, just the two of us.

The sunlight pierces my eyes, as it did the last time I left Enduvida. I was not meant to be out here, looking like a human.

But things change.

We walk in silence until we reach the opening of the icy passage.

Strangely enough, the further away from the cave entrance Melisa gets, the quieter she becomes.

At first, I thought nothing of it, but then I caught her looking back at the mountain's entrance as if she had forgotten something.

When she catches me, a mask covers her worried features.

"What—"

"Can I carry something?" she interrupts me to ask.

My brows furrow. "It is not wise. The trek to Zlosa is long, as you've already seen. I am perfectly fine. You should conserve your strength."

Melisa bites her lower lip but says nothing more. She steps closer to me as the chill of the ice blankets us. I do not find it much colder, especially since we are out of the wind, but I understand her reaction.

She continues to walk at my side, somewhat subdued. I think of how she'd looked coming to Enduvida—full of wonder. But now that expression is gone and is replaced with a haunting worry.

Glistening blue and white glaciers stretch above us, and the sound of the wind hits the ice just right. It almost sounds like a song.

For a second, I marvel. Then my head turns to the woman at my side. A bitter taste coats my tongue.

I'm taking her back to be tortured.

Why had she insisted? The decision seemingly came out of desperation. But I can't know for sure—it's all a part of the mystery that keeps her just out of reach.

Unknown by me.

"When we get back to Zlosa, are you truly planning to go with your master?" I ask, breaking the silence.

She freezes and looks up at me. We stop walking all together, and her eyes quickly shift through different emotions.

"Yes."

"Why do you want to go back to Zlosa so badly?" I ask through a tight throat.

Her hands bunch in her skirts. "I want to help the Enduares."

"Bullshit," I say.

Her face switches from shock to anger. It's like an entirely different person emerges from the recesses of her mysterious soul.

"What is that supposed to mean?"

"You want to return to a life you hated—a brutal, cruel life—for people you hardly know?" I press.

She frowns."You're right. I don't know you very well, so I don't need to explain myself to you."

"What kind of response is that?"

She glares at me and continues walking.

I clench my fists.

"Are humans truly so fickle? You confirmed you were interested in me just a few days ago. Shouldn't you want to share your thoughts with the man you desire?"

"Ra'Sa, I don't wish to speak about this with you. Please, drop it," she says.

"But I'm saying these things because I want to help you."

When I catch up to her side, I see her nostrils flare, but she doesn't say anything more. She just continues walking.

Frustrated, I drag a hand over my face and follow her. Women make no sense. This is why I shouldn't court one.

The stone was supposed to sing and make this easy.

"Are you worried?" I ask finally when I catch Melisa's hands grasping at her red dress.

Both arms drop back to her sides. "Not at all."

Her words have a tang of falsity, but I give up.

If she is nervous or worried, I won't pressure her with more questions. I square my shoulders and continue to push through the narrow channel.

When night falls, I finally start to relax. There's something about the darkness that reminds me of the caves. It makes the wide open space feel smaller—almost like an embrace.

I am quiet as I set up our small camp. I clear away snow, lay the bedrolls inside a leather tent, and then return to the ground. As I kneel, I let my hands rest upon my thighs, palms facing upward. The stone beneath my fingers shifts. Each particle vibrates to the same tune as my mind. My eyes see further than the physical world, aided by my other senses. Slowly, I raise a few bits of stone from the frozen topsoil.

While I cannot call upon the earth's molten rock like Teo, I can heat the stones to make a surface suitable for cooking.

As my makeshift stove is complete, I scoop snow into a pan, pick out the debris, and put in the dried ingredients.

It isn't until I sit back, the meager meal bubbling, that I look over and see Melisa watching me. She's curled up in one of the fur blankets, and her eyes sparkle in the dim light.

"Food will be ready soon," I say.

"So I see. Thank you."

I nod.

She smiles, and my whole chest warms. After our fight earlier, I've been stewing in my distress, but all her nerves and irritation seem to have ebbed away.

"Will we be sleeping in that tent together?" she asks bluntly.

I nod again, trying to hide my racing heart. "Yes. It will keep us warm. It's efficient."

She grins. "My dear Ra'Sa, I told you once before: I wouldn't mind lying on top of you to help save space."

I sputter. At least she's feeling better. She was so quiet on the walk here.

"Well, if you really want—"

"Relax, Ra'Sa. I was merely joking."

The lightness in my chest falls flat. "Of course."

She is silent for a few minutes. "While I'm grateful you've come to help me, I know how… *eager* you all are to have mates. I won't keep you from your future woman."

My brows furrow, and I refrain from saying the words that have slowly snuck into my head.

She could yet sing for me with a stone in her chest. But that's madness. To speak it is futile.

"I would never pressure you—"

"Again, I am grateful you came with me on this trek. Not many men would help a woman who belongs to another," she interrupts.

I blink. "Belong? You remain unmated, do you not?"

"Correct."

I meet her gaze. "Then you belong to no one. You are free."

She tilts her chin up. "I am Eneko's whore, or did you forget so easily?"

I make a face, but she shakes her head.

"Believe me—it doesn't hurt me to say it aloud. He plucked me up a year and a half after I was first conscripted to the breeding pens. It doesn't matter that we escaped; I still belong to him. And I will be every second we are in Zlosa."

Unless he dies.

My jaw tightens. Killing Eneko too soon would cause the whole mission to fail. But once the mission is done, we will have what we need, and the giant slaver will be all mine.

"If that's how you feel, then fine. Everyone is grateful for your sacrifice."

Sacrifice is one of the many things that a man should be comfortable with. Yet, seeing her take on this burden makes my gut churn.

I felt the same when my brother Tirin sacrificed himself for the humans.

No one tells you how agonizing such gifts of self are for those left behind.

Memories of the past swirl as I stir the dried meat into a stew, and silence settles around us.

A small beast emerges from the bushes and bounds through camp, only to stop in front of Melisa. It has strange ears and a white coat. Another one of those mesmerizing smiles graces her lips as she reaches out and pets the creature.

"When we traveled before, Niht was always inundated with animals. It seems they like you, too."

She nods. "Animals have always come to me."

I smile.

"I used to work with them before," she says, almost hesitantly. "I enjoyed their company."

A part of me wonders if that is true, as so much of her is shrouded in mystery, but she says it with such reverence. I can't help but believe her.

"What is that one called?" I ask lightly.

She brushes back one ear of the animal and laughs. "A rabbit. Sometimes I forget how much you don't know about the world outside of your pretty caves."

"You think me an ignorant hermit because I have little family and no mate?"

I shouldn't be so bitter, but I am stuck between duty and desire.

It's becoming agonizing.

She stops petting the creature, and it bounds away.

"I didn't mean my words to sound so cruel," she says.

I shake my head. "It is fine. Rest."

We are quiet for the rest of the night, and when I approach my bedroll, I slip in and put as much space between us as possible.

CHAPTER 12

RA'SA

Terror claws at me as dark shadows pass before my eyes.

When one of the cold monsters reaches out and grabs at my neck, I black out. I see Teo's face as he approaches my mother and me.

He tells us that Tirin is dead.

Young Ra'Tirin. My baby brother. I held him in my arms when my mother and I escaped the volcano.

No…

I bolt upright, panting. The tent is cold, the space humid. I drag a hand over my face, looking over at Melisa.

She still sleeps soundly, surrounded by blankets and pillows.

I let out a long breath.

Need to get out of here.

The sun has not yet risen over the horizon, so I move as quietly as possible. When I peel back the tent flap and walk into the world, the cold air soothes the tension in my muscles.

Since I didn't hold my glamour stones, I've shifted back to my Enduar form. I harbor no desire to return to being a human just yet.

My hands ache with the need to do something other than lie on my back, so I decided to hunt and make breakfast.

Melisa didn't enjoy our meal last night, and there is still a long way to go. She needs her strength.

I gaze across the snowy forest. A few rabbits Melisa showed me hop across the ground. They seem decidedly plump, but my magic hesitates. Ulla disliked us killing the creatures. I wonder if Melisa would have the same qualms.

Glancing back, I contemplate asking her. To my surprise, she rolls over in her sleep. Her arm reaches out to the spot where I was lying.

Something pinches my chest, but I continue forward.

It doesn't take long to catch two rabbits, skin them as I would a *ruc'radh*, and put them over my makeshift stove.

The wind makes cooking challenging. But thankfully, the sun is just beginning to crest over the mountain. It takes away the bite of cold while I shield the sizzling meat.

When I am finished, I turn back to the tent.

"Melisa?" I call, wondering if she would need me to shake her awake. Would that frighten her?

She makes a soft sound that echoes in my ears and warms my chest.

"Melisa, I have food."

Slowly, she stirs from her slumber. Her arms stretch out around her as she sits up. One side of her face is red from being pressed against a pillow. She casts me a sleepy smile, smoothing the hair out of her eyes.

I can't tell what is so charming about this sight. Objectively, she looks puffy and unkempt as she wakes, but I wish to see it every morning henceforth.

"You must forgive me," I say a moment after.

Her smile drops. "Whatever for?"

"I killed a few of your rabbits." Her brow furrows.

"They weren't my rabbits. And besides, we needed to eat. Put it from your mind."

I like that reasoning and hand her a small leg of meat. We eat in relative silence for a few moments until I can keep my mouth shut no longer.

"I have thought a lot about what you said yesterday. I do not understand why you insist on going to Zlosa, but I have agreed to watch over you. An Enduar never breaks his word."

A half smile crosses Melisa's lips. "That is good to hear."

"However, while I look like one of your kind, I know nothing about your customs."

While I am interested in learning about humans, a deeper part of me just wants to know more about her.

Melisa looks at me and takes a bite. I keep myself from letting my gaze dip down to watch her mouth.

"What customs? Ra'Sa, we are slaves. All you need to know is this: don't talk to anyone, don't touch anyone's things, and do as you are told," she says angrily.

"And what of my height?" I ask.

She waves her hand. "You can be the bastard son of some giant commoner."

I curl my lip. "There is no cursed giant blood in my body."

She rolls her eyes. "Who cares if you do or don't? It will solve the mystery of your height. Being part giant is rare, but half-giants make excellent workers."

I think of my father. He hated the giants just as much as any Enduar, as did Tirin. Would playing such a role hurt either of them if they were still living?

"I don't like it."

"Ra'Sa," Melisa says, tone serious. Her foot brushes my leg, and every thought swirls straight out of my head. "You will need to find work as a slave somewhere close by while I'm tending to Eneko. That's how you'll blend in."

Something ugly curls around my heart.

"Tending to Eneko…" I repeat. "What exactly will that entail?"

She snatches her foot back.

"Please, I'm not trying to be cruel." This question is borne of something much more petty: jealousy.

She looks at me. "Eneko only talks after a good fuck. So that is what I will give him, as many times as it takes to find out all the things your king needs to know."

Dread twists in my gut, but I push it down. A man should know how to deal with the harsher truths of life. And she clearly doesn't want sympathy. She just continues to eat.

"So, we will arrive in two days. Likely from the north. What is our plan?" I ask, wanting to keep her talking.

Her eyes search the snowy forest as she grabs another piece of meat.

"Arriving from that direction means that we will get to the northeastern lumber yards. That's where Eneko is a foreman. Though, he's not the only one, of course."

"I assume you know exactly where to go?"

She flashes me a smile. "Naturally. Now, when we arrive, I had better do something to gain his sympathy, or I'll spend a week in the pit."

"The pit?" I repeat.

She nods. "It's one of the other torturous ways we deal with things in the northeastern lumber yards. Whipping is useful for slaves with active jobs like healing, chopping, or cooking. Those with more passive jobs are sent to the pit, sometimes without food or water."

"Why?" I ask.

"Because if you cover a comfort woman's back with open wounds, she can't lie down. Starve her, and she'll be lethargic, to be sure, but she'll still be good for a rut."

I recoil. "Why the hell would you say it like that?"

"Because it's true. It's not like I have a choice in such matters."

The truth settles between us like the snow settles on the ground.

"I—"

"I don't need your pity, troll. There are worse masters than Eneko," Melisa bites out, tossing her bones in the embers and standing. "Now, I'd like to continue."

My mouth falls open with unspoken words. I want to offer her comfort, but I don't know where to begin.

I don't know how to care for a woman.

Deflated, I watch her slip inside the tent and start taking down the evidence of our stay.

I swallow hard and follow her lead.

The road to Zlosa is a long, three-day trip despite the excellent conditions we've been blessed with. No malicious creatures or weather mishaps have slowed us down.

I've stopped applying my glamour, as I find little point in it when my true form is much stronger.

The white snow is blinding under the light of day, and I am more than grateful when the cursed flaming orb sinks beyond the trees.

A fox follows Melisa as we walk. I watch her trek on, head high and uncommonly quiet. She doesn't say anything more, and I don't have sufficient words to speak with her, so we continue in silence.

When there is rustling in the trees, I ignore it, partly because of the animals Melisa enjoys petting.

We need to sleep soon, and there is a clearing just ahead. There is enough space for our tent and a fire between a few trees. I can make her a proper fire instead of a cooking stone tonight.

It takes Melisa a few moments to realize I am no longer beside her. She stops, lets out an exasperated breath, and turns to look at the area.

"Are you ready to set up camp?" I ask, taking note of the fallen branches and large stones.

"This seems as good a place as any," she says at last.

Then the words dry up again.

After the sun finishes sinking beyond view and the sky fades from a pinkish purple to an inky black, I hear rustling again and pause. When it doesn't make another sound, I stone bend a small heat source to cook more dried food.

"When we arrive at Zlosa, we'll need to get rid of our supplies. Estela showed me a hollowed-out trunk where she used to hide things. We can take your weapons and anything else there. It's secluded enough that it won't be found," Melisa says, speaking more than she has the entire day.

I nod my agreement, still preparing the meal. "Thank you."

Another rustle comes from the trees to our left. It's a little too close and a little too loud.

This might not be a mere fox or rabbit. I stand, leaving the food to boil.

Melisa busies herself with the bedrolls.

"What are you doing?" she asks as I move away from the fire.

Holding my finger to my lips, I creep to the trees. I call the stones to fashion a short blade from the earth.

My heart gallops as I approach the thicket where the noise is coming from. I reach into the ground with my magic and send a light tremor to sense the exact location.

There are the small bodies of a family of mice, the four legs of a rabbit, and then… four paces away, obscured by two large tree trunks, I feel two feet, and one hand supporting a much larger body in the snow.

Shock precedes the searing protectiveness that sends electric pulses up my limbs. Without waiting, I enter its hiding place.

A hiss fills the air. Red eyes peek out from behind the tree.

"Vaimpír!" I shout at Melisa. "Get in the tent!

The creature charges me.

It knocks me on my back, breaking my focus. The makeshift weapon I crafted scatters around me. A glinting set of white teeth open just above my neck.

"Ra'Sa!" Melisa screams.

Can't let it bite me.

I shove the beast away. A few twitches of my fingers have stone shards levitating off the ground. They swarm around the creature's head before piercing its gray skin.

It screeches and falls to the ground next to me. I shove it further away.

Rolling over, I see Melisa frozen at the tent's entrance. No defensive stance. No weapon.

I curse, realizing she doesn't know how to fight.

Gods on their stony thrones.

The creature stands, black blood oozing down its bare torso.

Holding my breath, I summon as many stone sharps as possible. They make a whizzing, high-pitched sound as they compound into a blade.

The creature and I charge each other at the same time. It wields tooth and claw. I raise my stone blade above my head.

I bring the weapon down swiftly.

With the intensity of my force, his head and left shoulder are cleaved from his body.

Melisa cries out behind me.

I whip around as the two pieces of the vaimpír's body fall in heavy thuds on the snowy floor.

Melisa's breath is rapid and shallow, one hand on her chest and the other over her mouth. I let the stones of the sword fall back to the ground and rush over to her. She's trembling, and her face is pale.

"What's happening? Are you hurt?" I demand.

She swallows. "I might… my chest hurts."

My hands trail over her shoulders, and they are soft and pliant under my palms. When they reach the impossibly smooth skin of her neck, her flesh is clammy.

"You're in shock," I say.

She shakes her head.

"No—this—" When her words don't come easy, she leans toward me. Unsure what else to do, I pull her in and rub my bloody hand up and down the back of her thick cloak.

Her frozen hands rest on my chest.

"Tell me what you are feeling?" I try again.

She lets out a gasping cough.

"Melisa—"

"This… it happens sometimes. My mother called them waking nightmares. It's just… it will… pass," she stumbles.

My brows furrow. "It is an attack?"

She nods. "Of my nerves. Please, it will p-pass."

Instinctively, I hold her tighter. When I agreed to take her to Zlosa, my duty was to protect her by any means necessary. I defended her from the vaimpír, and now, I will defend her from her own mind.

"All is well. The worst has passed. Nothing else will bother us this evening. You will rest well, and then we will continue in the morning. You are strong. You are fierce. You are capable."

I will confidence into my words as her walls crumble. Another mystery unravels, revealing her fear of letting another person see her so vulnerable.

My hand works its way up and down before venturing to her uncovered hair. Its silky softness is pleasing as it slides against the pads of my fingers.

Finally, with one long exhale, her body relaxes. But when she tries to pull away, something clicks in my chest, like a lock opening, and I resist.

"Ra'Sa, I am… better now."

My throat bobs. I still don't release her. Holding her through her shakes made me face her fragility. I fear we'll both fall apart if I step back.

How can I let her out of my sight, knowing anything could trigger one of these attacks? What if I'm not there to hold her together?

I can't lose another person I care about, not that I love this woman…

But my brother.

My father.

My three sisters.

I—

"Ra'Sa," Melisa's gentle voice calls again. She takes one of my hands and places it over her breast. Beneath my palm, her heartbeat pumps. Steady.

Whole.

Alive.

It doesn't matter what she is or where we are going. I can't deny what I feel. I soften, and my index finger traces her bare flesh just above her gown's neckline.

She gasps, but I do not.

If I had thought my blood was pumping hard before, it would be nothing compared to the reaction elicited by the feel of her beauty.

It is one thing to gaze… another to touch.

Gods, I had never touched a woman like this.

As my thumbs stroke the side of her breast, she gasps again, and blood rushes straight to my cock.

The suddenness makes me feel like a molten man. I am impossibly grateful that my brother believed in the worth of humans when I did not.

I want everything all at once: her mouth, her neck. I would bare as much flesh as she would allow in the open air to explore and warm.

Melisa stares up at me with a slightly parted mouth. Then she swallows and steps back, shaking her head. My hands stay frozen in the air where her body was seconds before.

Battle makes the rush of lust that much more potent.

"I am okay, Ra'Sa," she whispers. Then she bites her lip, and her reaction cools the lust pumping through my veins. As anticipated, the chiding comes, "You shouldn't—"

But it is my turn to interrupt her. "We need to burn the body."

She grows silent and helps me as we scour the ground for wood. We dust off snow, and add branches to the pile of the embers in the middle of the camp. Once the flame is sufficiently large, I toss the halves of the body in.

Melisa watches, eyes wide, as the fire eats away the cursed flesh of the creature.

I don't want her to stare at the flames. So, instead, I say, "You don't know how to fight."

She pauses, looking back up at me and wringing her hands.

"No. It's dangerous to give the slaves weapons," she says wryly.

Perhaps it is borne out of the desire to be near her once more, but I say, "Let me teach you. You won't be a master blade wielder, but you should know how to stab someone lest they get too close."

She opens her mouth, one side curling upward as if she were going to make a smart comment, but then… she stops.

"I don't have a blade."

I shake my head, holding out my hand. My wrist dips and pulls upward from the earth, bringing forth a long, jagged stone. Using my magic, I smooth the handle to protect her small hands and let it fly to my palm. Taking out a spare leather scrap, I wrap and tie it around the handle before passing the makeshift blade to her.

She takes it gingerly.

"You won't hurt yourself if you only touch it from here," I say, measuring her breathing to track if she starts to panic again. "My mother had attacks, as you have. They were worse after we escaped from Ruhsavida. Much later, I learned that they came when she felt like she had no power and control. Learn to fight, even a little, and you give yourself more power and more control."

Melisa bites her lip. Her displeasure with me has hung like a cloud over us all day. Seeing it melt away into the clear, brilliant skies of her smile makes me feel like Grutabela herself has blessed me with her light.

My stone doesn't sing, and there is no searing pain from my mating marks, but I am happy at this moment.

Happy to help Melisa in any way I can.

It's an emotion that's evaded me for far too long.

"Where do we start?" Melisa asks, stepping forward.

My smile grows at her courage.

Brave woman.

"First, stand. You can't fight someone if you aren't solid on the ground. Come here."

Her eyes flash at the command, but she comes.

I stand straight, feet close together, and then gesture at her. "Try to push me over."

Her brows furrow. "You can't be serious. You are at least two heads taller than me!"

I smile. "Trust me, *Ruh'flor.*"

She glares at the name, and a part of me can't believe it slipped past my lips: cave flower. Why give such a name to a woman who has barely spent any time in the caves?

Before I can analyze it any further, she shoves me. I laugh in surprise at the power of her blow and bend backward.

I had anticipated her to make me sway a little, but I tumble onto my ass mere inches from the fire. My tail stops my fall, and my short hair falls in my eyes. I brush it away.

She looks down at me, half-horrified, half-amused. "Ra'Sa—I'm sorry—"

I smile, getting to my feet and brushing the snow off my backside.

"No, it is a good lesson. The more rigid you are, the easier it will be to knock you down." I adjust my stance, with my feet shoulder width apart, knees slightly bent, and weight balanced.

"Now, try to push me again."

She raises an eyebrow but does so. While my torso twists and bends, I remain standing.

Her eyes study my movements. "You are more flexible."

I nod. "Exactly. The blows won't knock you over, and you can move forward and backward." I demonstrate. "Now, you try."

She chews on her lip, then begins to shift her body. Her eyes meet mine again when she finishes copying how I was moments before. "Like this?"

I like the determination in her voice.

"Yes."

I fashion my own short blade out of stones.

"Next, footwork. Fighting is not just about being able to stand in one place; it's about being able to move. You should learn to advance." I shuffle forward. "Retreat." I mirror the movement backward. "Sidestep." I calmly move to either side.

"And lastly, circle an opponent." I start to move around her, holding out my blade. "If you only attack straight on, you will get hurt more. Movement leads to success in a battle."

I smile. "Let's practice. Shuffle forward."

After a few more minutes, we have practiced each of the steps. I'm strangely proud to watch her catch on so quickly.

"Try an advance, sidestep, and then circle me," I call out, smiling.

She does so, and when she hits each movement just right, she thrusts a playful jab toward me and smiles. Her laugh lights up my heart.

"I did it!"

"You did," I say with a smile. "You have good instincts. What you just did with the blade is called a thrust, but there are other things. You could've slashed at me or parried my attack."

I show her each one, even throwing in feints.

When she slashes a little close to my chest, I reach out and disarm her. Her blade falls to the ground, but her wrist stays locked in my hand.

So many touches. I'm turning into a greedy man.

But then I remember everything she's told me about Zlosa—about Eneko—so I drop her hand, respecting her space.

Her face is flushed, and she pants, smile falling just a touch.

"I think that is enough for tonight," I say solemnly.

She nods her head. "Of course."

I smile back at her. "Well done today."

"Thank you."

"Let's eat."

CHAPTER 13
MELISA

Heat courses through my body. The pressure between my legs is the sweetest torture. A hand skirts over my sensitive flesh, making me impossibly wetter.

A finger skims over the sweet spot at the apex of my thighs.

I really need to tell Ra'Sa to stop or I'm going to break my only rule. But the fire coursing under my skin only makes me want to lean into the sensation.

When I open my eyes, Ra'Sa is under me. He looks up at me with such intense abandon and his fingers thread through mine. He's large, but not to the point of awful pain. Gentle, but rough when his passions take over.

This was right. This was good.

When I move my hips, sweet friction from his cock causes my center to hum with pleasure. Tension is building that I've never felt while riding a partner.

Not the first time a man took me in the breeding pens, and certainly never with Eneko. This is something more intimate than sex—this is release.

He lets go of my hands, and his tail wraps around my wrists. Pinning them behind me.

Ra'Sa hitches up his hips, meeting my movements with an alarming focus. My head falls back as the friction of his body against that small bundle of nerves causes insistent, sweet ripples of pleasure to pull across my skin. I feel like I'm going to fall.

Fall into him.

Fall for him.

No.

The insistent voice causes me to wake. Sweat clings to my brow, and I can feel the slickness between my thighs when I shift.

Fuck.

From the ebbing ache between my thighs and the frustration knotted in my chest, it seems that I stopped, quite literally, just in time.

I look at Ra'Sa over my shoulder, heart pounding and mind racing. I want to go to him.

Again, *no.*

When my mind finally clears from my intense wet dream, the reality of life crashes down once again.

We'll arrive at Zlosa tomorrow.

And I… I can't stop thinking about him. I'd thought all hope was lost after he told me he wasn't interested if we weren't mated, but he's changed on the trek.

He held me last night.

Tightly. Sweetly.

And now, I lie next to him. He is close enough to roll over and straddle. If he's started to change his opinion about mates—about me—then I risk everything by not solidifying this relationship before we set foot on giant soil.

I pull out the small gem that Estela gave me before we left. I admire its red color in the faint spell like Ra'Sa cast. Some grow to hate the color they wear as a comfort woman, but I don't. Red is pleasing. Lucky.

My fist closes around the stone, and my eyelids shut. The image of Ra'Sa holding me after my attack passes over the back of my eyes with excruciating detail. I feel the way his arms wrapped around me.

A flush creeps up my skin.

His care is gentle.

I see my dream again, riding him within an inch of either of our lives. The heat that had come over me was as exquisite as any night I'd gone to my bed and taken care of myself.

Mierda.[1]

I take another deep breath, and my hand brushes down my soft belly. Nine months after the breeding pens, I wrapped my midsection and went to the farms to help prepare animals for the slaughterhouse. It was miserable. But, in time, a giant came looking for someone to warm his bed.

Eneko.

He passed by me every day for a week, and then guards showed up at Griselda's house to take me away.

Griselda hated me for going willingly, but by not fighting back and controlling my emotions, I secured a measure of safety for three years. Making the choice to save my family helped me live with myself.

Ra'Sa had been right about something he said yesterday—that the attacks lessen when I feel like I'm in control.

Now, I'm in this tent with this Enduar man. I chose him for logical reasons, but my heart flutters at the nearness.

"You belong to no one."

He doesn't understand that for a woman, belonging to a man is often the only way to have some semblance of safety. And for me, a person prone to falling apart when the world spins out, controlling this would be better than not.

I'd like to belong to him. But the rules still apply.

My eyes close to block out the images, but my mouth is dry, and my skin is oversensitive.

I breathe in and out.

The space between my legs throbs.

I open my eyes and grit my teeth. This problem must be resolved.

It's too cold to go outside, and the tent is small.

What would he do if he woke up and found me like this?

Goosebumps cover my body.

Maybe if I get this out of my system first, it won't mean anything. If I act before letting my lust consume me, my head will clear. I will cement our relationship while keeping some perspective.

Restless, I roll over and look at the large sleeping form on the other side of the tent, pretending not to notice how my heart picks up in speed.

This is just business. Just me ensuring my future.

Slowly, I bring myself to my knees and lean over him. I pause, my hand connecting with his large bicep.

I can't help but appreciate the difference between my average-sized hand and his large shoulder. With Eneko, I've always felt too small. Too breakable.

But with Ra'Sa, I am just… delicate.

I ignore how much I enjoy that. Instead, I stroke my hand to his wrist.

"Ra'Sa."

He stirs, and I watch as he shifts onto his back.

"I can't sleep," I say.

His eyes fly open, and he bolts upright. Our tent isn't big, so he almost knocks it all over with his quick action.

I put another hand on him just as he says, "What's wrong? Are you hurt?"

Ignoring yet another blatant sign of care, I fall into his lap and position my legs on either side of his hips.

He stiffens beneath me, but I keep both hands on his shoulders and look up at him, biting my lip and softening my expression. The movements come easy—I've done them at least a hundred times.

"Melisa, what is this?" he asks, but his voice grows deep and soft in a way I haven't heard before.

It eases something inside of me, settling like sand at the bottom of a river.

"Like I said, I couldn't sleep."

"So you've come to me? How can I help with that?" he asks, and the sound of his voice washes over me in soothing waves.

Men are easy to mold. You don't need to lie to them to make them love you. If they care for you enough, they will lie to themselves.

My fingers trail down his arm, and he blinks before releasing my waist and reaching over to grab my wrist. I gasp at his warm hand against my skin.

He breathes deeply, nostrils flaring."Melisa. *What is this?*"

My chest rises and falls between us, breasts just barely brushing his chest. I swallow, trying to return moisture to my mouth. My body is eager, but my mind is wary.

Go on, Meli. Kiss him. Use your tongue. Be the whore you are. He'll like it, and you'll stop dreaming about this.

And so I lean in.

When my lips brush his, they are stiff. Frustrated, I brush my tongue over the seam of his mouth. It catches him off guard, and he parts his lips for me.

I kiss him harder, pouring every trick I have into the action. My hand trails over his shoulder and down his spine as best I can—light touches meant to drive him wild.

Then I bite him once.

The evidence of his arousal pushes up against my ass, but he doesn't grab me. If this were Eneko, he would throw me down, taking this as enough of a hint to fuck me, and do as he pleases.

Ra'Sa *waits.*

Growing angry, I pull back.

His mouth remains slightly puckered as the gem in his chest glows and his eyes open.

"Melisa," he says gently.

I shake my head. He just told me he cared for me, but he does not act like a man who desires a woman. He needs to want me.

"If you do not want me, I will leave you be," I say crossly, fully pulling back.

"Wait," he calls out, reaching for my face.

Good. Let him chase you.

When I extricate myself from his lap, I fall backward and roll over. Pain spreads through my side, and I cry out.

"Maldita sea,"[2] I curse.

Large hands scoop me up, and a brighter spell light glows to life above us. Ra'Sa looks down at me with wide eyes and a slightly parted mouth.

"Shit. Don't move," he says.

"Don't touch me," I bite out when his hand reaches toward me.

My brain is foggy, stuck in a place where I'm more instinct than sensation. I hurt. I don't need him making it worse.

His hand retreats like lightning, and I swallow hard.

"Forgive me. I merely wished to help care for the wound," he sputters.

When I look down, I see a nasty gash caused by the stone dagger I'd left near my bedroll. Blood soaks into my dress.

I'd been careless.

"Fuck," I sputter. "There's so much blood."

"May I? I will move slowly," he coaxes.

My hand presses to the bleeding wound as I pant.

"I did this to myself. You don't have to fix me," I say through gritted teeth.

Ra'Sa's nostrils flare in the dim light. "Melisa, please."

That word. It causes a crack to bloom up the walls to my heart. I sigh and angle my body so that he can approach.

"If you must."

Ra'Sa doesn't speak as he nears. Just slowly lays his hand on my ribcage so that he can see the wound better. I hiss as his thumb prods at it.

"Gentle," I growl.

He makes a clicking sound with his tongue.

"You do like to goad me, don't you?" he says at last. "Remember, I'm helping."

My mouth opens and then closes. He's not wrong.

Ra'Sa's rough fingers trail up my sides. Not lightly, but not bruising, either.

"I need to get a better look at the cut. It's quite deep."

I sit there for a second, dumbstruck.

"If you wanted me to undress, you should've done something about it when I was in your lap. I could be naked and riding you right now," I grit out, half-goading but also trying to distract myself from the inevitable pain. He doesn't have to know that was something I *longed* for in sleep.

"What is wrong with you?" he demands, letting go of my ribs and leaning away from me. "You draw me in, then push me away. Now, you wake me up and are frustrated that I didn't make love to you less than two days before we arrive in the giant territory? Before I hand you off to another man?"

I look at him, furious, as the blood dampens more of my dress.

But then his eyes widen. "Are you trying to do this?"

I inch away from him. "What on earth are you talking about?"

"You keep too many secrets wrapped up in the layers of your mind. You're playing a game," he says.

This isn't a game—this is my life. My survival is valuable, for it sustains the two girls back in the slave pens.

"I care for you," I say.

"But you care more about whatever game you are playing, right?" he says at last.

Something nudges me, suggesting that he might be more generous with his opinions if I tell him the truth. But that would leave me exposed. What if he changed his mind about helping me?

"You're angry with me," I murmur, unsure what else to say.

"Yes." He pauses, "No. I'm angry with myself and frustrated that I didn't see it earlier."

"Ra'Sa, I am not playing a game. I like you," I say. I'm almost afraid of how quickly that is becoming truth.

He looks up at me. "Really?"

"Yes."

He grows strangely silent after that.

"You know, I could help ease your frustration." I wince as I apply more pressure to the wound weeping at my side.

He frowns. "Will you stop that? Now, take off your dress. Or better yet, don't. You only need to expose your ribs."

I clamp my mouth shut and then allow him to assist me in removing my arms from my sleeves and pushing the dress below my breastband. The chill of the night bites at my skin, causing my nipples to pebble.

He reaches for the cloak and drapes it over my shoulders.

"Tell me if you get too cold," he murmurs.

I swallow back another comment, and he places me atop the packs he carries, leaning me against one of them as if it were a pillow. With my back on an incline and him between my legs, I feel the heat crawl up my neck.

He sifts for a few things out of his pack, withdrawing herbs. I recognize some of them from Estela's stash.

"Have you been taking lessons with the human queen?"

He exhales, and his warm breath skims along my bare torso. "More like with Ulla."

Absent-mindedly, my fingers close around his wrist.

"Is it more appropriate for you to be with an Enduar woman?" Even saying the words, I know I'm grasping. But I'm angry and raw over his rejection.

He stills. "What?"

"I kiss you, and you barely react. You come with me because I ask you, but you also treat me as though I annoy you."

He looks back up at me, and bright blue eyes pin me in place. No one has ever looked at me this way. His noble tendencies are aggravating. And yet, I don't try to run from this moment.

"I do not wish to court Ulla, or any other Enduar woman. She is nothing more than a good friend. She is also quite a bit older than me."

I pause. "Would you not be with an older woman?"

He growls. "If I fancied her, I would not care for her age."

"So you do not fancy Ulla?" I say.

His nostrils flare. "Enduar women do not want me."

"That wasn't an answer."

He sighs. "No, I don't care for her like that."

"But you desire me."

He presses a bunch of herbs against my wound, and I squeal, letting go of his wrist.

"That was cruel," I say.

In response, his fingers skim the underside of my breast, and I gasp.

His eyes snap back onto mine, and the moment's intimacy strikes a chord in my chest. I've had men lay over me, move inside of me, and yet, this closeness… This tenderness is nothing like any of that.

The two of us are using up all the air in the small tent.

My dress falls a little lower.

His eyes drop back to my body. His fingers continue to trail over several silvery scars on either side of my belly.

Fuck, I forgot.

I hold my breath as his brow furrows. Then I place my hand over the marks caused by overstretched skin. He doesn't need to witness all my imperfections.

He grabs my hand, exposing my bare arm.

"You have so many marks. What are all of these?" he asks, brushing his fingers over faint, slightly sunken lines up my forearm.

I grit my teeth. "Battle scars."

He lets go of me, and his eyes find mine again.

"Battle is painful—I cannot imagine what it must have been like if you did not know how to fight. I am sorry you've also endured that."

A question sits on the tip of my tongue, and I try to resist asking it. But in the end, I hear myself say, "Have you been in combat?"

He takes a deep breath, then returns to bandaging my wound.

"Aside from tonight? Yes. A few times, but always against giants and spiders. Only one encounter left a scar."

"And that was…?" My question breaks off with a hiss. His fingers rub at the hurt, soothing the sting.

"Before you came along, I had a brother named Tirin. He was young—barely a baby when we escaped one of the surrounding cities during the Great Eruption."

I listen intently, grateful when he continues.

"Tirin was a young hunter and what we called a '*Ruh'duar*.'"

My eyebrows draw together while hearing him say a word in his native tongue. The way it flows from his mouth is mesmerizing.

He notices my attention and continues, "It means 'cave born'. He did not know the ways of the old trolls."

"What do you mean? Most of the stories I've heard of your people involve flesh-eating and human ravaging."

Ra'Sa laughs bitterly. "We have never been cannibals, you strange woman. We were people of strict tradition. A cold people, but a successful one. Tirin was too eager—too optimistic."

I bite my lip, realizing the bandage around my middle is complete. I could move away and put my clothes back on, but I do not wish to. Especially since I find I enjoy the sound of his voice.

"I don't see how this left a scar."

He purses his lips. "Patience, *Ruh'flor*." Ra'Sa spreads his hand over my bandage, coating the wound in a delicious warmth. "When the humans came, he saw our people's salvation. But not for himself… for me. For his quiet, brooding older brother."

My breath catches.

"He is a good brother," I say gently, despite realizing that he's only used past tense verbs to refer to him.

"*Was*," Ra'Sa grits out. "And he *was* beheaded by my king to save us from an attack from the giants. His head was given to the giant king to stop a war that came anyway. I raged against the heavens and cursed my gods. But in the end, I realized how I could honor his death. You see, we lost our father and sisters in the eruption. He wanted me to have a chance at what we lost."

The story pours out of him, and I wonder if he's ever told it to another soul.

My mouth goes dry, and every cell inside of my body goes deathly still. I don't need to know this about him. Too personal.

"I'm… sorry," I say softly.

"It is the only scar I bear on my soul and serves as a compass for my purpose."

Somehow, he's drawn close to me. I can taste his breath on my lips.

"And what is your purpose, Enduar?"

"To find a mate. And from my future matehood, I will have children."

I pull back.

Children.

That word radiates through me like lightning. It reminds me of screams, and pain, and laying on my back alone. No one knew where I was; no one even knew that the girls would be born, save the wolf who protected me.

I hurt and bled and starved. And then I vowed, 'Never again.'

His wanting children changes things for good.

"And what if you are mated to one of the pregnant women?" I ask, my voice a slightly higher pitch.

The Enduar looks at me, brows furrowed and confused by my distance. "I would care for the child."

"But you would want your own?"

"Yes. Someone to name after Tirin."

Fuck.

Ra'Sa wants… *children.*

I can't be pregnant. I won't ever be able to handle that again.

Ra'Sa is dangerous—far more than I ever realized.

I'd been a fool for thinking he could be swayed. I'd been a fool for thinking I could ever control any part of this. I need out. I need to get away.

I shake my head and push away. “I can’t be your mate.”

“I never asked—”

“I can’t—I can’t.” I look up at him. “If a song sings between us, I don’t think I would accept.”

He grows defensive. “Was my kiss so repulsive?”

I swallow hard. “I—You—You don’t know how to care for humans.”

What the fuck kind of answer was that?

The damage hits him square in the chest anyway. His face falls into a grimace.

You weren't meant to be a mother.

I’d heard that my whole life. It seems I wasn’t meant to be a mate either.

Slowly, he pushes me off of him and helps me replace the sleeves of my dress. Once I’m clothed, he stands and pushes out of the tent.

“Ra’Sa,” I call. If he leaves me alone out here, wolves could find us. Or more of those pale, red-eyed creatures. "Please. I didn't mean it like that. Forgive me—”

“Sleep. I will be near.”

1. Shit.

2. Damnit.

CHAPTER 14

RA'SA

"Move your wrist faster," I grumble as I carry Melisa through the snow.

"Put your glamour back on," she retorts.

I find it's easier to travel with my skin blue and my tail long. This morning, I was weary from the poor rest, so I didn't even bother using Thorne's glamour.

"No. Now move faster."

Melisa practices her knife work while nestled in my arms. Perhaps it's masochistic to keep her so close to me, but I can't help myself. She is injured. There's no way I would have her walk like this.

"It's disappointing that this is the only way you wish to wear me out. I swear, there are much more fun ways to work up a sweat," she pants.

I try not to notice the way her black hair sticks to her skin or how the cloak parts to reveal her soft, full hips and thighs in the red gown. Especially because of what she said last night.

"There is no better way to prepare to enter Zlosa than by ensuring that you know how to defend yourself," I retort, and she falls silent.

The quiet doesn't bother me much. It helps to think about our exchange.

Or rather, her rejection. If it had been anyone else, I would've believed it and left her be. Cut myself off.

Optimism does not come easy to me. I tend to see the worst in people. But Melisa is decidedly different. I'm not sure why. All I know is that a sensation deep in my gut tells me to hold on.

I want to help her.

"If you insist on being prepared, perhaps we should work on finding a way to send each other messages," Melisa says, effectively tearing a hole in my thoughts.

I look down at her. "We will not be able to see each other?"

She avoids my gaze as she straightens her clothes and returns the dagger to the folds of her dress.

"No. When we return, you will take me to Eneko's cabin, where his whole family lives. You will go to work with the other slaves. We might be able to meet at night every few days."

Silence hangs in the air between us.

"We should have a method in case something more serious arises," she says.

The reality that we will make it to Zlosa within the next day begins to weigh on me. Even thinking about her in the home of that monstrous giant makes my skin crawl.

Instead of voicing my displeasure, I ask, "What do you have in mind?"

She is silent for a moment.

"I think it would be best if we use a code my family and I invented. Basically, it's a pattern of rocks and sticks. It's easier to disguise than other methods. Each letter has a series."

The world around us continues to be quiet as we trudge along. The hours spent listening to her voice are strangely calming to me.

It causes me to smile. That expression doesn't go unnoticed.

"I didn't know you enjoyed pebbles and branches so much," Melisa teases. "Or perhaps you are just one of those quiet types excited by secret codes?"

I sneak a sideways glance at her. "Perhaps I am merely *excited* by the sound of your voice."

When I look at her, she seems as bewildered as a cave rat before a fire.

"What? You are the only one allowed to tease?" I ask.

Her mouth curves up into a smile. "Not at all. I'm just surprised."

I hum, pleased. "Tell me more about your sticks and stones."

"Are you sure it won't be too complicated?" she asks. "I worry for your tiny brain."

"I can proficiently speak five languages. They come to me quickly. I know the alphabet of the common tongue."

More silence passes through the space between us. The birds fly overhead, and the blasted sun continues to crawl into the sky.

"Fine, I will teach you. Put me down. I think I am well enough to walk."

I reluctantly oblige, casting her a sideways look and drinking in her unusual beauty.

"Tell me how to recognize an *A*. We have plenty of time before we arrive to memorize a few dozen measly letters," I say with a smile.

She laughs and shakes her head. The sound is sweet. I wish I had a million days to walk through these woods and learn every secret she keeps hidden.

"A would be a rock and a stick," she says.

I smile. "Next."

"B is a stick and two rocks."

We continue on like that for hours, reviewing her letters until we are half a day away from Zlosa.

"Tell me how to say… Melisa is the most beautiful woman in the world," she says.

I laugh. "That message is too long."

She grins. "We have time."

I shake my head. "Two sticks, one stone, another stone then a stick followed by two stones, two stones—"

"What's that smell?" Melisa interrupts, looking away from me.

I stop walking and take a deep breath. The air is thick with charred wood and the roasted smell of burnt flesh.

Acid pools in my stomach.

"Melisa—" I start.

"The sky has been pink. I just thought it was an extended sunrise… oh gods. That's smoke, isn't it?"

I swallow, looking up at the sky. Sure enough, the heavens have an orangish hue.

"I am not a land dweller. I hadn't noticed anything amiss."

Her eyes widen when she looks at me, and I see past all her walls. "They are burning something. Or there is some massive forest fire. Either way, we must get to Zlosa."

She picks up her pace, no longer looking at me.

"Melisa!" I call after her.

When I reach her side, I see a column of smoke billowing above the trees. I grab her shoulder, and she whips around to look at me. Small strands of hair puff out around her face as she pants.

The deep, golden skin that usually glows with health has taken on a grey tint.

"Is this another attack? One of your waking nightmares?"

"They're burning Zlosa!" she yells. "We have to get there tonight."

I look at the sky and see the ash. "Slow down. It will still take us at least half a day to arrive."

She yanks out of my grip. "Put your glamour on. They might find us in the woods."

Reaching into one of my pouches, I grab a glamour pebble. I close my eyes and speak the elvish word that calls the magic on command.

"Blàth," I murmur.

In seconds, my skin begins to tingle. When I open my eyes, the blue slowly fades and morphs into something more human. A discomfort comes as the magic spreads across my chest and back, and my eyes burn.

When it is done, I drop the small stone. It has become dull and barren. A part of me is sad to leave it behind.

Then she continues walking. No attempts at reasoning will draw her off course. We skip lunch and continue to walk at a breakneck pace in frenetic noiselessness. She swats at me when I ask to check her bandage.

The hills are much more challenging to climb in this cold weather. I had thought that my physical condition was adequate, but we are both out of breath when we reach a hill that looks down on the valley.

It is late at night, but light pours from the city and palace.

The slave pens come into view shortly after. While we cannot see much further than the northeastern lumber yard, the charred houses are easy to see from here.

It looks eerily similar to the homes that were overtaken by lava. My heart skips a beat.

"Melisa," I start. "Are you all right?"

When she finally turns to look at me, she frowns.

"They did not burn Eneko's section," she says at last.

"That's… good?"

"That is everything."

A part of me balks at this. Though I am not the most expressive individual, I can hardly believe she would see all this destruction and not be affected.

While I study her, I think of what she said. She constantly extinguishes her feelings and puts them in some dark corner.

"That's all you have to say? Melisa, they burned hundreds of your people. Maybe thousands."

She turns away from me, and I notice that her breathing is oddly stilted. When she reaches down and picks up a handful of snow, I move to touch her again.

"Ra'Sa, we've arrived. It's time to prepare to see Eneko. He's already going to be angry that I've been gone a week. I need to make this believable. I'll worry about the others later."

I clamp my jaw shut as she tears the hem of her dress and soaks it with ice. She smears frozen mud over her garments and coats her hair in the thick filth, along with her cheek, collarbones, and fingernails.

I come behind her to help her warm up.

"No. I must be chilled as if I'd been left outside for days," she says.

My brows draw together.

"That would be impossible. If you'd been in the snow for a week, you'd be frozen solid."

She practically snarls and presses her hand to the waistband of her dress. Her eyes are blank, haunted, when she lets go of the wound soaked in red.

The bandage has been leaking this whole time.

"Melisa," I growl, grabbing onto the side of her ribcage. Why didn't I smell it? The fires must have altered my senses.

She gasps and shouts, "Fuck!"

"You do seem to love that word," I say, and she glares at me. "Why didn't you tell me you were hurting?"

"When I saw the smoke I…"

"Had a plan. Of course. I should've known you were thinking far ahead." I sigh. "The good news is that you are dirty enough for them to believe you haven't had a bath lately. I would stand firm on you being an icicle if you'd been outside, though."

She bites her hand. "You should hit me over the head. They'll be so focused on my wound, they won't question everything else."

I recoil. "Absolutely not."

"Ra'Sa, if you want me to include you in my plans, you must be willing to play along," she says.

I grab her wrist. "I have my limits, and injuring you is out of the question."

It still hurts to think of those scars along her belly and up her arms—not to speak of the scars slashed across her soul, where no one can see. She's been hurt too much.

She smiles sweetly, as she has done dozens of times. I realize it's been a mask.

"What if I ask kindly and promise to wrap my lips around your cock?"

A spike of adrenaline rushes through my veins.

"Again—No." Then I bite my lip. "I will carry you. You pretend to sleep in my arms. Final offer."

She sneers. "Fine. But I won't forget this."

"You won't forget that I refused to hurt you?" My eyebrows scrunch together.

"If they don't buy our story, they'll kill us both," she spits.

I clamp my jaw shut. "I'll be convincing."

"Hide the gear. We're leaving the trees."

I suck in a sharp breath and do as she says. Once finished, I turn back to Melisa, she wraps her arms around my neck. I bend down, slide one arm under her legs, and hoist her up closer to me.

"I am sorry for your people," I say softly.

She meets my gaze. "Me too. Now, head down this hill and turn to the left. You'll see the slave pens. Before you arrive, there is a hill with a fence surrounded by tightly packed trees. Eneko's cabin is in that area."

She adjusts her grip, clearly waiting for me to move.

I take a deep breath.

Our short time alone together is gone. It's been… it's honestly been a mess.

As I look back out at the smoking remains of the slaves and the burnt houses, I think of the gruesome things giants had done to my people in the past. The ravaged villages and dead women.

They never stopped being awful. Their lies poisoned an entire generation against us.

A new future gapes before me like the maw of a venomous beast—one that we voluntarily enter. When I take my first step, it is because of the human woman in my arms.

I move quickly. She is silent when we hurry past the first people we've seen in days. I grimace when I see a large bonfire in the corner.

Human bodies are stacked atop each other.

I turn away, shielding her from the shock.

What is this hellish place?

When we finally reach the small thicket of trees where Melisa says that Eneko lives, I slow.

The house itself seems ordinary enough. There are no heads on spikes or bloodstains in the snow. Two small children are playing outside.

As giants, they are nearly as tall as Melisa, though neither could be older than a decade or two.

Melisa's arms go slack, and one hangs down pathetically. When I glance down at her, I see her eyes close. The need to adjust her is strong, but before I can, one of the giant children catches us.

"They're humans!" one hisses.

The taller and presumably older of the two steps forward. "Da said you can't come here after dark. Get out, or we'll throw rocks!"

Though the warning had just come, one of them throws a stone the size of my foot at me. It connects with my leg, and a burst of pain radiates up to my hip.

I curse in Enduar under my breath and step forward.

When I do, one of the children screams.

"Ma!"

When the elder one sees Melisa limp in my arms, he grabs his brother. "Shut up. It's Da's human."

Something hot and angry stirs in my chest, but I keep it clamped down.

The front door to the cabin flings open, and warm yellow light spills into the night. A giant woman with rich, brown hair stands in the doorway.

It's clear that she's older, from the wrinkles across her forehead and near her eyes. Decorative scars are carved into the tops of her breasts and around her cheeks. Some of them have been painted red to match the flowing red gown that covers her figure. It resembles what Melisa wears, but the cloth is a finer weave.

"What's all this?" she demands, moments before her gaze lands on Melisa.

Her frown deepens, verging on a sneer. Quickly, she steps out into the chilly air and pulls the door shut behind her.

"Boys! Go around back and get inside. Tell your father nothing, and go straight to bed."

She waits for them to abandon their wooden cattle, warriors, and spears before she looks back at me.

She marches over. The woman is tall enough that I have to crane my head to look up at her.

"Get her out of here, or I'll slice off your cock and feed it to you."

My mouth drops open to say something as my grip tightens on Melisa. I don't want her to be touched by these people. Leaving her with them is as preposterous as leaving a newborn outside.

"Are you deaf, you niggling twit? Get away!" she whisper-hisses.

I take a step back. As much as I would love nothing more than to run away with Melisa still in my arms, she was determined to come here. She made me promise that I would be with her as she completed this mission.

I gave my word to her, and I gave it to my king. My duty lies with them.

"She belongs to Eneko," I grit out, trying to swallow down the sour taste the words bring.

She sneers. "I don't want her anywhere near my husband."

The door opens again. "Hibsej, my dear, what is all this?"

Another tall giant walks out. He is much older than Hibsej, much older than I would've anticipated. His frame is large, scarred, and stocky, as most giants are. Though, for a commoner, he is much more neatly groomed, and his clothes seem to match his wife's.

Hibsej glares at me, then turns around, her glare melting into a smile.

"Nothing, dear. I was just taking care of something."

He peers out past her, first seeing me, and then his gaze drops to Melisa.

"The whore's come home!" he calls, clearly excited. "Thank the gods. I thought she'd been killed with the others."

The crass title has me tightening my grip on Melisa. How can I leave her with this brute?

"Eneko—"

"What's wrong with her, boy?" he demands.

It takes me a few moments to realize he's talking to me. I meet his eye.

"I found her near the northwestern lumber yards. It looked like she'd been left there to die. Silvester told me to bring her here." The lie had been carefully practiced, but a part of me worries it will be rejected for its obvious flaws.

Eneko looks at me long and hard, and I try to erase the hatred I feel from my face. When his gaze dips back to Melisa, I resist the urge to cover her.

"Silvester sent you?"

I pause, then say. "Yes, Foreman."

He nods. "Good. High King Rholker has been too busy to find me a new comfort woman, and I'm desperate for a rut. Khuohr knows that my saggy old wife is no good after two sons. Take her to my bed."

I freeze. Confronted with my reality is like being stabbed repeatedly in my stomach.

"Foreman, she's unconscious and injured. We found her with a cut on her side."

"Godsdamnit. Then put her in the back room."

I hesitate, and he misinterprets the action.

"Fine. I will show you the way, as I suppose I'm meant to do godsdamned everything around here. Hib, go take care of my sons." Then he starts walking into the house.

Inside appears exaggeratedly large with high walls and spacious rooms.

"You're quite tall for a human," Eneko says after a moment.

I don't respond.

"I didn't realize there were so many giant bastards with Silvester. I knew that he helped the king's halfblood."

"Bastards aren't well-liked in the yards," I say, unsure exactly how to have this conversation.

He snorts. "Damn shame. Your kind is twice as strong as the others."

We continue walking, but he stops abruptly at a door leading to a room tacked onto the rear of the house. I pull it open. Everything inside is small, hardly tall enough for him to walk inside.

"We've lost a few thousand of you in the last week after those humans escaped," he says before I step inside.

I turn around and look at the man. I hate him as I have never hated before. Every inch of him. May his sons grow up and kill him.

Or, better yet, I hope I do it with my bare hands.

"We are short on slaves in our yard as well."

"My apologies," I grit out.

"Work for me. I'll give you better meals than they do over there."

I freeze. This was exactly what we wanted.

"My master will not be pleased."

He frowns. "I'll tell Old Silv if he asks. In fact, it is decided. You will stay and help my crew. Head over to the slave pens and look for the biggest hut at the end of the path."

My stomach growls.

He smirks. "Just toss her on the bed. I'll have Hib give you some bread before you leave."

I nod, then walk into the room. It is chilly in here, and I worry about the temperature. When I place Melisa on the bed, I try not to linger. Not with her master watching me closely.

The only thing that causes me to pause is when one of her fingers brushes over my hand.

It's a bit of comfort for a woman who asks for little.

My heart aches.

Risking it all, I covertly squeeze her digit and hurry away.

Once out of the room, I watch him remove a lock and shut her in. I bite back questions, keeping my gaze down.

Silently, we return to the front of the house. Eneko momentarily disappears and comes back with a half loaf.

"Frigid woman. It will be nice to have some soft flesh to touch once more," he mutters, more to himself than me.

When he offers me the bread, I almost don't take it.

So much anger simmers beneath the surface of my skin.

I could kill him.

But we wouldn't get the information we need, and we would lose. There would be no news on the giant king or his court, and we would be clueless about how to get humans to Enduvida.

So finally, I take the loaf.

"Meet in the northeastern yards at daybreak," he commands before leaving.

I make to walk away from the cabin, but pause. There is a window near Melisa's bed.

Making sure I'm not being watched, I rush back and organize a quick message with stones and sticks, just as we planned.

Once I am done, I unlock her down and hurry away. When I reach the pens, the stench of unwashed bodies lingers in the air.

Everything is damp and chilly.

There was no way in hell I would eat food from that man, but wasting such a commodity would be cruel, so I stop in front of one of the dens and throw the loaf inside.

I look for the men's quarters. It is essentially a large building with dirt-packed floors and scraps of oiled wood to keep some sections cleaner than others. At least a hundred men are crammed into one area, and I navigate between them.

When I finally find an empty spot, I lay down and work on securing myself and my pebbles, clutching one so I won't shift in my sleep. Then I close my eyes.

Sleep refused to come despite knowing that tomorrow would be filled with back-breaking work.

I can only think of leaving Melisa at that cabin with those monsters—but that was always the plan.

We made it to our mark. We are in Zlosa.

May the gods keep us all as we journey through this valley of darkness.

PART 2

CHAPTER 15

MELISA

The sound of scratching wakes me up, followed by a whine.

When I open my eyes, the weak early morning light paints the walls around me blue. I recognize the brown wood filled with knotty bulges and streaks of gray—winter elm.

Back in Zlosa.

Another high-pitched cry draws me to my feet despite my sore limbs. When I pad to the door and pull it open, a medium-sized gray wolf stands on my front step.

"Coco," I say, exhaling. "How did you know I was here?"

She lets out a frustrated huff and pushes past me into the room. Closing the door, I stumble back over to the bed just as she jumps onto the mattress.

Once I flop back down, she curls up beside me, resting her head on my legs.

"You should be taking care of Thea and Wren," I say sternly. She looks at me with those large, pleading eyes, and I sigh. "Yes, yes. I'm sorry. I missed you, too."

She snuggles into me, sniffing.

"I have been to so many marvelous places, *mi amor,*"[1] I say, stroking the fur around her ears. "I'm sure I smell strange." She makes a grumbling noise, as if trying to talk. "How are the little ones?"

As I rub the poor creature's neck muscles, I feel the tension that likely has been building since I left.

A pang of guilt pricks my chest, and I let her lie atop me as her eyelids droop.

"How much have you been sleeping lately?" I whisper, stroking behind her ears.

Hibsej would be furious if she found her in my room—animal should piss and shit outside—but I hardly have the strength to push my wolf away. Eneko doesn't do morning visits, so we'll have at least a few more hours of peace.

I'll move her as soon as I can stand again.

Soft, deep breaths come from her mouth, and I look out the window. The sun is barely peeking over the trees, and my room is cold.

A weight sinks down on me. I hate being back in this room. It was added after the cabin was built for a newlywed couple looking forward to a lifetime of love.

Well, as much love as giants can conceive of.

Hibsej and Eneko had been married over a decade when she got pregnant with her oldest son, Relmos. Eneko more or less tended to his wife during the pregnancy, and a son was born. Strong. Healthy. Sadly, his mother had been left to suffer on bed rest.

It took less than a week after her birth for Eneko to call in a whole troop of slaves and start building this small, drafty living space—or so she'd told me the first few days I'd come here.

She told me that she begged Eneko not to petition the Second Prince for a comfort woman, and he obliged for a time.

Then she gave birth to Urdort.

I arrived on the day of his birth, a little over three years ago. A handpicked present: a woman to fuck under the consent of the prince. Hated by humans and giants alike.

Despite this room's sad story, it offered more protection from the elements than traditional slave dens, and the walls connecting to the house were thick enough not to have to listen to their every movement. I was slow to complain the first year.

But this life wore down on me, like grains of sand rubbed over rust.

When I'm not called to the main house to whore, I do Hibsej's bidding. I have been paraded around in front of slaves, humiliated, and have endlessly washed every scrap of fabric in that house, from the bedding to the undergarments. I did it all while concealing the anger growing in my heart.

It's strange how physical proximity to a location can mold your whole personality. When Estela told me about the caves, not only did I see a better life for my family, I saw an escape from what I was.

It worked—for a few days. But now I am fully entrenched in the same place that turned me into a smiling viper.

Coco's head is heavy against my legs, but I feel more awake.

I take a deep breath and push up to a sitting position. The place where the knife sliced open my flesh stings in pain. Much worse than when I first woke.

My hand flies to the hot, puffy skin. It's likely irritated from walking. I wince, take a deep breath, and look up at the ceiling.

Coco awakens as I bunch the fabric of my dress. She watches as I pull it up until my stomach and wound are exposed.

I bite my lip and feel around the packed leaves that Ra'Sa left. I can almost hear his voice telling me to leave it be—can almost feel his fingers against my skin.

For only a minute, I allow myself to luxuriate in the memory of him carrying me across the yards. I think of how quickly he moved and how careful he was not to jostle me. Like I am precious to him, even after our fight.

I squeeze my eyes shut. This has turned into such a mess.

You draw me in, then push me away.

Something hot and indignant sparks in my chest. What the hell does he know about attraction and want?

I hope he finds a mate while here, one ready to give him the family he so desperately wants, and I can forget ever wanting him in the first place.

Coco whines again as I take another deep breath and peel away the herbs. I suck in a sharp hiss, and she tries to lick me.

"Coco, no. *Bad.*"

She looks up at me with large eyes, and I sigh.

"Licking makes it worse."

She leans back. Shoving her off proves fruitless, so I settle for her watching as I prod at the wound. It hurts. Definitely irritated, but it doesn't look infected.

Good.

A gritty film covers my skin, and when I shift my legs, I feel a deep soreness. Damn. Cleaning days of sweat and dirt will likely help stave off some of her fury.

Eneko will be gone at the yards until the early evening, and I have somewhere to visit.

Yanking my dress back down, I find the knife from Ra'Sa and the gem from Estela; I'd been given few precious gifts in my life. I move out of bed. Coco follows.

My wound aches as I lift the mattress and put them in the back corner. It was a kind thing to teach me how to use the weapon, but I'll have little use for it now.

When I stand, I almost fall back onto the bed. Coco casts me an incredulous look, so I grit my teeth and gesture to the door.

"Go. Watch over the twins," I say.

She looks up at me with sad eyes, but follows when I cross the room and open the door.

After she leaves, I move to the window to see if anyone is around. I'm pleased to see the backyard empty as my wolf leaves.

Thick trees surround this cabin to give the foreman's family privacy, and the entire backyard is still dusted with a thick layer of snow. Sadly, I must admit the evergreens look pretty next to the stark white. Rows of wooden dowels are organized between several trees. I use them to hang the family's washing.

My eyes land on the well I'll use to draw water for a bath, and I take a deep breath. After a few minutes, and no sign of Hibsej or her two terrible sons, I draw up all my resolve and pull a cloak out of my wardrobe.

There are different kinds of comfort women. Some spend their days working as a slave, only to go to their masters when called.

But foremen are typically given comfort women like me—we live in the homes of the masters we serve and help the household during the day. Despite this, my wardrobe is much nicer than the other women in my position. Eneko is favored by the new king, and I'm always carted out to parties. The foreman takes great pride in having both a sturdy wife who gave him two strong sons and a pretty human to warm his bed.

I select my red cloak and slip it over my soiled clothing.

There are two weighted buckets next to the simple metal tub in the corner of my room. Once dressed, I grab them and pull open the door. Limping, I slip into the chilled morning air.

The sun is still just barely sliding past the horizon line, and I sigh, wishing I had rested more. But I've always been unable to sleep for more than a few hours despite my soreness weighing me down.

Stepping out of the cabin feels surreal. It's all the same—the crunch of my boots against the snow, the red clothing, the smoke coming from the front house where Hibsej is no doubt burning bread just for me—but I am different. I have a purpose.

Soon, this will all be worth it.

I can feel the end of this horrible life like a song playing in the wind.

It reminds me of the faint melodies in the Enduar caves. Thea loves music. I can imagine her refusing to sleep, sitting in front of a crystal and soaking up every note it offers. Wren will become cross, insisting that it's time to play. Perhaps they'll be able to make friends with the other children, and she'll be placated for once.

A small smile crosses my face. Then I look down and see several lines of scattered sticks and stones.

I pause, my brows furrowing as I read the message.

Please, rest. I will be near. No one will hurt you.

A tender emotion pricks my heart, only to be replaced with irritation. I kick the message around and scatter the pebbles.

We were only supposed to leave messages for each other if there was an emergency or a need to meet. He shouldn't be risking our cover to play the hero.

I let out a 'bah' as I walk over to the well.

No one will hurt me?

Foolish man.

My leg and back muscles scream as I bend over to attach the bucket to the hook at the rope's end. As I lower it—slowly so that it doesn't make any loud noises and call Hibsej from her home—I look up.

From this spot, there is a small gap in the trees. Eneko's house is on a hill, and down below, in the valley, I can see the slave pens. Griselda's home is there. It is unharmed. I knew that it would be; the burnings didn't touch this area of land. They could start tomorrow, though.

I let out a sigh.

Let's hope not.

While the tension on the rope grows taut, I spare one last glance at the elm that grows near Griselda's den. The tree has been there since I was young. Strangely it hasn't been cut down as most of the trees in the pens have been.

I need to visit. The girls' birthday is next week, and I want to visit them before then. Maybe I can even glean a few things to send back to Estela.

While I pull one bucket up and attach the other, I think of everything we saw on the way here. The stacks of bodies, the charred dens burned en masse. The thoughts spark inside me, and I welcome the anger like an old friend.

Once I have both buckets filled to the brim, a bit of nausea gathers in my belly at the thought of Thea and Wren, but I banish it with a deep breath.

It's been a while since I've seen the girls. Surely, they'll be happy to see me.

Who doesn't enjoy a visit from their mother?

1. My love.

CHAPTER 16

RA'SA

Sleep didn't come easily. Throughout the night, I clutched a tiny stone in my hand, desperate to ensure that my glamour doesn't fade. At some point, my Fuegorra started to burn, and I rolled over to ensure it didn't wake anyone. It was an uncomfortable way to rest.

The hut that the working men are meant to share is large but overcrowded. It's a combination of mud bricks and wooden sheets that lay precariously against each other and do the absolute minimum to keep the chilled air out.

There is a smell that seems to cling to the walls like a man hanging onto the side of a cliff for dear life. It is musty and pungent, like unwashed feet.

The room is cold enough that my breath is visible. I adjust on the poorly made bunk, my feet hanging off the edge. There's barely enough space for me to stretch my shoulders, as there's a man on either side of me.

When the other men stir, I sit up, grateful to stretch out my sore, cramped limbs. Their movement causes more smells to ripen in the air, but the stench doesn't bother me so much. The eerie silence does.

No one speaks as we pull on our boots and soiled shirts before shuffling out of the room.

Men of all ages are around me, but I tense when I see a few children sporting the faces of men as they dress and grab their hats.

Children.

They should be playing in the woods, not destroying them.

A few people cast me confused glances as they crane their necks to take in my full height. Others bare their teeth, and I think about what Eneko said about those with giant blood. It won't be easy to make friends.

When we walk outside, I follow a silent group until we reach a large fire. Three giants are standing behind red-faced humans tending to an enormous iron pot covered in cooked-on fat and scorched food.

The guards watch us as we approach the dozens of long wooden tables. There are no chairs, and the closer I get, the more I realize the weathered surfaces are covered in a thick layer of grime. My lips pull back at the dreadful conditions.

Inwardly, I grimace, dreading whatever slop they intend me to put in my mouth. The closer I get, the stronger I smell soured meat.

I watch the men and women dribble out of their dens, step in front of me, and shuffle past the table. Each takes a bowl and waits for it to be filled before scattering. Some go back to the half-wood, half-mud houses; others go to lean against some of the trees or find rocks poking out of the snow to sit on.

After I'm served the slop, I find an unoccupied tree and grab a crudely carved spoon. As I bring the mush to my mouth, I nearly choke on the smell.

This goes beyond soured meat. Something akin to too-sweet berries burrows deep in my senses. The food is definitely poisoned. It is likely not enough to kill everyone, but enough to kill a few.

When I sneak another glance to survey the other slaves, some eat like normal.

Interesting. I'll need to wake up earlier tomorrow and hunt something.

You should get food for Melisa, too. Now that you know what she likes…

I bite my lip. Hopefully, she is well.

Perhaps I shouldn't worry so much about her. She's made it clear that she doesn't think I would be a fit mate… but she let me hold her through her waking nightmare and bind her wound.

Something deep in my gut wants to stay away, but I need to check for messages tonight.

I'll leave my thoughts about her until then.

I inhale deeply and smell a river nearby. It's large, and the water rushes violently. It's cold, but not cold enough for it to freeze. I make note of that and survey the other slaves.

Not all of the humans are blind to the poison. I see half a dozen humans throwing their food on the ground and kicking snow on it, or disappearing to the latrines and coming back with empty bowls. I follow suit. Then I bring the dish back to a large vat of hot water where several teenage slaves with blistered, bright red hands are washing.

I take one look at those hands and grab a rag and soap from a bucket.

They cast strange looks at me, but I refuse to let adolescents wash my plate when it will cause suffering.

One of them passes me a gourd to fill with water. I thank them, and then, after finishing up, I head to the lumber yards. It's a long walk. The sharp smell of fresh air fills my nose as the sun rises in the sky.

Several other humans walk near me on the beaten path, all quiet. There is a large open space between the tree trunks and, of course, more giants. Six stand near a rack of axes.

I let out a long breath and keep walking, scanning the other men who've joined us. There are around three hundred in total, and it hurts my heart to see some of those young boys follow us out.

Good hell.

It isn't long until I see Eneko. He sits on the back of a cart, drinking something from a steaming goblet. His hair has been brushed out and pulled atop his head. His clothes are clean, and he is well-protected against the chill.

He laughs at something one of the other giants says. When he tilts his head back to finish off whatever was left in the mug, I see the scarred column of his neck on display. It would be so easy to slit.

Melisa would be free of him and his bed.

I grit my teeth and shove away the thought. It will not be me who ruins our mission.

All of us slaves arrange ourselves into rows. This time, however, we wait for dull tools instead of poisoned mush.

With one last violent tip of Eneko's head, he slams his cup on the top of the rack before approaching us. His hand goes to a coiled whip in his belt.

"We are behind on our quota," he says after half a dozen paces in rough silence. "The palace asked for five thousand trees this month. High King Rholker is preparing for a massive expansion that will bring honor to the giant kingdom; they need lumber to build. Looking at our numbers, we are halfway into the month, yet have a quarter of that. What holds you all back?”

The air fills with dread. It leaks out of the pores of every man here.

“Well?” Eneko calls. “I let you eat two meals a day. We protect you from the wolves and bears that lurk in the forests. All of you have a roof over your head, do you not?"

No one answers.

He holds out one hand, gesturing to us and then presses his hand to his forehead.

"All that we ask is that you do your fucking jobs. Why so slow?”

Still, no one responds. No one even moves.

Displeased, Eneko pulls out his whip and cracks it on the ground.

“I don’t like using this. You know that.” He places the whip on the ground. “Bring home over a hundred trunks today, and I will do what I can to keep you off the racks. I don’t want to see any of you on the chopping block—but if you won’t work, then I can’t prevent that.”

One quick glance shows that the men around me are resolute.

“I’ve even brought in help.” Eneko raises his hand and points it at me. “I found another slave with giant blood. He should be able to carry an entire log himself, but don’t take advantage. You all know how I feel about fighting.”

More eyes on me. I clench my jaw and give a nod just as my stomach grumbles.

They glare, equal parts angry and weary. Then the attention is taken away, and the butts of spears shove men forward.

“Move, mangy rats, or I’ll peel the skin from your balls,” one of the guards shouts.

The others follow without resistance.

One by one, we approach to take our tools. When I pick up an ax, I look at the dull blade and hold it toward Eneko.

"Foreman," I say, and Eneko raises an eyebrow. "Do you need me to sharpen this?"

He lets out a laugh. "Why would you need a sharpened ax?"

"To cut trees."

He shakes his head. "Fucking halfblood, know your place. You'd sooner cut one of us with such a weapon. Now join the others before I regret bringing you into my region."

I bite my lips and fall into line next to a few slaves. The one directly at my left, two heads shorter than me, glares. His deep brown skin is rough and spotted from the sun, but his black eyes are backlit by flames.

"The Foreman seems to like you," he says.

I raise my eyebrow. "He seems to like my height."

The stranger doesn't like that answer. I can feel the displeasure radiate off him.

"You look well-fed. Where did you come from?"

"They call me Ra'Sa. I come from the northwestern yards."

The man continues to stare rather rudely. "I've heard some of the slaves talking about that area. They had even more poisonings than us. Makes no sense that you would have so much meat on your bones."

Damn. I genuinely don't know what to say to that.

"I am good at scavenging."

He scoffs. "Likely story. Watch yourself."

I pause. "Why would I need to do that?"

"We don't take kindly to halfling bastards." He pushes away from me, and I walk alone once more.

CHAPTER 17
MELISA

Once properly bathed, I open the wardrobe—the largest piece of furniture in my entire room—and look at the excess of red and white.

Dozens of gowns, jeweled headpieces, and nighties are hung up on plain metal hooks. While the red colors are all rich in hue, the texture of the heavy cotton fabric is scratchier than the silky dresses that I wear to parties.

I despise this wardrobe for the long gowns, heavy underskirts, and thick stockings.

For a few days, I was free from breast-busting wraps that restrict my breathing. In Enduvida, they wear soft leather clothing and I even tried pants—gods, I miss the pants and practical shoes. The boots that line the bottom of my wardrobe have small, thin heels at the end to make me that much taller.

It's a pitiful attempt to breach the difference in size, but the giants still try.

My hand brushes over the dresses. I chose this color when my first dresses had been ordered.

Red.

Serpents often use their colors to warn away other creatures. Each hue dictates the level of danger, like the orange bands of the kingsnakes that lurk in the woods.

Red was like that for me. I could use it to show people exactly what I was—a temptress. A whore. If others judged me for wearing it, at least it was my choice.

Today, though, needed to be different. At least for the morning. Eneko would be at the yards until the afternoon, and I needed to visit the girls.

After selecting one of the simpler dull, red-brown gowns without any petticoats, I put on the underdress leggings, coil a black scarf around my neck, and slide on a black cloak before heading out.

Closing the door quietly, I sneak past the fence and into the woods.

Heading to Griselda's house through the trees takes longer than the beaten path, but using it means that I avoid the guards. Usually, I'm not punished for leaving the house, but the guards are unpredictable.

The walk used to calm me, but today, my nerves are shot and frayed. It's been more than a week since I've seen the girls. I put my hands into my pockets and brush my fingers over the crystal that Estela gave me. It gives me a measure of comfort.

It takes me nearly an hour to reach the slave pens. I duck under the hidden hole in the fence. It smells like unwashed bodies and human waste.

Exhaustion hangs in the air. We're all used up, worn out, and tossed aside. The dens' squat, crooked walls and uneven floors remind me of my childhood.

Golden late morning light spills through the small spaces between homes. A few slaves who no longer work due to age or illness are scattered around the crumbling buildings. They are wrapped tightly in threadbare clothes barely covering their skin. They sit in front of dens, staring at each other—almost as if eager for connection, to remember that they are not alone in this awful place.

Some look up from their idleness and scan me with eyes that are far too intelligent for their run-down bodies. As soon as they glimpse the reddish color of my hem, they frown and look away.

Despite that, I cast them small smiles, an uneasy pit forming in my stomach as I hurry to the den next to the elm. When I reach Griselda's house, I hesitate. My stomach churns as I lean forward.

"…Don't understand how it gets so tangled. It's not like you do anything all day. I am the one who works around this house…" Griselda says in the human tongue.

Gritting my teeth, I push open the door.

The woman's surprise starkly contrasts the frown lines etched into her face. She isn't more than fifteen years older than me. I'd heard that some thought her beautiful once—we share long, pin-straight black hair, piercing brown eyes, and an elegant nose—but all I'd ever known was the sour woman sitting on the chair I gifted her.

A child stands in front of her. On the other side of the room, another girl sits with Coco, her hair freshly braided.

My throat tightens. They both have their faces downturned, and I can see the streaks of tears from here.

"What the hell are you doing?" I demand.

Thea's sadness melts away when she looks up at me from her seat across the room.

"Mamá!"[1]

That word. I don't deserve it; I haven't been able to be her mamá once since she was born.

Wren, still caged in by her grandmother's claw-like hands, smiles up at me.

"Lita me dijo que no ibas a regresar,"[2] Thea cries as she wraps her scrawny arms around my legs.

I reach down and gently touch her hair, worried that I'll hurt her. I know firsthand how one's scalp can hurt after Griselda's styling.

Instead, I touch her back and feel her spine. My nostrils flair, and my jaw tightens. Heat splashes through my limbs. Neither girl looked so starved the last time I was here.

My gaze locks back onto Griselda.

"Why is she so thin?"

"You were gone for over a week. Your masters stopped bringing food—and there's poison in the regular food. There was no way for us to eat," Griselda says, sucking on her teeth. Her eyes are more sunken, and her jaw more pronounced.

"I gave you extra supplies before I left," I say.

She shrugs. "They eat too much."

I grit my teeth. "Did you sell it? What did you get this time? Ayole powder?"

Ayole was a drug scraped from the tops of mushrooms that grew on the tallest trees. Griselda had dabbled in it when I was a child, but I thought she hadn't touched it in years.

My mother turns and looks at me. "You know, bread mysteriously showed up on our table last night. I don't even want to think about what you did to get it."

"Don't change the subject. Did you feed them while I was gone?"

Griselda leans back. "I did for the first few days."

I stand there, breathing deeply, wanting to scream and pull out this woman's hair. The agreement had been that I would provide for the family, and she would take care of my daughters. For most of the last three years, she's done just that. But I've been growing worried.

"What the fuck?" I seethe.

"Don't curse in front of the children," she spits back. "Remember, I do this out of the goodness of my heart. You didn't want to live with their father, and I helped you hide them. No one cared for you. No one let you in except me."

She's partially right. Once a slave has a child, they make you stay with the man who sired the babe. There was no way in hell I'd share Thea and Wren, even part time, with the sweating, disgusting man who'd raped me on a cold table.

The stakes only rose when Eneko picked me. He'd known that I'd gone to the breeding pens, but believed me childless. Working all day with a wrapped stomach made me lose most of the softness in my belly quickly, and Hibsej made me wear a dressing gown that covered the marks to sleep with him.

But Griselda doesn't need to know that. She's already started to become more reactive and less attentive, which is why I went to find the girls a new home. If she knew her watching them had anything to do with the giants, she'd cast us aside out of spite.

I didn't realize she would change so abruptly.

"Tell me you won't do it again," I say, my voice low.

"I fed them this morning."

"Promise. Me," I demand.

When she turns to look at me again, brown eyes burning, I see the woman who raised me and hated me for it.

“It isn’t easy to raise two young children alone.”

The room spins, and my stomach sours. Words sour on the tip of my tongue, ready to be spit out.

Don’t bring her with you to Enduvida.

My shallow breaths echo in my ears, and my jaw aches from clenching and grinding my teeth.

“I have provided food and peace for you and the girls for the last three years,” I snarl. When I take a step forward, pushing Thea behind me.

Griselda tightens her hands on Wren. I watch her dig her fingers into the taut flesh around Wren's neck.

“Yes. And how have you done that, *mija*?” she throws back, eyes narrowing.

“I did what you told me: I found work.”

“I told you to become a whore?”

I cross the rest of the way, letting Thea stand with Coco as I yank Griselda’s hands off Wren.

“You told me that you would take care of the girls if I could take care of the family,” I shout.

“Yes. I did. You knew I was the better option because you aren’t fit to be a mother. Hell, I wasn’t either when they made me have you—but I learned. All that learning has benefited these two. Is it so wrong that I seek a godsdamned moment of peace?” Griselda stands up, her knobby joints cracking and her face turning red as she yells back, finger pointed.

“Yes. They need you all the time because they are *children!*” My voice cracks on the last word. Legs that had held strong start to tremble, but not from fear.

"Well, you—" Griselda starts just as the girls cling to my hips. Griselda makes an irritated sound and rolls her eyes. "Thea, Wren, stop that."

A soft "*mamá*" sounds behind me, and I hug the girls close. Gods, they're walking so well.

I feared this woman until I went to the breeding pens—her dazed indifference often followed fiery anger. I'd thought she'd gotten better when she started taking care of the girls. In the beginning, she was softer, *kinder*. Sure, she was furious with me, but that didn't extend to Thea and Wren.

"I came back. You're being fed now. I wanted to see them. If my presence offends you, give me a quarter-hour, and I will be gone before you return," I seethe.

"This is my house. I refuse to leave it for you," she says. Those amber brown eyes turn up at me, burning. "In fact, don't come back at all. We were better off without your visits—all we need is the food you send."

My mouth parts. Sometimes she's like this—she says things she doesn't mean—but this time, I don't know.

If I could, I'd take them now.

"The food you're given comes with my visits," I insist.

Griselda narrows her eyes. "Get out."

That awful, choking emotion rises inside of me. My shortness of breath returns at the thought I won't be able to see them.

"But—"

"Mamá," Thea whimpers, fingers digging into my skirts.

"Get OUT!" Griselda yells, waving her hands. "I don't want you back here, mucking up my home with your filth."

My hands go to my daughters' heads. I look down at them. Wren's brown eyes meet mine.

She looks afraid. Unsure.

I choke when I think about raising them. I wouldn't be a good mother to them—I don't know how to take care of their needs. Hibsej would probably try to have me killed if she knew.

The Enduares know how to care for children, and I'd thought I found someone prepared to do just that. But Ra'Sa told me he wants a mate to have his own children. Not some human man's cast-offs.

I take a deep breath, barely swallowing down the panic creeping up my throat. When I look at Griselda, she's still fuming.

"¿Me escuchaste?"[3] she seethes.

"I will go, but I will find a way to check on them. And I swear, if they don't start to gain weight, I will take them far away from here—from you. You will be alone, without any of the benefits my whoring brings you."

It's a bluff. I don't have anywhere to take them yet.

Griselda opens her mouth, but I turn away and drop to my knees. I take both of my girls' faces and kiss their cheeks. Thea's eyes go wide and her lip wobbles.

"Mamá, no te vayas. Por favor mami,"[4] she says in rapid-fire succession through bubbly tears.

"Shh," I murmur, wiping away her tears, and then kissing her forehead. "This isn't my last visit."

Then I turn and kiss Wren, who has grown sullen and silent.

When I stand and face Griselda, my chest heaves. "Make sure you're teaching them the common tongue. They can't speak the human language forever."

Griselda scoffs, all of her red-hot anger simmering down to numb nothingness.

"Leave," she says weakly.

“Remember that I love you,” I tell the girls as I walk out the door.

The phantom of the girls’ clinging to my dress remains as I straighten my cloak and step away from the den.

The girls’ tears hit me like a wave, almost making me turn back to barge into that room and comfort them as best as I can.

Instead, I break away and head back into the thick patch of trees past the gate. Once far enough away not to be heard, I kick the tree. It feels good. Hot breath pours from my lungs as I hit the tree again—funneling my frustration into the blows.

It hurts.

The skin on my right hand breaks, and I stop, gasping at the blood.

The sound of a hundred men marching makes me stop.

Fuck. Eneko will be home soon.

I need to leave, but something holds me back. *Someone* I shouldn’t give a damn about. Ra'Sa should be marching with these men.

And gods… he is.

Perhaps it’s the need for gentleness after being yelled at, but I watch him move and long to be held.

He walks at the front of the group. His tall, muscular arms are bare despite the winter chill. He carries his shirt in his arms, and his short hair hangs in mangey strands around his face as he shakes out the snow. The afternoon light seems to bend toward him and his tall frame. Everyone bends toward him.

He turns his head to the side, showcasing the graceful lines of his neck.

When he leans over to say something to one of the men, it's almost as if I can feel the ghost of his breath on my neck. And when he graces the world with another one of his beautiful smiles, my heart constricts.

My head tilts to the side as I watch him go, and I slip around the back of the tree. He's a mountain among men.

No, that sounds like a giant.

Ra'Sa is a volcano. Tall and stoic, but deadly.

He easily towers over the others. He would keep me safe.

But he wants his own babies.

I clutch my cloak tighter and hurry back to the cabin. I curse myself the entire way for wasting time.

When I make it through the copse of trees, my heart stutters, two shadows are visible through the curtain of the living room. They are shouting again.

"So that's it? You're going to fuck her with a stomach wound? I saw it—she can barely move. That's why she's not helping me with chores today!"

I hear something crash.

From one mess to another…

I inch closer to the house, sneaking around to the back, where I see the boys playing. They chase each other around the front of my room. An icy chill spreads from my spine down my arms. Was I gone too long? Did Hibsej try to check on me?

"She belongs to me! Just like your pots and pans belong to you. If I need her, I will use her," Eneko yells.

"Not until she is healed!"

"And how long will that be? If I know you, this is a scheme to get me to touch you. Is it not enough that I sleep next to you, night after night? Am I condemned to my hand for the rest of time?"

"You will do anything not to fuck me!" she shouts back.

I creep forward, thinking that the boys are otherwise distracted, only for their eyes to snap onto me as soon as I exit the trees.

"Who's that?" the youngest asks.

I drop the hood of my cloak. "Easy, boys. It's me."

They stare at me. Neither moves to approach.

"Ma left you something," the oldest says.

I let out a long sigh and walk into my room. When I do, I'm greeted by three bags of laundry.

"Oh, for fuck's sake."

Pressing my hands to my face, I hold my breath and inspect one of the sacks. The smell of sweat and old clothes hits me square in the face.

I cinch back up the bag. If I let it stink up the whole room, it'll be a miserable night for sleeping and it's too cold to simply throw them in the snow. Using all my body weight, I shove them to the side as far as I can, and look around the room.

I pause.

Hibsej has been here, but no dinner?

As if on cue, the door behind me opens again. The doorway looks small in comparison to Hibsej's form. Irritation and anger radiate off her in waves.

"Where the hell have you been?" she says.

I pause. "I had to visit my mother."

"Fine."

Hibsej enters the room and lights one of the torches on the wall. When the light splutters to life, the now-dried tear trails are still visible on her ruddy cheeks.

She holds a plate of food in her hand, which she throws on the table with a loud clatter.

“She told me you stopped leaving food,” I breathe.

Hibsej gives me a scathing look. “Of course I stopped giving her food.”

“But why?”

“Khuohr’s bloody mercy, girl. We all thought you were dead.” She laughs bitterly. “Taking on a comfort woman is meant to symbolize fortune. But really, it’s just a burden. We have no other slaves that tend to the house—other than you—so I must cook and give up parts of my pantry so you can steal my bed. I don’t do it out of the goodness of my heart—it’s an exchange.”

My gut twists as she speaks.

“Forgive me, Mistress Hibsej. I am very thankful for your generosity to my mother and sisters.”

“Fuck off.” Hibsej turns to look at me. “My husband has been invited to a feast of the lords and foremen tomorrow. Something to take everyone’s mind off of the godsdamned tension after the recent confrontation. You are going, so clean your finest dress while you work on all this.” She gestures to the bags of soiled clothing.

Tensing, I dip my head. “Understood.”

Her mouth hardens into a thin line, and she turns to leave. “In the morning, make sure to bandage your wound tightly. Eneko wants you in his room after the meal.”

“I will be prepared at nightfall,” I say.

She sucks her teeth and leaves.

I turn back to the table and find a burnt loaf and a few slices of meat. Weary, I pick up the food and the jug of water I keep inside my room. As I eat, I think of the girls. How had Griselda been so cruel?

My mind wanders through memories of the past. I think of the times when she was gentle before she'd ever called me a whore, when she told me that I was too pretty to let my hair get matted up like the other girls my age.

Griselda would tell such fine stories while she braided my locks, taking me on a thousand adventures.

I loved her. How could I not?

When she let me in, the light of her soul warmed me.

I shake away the thoughts. She isn't that woman anymore—she hardly ever was—and she doesn't have to come to Enduvida. Right now, all that matters is that my daughters are alive. Soon, I'll be able to take them to a better place.

I'll need to send a message to Ra'Sa. We should meet tomorrow—I'm sure I'll have something to share after the feast.

After I'm finished with Eneko.

1. Mom.

2. Grandma told me you weren't coming back.

3. Did you hear me?

4. Mom, don't go. Please mommy.

CHAPTER 18

RA'SA

"When I finally cut down my first branch, I thought I was going to die. The tree shoved to the left, and one of the splinters cut my arm," Nicolás, the climber on my cutting team, says animatedly.

I smirk at his excitement, shaking the sweat out of my hair. He's got all the youthful hope that Tirin had. In fact, the more I think about it, the more I see bits of my late brother in this young man. From how he grins despite the generally gloomy mood of everyone around him, to how he makes wide gestures with his arms without taking into account those next to him.

"We'll fell two trees tomorrow!" Nicolás continues, hand crashing into my forearm. "They'll give us each a leg of lamb."

I have the strangest urge to reach out, grab his shoulder, and remind him to temper his enthusiasm.

Abet, another cutter, does it for me. "Quiet, boy."

We continue to trudge along the trail, and Nicolás' head tilts further and further down. His blond hair falls in his eyes, and I feel bad for Nicolás. He's just proud of himself, as he should be. It was a job well done.

To help him feel better, I pat him on the back.

I glance at Abet and ask him with the lowest voice I can muster. “Why is everyone so quiet?”

He looks up at me. “They execute the ones they think are conspiring to rebel.”

I blink.

A rebellion?

Deep gray plumes of smoke return to my mind, as does the sight of slaves throwing poisoned food under patches of snow to rot. The situation here is worse than I expected. But King Teo wanted me to help the humans, and I keep my word.

"In my last yard, they started burning dens without warning. What caused all of this?" I lie.

Abet bites his flaking lips and looks at me sideways. Our pace remains steady as we pass through the gates leading us back to the slave pens. Abet spits on the ground and then coughs.

"An entire breeding pen full of women escaped."

Obviously, I knew this. I open my mouth to find out more—anything that I could send back to Enduvida—but I am quickly silenced by another look from Abet. He jerks his head to the right, directly toward a line of giant guards waiting for us to arrive.

After giving them a long, appraising look, Nicolás—who stands on my other side—leans over.

"Standing at attention like that, they almost look like uncooked sausages. Some days, I can’t believe they’ve got skin so pale and ruddy," he says.

Thank the gods, his voice was low this time, but I can't help but grin. To hide the emotion, I pull on the shirt I'd sloughed off hours ago. As I do, I feel eyes on me from somewhere nearby and gaze out into the woods.

A small hooded figure stands just behind a tree. Dull red skirts peek out from the heavy black fabric, and slender, umber fingers are splayed across a tree trunk.

Melisa.

She turns and hurries away, and the urge to follow her ripples through my entire body.

I almost do.

Somehow, the ghost of her scent comes over to me, and I… ache.

"Did you see the whore sneaking around?" someone behind me says, almost too low for me to hear.

I grit my teeth.

"Wonder who she came to fuck this time," another says. Low laughter swells through their group.

Heat prickles on my neck. When I look back, I find the man who threatened me this morning. What the hell is wrong with him?

I ignore the rest of the group as the guards lead us to the eating station. A fire is lit this time, but most people disappear into their houses after getting their food.

The grainy, gray slop is still just as unappetizing as before, but thankfully, the sickly sweet smell of poison isn't present. I shovel some into my mouth. The taste of tree bark and meat mashed together is disgusting, but at least it's something after a long day.

"You were quick to eat that," the crude man from before remarks as I head over to the large den where the men sleep.

My fists tighten while I think of what he said about Melisa. His head is cocked to the side as a bald man trails just a short ways behind him.

They were the ones who spoke poorly of Melisa.

I nod once, keeping the sneer of my face, and bring another spoonful past my lips. “It doesn’t smell off.”

“You can smell that?” His brown eyes seem to glitter.

I raise an eyebrow. I’d definitely seen other slaves throw the mash away. “You can’t?”

His intrigued expression melts into a glare.

“If we could, there probably wouldn't be so many dead." He steps forward, away from the trees. "I wonder where you picked up such a skill. Where did you say you were from again?”

The bald man from his cutting team stares at me through narrowed eyes, and a third joins them.

“The northwestern lumber yards,” I say.

His eyes narrow. “It was a massacre over there. Hundreds were slaughtered in one day between the fires and food. And yet you, a halfblood, survived... and came here. Interesting.”

Others start to pay attention. Not just his cutting team but old crones, young children, and shadowy faces of other men and women.

“I survived because I worked hard,” I say at last.

The man in front of me smirks. “We all work hard, and most of us still die. Who, exactly, do you work for?"

My teeth grind together. “What is that supposed to mean?”

“Do you work for the giants or the humans?”

I purse my lips. Well, shit. I’m too tall, too strong, too suspicious.

“I came here because I found the foreman’s comfort woman and brought her back to him. I wanted out of my old area. Too much death.”

The man’s gaze shift, and he lets out one huff. “You brought back the whore?”

My fists tighten. “Don’t call her that. It’s disrespectful.”

His eyebrows raise. “Did you rut her, too? Be careful. Can’t trust the ones who work with the giants.”

More than anything, I want to smash the asshole's face. But I'm already standing on dangerous ground—ice so thin that if I don't tread carefully, I'll be plunged into the dangerous, frozen depths.

“No.”

The slave’s smirk grows wider.

“Ah, but you want to. I respect that. My name is Rodrigo—people look to me as their leader.” He comes over and claps me on the back. “Don’t do anything stupid in our pens.”

I remain unmoving as he turns back around and walks away with his group. The man who was leaning against the beam moments ago gives me one last up-and-down before he lets out a huff and turns around, too.

I’m left standing there, feeling slightly off balance. That sensation follows me as I clean my plate and head back to the men's den.

When I find my bunk, I crash against the wobbly surface, nearly breaking it, and groan.

Today started poorly, but it was interesting to speak with Nicolás. Catching Melisa watching me makes me feel guilty. We hadn't been kind to each other.

“I saw you talking to Rodrigo. Be careful with them,” a voice says from one of the cots.

I look over at Abet. I’d assumed he was already asleep.

“I wouldn’t have gone near them otherwise,” I murmur. "They spoke to me first."

He snorts. “Good instincts. Just leave them be, and they won't bother you too much.”

While I look at him, I think about dinner. He wasn't anywhere near me, and I didn't see him grab a plate.

“Did you eat? This one wasn't... soured,” I say.

He shakes his head. “Not hungry.”

My eyebrows shoot up. “Even after all the work we did today?”

"Leave me be, Rasa,” he says, pronouncing my name like some of the other humans.

"I can get you food," I say gently.

He is silent for a long while, and then I hear a snore from him. His lack of response worries me, but I'm reluctant to wake him.

After a few hours of lying awake while the rest of the men drift into sleep, I sneak out. Now would be a good time to check on messages from Melisa.

It would be good to find some real food. I might even share with my cutting team.

The closer I get to Eneko’s cottage, the more my stomach aches.

Is Melisa with Eneko now?

My breath comes in shallow pants. How had I not considered that before leaving?

But when I arrive, I find every light off.

As I creep forward, the windows are as dark as the night sky. No… explicit sounds can be heard anywhere.

That brings me comfort. But I still creep closer and closer to the back room.

Her room.

The lock on her door is open, and my heart skips a beat. I listen at the door. A small hiss sounds without warning, and a warm, yellow light filters out through her small window. The glass is cloudy, nothing like the fine workmanship in Enduvida.

I wait a minute, and then another, to see if a giant's form crosses in front of the slight square opening. Eneko never materializes, and I let out a long breath. My fingers itch to look through the window again to see her beauty.

Instead, I look at the area where I gave her the first message. To my surprise, she left me something.

Meet me at midnight tomorrow.

Warmth spreads through my chest, and I arrange my own message.

Of course. Be well.

I press my hand to the side of the wall that connects to her room. It isn't the same as touching her skin, but the connection, fleeting as it might be, is satisfying.

The stirring in my gut makes no sense. I have no claim over this woman. Our song did not start the first time I saw her.

But then she let me hold her through her panic. She kissed me. Gods, I'd never tasted anything so sweet. I was surprised when she let me teach her how to fight and bind her wound.

She'd told me that I didn't know how to care for humans.

I wasn't practiced in matters of the heart, but the thought of drawing her close to me and holding her seemed nice. Even if it was likely she'd reject further advances.

Not wishing to dwell any longer, I get up to hunt. It doesn't take me long to find a rabbit. It takes even less time to kill and clean it with a conjured stone knife.

When I start walking back to the camp, I try to follow the same hidden path. I assume there are no giant warriors. But as I cross over the fence covered in foliage, I am abruptly pulled back by a large hand.

"Where did you get that?" the growling voice of one of the giant guards demands.

I look up at his towering form. His dark cloak blends in with the shade between the trees, and his dark hair is even harder to spot.

Though Melisa hadn't mentioned hunting as something to avoid, I've obviously made a mistake.

"I got it in the forest," I swear.

He spits on the meat. "You know that hunting is against the rules. You eat what's given to you."

A smart remark sits at the tip of my tongue. Seeing the men today was bittersweet. These people look at death like it would be a merciful escape from life. I should keep my mouth shut, I really should, but...

I'm not good at *not* voicing my opinion.

"So I can either eat poisoned food or nothing," I bite back.

That earns me a violent shove to my knees. The gritty snow bites into my flesh, and the knees of my pants tear. Cold dampness soaks through, stinging my cuts.

"Shirt off," the guard demands and draws out his whip.

It's dark. I could kill him. The hunger for his blood brews under my skin, but Melisa's face enters my mind. All the strange emotions from earlier return. If I kill him, I'll be taken away, and then how will I be able to protect her? She would become just another person I couldn't save.

Midnight also draws near. I have one of the glamour stones in my pocket, but I worry it won't be enough.

Slowly, I take off my shirt and angle my chest away from them so they don't have any chance of seeing my glamoured Fuegorra.

The first lash comes, but I don't cry out. Not even when the skin splits, and I feel blood run down my back. Painfully hot. When it's over, he kicks his dirty boot into my back and pushes me fully into the icy ground.

"Next time, your punishment will be worse," the guard bites out.

My back aches, but I remain there on the cold, hard ground.

My Fuegorra begins to heat my chest, and I worry about what is or isn't visible with this glamour.

The guard leaves, sure to kick me in the ribs one last time.

I want to snarl at him, but instead, I wait until the Fuegorra finishes healing my back and let him walk away.

CHAPTER 19

MELISA

The next morning, I find the herbs I had carefully tried to replace after my bath are gone, but I'm pleased my wound isn't infected. A thick, deep red scab has formed.

Hibsej told me to wrap it well because I would be going to Eneko tonight.

Pulling on a new dress, acid pools in the pit of my stomach.

I had known that this would happen upon returning. Normally, I would do it without flinching, but a part of me hesitates. A taste of freedom soured my reality.

Foolish, foolish woman.

Stepping into the early morning, the brisk chill of the air greets me like a rough slap in the face.

A new message sits in the snow. All of the dozens of rocks and sticks add up to say that he would meet me. It also says, "Be well."

My foot hovers to kick the words away—half furious with him for leaving a kind message. But I pause.

Be well.

No one thought about what I needed. Before Estela and her kindness, I built relationships with others, not the other way around. With Abi, Paoli, Daria, and Alisa, I gossiped and shared secrets about our masters. I knew their dreams and thoughts, but they never knew mine. They didn't even know about Thea or Wren.

And I sure as hell never told Ra'Sa. He saw the markings from the pregnancy and thankfully didn't recognize them. He'll know soon enough when it's time to escape though.

My mind turns in circles. I was supposed to seduce him before we got to Zlosa, and that did not go according to plan. Instead, he cared for me.

And now... I will have to see him after spending the night with Eneko. Not that it matters.

"You're a whore," my mother's voice echoes.

I push it away.

But as I walk by with the buckets towards the well, I leave Ra'Sa's message on the ground. I can't bring myself to erase it.

"Be well," I whisper to myself.

A faint ghost of a memory whispers back to me, "You are strong. You are fierce. You are capable."

Damn. It. All.

Why did he have to be so gentle?

I'll have to haul the laundry bags to the river with Daria and Alisa. Fortunately, I'll be able to hear the latest news from them.

Just as I pull the bucket back up, there's a faint burning along my wound, and I hear the sound of small giant feet and laughter. When I turn my head, I see Eneko's eldest son, Relmos, and his younger son, Urdort.

They run at high speed around the outside of the house, utterly ignoring me, and push onward through the trees. They are still small enough to walk between the elms and evergreens, but I resist the urge to call after them when they nearly run head-first into one of the branches.

Good choice, because seconds later, Hibsej's voice fills the silence. "Slow down! You're to come with your father tonight. I don't want you bruised and cut for the king!"

I tense. “Good morning, Mistress Hibsej.”

For the past three years, the feasts have always been the same. We all go together and enjoy the meal, and then Hibsej and her sons return to the house while I stay at Eneko's side to be leered at and pinched.

“Here’s your food," Hibsej's rough voice bites.

Her red-painted scars stand out from her pale skin, and they almost look like fresh burns. Her chestnut brown hair has been arranged at the top of her head, and gentle curls fall around her face.

Under everything, I pity her. I’ve never truly been able to hate her because… well, she’s a good mother—the kind of mother I’ve always wanted to be.

I pull the bucket out of the well and take the plate, mumbling a soft thanks.

She rolls her eyes but doesn't leave.

I lean against the barrier and look down at the small plate with cheese, bread, and berries. I’m surprised by the cheese—it’s a delicacy—but my eyes narrow at the bright red balls.

Bayas agridulces. Poisonous to humans.

I take them off the plate and toss them as far out into the trees as possible.

"You should be more careful with your poison. Urdort or Relmos could find them by accident."

"My sons are smarter than that." Hibsej snorts.

I raise an eyebrow. "They are children."

She glares at me but lingers. "Finish, so I can take my plate back to my kitchen."

Sighing, I grab my food and dig in. The bread is finished first, followed by the cheese. As I take my first bite of the smooth and salty deliciousness, Hibsej, who's been looking around to keep her attention anywhere but on me, freezes. My muscles tighten, and my senses heighten as I watch her gaze. It lands directly on the sticks and stones near my room's window.

Ra'Sa's message that I hadn't kicked away out of tenderness. I bite my lip as she stomps over.

"What's all this?" she demands, then looks back at me. "Witchcraft?"

My breath whooshes out of my lungs.

A few months ago, six hooded women came to Zlosa. It was only recently revealed that they were human women with cursed magic. The Six, they called themselves. We humans called them *Brujas*.

Regardless of their titles, the giants have been uneasy over the king's alliance with such women. Before I'd left, there was a small-scale hunt for any such magic-wielders living amongst the slaves.

I meet Hibsej's eye and shake my head.

"Not at all. I think the boys were playing near my room last night," I say.

Her eyes narrow further.

I finish the rest of the food, despite how it turns from appetizing to bitter ash in my mouth.

As soon as I'm done, I hold out the plate, and she yanks it from my hands. She says nothing more about the sticks. Then she calls out in giantese.

"Come!"

The boys bolt to her side, and I watch the three of them storm off before I let out a long breath. I suck in more air and then repeat the action as many times as possible. The attack doesn't wane, unfortunately. It waits until I've lugged the bucket inside before it starts to unleash its full force.

Sinking to the ground, I let my thoughts race.

I will take the laundry to the river in a second.

I just need to... breathe.

There's a knock at my door.

"Melisa," Eneko's voice says, shocking me out of my attack.

Usually, he's gone by now. Why has he come to my door?

"Yes, Foreman?" I call.

"Dress. I've missed your company and would enjoy a day with you on my cart."

I stand and straighten my dress.

"She has work to do," Hibsej's voice hisses in the background.

"Worry not, woman. I'll have her home with time to spare."

CHAPTER 20

RA'SA

I can see the inky dark blue sky above me. There's a poorly patched crack in the crumbling roof, and it reveals the outside world in a way I'd never seen. Usually the open sky is vast and uncomfortable, but this—barely a sliver—intrigues me.

Clouds the color of steel and stone float through the sky, framing the stars. While I lie there, something in my magic stirs. Enduares believed that stars were faraway realms for our goddess to inhabit. Spheres of stone, like the world we live in. Grutabela picked one for her home. She built a throne of stones and began to sing to us across the distance. It was always a comforting thought for me to think of her as bits and pieces manifest in the crystals.

The more I think about it, the more curious I am that we have taken to the underground as much as we have, especially as I realize, looking up at the celestial realm, that I enjoy it.

In small doses.

Strange.

I'd never considered myself so changeable. But perhaps I've merely denied myself the space to find out what I really want over what others have wanted for me.

One of the slumbering men on my left stirs with an abrupt snort. I don't recognize him, but the movement causes me to adjust and feel the sweaty, blood-crusted clothes clinging to my body.

I grimace.

My eyes fix on the heavens once again, only to find the shade of blue much lighter. The sun awakens, meaning I must soon work.

Images return—blood-soaked memories—of bodies stacked on top of each other, and the world around us swirling with smoke…

Long ago, we lived in a small village near the old Enduar capital, Iravida. Ruhsavida was a collection of caves in a forest up north. We were in one of the few places that had easy access outside of the mountains.

We'd been home the day the world ended. I'd been helping my father clean the roof from lichen that had started to build up. Mother was downstairs, feeding Tirin, but my sisters weren't home. Sera, Orena, and Anina had gone off to art lessons with one of the painters in the Royal Art Institute.

Our house was covered with their paintings. Bright glowing blues and greens covered every surface. They painted the world beyond the caves, and our family, too. Mother and Father in fantastical clothing. Me, with dancing stones around my head and glowing eyes. Them with swords and ballgowns and books.

When the smoking started, Father recognized the signs. He'd worked with the great battalions tasked with guarding the king's treasures and understood, so he shoved me off the roof.

He shouted at me and told me to care for my mother. He would get my sisters and join us later.

I didn’t understand what he meant, but my mother was screaming and crying. I took Tirin, and we ran.

Ran until we couldn’t breathe.

Two quiet words are whispered to my thoughts, breaking me from the memory.

Be well.

It's Melisa's voice.

Rushing blood silences the world around me. I sit up and look around. She’s not here, but I hear her thoughts like a mate would hear its other half.

Melisa?

Nothing.

No song accompanies the words.

No marks burn on my neck.

… No more thoughts come.

When I stand up and start to make my way out of the den, I pause at the exit, looking for Melisa again.

Guards are littered around the area outside, but there is no raven-haired woman.

Several guards produce metal pots, and they start beating them with their spears. The awful clanging noise steals sleep from anyone who wasn’t already stirring. I wait for a group to form and follow them out of the sleeping area.

As we all shuffle outside and head toward food, everyone is quiet. The morning is crisp. The air awakens me entirely, making my body feel more like unsettled energy rather than a man who didn't sleep long enough. I stretch out my cramped joints and lumber to the large pots.

When I approach, one of the giant guards turns around. My hair stands on end when his eyes go straight to my face. I'd only caught glimpses of him in the corner of my eye, but I'm sure he's the one who held me down and whipped me. He gives me a sneering triumphant look as overcooked grains are spooned onto my plate.

Once finished eating, I follow the same process of washing my dish myself before exiting. When I begin the dreary trek up to the trees, Abet and Nicolás find my side. I look over with a pleasant expression as I say good morning, but only Nicolás smiles back.

When I reach the lumber yard with my cutting team, I see Eneko.

A hot, ground-rending anger spikes at the sight of his face.

He stands tall and grim, with at least a dozen giant guards, including my tormenter from last night. Behind him is a cart pulled by oxen.

A head of deep, raven-black hair is visible above the walls of the cart.

Melisa.

My heart races, waiting for her to pivot and see me. Eneko turns to a warrior, retrieving something from a guard while the slaves fall into formation.

A few whispers sound next to me. Most of their words mimic the rustling of trees, almost impossible to perceive, but I make out '*woman.*'

I clench my jaw. Her voice… it'd been in my mind.

Had I imagined it?

"We have news from the king," Eneko calls out, one hand on his hip, the other clutching a piece of paper. "I warned you all that your lackluster performances yesterday would have consequences.

Today, every group is expected to cut down three trees, or your group will be subject to the racks."

The crowd around us is silent. The rack means death.

Clearly shocked, Melisa finally moves. She twists around in the cart, brown eyes wide and red mouth parted as she looks at Eneko.

In the silence, someone says something too low to hear.

Eneko's eyes snap over to the direction of the noise.

"What was that?" he demands.

Everything is quiet for a moment.

Then, a man yells from the back of the group.

"Kill us for serving you? Soon, you won't have any slaves left, Foreman. What does his Royal Highness think about chopping his own wood and cleaning his own shit?"

Eneko sneers. He lifts his chin, still frowning, and waves his hand lazily toward the slave.

Two guards rush forward. One grabs the man by the arm just as he starts to run. The guard yanks backward mercilessly, and a loud pop fills the air as the man is slammed into the ground. The human roars as he's dragged by the back of his shirt to the front of the group.

Melisa's hand covers her mouth with fear written all over her face.

The slave tries to stand, but he is kicked back to his knees by the second guard, who holds a short whip—the man who tore my back apart. The human cries out from the force of his second fall, knocking into the rocky, snowy ground. The rest of us watch as it happens, feeling the echoes of the screams through the air and holding our breath as the whip lifts.

The guard's lips turn up at the sides when his hand cranks back before beating now-bare flesh. The man lets out an agonized growl through his teeth as his body curls forward under the shock of the pain.

Another lash comes down with bone-cracking speed. And then another.

The hunger on the guard's face is ravenous. As if the blood were a thing to be celebrated. I wonder if he looked the same when destroying the skin on my back.

My eyes travel to those around me. I look at the men. Some watch with a sense of indifference and tight lips. Others watch with the rage of men plotting revenge.

The giants treat these men as disposable sods. Through them, they feel their power. They can manipulate their lives with the breeding pens, control them in their homes and daytime hours, and finally, end their lives. The giants have made themselves the gods of the humans.

Such bloody, ruthless gods.

Melisa's eyes finally meet mine. No tears mar her flawless skin, but the horror is apparent. She never looked like that in Enduvida.

I need to get her back to her new home. One that exists because the stones sang a new future for us all.

Even without Fuegorras, those humans heard their own hope in the stones. They whispered it in back rooms and told the others. Little do they know I stand among their people. And my king sent me to help.

I know the ways of strategy. I have led before.

"Anyone else wish to question my words?" Eneko snaps. "No? Very well. You have your orders. You alone decide if you will die this evening. I suggest you work quickly."

The man lifts himself off of his knees, blood streaming down his back and dripping into the snow, face pale as ever. We all watch as he struggles to get back to his spot in the line. No one helps him, for none wish to risk the pain that might come from it.

I am moved to compassion.

I break away and help him to stand. The humans watch as I pull him up.

"Let him walk by himself!" the guard bellows.

I continue to move, glaring ahead as the injured slave hobbles next to me, heavily leaning on my arm for support. The other slaves shift their spots as I bring him to stand near me.

Eneko watches me with hooded eyes.

"Let him be, halfblood," Eneko says.

I look back up at him. "I am merely ensuring we get all the trees you need. You need every slave."

It breaks my heart to feel the man at my side pull away. He doesn't so much as nod, not that I blame him. I can understand why he might not want me to assist him.

The guards push us forward to get our working tools, and I watch him go.

When I'm at the front of the line, the smell of roses and cinnamon engulfs me.

I reach for my ax, and Eneko stops me.

"Remember that there are no winners in this game. You may help him walk now, but you will not save him from death at the end of the day. Without a fourth, his chopping team will be helpless. You don't want to be grouped in with such people."

I look up at him. "I meant what I said; I want to ensure we cut enough wood."

Eneko continues to study me, and I wonder if he regrets bringing me to his lumber yard yet.

He certainly doesn't know that I want him dead. Dead for what he has done to the humans and dead for the woman who sits behind him. On his cart. Sharing his bed.

The forbidden woman I should've never touched—should've never started to care for.

"I heard you cut fast, pair that with the kinship we share in blood, and I find I am hesitant to punish you. But act out like this again, and I will not spare my hand."

I grit my teeth.

He seems fixated on the fact that I have this giant blood. I am not above playing into that.

"Why would I side with the humans when the same blood that runs through my veins also runs through yours?"

He purses his lips. "Good words. Make your goal."

I nod, leaning forward to grab the blunted ax. The air changes as I reach out, almost as if I were reaching for Melisa, not a pitiful weapon.

I would kill every last giant in this field and hold her close while the humans run. Far, fast, free.

But then my hand wraps around the worn handle, and I'm drawn back into the real world, where they give us dull weapons and whip us.

On the trail, I spot one of the leather wraps that climbers use to attach themselves to trees tossed on the ground. With no attention focused on me, I reach down, snatch it up, and hurry in the direction of the others.

"That was foolish," Abet says when I get close enough.

I ignore him, looking back in the direction where the bloody man went.

"Let's get to work," I say.

Nicolás begins to wrap the leather around the trunk and climb. Then, I connect myself to the tree and follow him up.

"What are you doing?" Abet demands. "You are full of foolish ideas today."

I shake my head. "We have three trees to cut. We need to work quickly. Just stay on your side and there will be no problems."

"The tree will move too much with you both cutting!" Abet calls up.

I poke my head around the trunk.

"Hold on tight. Balance and strength first," I say to Nicolás.

He nods, and we continue.

When we reach the top of the trunk, it doesn't take long for him to start chopping. When I feel the vibration of his first cut, I wait for his branch to crack and fall.

The tree sways slightly under the loss of its limb, but I hack at another branch before it has time to recover. With one powerful chop, the branch splinters and falls.

"¡Ojo!" [1]I call down as it tumbles, selecting the human word they use in warning.

"Hostia puta," [2]Nicolás murmurs from the other side of the tree.

I look around at him and grin. "I'm fast."

"You're something, that's for sure!" he calls back.

We follow the same pattern as we move around the trunk. Branch after branch hacked away in record time.

When the last branch is done, we climb down.

Abet lets out a bitter laugh and curses under his breath.

"Fine. If you want to risk your life to make sure we don't die tonight, be my guest," he grumbles.

“Thank you,” I start, rolling my eyes.

Turning sideways, I see Eneko standing near a group fifty paces south.

My eyes look for his cart, searching for Melisa, and I find it nearby. There are a few men speaking to her as their climber hacks away at branches.

Turning to my team, I hold up my hand. “I’ll be right back.”

Abet purses his lips. “Off to take a piss?”

“Something like that,” I say over my shoulder as I stride toward them.

As I approach, Melisa looks up, and I see the glittering, polished smile she seems to put on for everyone. It’s nothing like the fear, the desire, the fury I’ve seen painted on her face.

My blood goes hot.

“My my my, what have we here?” she says, conversationally.

The men turn to look at me and sneer.

“Fuck off, halfblood,” one of them says.

I glare at him.

“No.” I look back up at Melisa. “What is happening here?”

“We’re just chatting,” she starts.

“You do realize that you will die tonight if your work is not done,” I say to the other men. “Leave her be.”

One of the men grins. “If it’s my last day, it will have been worth it for a minute between the fine lady’s thighs.”

White hot rage flashes through my veins.

"Get back to work, or I'll call for the foreman," I say through gritted teeth.

The men grow hostile. "You would deny us a moment of pleasure on our last day?"

"It's not your last day yet. Get back to work."

"Fucking bastard," one of them hisses. "You probably don't even know the touch of a woman!"

I frown. "And you'd be right. Now leave."

This time, they do.

It takes everything in my soul not to turn and look at Melisa, to savor her scent.

"Ra'Sa…" her voice says, gentle and sweet.

I keep walking. No more playing with fire today.

When I approach my team, Abet is still working.

"I'm back," I say irritatedly.

Abet looks up at me, lips pursed. "Took you long enough. Ready to work?"

I give a noncommittal grunt and step into my position. Emilio starts counting our turns.

"Uno!"[3]

I give the most rigid chop I can muster, and the angle of the blade lands nicely. The cut is far deeper than Abet's. His eyes widen, and he looks at me, missing his turn.

"Whoa there, easy on your back," Abet says.

When it's my turn again, I slam my ax into the wood. On and on we go, but the time it takes to slice to the tree is much shorter than the day before.

When the wood starts to splinter, Abet yells, and we run from the tree. Those weightless moments before the trunk's thunderous landing, capable of killing, are exhilarating.

"Let's get started on the next. We can carry when the sun starts to drop through the sky," I tell my team.

A sheen of sweat coats my body, and I remove most of the layers before I harness myself to the tree and follow Nicolás up.

The second tree comes down faster than the first.

The third drags, but only because the others grow weary. I've always been brawny, but today, the purpose pumping through my veins makes me far stronger.

That is, until I look over and see the other laborers struggling. They are panting and sweating, defeated.

It hurts my soul.

I spot one of the boys in the same team as the man who was whipped. The boy is small, dirty, and frowning, while the man has dried flaking blood all down his back. I approach and find them standing around a single tree fallen across the snowy forest. There's no way in the world above or below that they can chop a second.

I turn back to my group. "I will return soon to help you carry."

My footfalls are heavy when I reach the next group, huffing. They look up at me. A few of their gazes drop to the ax hanging in my hand.

"Let me help," I say.

They narrow their eyes.

The young boy is the first to speak. "You want to get killed?"

"I saw him speaking to the foreman. Likely, he wouldn't be killed, but we will be. And they'll still get our lumber."

My skin crawls with anticipation. "Please, I just want to help."

Looks pass between each of them.

Then, at last, a cohesive *"fine"* passes their lips.

Relief.

I tell the other cutter to get in place and get back to work. The afternoon is long, and my muscles strain until I fear they will tear.

But somehow, pulling on the strength of my magic, I help them cut two different trees.

When we are all taken back to the clearing, I feel lighter. Better.

While I saved my group and another, I see the pile of timber much less full than it needs to be. Many accomplished what was necessary, but many did not.

The same desperation bubbles up in the space between my bones and flesh. As we are sorted between those that pass and those that do not, I bite the inside of my cheek.

Eneko is, surprisingly, absent from this ordeal. He's gone.

With Melisa.

My agony is compounded with the fact that more than fifty of our three hundred men stand on the other side of the yard, awaiting their death.

I picture their blood staining the ground. I picture Melisa kissing that horrible man.

It shreds my heart, my lungs, my head.

Somehow, something needs to stop. When I start to take a step forward, Abet stands in my way.

"I didn't stop you before, but I will now. You saved seven men today. Let it be enough."

I look at him long and hard while my insides churn in pain.

What is seven in the face of three hundred? What is it compared to ten thousand?

My thoughts never find an answer as the guard calls out, "We will now all go to the racks. Attendance is mandatory."

And thus we go.

It shreds my insides to see the merciless gore. One by one, they are sent to the front and beheaded. It is somber.

With each death that I did not stop, I feel it stain my soul. So much death.

Like a light, I remember that I will speak with Melisa in a few hours. It should be more pain, but I don't care what she's done. What she's learned.

I just want to hold her, as I did the night of the fire.

The emotion is just as natural as breathing. It strikes me as futile to believe it would fix anything… But the comfort in another's arms certainly would make it easier to withstand another day.

1. Watch out! (But literally translated as "eye")

2. Holy fuck.

3. One!

CHAPTER 21
MELISA

You are strong, I tell myself while lighting flames that damned near refuse to spark.

You are fierce, I whisper while I wait for the buckets to boil.

You are capable, I insist as I place the gem for the girls in a drawer near my bed.

The words repeat as I clean my teeth with a citrus tree stick. Eneko hardly kisses during the short nights I spend with him—he prefers my mouth on other parts of his body—but something about it eases my stomach.

Once finished, I crush a few of the mint leaves I'd found with Estela's herbs until a powder forms that I apply to my teeth and let it sit while I finish preparing my bath.

I add the rose-scented oil to the warm water. I scrub every inch of my body, paying extra attention to my fingernails and toes. Then I get out of the tub so I have enough time to dry my hair.

The warmth from the hearth is welcome as I plop down, boar hair brush in hand. While I stroke my tresses, I think of how Wren looked while getting her hair combed out. Griselda had taught me how to pin my stick-straight locks into curls around my head.

Once my hair shines, I tie it back with a red ribbon. Then, I dress, being sure to bind where my wound has scabbed over, and dab the red rouge onto my eyes and lips.

When I look at myself in the mirror, I can almost feel my mother looking over my shoulder.

Whore.

Griselda can think whatever she wants about me. One day, I'll leave her behind.

I square my shoulders, inspecting my body with an almost clinical scrutiny. My breasts are appropriately pushed up, my dress remains unwrinkled, and my face is pleasing by giant standards.

You are strong. You are fierce. You are capable.

You are... a whore.

My chest squeezes.

It doesn't matter what Ra'Sa thinks about me tonight, or any other night. But then today… he got those men away from me.

"You probably don't even know the touch of a woman!"

"And you'd be right."

Did that mean… that he'd never made love to a woman?

I shake my head. None of it matters. I didn't sleep with him before he arrived, and I'm glad I didn't. There will be other men. There will always be other men.

The Enduar fantasy of being mated and finding someone to care for you unconditionally... It isn't for me.

When there's a knock on the door, I let out a long sigh. I place the beaded headdress atop my locks and then grab my cloak. When I reach the door and pull it open, Hibsej waits on the other side, dressed finely. Her frown deepens when she sees me.

Without a word, she turns on her heel and begins to walk to the front of the house. I hurry out outside, locking the door behind me, and follow after my master's wife.

Eneko's cart waits, prepared for us to go to the feast.

The two boys, Urdort and Relmos, are already sitting on one of the benches, wearing fine clothing. Eneko helps his wife to the front of the cart, so that they might sit next to each other, and I am left to haul myself into the back. It smells of sweat, wood, and something foul that I'd rather not inspect too closely.

The boys continue to poke and prod at each other as I settle on the bench opposite them. I take a deep breath, trying to ignore their fighting. It isn't my business to help them. When they look over at me, the youngest smiles and the elder one hits him squarely on the shoulder.

"Don't speak to her," he hisses.

I let the remarks go and brace myself against the wood as the ride gets bumpier. We pass the trees and slave pens until we make it to the road. I try to look for Ra'Sa to see if I might get a glimpse of him before the feast, but no slave is in sight.

A sensation creeps up my lower back and moves all the way up my spine.

Tonight. You'll see him tonight after—

Enough! It doesn't matter. This is the mission.

I let the worries roll off of me like snowflakes that float to the ground. We travel past the snow-covered trees while I clutch my cloak closed. I watch as Urdort leans his head against Relmos' shoulder, and something inside of me softens. They are generally monstrous boys with horrible parents, but they are still children.

Even I was young and monstrous once.

It's not hard to understand why Hibsej hates me. If I were in her position, I don't know how I could share the man who had promised to be mine. Especially not after I'd willingly given him babies.

To be honest, I don't even fully remember all the details of the man who gave me Thea and Wren. I remember the color of his hair and the sweat that slicked his skin, but everything else faded, like the pain of giving birth.

I hate those memories. Most of the time, I keep them buried deep.

But it's hard not to compare such a time to Ra'Sa's fingers skittering across my skin as he packed the wound. My mind pictures Ra'Sa over me instead of the other two men who have held that place. His eyes would be focused on me instead of his own pleasure.

Just like he had in my dreams.

Fuck. Those dreams.

Like pine sap catching fire, a new ache spreads through my chest. What if he had been Wren and Thea's father? I scarcely need to ask the question to know how different life would've been. How much gentler and sweeter *everything* would've been. He wouldn't have made me fear motherhood.

But I've lost my opportunity. He wants new babies… his babies.

My eyes squeeze shut. Hope is the cruelest of emotions. I cast the painful thoughts aside, but they don't sink into the cracks on the road. They cling to my skirts, like the smell of smoke clings to my clothes as we approach the palace.

I see some of the other foremen from other regions approaching the palace in a similar fashion.

Juan, the human foreman that Abi used to belong to, has a new woman at his side. At least he doesn't have a family to insult with her presence.

This human is sullen and thin—the opposite of Abi's thick, full body. I try to catch her eye. When I manage to, she quickly looks away.

I frown and twist my hands in my skirts.

There are over twenty foremen scattered around, but I hardly recognize any of their women. Abi and Paoli made feasts like this the faintest bit more tolerable. At least we could cast each other covert rolls of our eyes when we were drawn into our masters' laps.

Colorful dresses begin to reveal themselves from under thick woolen cloaks as men and women are escorted up the palace steps. I hop off the back of the wagon unceremoniously and follow closely behind Hibsej and Eneko. Hibsej looks disgusted when she sees me trying to get my footing right.

"At least act like you are a lady," she sneers.

I take a deep breath, nod, and quietly thank her. There's no reason to make anyone mad tonight; it will only worsen things. The boys join their mother's side while I attach myself to the back left of Eneko—his little, human shadow.

We continue up to the top of the steps, and I straighten when one of the men collects my cloak. The human frowns at me, but I let his unpleasant glances bounce off me.

Fuck him. I could fret about the giants finding me desirable, or I could turn my looks into a tool to feed my family.

If I had to do it all over again, I would.

As I step forward and Eneko is announced to the party, the warmth washes over me, a welcome respite from the frosty air outside. As I take a deep breath and fall back into my place at his side, most of the prying eyes find new targets.

We approach the festivities. The human playing a harp in the corner accompanies the lines of people seeking different kinds of food. Roast boars and bulls are laid across the tables while the wine flows freely into glasses. Long tables are situated at the back of the room for the foremen, while lords are afforded more dignified tables near the top of the enormous room.

High King Rholker and his new queen, Marej, sit side by side as humans serve them delicacies from silver platters. A few men and women sit on the sides of the elaborate thrones encrusted with gems. A host of women sit at the king's feet, all dressed to match his golden suit.

He ignores their touches and laughter, already looking irritated and bored.

We walk up the carpet reserved for paying respects to the royalty. I think of the days I spent being ordered to wash and dress Estela. Eneko had been upset at the request, but who says no to their king?

As we approach, his gaze snaps onto me and narrows. My skin bursts into flames, but I keep my head down and bow low enough to touch my nose to the ground.

"Foreman Eneko, welcome. Thank you for coming with such a hasty invitation," King Rholker's voice rumbles through the distance between us.

"It is I who should be thanking you, my king. Thank you for inviting my family to this splendid feast," Eneko responds.

My gaze remains locked on the pristine fibers of the decorative rug beneath me. My thighs and ribs burn as I stay in the position, but I resist the urge to move.

At last, High King Rholker speaks. "I'm glad to see your woman hasn't escaped like so many other humans fleeing our lands."

The heat flashing across my skin intensifies as the seams of my dress suddenly feel too tight. I try to ignore the sensation as I slowly rise with the others.

When I look up, the king smiles at Eneko. "Go, enjoy! Later this evening, I may require a minute or two of your time, along with the other foremen."

Eneko nods deeply, as if nothing would make him happier.

We are dismissed, and Eneko and Hibsej walk away from the throne. I hang back for a half-second to look at the new king. His wife notices and pins me with an icy glare.

I bend into my quickest curtsy and hurry after my master.

Soon, each of us is given a plate. The giants fill them with food, but I hardly eat. Too much food will make the rest of the evening that much worse.

After settling on a roll and a bunch of grapes, I sit. Slaves bring out even more bottles of wine. It's not my intention to overindulge, but I can't seem to help myself.

My chest ties itself into another knot each time I picture Eneko's bed and his naked skin. I chew on my lip. None of this should worry me. I just need to focus, get my head into the right place with a little more wine and let myself relax.

That's all.

Throughout the feast, I watch the others enjoy the music and dancing. My hand hardly leaves the goblet. Usually, a bit of alcohol helps to dull my senses, but tonight, it enhances every detail.

The candlelit chandeliers glittering above are too bright, as are the torches on the wall and the fires held by the statued consorts of Khuohr—god of war. The music makes my ears ring, and a sense of irritation nestles itself firmly in the center of my soul. I fix the fake smile I've pasted across my mouth and take deep breath after deep breath.

Different variations of *'More wine!'* and *'Faster!'* prick at my ears from the dancers.

Too loud. Too bright.

I snap out of my dread when Hibsej returns from the dance floor, cheeks flushed, and a smile spread across her face. Her chestnut hair looks windswept from the lively music, but it suits her, as does her gown and makeup. Her eyes land on me, that twinkle fades. It snuffs out completely and turns into all-consuming darkness when Eneko lets go of her hand, steps away, and nods.

Even I'm annoyed at his brashness.

That tree fucker.

Hibsej's fingers clutch at her skirts, and her shoulders rise a fraction of an inch. "What? You want me to go now?"

He casts her a look that warns his patience wears thin. "The king requires an audience with me. The rest of the night is my own."

Hibsej opens her mouth and then snaps it closed. "Very well, husband."

He gives her a peck on her cheek, which only hardens her glare, and walks over to the boys, who are curled up on a bench after hours of chasing each other around and playing battle with the other giant boys. They continue to sleep as she picks them up.

An ache blooms in my chest as I watch her leave. It doesn't matter that she glares daggers at me; I hurt for something I never had. My womb was once full, but my arms have long since been empty.

"Wait here," Eneko says, addressing me directly. "I must speak with the king, and then I will return."

I can't say that it's normal for the king to stop his party-goers mid-festival, but any information is good information as far as I'm concerned. I let out a huff of a laugh and pour myself another glass of wine. This should be the... third? No, fourth.

The rest of the foremen filter out the room, and I tip my head back. The men all leave behind women like me, dressed in bright colors and accessorized with wine glasses. One comfort woman catches my eye, and I raise my goblet to her, but she shakes her head and looks away.

I sigh.

"Tough crowd," a voice says to my left.

I turn and see Alisa, one of my allies, occupying the seat next to mine. Her brown hair is graying at the root, but she has a pretty round face and rosy cheeks.

"Gods. It's good to see you! Where have you been?" I slur, slightly. "Neither you nor Daria have been at the *cesto de lavado*[1] to wash clothes with me."

"Sorry, love. I wash on Thursdays now. And Daria and I have missed you, too," she says, grabbing the bottle from the table and trying to pour the glass, only to find it mostly empty. She frowns.

"You're anticipating a nasty rut tonight, then?"

I look at her and cast her a crooked smile. "Eneko isn't ever gentle."

"Neither is Forik."

Something about the way she says that makes me sit up straighter.

“Did he make you bleed again?” I ask as if this were a normal conversation. Old friends, and all that.

She winces, but then she nods. “You certainly are drunk tonight.”

“A friend showed me a bush with pale blue flowers. Boil it —it will help you heal,” I say.

Alisa smiles. “Thank you. That’s… It’s kind of you to think of me.”

I don't respond.

“So,” she starts. “Can I ask where you went?”

I sigh deeply, sipping more wine. “I think you know.”

Guilt pricks at my chest.

I look at the woman. Why did I pick Abi and Paoli over them?

They were younger than me. Newer to this life. They were hopeful in a way Alisa and Daria have lost, just like me.

“Perhaps I should try to switch the washing days so Daria and I can meet with you.”

But maybe I was wrong.

“That would be a good idea,” I respond, turning back to the ballroom.

While the families of the foremen have left, many noble couples remain. Even still, there’s an imbalance in the ratio of men to women. It isn't long before dedicated, *loyal* husbands start casting glances our way. Every minute that passes makes me feel more anxious for Eneko’s return.

Giant Lords don't want us for their homes, but that doesn't stop them from wanting a taste. A touch here or a grab there.

All's fair in the name of fun.

Finally, one breaks away, walking toward us with a purposeful swagger that tightens my chest.

Lord Veklor. He's quite an important noble—he owns a decent chunk of the eastern and northern yards. Insulting him would be foolish.

As a sculptor might carve out a perfectly demure face on a statue, I adjust my position, straighten my dress, and arrange my face into the sultry fantasy that men have projected onto those in my station. He takes my movements as pleasing and flashes me a smile of his own.

"It's a shame that your master has left you here all alone," Veklor says. His eyes pass quickly over my body, starting at the glittering headdress and landing on my feet, which have been tactfully kept out of sight.

Giants love neatly groomed, delicate feet.

I smile at him as sweetly as I can muster. "I'm sure he'll be back soon."

Veklor's smile deepens.

"Perhaps." He draws one hand out from behind his back and offers it to me. "And perhaps you'd enjoy a dance while we wait for him."

I refuse to let my lips twist downward even a fraction. "I don't think that would be wise."

He lets out a laugh, but his eyes narrow. "And why would that be?"

I breathe through the wave of nerves washing over me. I always thought that this part would go away—that I would once be able to feel as at ease as I look. It's a testament to my skills that the men never notice. Or perhaps... they don't wish to see.

"Truly, your offer honors me. But I'm sure that Foreman Eneko will return soon. We will likely leave after," I say as softly as possible.

He smirks. "Yes. I'm sure he'll keep you quite busy."

"I will," a voice rumbles out from behind him.

The tension in my chest continues to mount. I breathe in.

You are strong. You are fierce. You are capable.

I let the air out of my lungs.

Eneko steps into view, and Veklor casts him a long suffering glance. "Ah, the devil himself."

Takes one to know one.

"It's a pleasure to see you, Lord Veklor. I hope that the lumber we've been sending is sufficient." Eneko's words run together a little. He hasn't been gone that long but it seems he's managed to drink his weight in wine.

We need to return to the cabin so I can get him talking before he crashes. Without speaking, I gravitate to my place at his side. It's more habit than anything, but it's still necessary.

They continue talking for a moment before a slave appears with a tray of wine glasses. The tension knotting up in my stomach makes me nauseous as we stand there.

They talk about lumber and slaves, and I listen to them discuss the different parts of the trade. I hear about the thousands dead, and sadness snips at my heart. Eneko ordered dozens to be murdered while we sit here partying.

"They can try to do whatever they want, but it will be useless. We've got them backed so far into a corner that they would be fools to try to get out again. As you probably heard, the king is making good on his promises to cut out the rot at the root. With any luck, the next generations of humans won't be so bitchy," Veklor says.

Eneko pauses. "And what will we do without workers?"

We humans need to get the fuck out of Zlosa.

The sooner, the better.

Veklor makes a noncommittal sound. "We'll be fine. They breed like rabbits and mature quickly. We have more across the kingdom that can supplement the more arduous tasks like chopping and butchering while they repopulate."

I memorize every word, knowing that I must remember it for my meeting in a few hours.

We need to leave. I don't want Ra'Sa to wait all night; he must rise early.

Every nerve in my body sparks to life as Eneko leans down a half hour later and says, "Time to return."

1. Washing basket.

CHAPTER 22

Melisa

NOTE: In this chapter, there is a serious trigger warning. When you see **, you will know it's starting. The same symbol will show it is over.

Eneko's breath stinks of fermented grapes, and wine churns in my stomach. The lack of food was a mistake. It almost feels like my belly is trying to crawl up and nestle in my throat.

When we at last near the thick patch of trees that hides his home, I lose feeling in my hands. Invisible needles stab at my skin.

Enough. You've done this before.

When Eneko's hand slides down my back, I tense. His touch is rough and possessive. Ra'Sa's was gentle and careful.

I smile sweetly, blinking rapidly to erase that thought.

Eneko stands, swaying, and holds out his hand. Between our nights together, he couldn't care less about me, but now his eyes watch with such care.

Each movement feels like someone else is puppeting my body. When I walk over to take his hand, it is warm—too warm—as he helps me down.

He smiles. "You're nervous again. It's been a long time since I've seen such shyness from you."

"I am sure I have no idea what you mean," I respond.

He purses his lips. "You wish to play coy? Very well. Come. My wife has been crawling all over me for the past week. I require release."

He guides me to the cabin's front door. Every sound is hauntingly familiar as we walk up the three steps and gaze into the dark home. Somewhere, Hibsej waits, and the boys sleep.

But I don't need to think of that right now. All I need to do is appear willing.

He stumbles around the table and past a few upholstered chairs as we move to the master bedroom in the back. I follow along—dutifully—as he casts me his greedy smile.

Just as we reach the master bedroom, one of the doors cracks open. Eneko is too drunk to notice, but I turn back to glimpse Hibsej. She glares at me.

I wish she would leave and spare herself from hearing this.

But she doesn't. She never does.

I let my gaze fall from her face as I am pulled inside. When the door shuts, the rest of the world goes quiet.

*****Serious Trigger Warning Starting*****

Eneko removes his coat before tugging his shirt over his head. Then comes his undershirt and the rest of his clothes. He stands before me naked and ready for servicing.

The giant stumbles over to the bed and sits down. I grab my headdress and give him a sly smile.

He grins and holds up his hand. "Wait."

I let go of the headdress.

"Dance for me."

Breathe. In and out.

"Yes, Eneko."

His eyes blaze as I finally speak his name, which is only reserved for these four walls.

My dancing is decent enough. I can move my hands over my head in a graceful arc. Even stepping side to side comes naturally to me. When I take my headdress off, it's with a flourish, followed by unbinding my hair.

He watches, mouth slightly agape, before he begins to touch himself. I look away, focusing on the task at hand. Slowly, I undo the front-facing laces of my dress. I make a show of pushing off the straps before I let the gown slide and fall to the ground.

Eneko grins as I stand before him in the thin nightgown I wear to these meetings.

If this were a regular night, he should tell me to stop here so he can splay me across the bed. But the seconds stretch on, and he doesn't.

Just continues to work himself frantically. Watching, lusting.

Panic claws through my mind. My throat closes, and my eyes burn.

Dear gods. Ra'Sa, please come for me.

Kill him.

Please.

But my thoughts belong to me alone. He can't save me. No one can. So I cross the space between us.

When I reach over and place my hand atop the one he uses to touch himself, he smells of sweat and wine. He groans. Slowly, I lower my head. My mouth connects with salty flesh.

He grabs my hair and pulls me back. Then he surprises us both with his choked grunt as he comes.

I force myself to look at his eyes as it happens, trying to keep the disgust off my face.

He slumps back.

"I really did wait too long for you to return. We should've done this the night you turned up."

"Yes, Eneko," I say softly.

He adjusts himself on the bed.

"Sit—wih me," he slurs.

I do, gently brushing the hair out of his enormous face.

"The king wants me to leave," he blurts out as he often does.

I continue stroking despite my shock. The Enduar King wanted me to find out if there is tension within the giants, and he wants to know if Rholker will attack him.

"He'd take you away from me?"

"Rholker doesn't like his new advisor," the giant breathes.

"I don't know much about Regent Uvog."

Eneko closes his eyes. "Regent Uvog is dead. Lord Fektir has taken his place."

I recognize the name. It's Queen Marej's father. He owns most of the northern yards.

"That's awful for the regent," I continue.

"It's a fucking shame," Eneko says. "And now, I have to go to the Ogre Swamps to visit some mine. Hibsej will be furious. She's going to nag me from the second my eyes open."

I let him speak, waiting for him to pause before I ask, "Why the mines? To retrieve tools for the lumber yards?"

He shakes his head. "No, there's something valuable there. Something the Elf King cares about."

The Elf King. Gods.

“The elves look at us like we are brutes. I don’t care for the new king, but Rholker insists he needs the alliance. If I were king, I’d kill them all, alongside those damned trolls. We giants don’t need allies, we need to expand.”

The words tumble out of him, and I try to breathe evenly.

“What’s wrong?” he asks.

My shoulders tense and shivers run over my arms. “Forgive me, Eneko. I am merely sad to see you leave again. Especially so soon after we were reunited.”

He sighs. "I cannot bring you. I already asked."

I relax. "I will miss you. May I ask how long you will be gone for?"

He grunts. "Two weeks. And I leave soon."

"How soon is soon?"

"In the morning," he says.

I force myself to stroke up his arm. "That is soon."

He nods under my hand. "Killing your people isn't enough, you know. The others, they are too stubborn—don't accept their fate. Not like you. You are the best of them."

Silence, and then he whispers, “I missed you.”

I listen to the words, humming my agreement as I pet him like a dog.

"You are a kind foreman. You think of your men. It is a shame they do not return your favor."

Like this, stripped of his pomp, I hate him more. I hate his weakness. If the world saw him now, they would see him for the pathetic, leashed pup that he is.

"Stay until I fall asleep," he says, wrapping his arm around me and pulling me close. "I promise to give you a proper rut when I return."

Godsdamnit. I need to get out of here.

I say nothing; I just lay next to him, tracing his arms and giving him the comfort he needs to sleep. Once he begins to snore, I extricate myself from him and push away.

End of Trigger Warning

I grab my clothing, deciding to wrap my cloak around me instead of getting fully dressed. I can survive the short walk to my room. Only then do I notice some of his seed on my clothing and flinch.

Grabbing the area of fabric between my thumb and finger, I hold it off my skin.

With one hand pressed to my mouth, I rub it against one of the chairs. I close my eyes, trying to breathe deeply, and slip away.

Even after it's wiped off, the feel of it clings to my skin. It lingers like a ghost when the damp fabric brushes over my belly.

When I touch the door handle, my hands burn from what I've done. I see Eneko's face over and over, wanting me.

If I could peel away the areas of me he touched, I would.

I hurry out of the damned room and start to run. When I leave the cabin, the cold air lambasts my burning skin.

Kneeling, I grab a handful of snow and press it to my feverish cheeks. It burns, but then the sharp pain is replaced with… nothing.

Numbness.

I use the gritty powder to scrub my mouth clean of Eneko. I rub until my lips and tongue feel raw.

Only then do I stand and walk to the backyard.

My room is unlocked. A fire is already burning, too.

Taking a deep breath, I enter and find Hibsej sitting on my bed with a knife.

She looks at me with tired, hate-filled eyes. "Finished so soon?"

I open my mouth. "My Lady, I—"

"Shut the fuck up." She holds out her hand, reaching for my arm.

I let it fall out of the cloak, revealing my shift. She grabs my hand, jostling me all the way to the shoulder, and pushes my sleeve up. Dozens of cuts are exposed.

Notches. A reminder of every time I touched her bed.

Sometimes, it's a quick slice, only lasting for a few days. Other times, it's deep. It burns and refuses to heal for weeks on end. I almost cried the first time she did it, but it's been a long time since I cried over something so trivial.

When she pulls out her knife—a regular kitchen knife she brought from inside—I look the other way. The sharp sting causes a hiss to push past my lips. Instead of fading into a dull ache, it intensifies.

Forcing myself to look, I see the wound spans the entire circumference of my arm. She still holds the knife to my skin. My mouth parts in horror, but she looks at me with such fierce disgust.

"For a week, I had my family all to myself. You shouldn't have come back," she sneers.

I meet her eyes, enduring the pain. "My Lady, please—"

"Speak plainly. I'm no lady, and I tire of your pandering."

For a minute, I am silent.

“You know that if I hadn't returned, he would've found someone else."

She shakes her head, but I see the shine along her waterline. "Before he saw you, he never wanted anyone else."

Pity flourishes in my chest, like a drop of ink spreading through water. Another drop is added. And soon, it’s too murky to see.

"Hibsej…" I say softly.

For whatever reason, the sound of her name coming from my mouth makes her remove the knife from my skin. I ignore the burn and how the blood feels running down my arm. I pretend not to hear how it drips onto the floor.

“Eneko built this room before he ever knew I existed. If it hadn't been me, it would've been someone else. He's told me that children ruined your body.”

The irony of that statement has always struck me as unsettling. Although she and I have had the same number of children, Eneko can’t tell because of our size difference.

It makes me sick.

As I’m lost in my thoughts, Hibsej inhales sharply.

"But they were his children who hurt me. I did it for him,” she murmurs.

Hibsej is complex. She’s cruel and sharp, but sometimes… I think I’m the only person she can talk to.

I can't bring myself to hate her. Not when I've seen how she’s treated, pitted against me, and always—*always*—given the short end of the stick. In a way, I envy her. She cares for her sons in a way I wish I could care for Wren and Thea.

"I know,” I say.

Her look of surprise is filled with hatred. "Why?"

The question isn't for me. She gave Eneko so much. Her body, her time, her talents. She gave him strong sons.

Why does he betray her?

"Because he doesn't deserve you," I say at last.

She purses her lips as the tears well in her eyes. “I hate him.”

I nod. "I know.”

She stands, and I still see the conflicting emotions war across her features. "I don't need your pity."

Right now, she isn’t just my master’s wife, she’s a fellow person. Someone I know very well.

“And yet, I feel it all the same.”

She brushes out of the room, knocking a bucket of water on the fire she'd lit, and ensuring it won't be dry enough to heat my room tonight.

CHAPTER 23

RA'SA

I lie under the stars, waiting until it's time to visit Melisa and thinking about the day.

I see the faces of the men strapped to the rack and whipped to death, and my heart aches. I am a man who hated the open sky of the overworld, but now, lying in the snow, I watch the stars glint with a swollen, bleeding heart.

Melisa asked me to come tonight—which means she has information. I know how she got it, and I want to tear a tree down at the root.

I try not to think about it.

Try not to picture.

I fail.

What I feel for her shouldn't be felt between two unmated people. It will only end in sadness. If only…

A flash of panic shocks me to a sitting position. My cot creaks under me. My heart races, and my stomach lurches.

Dear gods.

Melisa's voice is as clear as day.

My mouth parts.

No, it can't be.

When I heard her murmuring this morning, I dismissed it as wishful thinking.

My breath comes out in crystal puffs as I press a hand to my chest. There, in the center of my soul, a little bond wraps itself around my heart. I *feel* her. A song starts up. It rumbles, like thunder, and wakes up my senses. It guides me to her.

A conduit opens between us, and every emotion rages along the line. The shock. The panic. The raw, undiluted fear.

Ra'Sa, please come for me.

I stand, more instinct than thought. I whip around, facing in the direction leading me to the woods.

Melisa is calling to me.

Melisa is my…

My mate.

Sunlight floods my being. Of course, it would be her.

I can't find it in myself to figure out why it took so long. I'm going to her side, and I will never leave.

I'm coming, Ruh'flor.

CHAPTER 24
MELISA

I pull off my nightgown and use it to staunch the wound on my arm as I look for another dress to wear to meet Ra'Sa. Judging by the moon's course in the sky, he might already be waiting for me. The smell of blood fills my nose, giving me a light headache.

At least the gash on my ribs doesn't hurt so much.

Estela once told me elm tree sap can help with wound healing. There's one near my room. At the very least, I imagine it should help stave off infection.

Reaching for a chilled bucket of water, I wash my skin and then pull on a new dress. My body warms in mere moments, and I am grateful for the change of temperature.

As I walk out of the house, I continue to think of Estela. She'd shown me friendship when I let very few see me. Not Hibsej, not most of the other comfort women. She was like Seranya, in that regard.

The memories of two women, both important to me for very different reasons, comfort me as I cross the backyard. Pausing at the start of the trees, the deep night presses against my skin and the backs of my eyelids as I sigh. Then I push deeper, looking for the tree.

Its silver and brown stripes stand out against the pines. Pockets of sap are scattered up and down the trunk, and I pop a few, coating my fingers in the sticky substance while holding up my arm to inspect the wound. In the dim light, I see some of the blood has started to clot, but the wound is hot and tender.

I hiss as I smear the sap over it.

A branch cracks from behind the tree. Out steps Ra'Sa. A light flickers dimly in the center of his chest, almost like the flicker of a pixie.

“You’re hurt again,” Ra’Sa says.

His Fuegorra mixes with the moonlight, illuminating his features. Harsh lines bracket his mouth and tense between his eyebrows. He looks like he would burn down the entire forest.

But those eyes are blue, like the open skies. Panic flares up inside me, compounded by my shitty night.

"What the hell are you doing? Where’s your glamour?”

“Midnight passed—don’t worry, no one will find us. Now tell me what happened?" he demands, pulling me into the shadows of the trees.

We walk away from the cabin, away from the slave pens, until I can’t see any signs of Zlosa. Ra’Sa presses himself against a rough tree trunk, encasing me with his body as he looks at the wound. The gem in his chest glows brighter.

I panic more, placing my other hand over the glow, trying to hide it.

"Let me go, and turn that off," I whisper.

His head snaps up, but his fingers continue to gently cradle my injured arm. Blood weeps from the slash, staining his blue skin.

“Did Eneko do this?”

My anger fades at the look in his eye. It's too intense, too consuming. I spent my time with Eneko wishing he were Ra'Sa and now… now I'm here.

Heart galloping, arm stinging, and lungs constricting. I'd rather be anywhere else than seeing his face when he realizes where I've been.

"No. It's payment to his wife," I say softly.

His eyebrows draw together. "What does that mean?"

I worry my lower lip. If I tell him, he will be disgusted. Disappointed. He might even leave. Men only defend that which they think they've conquered. It's just how they are—territorial, cruel, jealous.

That's why heroes are dangerous. They deluded themselves into believing such behavior is honorable because they are the ones doing it.

My actions are not noble. They rarely have been. Even when I longed for the Enduar before me, it was out of selfishness, not love. I doubt I can even love like a proper person.

I'm merely a smiling viper who broke her own rules and allowed herself to... feel.

"Melisa, I know you were with Eneko. What happened?"

His blue eyes pierce me from the depths of my soul, but I stare back, fearless as the jaws of ruin open wide. One last breath pushes past my lips.

The waking nightmare comes swiftly. My heart beats at a frantic pace, and my palms start to sweat as the tips of my fingers turn numb. I try taking the deepest breaths possible, but the air simply refuses to enter my lungs.

This cursed man's arms wrap around me, pulling me off the tree and then holding me as close to his chest as possible.

"No," I choke.

He shouldn't touch me. I can't be the kind of person who is touched by one man and then another. I can't do this to Ra'Sa.

"Shh, I am here," he says. "I know how to help you through this, remember?"

A choked sob breaks out as I stand there, weak and defenseless against his kindness. "You don't know, Ra'Sa."

“Tell me what you needed to pay her for?" he murmurs.

I shake my head.

Just do it. He came with you to get information, nothing more. This is all a part of the mission.

I pull away from the Enduar. The perfect man with a kind soul and a smile that lights up the heavens looks at me with such tender concern I simply don't deserve.

I take my other arm and pull back the sleeves, revealing the hundreds of scars across my arms. They are so rarely on display.

“You’re right. I was with *him*, but Hibsej met me after. This is payment for laying with her husband," I spit out.

As the words leave my mouth, my head buzzes. I feel as though I am watching this exchange happen from the top of some tree.

I take another step back when Ra'Sa's bright blue eyes drop from my face to my arms. His large hand reaches up and wraps around one of my wrists, brushing against some of the deep scars that had been dangerously deep when they were made.

He soaks in the years of wounds.

"The long sleeves,” he murmurs, more to himself. “I thought that you only wore them for winter."

I don't respond.

He gives me the same look he did while we were traveling. Memories of his arms wrapped around me turn. He held me close while my attack raged. Cherished me. Whispered sweet words.

"Why are you still here?" I demand.

"Because I don't care about where you were—I care about you."

I laugh bitterly into his chest. "You don't know what I did. I used the same hand you now hold. I put my mouth on his cock. If we are being honest, I got lucky he didn't demand more tonight. I won't be next time. Will you hold me then?"

The sex would be awful, like it had been the first few months. But being held after? How could I live with myself?

Ra'Sa remains silent, and the absolute absence of sound drives me crazy. I try to pull away, but he refuses to let me go.

"Again, this is what I am, Ra'Sa," I say into his chest.

I expect him to finally drop my hand, to let me go, but he still doesn't. So I tear away.

"Melisa, I want to be with you," he says softly and steps toward me. "It's all right."

"All right? You are good. You want a family, and children to carry your bloodline, and a *mate*. I-I'm a leech—latching onto people who can secure my future. That's the whole reason you and I know each other!"

He shakes his head. "You're wrong."

I look at him, tears falling down my cheeks.

Tonight wasn't supposed to be like this; we were *supposed* to send a message to Estela. I wasn't supposed to tell him any of this, but he was so damned gentle. So kind.

I wanted to be comforted, not to comfort, for once in my godsdamned life.

“I’m a whore, Ra’Sa. Take my information, and leave me to my shame,” I spit at him.

The moonlight bathes him with such noble, beautiful colors. It makes my chest hurt. He must be young and stupid to approach me so swiftly, knowing that the woman he pursues is... me.

“While you were with him, there came a moment when you felt a waking nightmare creep up, wasn’t there?” he asks, voice low.

I don’t understand how he could know that.

“What?”

“While you were with him. You said, ‘Ra’Sa, please come for me’.”

Shit.

“I—I did,” I whisper as he approaches.

He is devastatingly beautiful, like some fallen god. He looks at me with the light chiseling out his features. There's no humor in his face.

I have never seen anything like this.

It puts me wholly at his mercy. I’m exposed.

Ra’Sa nods once. “I know—I heard it.”

“What the fuck do you mean?”

Melisa, I can speak to your mind, which means I am your mate.

A tentative smile crosses his face as my mouth parts. He looks at me like I hold the key to hope itself.

All the humans wanted this except me. They wanted perfect lives with pastimes and gardens and pretty jewels.

I just wanted safety.

“No.”

CHAPTER 25

RA'SA

I take another step toward Melisa.

"What do you mean 'no'?" I ask as hot panic slithers under my skin.

She shakes her head again. "I can't do this, Ra'Sa. I can't be yours."

The gods blessed me with a strong woman, and right now...

"Why not?" I demand.

Her breath shoots out in misty clouds, and her eyebrows draw together.

"Is it because I don't know how to care for humans?" I snap.

The bitter words had been spoken by both her and my mother. They rang loud, and the vibrations burrowed in my heart. Of course, she wouldn't want me.

But she shakes her head, and her lip wobbles. She throws a hand over her face, cowering in the crook of her bloody arm.

"You told me you think I am playing a game!"

I shake my head as regret pricks my chest. "I was angry. I felt used. I didn't understand—didn't see how you were treated here."

"And you do now?" she snarls.

I take a deep breath. "I'm starting to."

"Your goddess made a mistake. I am not what you want."

All the hurt inside me softens.

Her fears are my fears; they tied us together—inviting us to soothe the pain. How could I not reassure her?

"Can you lower your arm?" I ask quietly.

A deep, shuddering breath wracks through her shoulders, but then, her arm comes down.

Her eyes are red, and her cheeks glisten in the moonlight. Melisa stares at me like I should be running.

I'm not.

I'm exactly where I'm meant to be.

"I've never seen you cry," I murmur.

"Ra'Sa—"

"Melisa. He doesn't own you. The bravery with which you face the world should be recorded for generations to come. You amaze me—you survive while the world crumbles."

She looks at me like she'd continue to weep whether I touched her or walked away.

"You don't know me."

"I don't know some of you. I see mysteries wrapped up in your eyes, but I know you are my mate. I know that you like music and care for your family. You are good with animals—so good that they eat from your hand. You pick up new skills quickly, fear blood, and memorize secret codes. Above all, I know you are stronger than anyone I've ever met, Enduar or human."

Her pupils dilate.

"Fucking damnit. Why do you make me feel so safe," she says through another shaky breath.

"Can I touch your face?" I ask carefully.

She closes her eyes. "Please."

When I reach for her cheek, she flinches but doesn't pull away. Instead, her head pushes into me. Tears streak her face. She looks haunted and hurt.

I just want to help.

"Tell me what I can do," I say.

"Hold me like you did that night in front of the fire," she says, eyes blinking wide and eyebrows furrowed.

The words pierce my heart. She had been so fragile when her waking nightmare almost took her. To know that I could be there for her is the kindest gift.

"Are you sure that you want me to touch so much of you?" I ask.

"Some touches don't hurt."

My chest hollows out, and I slide my hands around her back. Carefully, so damned carefully, I bring her a few steps closer. My hand comes up to cradle her injured arm.

Once surrounded, she starts to shake. She falls apart in my arms, shattering into a thousand pieces that are only kept together by the cage of my body.

I kneel down before her. Even from this position, we are nearly the same height, so I pull her into my lap. She nestles against me.

I speak to her mind again.

Breathe. I am here. You are strong.

She folds into me. The difference between our sizes is stark, and a new instinct comes into focus. Protect. Nurture. I brush her hair away from her face and gather it over her neck.

Slowly, the shaking stops, but she clings to my torso.

"I will unwrap each of your mysteries, and I won't leave. You can't be rid of me. The stones have sung our fate," I say.

Marveling, I cup her face and tilt it toward me so that I can see her eyes once more. Her pupils are still large, swirling with budding hope.

"Kiss me," she says suddenly.

Shock floods through me.

To touch her is a gift. To hold her pain is sacred, but minutes ago, she was crumbling. Now she just looks vulnerable. Like she needs me to carry her away from reality.

"You want to kiss me like this?"

"I've never asked a man to kiss me. Let this be my choice—a real choice. Mark me as yours and erase him," she begs, hands twisting in my shirt.

I grab her behind the neck and pull her lips to mine.

The embrace is slow and full of low-burning heat that travels up my belly and warms my chest. She is everything in this moment. Her taste is sweet and smoky.

"That… should've been our first kiss." She pants against my lips. She eases against me further, accepting the care that I offer. "Again."

I don't wait before claiming her mouth.

Right now, I would take the sweet sting of our bitter story over the loneliness that has clawed holes through me my whole life. I'd have this, imperfect and dark as it is, over the ache that has followed me around since my family withered and died.

Hungry and desperate to seal this between us, I stand and muzzle her throat. I would make her smell like me, not him—*never him*.

As her mouth opens, she makes a sound that causes my cock to harden. I pull her closer. She whimpers.

"You are sweeter than honey," I say against her lips.

She doesn't respond. Instead, she feverishly returns to my mouth, just as twisted and desperate as I am. Our tongues brush, and my blood runs hot. I savor every inch of her tongue, and my hands swipe down her spine. They glide over the curve of her buttocks. Wrenching her up, her legs wrap around my hips.

One word reverberates as I let myself savor her perfection.

Mate.

Her hips grind against me, and her head falls back. New delicious sounds pour out of her.

"When you said you never knew the touch of the woman. What did you mean?"

My cheeks flush with shame, and it almost ruins the moment.

"I have never courted a woman, Enduar or human. No woman has taken her pleasure from my body," I say, chest heaving.

Her hands brush over my face."Then I will be your first?"

"I will be *yours*."

I press her back against the tree. She clings to me. My instinct dictates my movement, which is slow and steady. Following the action of her hips, my own sensations are wrenched out of me.

She pulls back, cheeks flushed. "Touch me."

"Where?" I gasp.

She makes a mangled sound and grabs my hand. She places it on the spot between her legs, where her heat invites me.

I find the fabric wet, and she moans into my mouth.

"What is this?" I ask.

The sound of my voice shatters the fragile connection between us.

She goes stiff in my arms. A look of confusion crosses her face, and she breaks away.

“What—?” I start.

Her face crumbles.

"I can’t—“

"Don't go, not yet.” I grab her hand. “I don’t want to leave you alone.”

“I got carried—This is too far. I can’t do this.” She presses her hand to her forehead.

“Did I hurt you?” I ask.

She shakes her head, darting away when I try to draw her into my arms again. Melisa’s face practically cracks in half with pain.

“Send a message back to Enduvida. Tell them that the Elf King has made a deal with Rholker. Send news of the deaths. Of the poisonings. They want to kill us all—Eneko told me the king’s new advisor, Lord Fektir, wants us all exterminated.” Her chest heaves. “Eneko will be leaving tomorrow to go to some new mines with the ogres. Tell Estela, and I will leave you a message when I know more."

“So this is it. You won’t meet with me again?”

She opens her mouth, but I step toward her.

Holding her hands up, she begs me. “Please!”

A sudden snarl comes from behind the trees.

I instantly push her behind me. My tail wraps around her as a wolf comes into view.

“Coco!”

Melisa struggles out of my grasp and runs to the creature.

Teeth bared, it growls at me.

"¡Basta ya!" [1]Melisa commands, stomping her foot, and the pup stops snarling to look up at her.

Confused, I step forward. The creature growls again, protecting my mate.

"I'm sorry," she cries before running off. The wolf gives me one last look and then trots after her.

I watch them go, unsure what to do.

A wolf? Another mystery.

Teo would've chased Estela if she had run like this.

Something in my blood tells me to do the same.

But she isn't Estela, and I'm not Teo. I must give her space. Reluctantly, I take an iridescent speaking stone from my pocket and bring it close to my mouth.

"Things are not… good," I start. "Upon arrival, we saw a pillar of smoke. Pens are burnt, men are rounded up and whipped, thousands are dead. Rholker is still here, and he has definitely secured a relationship with Arion. I do not know for how long the Elf King will stay."

I look for more words, but they escape me. The stone grows cold and dull as it hovers in front of my mouth.

I swallow hard and drop it, still staring at the tree where Melisa had been moments before.

All I can hear is the blood rushing in my ears.

All I can feel is the imprint of her body on mine.

I have a mate.

A mate possessed by that horrid giant.

We can't leave before the mission is finished, and I can't bear for her to be with him any longer.

Something has to change—I just don't know what.

1. Enough!

CHAPTER 26

MELISA

What was I thinking?

Comfort. I sought out comfort in him. It was a mistake.

It hurt so much—not the touches or the kisses. The care. It felt like he was sawing my heart in half with a blunt stone.

Coco and I reach the edge of the tree line before Eneko's cabin. I halt near, leaning against one of the trunks, and sink down to the wolf's level.

Taking her head in my hand, I press our noses together.

"Thank you, *mi amor.*[1] But I was all right—he wasn't hurting me," I say to my little protector, ignoring the knots in my stomach.

"Go," I pant. "Thea and Wren need you."

Coco leaves, hopefully returning to the girls, and I put one foot in front of the other. Alone at last, I can hardly breathe. I'm hot and tired and *unsatisfied* all at once. Pausing and pressing my fingers to my lips, I find them swollen and tender. I feel the spots where his sharp teeth nipped at me. They tingle with the phantom memory of passion.

Twice I've kissed him.

Twice I've nearly tossed myself off the edge of sanity and into the arms of a gentle, attentive lover. He was a way out of this wretched life.

Gods, he cradled my heart like it fit perfectly in the palm of his hand. And then, the pain stopped, and he made me feel so good. In a way I hadn't thought possible.

The air is still as I trudge through the thin layer of snow and an even thinner layer of ice, but I can't seem to pull myself away from the moments I stood there in front of Ra'Sa and told him to run from me. Confessing where I'd been had felt like sticking a live coal on my tongue.

You are my mate.

He had said the words into my mind, utterly invading my space. Taking up territory I did not give him.

My mind is a dark, filthy place for me alone. There's something painful and unnerving about being so utterly seen and knowing that the other person isn't interested in running away.

I told him where I'd been, and instead, he kissed me.

He held me tight as if letting me go would kill him. He tucked me into his arms as if I was something to be treasured.

He's never had sex, and yet he fucking ravaged my lips. I still can taste him.

For the first time being with a man, I felt… safe.

Gods. Fucking. Damnit.

Bad, Melisa. *Bad.*

I press my hand to my forehead to stop the raging whirlwind in my mind. When it doesn't work, I grasp onto my thin dress, looking at the cabin from the trees. I can't see into the master bedroom, but that's for the best.

I stop, leaning against a tree as my throat closes up.

With the world gone quiet, I still feel the imprint of both men. One very welcome, the other not, but both set against the backdrop of the cut on my arm.

Movement from my window draws my attention. All of the lights have been snuffed out except for one.

I didn't have a light on in my room when I left. Hibsej had thrown water over the fireplace. A crashing sound can be heard from here, and a slice of chestnut curls cuts into view through the window.

Mierda.[2]

I shove off the tree and run to the door. I grasp onto the handle, bracing myself, and push inside.

Everything is entirely torn apart. Clothes are strewn about, and my meager furniture is overturned. The mattress has been yanked off the bed, revealing where I hid the stone dagger Ra'Sa made me and the crystal that I tried to give to Thea and Wren. Their birthday is tomorrow.

Hibsej stands beside the lamp she's brought. She holds the dagger and the crystal, stares at me like she's never seen anything more awful.

"What the hell are these?" she demands, thrusting them forward. "Who did you steal these from?"

My mouth parts.

"T-they were a gift," I stammer, my chest seizing.

If she finds out where the knife came from, she'll tell the guards, and they'll kill Ra'Sa. There's no way I'll be able to get back to Enduvida, and I will be stuck here for the rest of my life.

Ra'Sa will be dead.

My heart starts to rip itself in half at the thought.

"Why are you here?"

“You left a shoe in my room. I had to walk in and find it near my bed, so I came to give it back to you and found you gone.”

She kicks a chair.

“Is one man not enough for you? Are you sleeping with some other lord?" she rages. "Were you planning to kill me? Or Eneko?"

I shake my head, opening my mouth but only being able to choke.

"Speak!" she barks.

"I-I would never," I stammer.

She narrows her eyes. "Humans are getting ideas about freedom."

I shake my head. "No, I have a life here." She sneers, and I quickly add, "A good life."

"I should have you killed for this."

My limbs start to ache, and I feel dizzy. "Eneko wouldn't allow it."

"He would if I told him that you were planning to kill him." She corners me against the wall, slamming the door shut. "Where were you just now? Consorting with the rebels? Performing witchcraft?”

I hold my short, shallow breaths.

Think, Melisa. Think.

"I was out looking for tree sap to cover the cut you gave me."

When I thrust my arm out for her to inspect, her eyes drop to my marred flesh. The cloudy substance clumsily covers my wound with several bits of bark attached.

She seethes.

"Did Eneko tell you that he's leaving in the morning?" I continue, trying to distract her.

Hibsej grits her teeth, trying not to take the bait. But I see her frustrated curiosity spike.

"For how long?" she says at last.

"He'll be gone for two weeks."

"And did he tell you to come to his bed when he returns?" she asks bitterly.

I look up at her, seeing the wealth of her pain and disappointment. "He did."

Her lips press into a flat line, and her yellow eyes sparkle with pain and rage. She lets out a tortured laugh. She holds up the knife, and her face scrunches up as she bears her teeth.

"The least I can do is ensure you are well-kept until he returns." She grabs my arm, fingers wrapping around the barely bandaged wound.

I shout in pain as she tears the flesh open further.

Ra'Sa heard me when I was panicked earlier. Had I opened my mind to him? If he sees this, he'll kill Hibsej. And then we won't learn what Eneko finds on his trip. I'll ruin everything.

Closing my thoughts to him, I shroud my mind. I bury every image in darkness, and keep him from seeing all of this.

"Hibsej!" I say as she pulls me out of the room. "Where are we going? Wait!"

My panicked voice doesn't reach her ears as she drags me away from the house. The snow pushes up above my boots as I dig my heels in and try to free my hand. Snow melts against my leggings and soaks my socks.

"Shut up. If you wake your master, I'll have to tell him what I found," she threatens.

I clamp my lips together, biting my cheek to distract from the pain in my arm.

When we cross over a path that leads behind the pens, I see our destination.

The pit.

Terror spikes in my heart and forks across my ribs, causing my lungs to stop working.

Two giant guards stand beside a wooden lid in a copse of trees—the lightless pit filled with filth and human waste.

"Please!" I say frantically. "You can't leave me down here!"

A rusted handle sticks up from the wood, and a smell emanates from the opening. It makes me gag.

“I will retrieve you when necessary." Her face is unnaturally blank and still. She thrusts me towards the men. They are both tall, wearing the winter warrior garb. The blunt ends of their spears rest against the ground.

One gives Hibsej a bored look. "What's this?"

She straightens, glaring at the both of them. "She needs to spend the next two weeks in there."

The guard pauses. "Cause?"

"She didn't please her master." Hibsej spits.

The men nod. One lifts the rusted handle.

The smell intensifies by a thousand.

The air is thick with decomposing human waste mixed with rot. The fumes choke me as I am shoved toward the mouth of the darkness.

The butt of a spear rams between my shoulder blades. I tumble through the entrance, and I crash into the damp, spongey ground.

Sharp pain from the impact radiates through my bones. I stop breathing. Save the few moonbeams streaming through the surface, I am surrounded by darkness and can only make out a few glinting surfaces of something wet.

I try desperately not to look too closely, wrapping my arms around my body, despite my stinging flesh.

I take deep breaths through my mouth and close my eyes, trying to ignore whatever lurks in the darkness. I look up to see Hibsej's face, along with the other giants. A short ladder extends down toward me a few rungs.

Not nearly low enough to reach.

"Please," I beg.

She shakes her head, nose wrinkled. "Gods, it smells like shit."

"We'll let it air out a bit," one grumbles.

She waves a hand and then leaves.

"Have a good evening, Hib," one of the men says, but I don't catch her reply.

A few more moments pass when I hear, "That's a comfort woman, yes?"

I freeze, panic rattling my bones.

"Yes," the other replies. "But she services that bastard Eneko. You don't want to taste that."

"Perhaps I might."

"Later."

They grumble something else too low to hear.

I scamper away from the light over something slimy. When I press myself against the wall, a wave of fear washes over me and grips my chest with an iron fist. My heart starts to race, pounding so hard I can feel it in my throat.

I can't catch my breath; it feels like I'm being smothered, and no matter how deeply I try to inhale, it's never enough. Sweat drips down my face, and the tremors in my hands spread to my whole body. Everything around me starts to spin.

I see Eneko's and Hibsej's faces.

Then Ra'Sa enters my thoughts, followed by my girls.

My precious daughters.

My stomach churns violently. There's no fucking way I'm going to make it out of here. The entrance is easily three times my height.

What is Hibsej going to tell Eneko?

What will Ra'Sa do when he can't find me?

He spoke to my mind, but I don't know how to do that. But if I could try...

Ra'Sa.

It's just as choked as if I would've said it aloud. Time seems to stretch, each second dragging on painfully. The light streaming in dims. I look up to see one of the giants poking their head in.

"Where are you, little human?" he taunts.

I stand tentatively. But then he starts to thrust his spear toward me. It reaches further toward the ground than I anticipate. Ducking out of the way, mostly out of fear, I slide and trip.

The crack reverberates through my skull as I land on the rotting ground of this stinking place. Then, all of the dim light winks out.

1. My love.

2. Shit.

CHAPTER 27

RA'SA

The imprint of Melisa is etched into my heart. I try to speak to her through our minds, but there is no response.

That is fine. Let her rest.

I'm not prone to outbursts of affection, but something akin to hope is nestled deep in my chest. It's a strange thing to feel after all the death and gore of the night before.

The softness of our romance defies the ugliness of this place.

Thoughts of her mouth on mine shouldn't exist alongside the memories I have of backs ripped open, but life is equal parts pain and joy.

I should be with her now, tending to her arm and holding her through the mornings so that she doesn't need to wake up alone.

Instead, I work.

I help the others check for poison. Fear, anger, and grief blanket all of the slave pens. A woman sits on the corner of the way, weeping for a son she says was killed on the rack. My heart continues to expand and bleed.

I trail along with Nicolás and Abet to the yards.

Nicolás clears his throat. "Are you well, Rasa?"

Pursing my lips, I clap my hand on his shoulder.

"Yes," I mumble. "Are you?"

The young man looks to the sky, his light brown hair falling in dirty tendrils over his shoulders. "When you disappeared last night, a part of me thought you weren't coming back."

His words are a chill seeping into my bones.

"I am not the kind of man who abandons others," I say quietly.

Nicolás gives me a strange look. "You don't owe us anything."

But my king had asked for me to help. While Melisa learns about the king, I was meant to learn about the humans.

How to express that without giving up my true nature is a challenge.

So I settle with saying, "I want to help you."

"And why exactly is that?" Abet says, interjecting into our conversation. There's mistrust sparkling in his irises.

I bite the inside of my cheek, trying to choose my words as best I can. "Call me soft, but I have no desire to see innocent men die."

Abet lets out a dark laugh. "Innocent according to who? The giants? Each other? Humans are just as capable of betrayal."

I think of all the humans I have seen. Most of them are poor creatures, living in a frozen, quiet fear that never quite abates because of their exhaustion. I think of them sitting around the fires, silent under the watch of the giants. I think of Rodrigo and his group of men. Plenty of people seem like they neither care to be saved nor wish for any special kind of treatment.

I watched my people die. My king believes humans need not suffer the same way, and I agree.

"I believe the world is more than black and white," I say at last. "It is hard to judge. We're all products of Zlosa. Who would you be if you'd been born in a different place?"

Abet lets out a bitter laugh. "I'd be just as bad as those who rule over us. I would scrounge for power and get as many men to cook my meals and wipe my ass as necessary."

Nicolás looks thoughtful. "I think I would want others to have what I have: an easy life."

"Perhaps you would be just as hungry for power as the giants. But perhaps not. I think men could work together in peace, but it will be impossible to know unless they can drink deeply from the cup of liberty," I say.

Abet continues to watch me with cautious eyes. "You sound like someone who has known such a life."

Memories of Enduvida well up and overwhelm me. The city didn't have the grandeur of our old civilization, and there were problems, but compared to this place...

But these men can't know about any of that yet.

I tilt my chin upward, getting a good look at the open sky I've come to enjoy. I see the creatures that so often fly overhead at this time. Grouse, as Melisa told me.

"Looking up at the birds in the sky reminds me of what it truly means to be free. When I watch their flight, their formations, I am touched by their sense of togetherness. I've never seen a bird dragging another around the sky. If one chooses to latch onto another, neither can fly, and they will both fall to their deaths."

We are silent for a minute.

"I would ask again: How can we know the nature of any of us, save we get a chance to be free? There is room for all in a place as vast as the sky."

The words sound like something my father would've said. Emotion clogs up my throat.

Abet gives me a crooked smile. "Your words are interesting."

"I'll say," a voice from behind us says.

I turn to see Rodrigo.

He gives me a strange look. "You sound like one of those scholars the giants are always going on about."

My skin heats. “I’ll tell you again: I have no love for the giants."

“Perhaps, but your allegiance isn't to the slaves."

I take a deep breath, retrieve my ax, and head to the yards. The next few hours are spent chopping as many trees as I can manage and then dragging all our logs away.

But it’s the same result as yesterday. There are at least twenty who do not meet the quota.

Abet leans over. “Think of the men who live because of you. Let it be enough."

I nod, watching the executions.

After the misery ends, and my stomach stretches taut from hunger, I leave my team and discreetly go to Melisa's room. The house is dark. I know she is not here when I knock on the door. My fear sparks.

Was she taken with Eneko?

No, that wasn't the plan. Pacing, I leave a message on the ground. But I can’t stay here.

CHAPTER 28

RA'SA

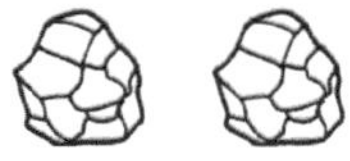

Melisa doesn't appear in the morning either. As the first rays of light begin to paint the sky with a pale wash of colors, I am still scouring through the forest. Two patrolling guards come into view. I press myself behind one of the trees, keeping my back flush with the scratchy, deep brown bark. They pass slowly, laughing to themselves in boisterous tones.

"You hear about the king?"

"The elven king?"

The first grunts in confirmation. "They say he'll return in the next few days."

I store each bit of information. I'd known that there was an official deal made between the giants and the elves, but my fists tighten at the thought of being close to King Arion. He betrayed my king and sold us out to the giants by revealing Estela's location.

Without him, this war wouldn't have started.

When they are out of earshot, I duck into the hole in the fence designed to keep the slaves in. Many humans are already awake, leaving their homes and shuffling over to get food. That's when I see the den Melisa had been visiting.

The only place I hadn't looked.

I'd never seen anyone other than her enter or leave. The windows are covered, hiding everything inside from prying eyes.

Had Melisa been here recently? Does she hide there now?

I raise my hand, prepared to knock on the door, and hear a soft bark inside. What kind of creature makes that noise?

A whining sound follows it. Inhuman.

It must be the beast that had interrupted Melisa and me.

Godsdamnit. I never should've let her follow a creature with teeth as sharp as a vaimpír.

My mind pictures Melisa lying on the floor, red lips gone pale and golden brown skin drained of color.

Without thinking, I push open the rickety wooden door and am greeted by three pairs of eyes. Two young children are playing with the four-legged beast.

My mouth drops open. They are alone and *young*. Young enough to need to be supervised at all times.

The girls look up at me from the ground, and the wolf growls.

"Coco!" one of the girls squeals. The same name Melisa used.

The one closest to me stands up in front of her wolf and points a finger at me. *"¿Quien eres?"*[1]

The creature makes another menacing sound, and I step closer. It doesn't look like a beast who should be anywhere near children.

The girl pointing at me slowly lowers her hand and pushes her hair out of her face, looking more and more fearful. The movement causes me to pause. The defiant curve of her lips, the sleek black hair, and wide brown eyes remind me of just one person.

Melisa.

I immediately drop to my knees as I softly push the door closed.

"Me llamo Ra'Sa," [2]I say gently, matching their language.

The two girls look at each other. Twins, I realize—both copies of Melisa.

They both look at me with hard, untrusting eyes.

"Lita está aqui,"[3] the girl near the wolf says.

I don't know who Lita is, but I'm sure I will find out soon.

"Melisa?" I ask, unsure how to form the proper sentences.

One of the girl's furrows her brow. *"¿Mamá?"*[4]

The word pierces right through me. As I look at these two girls, realization washes over me again and again.

"¿Melisa es tu madre?" [5]I ask.

One giggles. *"Hablas raro."*[6]

But the other says, *"Si."*[7]

Yes.

My head spins, and my heart beats fast. She never told me she had...

"I'm looking for your mother," I say, continuing to talk to them in their language.

They look at each other and frown. The one who isn't a veritable beast tamer steps closer to me and grabs my hand. I look down at her fingers. They are impossibly small.

"I miss *mamá*. Will you take me to her? She promised to come, but she missed our day."

The other says, "I can ask *Lita* again!"

My brows furrow, but I place my hand atop the girl's. "Who is *Lita*?"

"Wren, Thea!" someone shouts from outside. A woman joins us who doesn't look much older than Melisa. She looks like my mate, too. But, whereas Melisa is filled out and full of life, this woman's hair is tangled and mussed around her face. Deep hollows are in her cheeks, and some dust is scattered from her cheek to her nose, and she hastily wipes it away.

She gets one look at me, and her face twists with fury.

"Get out of my house!" she shouts.

I stand.

"I'm just looking for Melisa."

Her eyes narrow, darkening the circles under her eyes, and she grabs a metal rod from the wall. "I'll kill you."

I take my hint and back away, but don't leave.

The world tilts on its side. Melisa... has daughters. Two of them.

Memories blast at me, filling my thoughts.

"And what if you are mated to one of the pregnant women?"

"I would care for the child."

"But you would want your own?"

"Yes."

Then last night…

"You don't know me... You want a family, and children to carry your bloodline, and a mate… I can't do that."

Shit. I'd been stubborn and pigheaded. I'd acted like I wouldn't properly father children from another man.

That wasn't true. They were her daughters, and if the stones led her to me, then it was as if Grutabela herself spoke from the stars to bind them to me.

Starling children, as we called them in the caves.

A strange protectiveness flutters over me, growing in intensity before it settles firmly in my chest and demands my attention.

They are being watched by that woman.

She raises her weapon.

"Wait!" I cry. The woman thrusts the metal rod at me. I reach forward and grab the metal. "Are you all right?"

She spits on me. "I will be fine once you leave us alone."

"Melisa," I say again. "Where is she?"

Her sharp gaze dulls. "I have no idea where she's gone. But we haven't seen her in days."

I suck in a deep breath. "But you are her family?"

The woman barks out a bitter laugh. "We are bound by blood, nothing more. She does not live in this house, and I do not care where she is or what she does."

My gaze scans back over the creaky home, and the girls are confused at my presence. Her daughters. I look back up. Her mother.

The faces of my sister and mother flash before me, and something scratches at my chest, tearing holes. When I look back around, I see little food, but everything else seems to be tended to.

I want to stay.

But the men in the yards need me. If I don't help chop, I risk them looking for me. They could discover me and ruin the mission. Everyone in Enduvida would suffer, and the men who I've helped save would die too.

"I will leave," I start, and the woman relaxes. "But I will return."

Melisa's mother watches me go, and I have to physically pull myself through the door and away from the house.

My thoughts race. Melisa had been telling me all along—she had children. And I'd acted like an idiot.

Tirin. He wanted me to have children. I wanted someone to give his name to… But these girls had names.

Wren. Thea.

I'd heard their voices. Seen their small bodies. They didn't need someone to tack a dead man's name onto their heads—they needed a new life. Just like their mother.

Grutabela and Endu as my witnesses, I was going to give them that.

The further away I get, the more that I worry. Something isn't right.

My senses tingle when the sound of paws pad behind me.

I whip around to see the gray beast. Sharp teeth are bared at me, and I narrow my eyes, only pausing because Melisa cared for the thing.

Frustrated, it catches up and stands at my side.

"What are you doing?" I ask, as if it can understand me.

It doesn't close its menacing mouth, but it tilts its head to the side and whines. Its ears flatten to the side of its head, and it turns in the opposite direction.

I do not understand its grumbling sounds and continue on my way.

It trots next to me and breaks away as I exit the trees into the lumber yard. I look back at the creature.

It watches me.

I turn away and stand in the regular slave lines, but find other men whispering quietly as the guards bring in the racks of tools on carts. I let out a long sigh and glance between me and the other men.

Rodrigo is one of the men speaking to the others he surrounds himself with. I look away when his amber-brown eyes flick up at me and let my ears tune into his conversation.

"The whore's in the pit," one of them says.

Another hums. "So, Eneko is gone, and he didn't want her wandering. Shame."

Flames spread across my skin. Dozens of questions swirl. Why is she in the pit? What is the pit? Is that why she can't speak to me or hear me?

One of the giants notices the unusual chatting and puts a hand on his whip in warning.

"Quiet!" he calls.

Everything goes silent. I barely hear the giant's speech as they drone on, so I force myself to get my tools and go to chop.

1. Who are you?

2. My name is Ra'Sa.

3. Grandma is here.

4. Mom?

5. Is Melisa your mother?

6. You talk funny.

7. Yes.

CHAPTER 29

RA'SA

When I finish, it's nightfall. I go back to the forest to look for this *'pit.'* Darting behind trees and around different shadowy corners, a beast emerges from the trees.

That same damned creature.

"Coco?" I say, using the name Melisa and her daughters used.

The creature's ears perk up, tall against its broad forehead and narrow snout. It whines. Moving its head again.

My heart softens. "You wanted me to go with you earlier… to get to Melisa."

The beast stamps its foot on the ground.

Dropping to my knee, I hold out my hands for the beast, allowing it to smell me.

"Thank you," I say, noting how it looks at me with deep, suspicious eyes. When I move too fast, it bares its teeth and backs away.

I stand, following behind it. It leads me down the hill, away from Eneko's house and the slave pens, and then, passing a few more trees. I see two giant guards standing by two bars sticking out of the snowy ground.

A wooden lid and a foul stench are shadowed by the trees that backdrop the scene. Inhaling deeply, I sort through the smell of filth, excrement, and rotting food.

Under all of it... there it is. The sweet smell of cinnamon and roses.

I stumble, causing a sound to come from the tree I've been hiding behind.

The giants' heads snap in my direction, eyes squinting to see through the low, snow-covered branches.

"What's that?" one asks as the other approaches me.

Melisa?

I look for her through our bond. But there is nothing.

An idea sparks in my mind as I look down. A stone sits near my foot. I ease into my magic and out of my skin, sharing just a drop of my power with the stones scattered under the snow. Grabbing a hold of them with my mind, I cast rocks upward.

They shoot in every direction, raining through the trees.

"Fuck!" one of the giants yells.

They both start running away from my hiding spot. The sound of their roars and the readying of their weapons is like music to my ears.

I race forward as soon as they run into the trees and grasp onto the wooden door. I push it up, causing more of the miasma to blast me in the face. Immediately, I jump inside, crashing into the bottom of the pit as the lid slams shut behind me.

The crash makes me wince, and I wait a few moments after, trying to locate them by feeling through the vibrations of their footfalls, but they remain dispersed in the forest.

My eyesight is better than that of a human, and it's easy to see my mate laid out across the slimy ground. Fear slices through me. I fall to my knees at her side, feeling for her pulse.

It flutters against my finger, though her skin is clammy.

Melisa?

I speak quietly into her mind. I fit my hands under her and slowly try to draw her up.

"Melisa," I say, shaking her gently.

The smell of blood gets stronger.

Is it from her ribs? They should be mostly healed.

Perhaps her arm? But it has scabbed over nicely too.

Her chapped lips part, and she makes the smallest sound I've ever heard. Wrapping my hand behind her head, I slide her onto my lap and brace her neck protectively.

She's weak.

My thumb strokes the side of her head, and I look around for something—anything—that would help revive her. She's been down here for two days with nothing to eat, likely unconscious. I pull her as close as possible and try to remain still as I try to devise a plan.

At last, around midnight, I move. Shifting away from her.

My team wanted me to go drinking with them, but there's no way I'm leaving this pit. Not tonight.

My instincts war between desiring to be at her side and finding some way to improve her condition. As I stand, I reach deep into the layer of rock beneath us and start to rearrange the stones. I cannot move the depths of the earth as King Teo can, but I can clear away a scum-free area for her to lay on. She's cold but not as chilled as she would've been above ground.

This stinking, disgusting pit cannot account for much, but it can protect her from most of the elements while keeping her near the warm layers of stone. And for that, I am thankful.

Once she is arranged in the clean spot, I take one of my glamour stones and cover her with my sad excuse for a coat.

When I look over at the exit and the short ladder that is too far up for a regular human to reach, I crouch down and sense along the stone for the exact location of the men. I'm surprised to find them still gone.

That means I can stay with her longer. I am filled with something akin to ease.

Drawing her back into my lap, I let out a deep breath. Anyone could find someone like Melisa beautiful. But what we have is something much sweeter. To care for her in sickness is an honor.

The lingering scent of blood begins to fill the room seconds before she moves in my arms. She lets out a soft groan, and I freeze. As still as I can be, I look down at her, blinking twice as her sleeping form animates. For a moment, I worry.

Will she fear me?

Best to move slowly.

She moves again, and those lovely, deep brown eyes blink open. Even though confusion knits her brow, her gold-flecked irises dilate.

Her soul knows me before her mind, and that touches something deep in my being.

"Ra'Sa," she says, voice gravelly from disuse. "You're here."

Those three words are sweet.

"Of course, I'm here. I told you I would always be near."

She tries to swallow and winces.

"What day is it?"

My eyes burn as I stroke her cheek.

"It took me two turns of the sun to find you."

"Fuck. Wren and Thea's birthday." Then she lets out a pained noise. "Fuck. *Fuck!*"

Panic shoots through my body.

"What is it?" I demand. "Does your wound still bother you?"

Her hand goes to her midsection, and she barely sits up before doubling over my arm. I stroke her back, brushing her hair to the side.

"No. I'm going to—" She cuts off with another noise. "Bleed."

I draw her closer as she starts to shake in my arms.

"Where? What can I do?"

She lets out a frustrated noise. "Do you know nothing of women?"

I blink.

"My arm and ribs are fine. These are my monthly courses. They are irregular... but I bleed. It is starting." She grits out.

My brow relaxes. I know of such things. Enduares tend to bleed once or twice a year, and it is painful like this. But it also comes with increased attunement to their powers.

I peer at her as she curls up into a ball. Melisa doesn't look like any divine gift shines down on her.

"How can I help?" I ask, starting to feel something much worse than worry: helplessness.

She shakes her head. "Need to... relieve myself."

I nod, draw her up, careful not to press against her midsection, and leap toward the ladder that leads out of the pit.

She protests, but I shake my head as we climb out. I pull her towards a thicket of trees as fast as I can to keep her out of sight. She needs to remain in a place where no one can see her.

"I'll get caught. I'm supposed to stay here for the next week at least," she hisses into my ear.

"Fuck that," I retort, using the word she loves so much. "Tell me about Wren and Thea."

Her mouth parts. Then, her mask slides into place. "I don't know what you mean."

I take a deep breath. "Your daughters. I met them."

A fury I've seldom seen brushes across her features, and she pushes against me, with puffs of white clouds coming between us.

"What are you getting at?" she demands.

"Melisa, I am your mate. Your daughters are—"

“Do you mean my sisters?” she asks, voice hard.

“They called you mother,” I say, confused.

Her eyes go wide, frantic. “They did?”

I nod.

“They—I…” she stumbles.

I take her hand. “It’s all right. I know.”

A long breath wooshes out of her. “No one else can know.”

A word Melisa said earlier returns: *Birthday.*

When I went, they were sad that she hadn't visited. A pang goes through my heart—for Melisa, for what she is forced to do, for being pulled so far away from the young girls, and for the two little ones who live with that strange woman.

“Why do they stay with your mother?”

She looks away, silent for a while. “I… am not a good candidate for motherhood. But I was forced to have them. I suppose I could’ve stopped that, but then I found out, and after the grief and the worry, something flickered on in my heart. I was protective. I *wanted* them." She frowns, as this makes her feel ashamed. "I knew there were two."

Her hair shifts around her, disrupting the stillness of the night. She looks so defeated.

"Your mother doesn't seem to care for them well."

She looks at me. "She used to do a better job."

"Is that why they are with her?"

She sighs. "If I don't tell you, will you just rummage through my mind?"

The shock must be apparent on my face because she shakes her head.

"In the slave pens, if you fall pregnant, they tell the man. Sometimes, he lives with you; sometimes, he spends part of the time with you. I couldn't do that. So I worked. For as long as possible, wrapping my stomach, wearing loose clothes, and keeping hidden. There was never enough food. I was weak and thin. And then, when I had them, I didn't rest."

She hides her face. "I worked with animals. Not men—at least not yet."

I watch her, listening closely.

"Eneko picked me. He offered food for my family—a perk for whores. There still wasn't enough to eat for the four of us. Griselda's joints were always swollen. So I said yes. I left them as crying babes to join a man's bed."

I blink. "My gods, Melisa."

She peers up at me.

"You did your b—"

"Don't. Don't lie to me and tell me I did my best," she closes her eyes and looks away, as if it could hide away all of her shame.

It doesn't matter that it's wrong.

"Your secret is safe with me."

"Promise me, Enduar," she says, looking back at me sternly. "You say your kind always keeps your word. Swear it."

"I swear it upon our matehood," I say softly.

She nods, then shifts her weight from one foot to the other and curses under her breath. A second later, she twirls her finger. "Turn around."

I do and focus on something else as she sneaks away to empty her bladder. While continuing to keep my distance from her, I count the days until Eneko returns.

On the one hand, having her awake is a good thing. On the other hand, having her awake and having him return any day worries me greatly. I drag my hand over my face when I hear her curse again.

I turn back, debating whether I should say anything as I approach.

"Are you well?" The smell of blood grows thick.

"Stay away," she demands.

I pause. Biting my lip. Then I reach and tear off the mostly clean shirt under my coat. I begin tearing off the hem.

"Stop that," she says from her spot beyond the tree. "I have clothes back at the cabin."

"But you can't have them until you return. Take this," I hand out the strips to her, waiting for her small hand to reach out and take them.

A moment passes. "*Mierda*. Gods damn it all."

"Melisa," I insist.

"Fuck! Fine," she says, snatching them away from me.

I listen to the sounds of night until she emerges. Her face is pinched, and the corners of her mouth are downturned. I unhook the gourd on my belt and hold it out for her to wash her hands.

“Better?” I ask.

“I could be worse,” she replies.

"I tended to you," I say. “While you slept.”

Her chest rises and falls as she grits her teeth. "Why?"

I can't believe it. "Why? Was I supposed to let you rot in the filthy space?"

She lets out a frustrated breath. "You need to be more careful. If someone had caught you—”

From behind us, the laughter and footsteps get louder and louder. I grab Melisa and hold her close, expecting her to resist but pleasantly surprised when she melts into me. The tenderness of the small action makes my heart swell.

"She's down there... waiting," a solo giant slurs to no one.

I angle the both of us so we watch him as he moves toward the space at the entrance of the pit. Something sour coats my tongue like the sweetness of poison. It’s the giant who whipped me and executed my fellow slaves. He peels back the lid I'd carefully replaced and sticks his head in.

"Come out, come out little whore. Eneko's nowhere to be seen, and I'm ready for a rut!" he calls into the space.

I freeze at his crass words, my arms turning into a steel cage around Melisa.

"Where are you? I'm ready to sink into your soft little quim. Eneko shows you off too much for his own good,” he continues to ramble drunkenly.

Melisa is still. Her heart races. Then she lets out a shaky breath.

"I'll be right back," she says.

"No," I fume.

This haughty woman, the one who teases all and flirts with every man, the one who appears as an open book, could hide secrets, fiercely protect what she loves, and... be afraid. She was afraid of these men.

If she thinks that I wouldn't defend her honor, she's a fool.

I can kill a man easier than blinking. I've done it.

For the first time, she looks up at me with large, terrified eyes. Her eyebrows are drawn together, and I smile at her.

He'll find I'm gone, she pants. *I have to go back. I have to...*

Not this time. I can't save you from everything, but I will save you from this.

I feel her fear thicken through the bond.

I can handle this. Do you trust me? I plead.

Those beautiful eyes meet mine again. I stroke her soft skin and snarled hair. She finally says the one word that sets me free.

Yes.

Then stay here and close your eyes.

A flood of emotions open to me, but her thoughts shut. I slide away from her, and her eyes close tightly. I fashion a sword from the ground beneath my hands. Stones swirl into a thick, sharp edge, perfect for lobbing off the head of a giant.

The warrior lowers himself into the pit, sealing his fate as a dead man.

Confused sounds come from deep within the ground.

The heat of anger blocks out the chill of night, and I feel the way that the ground beneath him gives and moves in time with his steps. I whisper to the stones, telling them of his sins. Of his ugly, pathetic excuse for a life.

When I land on the ground behind him with a thud, the stones reach toward me, their old friend.

"What are you doing here?" I growl. My spell light illuminates the space.

He turns to look at me, then staggers back.

"You. What the hell are you doing here? Where's the whore?"

The giant's eyes land firmly on the sword in my hand. His eyes widen to the point of bulging out of his skull and his hand feebly goes to that whip on his hip, which carries the blood of gods know how many beings.

"Before you die, you should know you disgust me," I say calmly. "And no one will mourn your passing."

He protests, but I raise the sword and slice. It sings through his flesh, relieving the body of his enormous head. It falls to the ground, onto the spot I had cleaned for Melisa. I reach deeper into the ground, feeling the drain on my power as I let the stone take him. It opens and encapsulates him with ease, but I'm left panting in the end.

The long hours, the worry, and the lack of sleep while tending to Melisa all weigh on me, and I sag to the ground.

Ra'Sa?

It is done, Ruh'flor.

The sweet tones of her voice caress my mind. Her voice could call me back from death itself. I do not know how I ever existed without her presence.

I let out a deep sigh and reach toward the ladder, only to stumble and then sag back against the ground.

"Ra'Sa!" She calls, coming down with me, and fixing the pit's cover back into place.

She draws me up into her arms, but I'm barely aware. She lacks my strength, but her soft curves pressed against me is enough.

“What's wrong?” she asks.

“Too much magic. It's been too long since I used so much,” I say, swallowing to ease my bone-dry mouth.

She makes a frustrated sound, then brings us both on the ground. “Lay your head on me. Close your eyes.”

Obeying her words, I rest my head onto her lap. Instant relief soothes my aching head.

“You shouldn't have killed him,” she mutters.

I take a deep breath, enjoying her scent. “What man would I have been if I hadn't?”

She lets out a long breath. “I don't know what was wrong with me. He sounded drunk—I should've just flirted with him. It would've been over quickly and—”

“Stop that,” I say. “You don't need to do that again. Not for you, and not for me. You are your own person now.”

“I thought I belonged to you because of our matehood,” she replies.

My head throbs, and I wince. “You belong to me if you wish it. I will never force you.”

Her hands brush through my hair, but she is quiet.

“Thank you, Ra'Sa.”

“My brother was willing to do anything for others. I felt the need to watch over him, too. I hope, in time, you come to see what he never did,” I murmur against her lap.

She strokes my hair again. “And what would that be?”

"That you don't have to carry everything alone. We are in this together." The words slip from my lips, and my eyelids hang heavy. When I try to look up at her, she pushes my eyes closed.

"Rest," she says sternly.

My heart races, keeping me awake. I can't leave her and can't stay.

So I wait for her to sleep.

Once her body relaxes under me, I kiss her forehead, apply my glamour, and use what's left of my strength to leap toward the wooden lid. Once out, I check for the sun on the horizon. I find the sky blotted with the inky moments before the dawn chases away all of the black.

The other guard never returned.

I let out a long sigh. It's time to go and help the others.

I adjust my half-torn shirt and rush back to the slave barracks.

When I arrive, Abet is already awake, though he still lies on his bunk. His eyes narrow when he sees me, and I cast him a confused look before brushing my gaze over the men just starting to rise.

When I sit down, Abet makes a displeased sound in the back of his throat.

"Where were you?" he murmurs in the human tongue.

I look at him with my own narrowed eyes. "Why?"

Then he purses his lips. "*They* wanted you at their meeting. They will be displeased that you didn't come."

Unease ripples up my back, but I don't say anything more. I'll need to speak with Rodrigo. Surely, there will be another chance.

"What the hell happened to your shirt?" Abet continues.

I purse my lips. "Do you know where I can find another one?"

He sits up, nods, and grunts. "Fine. Let's get moving."

CHAPTER 30

MELISA

"He was here last night," a voice rumbles above me.

There are pains all over my body, but I grit my teeth and sit up. Ra'Sa is gone.

There's a sadness that accompanies that thought, but it's overshadowed by a pain pounding in my head. It doesn't take long for a cramp to squeeze my lower belly. I groan just as another voice filters through the wooden trap door above.

"So what happened to him? You weren't rutting around last night, right?"

Mierda.

[1]They are talking about the giant warrior who came into the pit while Ra'Sa and I were talking. Ra'Sa... killed him.

"We were here the whole time. A half hour ago, I went to relieve myself, and when I returned, he was gone."

The other man curses in giantese.

"So you're saying he's only been gone a half hour?"

The replying grunt comes instantly.

"You son of a bitch. Lying to me through your teeth already? I can smell the wine on your breath. You were careless—you left your post to do gods knows what. I don't want to see your ugly, warty face any longer. Report back to the barracks," the other warrior says.

"But sir—"

"I'll deal with you later."

It isn't until I hear the footsteps fade that I let out a long sigh.

My gaze drops from the wooden lid, and I realize I can see. There is a dimly glowing orb of light above me. I reach up and grasp at it, finding it identical to the floating lights all around Enduvida. A small basin has also been hewn from the ground and is filled with what appears to be clean water, almost like a fountain.

A small, rectangular hole has been carved at the back of the cave, which can function as a latrine. The strips of fabric left there are hard to miss.

Ra'Sa.

Ra'Sa did this. For me. While I slept in this slimy, disgusting place.

My musings dissipate abruptly when the pit's wooden lid is torn off, letting in gusts of chilled air. I shove the spell light into the folds of my dress. My heart races, fearing that I will be caught with contraband.

A giant warrior sticks his head in—Captain Truloj. Luckily, the small, marked improvements aren't enough for him to notice. The sun backlights his profile, showing how he curls his lip.

"You!" he calls in. "You still alive?"

I freeze in place, then force myself to crawl to where he can see me and put on a coy smile.

"I'm afraid I am," I call back.

Raising my hand to shade myself from the light, I peer up at his mousy brown locks and scarred face. His eyes are more burnt orange than the others. Even from here, I can see that his top lip is mostly scarred flesh.

He smirks. "Did you see either of the guards last night?"

I shake my head, and my breath feels a little tighter.

Are you well? Ra'Sa asks.

My mouth parts at the sound of his voice. It caresses my mind, sustaining me in the face of panic. Chills ripple down my spine as I let out a deep breath, and gooseflesh pebbles up my arm.

I nearly forgot to thank you for caring for me last night.

It was good I rested, Ruh'flor. *I very much enjoy the feel of your thighs against my mouth.*

My heart skips a beat. I press my thighs together at his innuendo, surprised at my body's response, and ignore him.

Fuck, get it together.

“You didn't hear anything?"

"I was asleep, Captain," I reply.

He pauses, considering my words, and then shakes his head, mumbling something about stupid humans. The top is closed, and I am left in relative darkness. I keep the spell light close to me for a long while.

It pulses lightly against my skin. Gentle reminders of the troll who protected me. A curious sensation creeps up my neck.

He cared for me.

My head throbs, and I lower myself to the ground.

Melisa? Ra'Sa says again.

I let out another long breath.

I'm fine. The giants came. They were just looking for... I trail off, remembering the sound of the giant dying. It was quick, but I knew what was happening.

Ah. I understand.

I don't know what to say to that, only that the entire evening felt like some fever dream. I can picture how the guard dropped into the pit, and Ra'Sa followed him.

Close your eyes. Don't watch, he said.

Why did he risk that for me? Does matehood also take away common sense?

Eneko returns soon, and I will go back to his bed. I need to know what he learned in the mines. He won't be satisfied with a quick hand and spilling over my dress.

My lungs seize.

Sleeping with the foreman has never been a particularly pleasurable experience, nor something to look forward to. But thinking about doing it when Ra'Sa is in my head, taking care of me...

It feels like... it feels *wrong.*

I rub my hand over my face. The plan was to find someone to take care of the girls, to make him care about me so much that he would do anything for me while I remained emotionally unattached.

I wasn't supposed to feel anything. Not the brush of butterfly wings against my heart when he says my name. Not heat at his touch or loyalty to him.

Fuck.

I feel Ra'Sa smirk in the corner of my mind.

Fuck off, I say darkly, recognizing that I'm having a harder and harder time of keeping my heart in my chest.

It sounds like you are feeling better, he says back. *Just so you know, I brought meat to the girls this morning.*

I brace my hands on either hip.

You did what? I growl.

They were hungry when I stopped by, so I found them some food.

Did they not have food? I demand, skin heating.

They did. But they're growing. They needed more.

Relief cools my hot skin.

Thank you, I grit out.

He smiles again, that little shit.

He barely smiled before, why does he have to be so... so...

Charming? he supplies.

I sputter. Am I so transparent?

You are anything but charming. When I met you, there were stones with more facial expressions.

And yet, you still followed me around.

I shut off all my thoughts and go back to sitting against the wall. He can't be in my head all the time. Except, it feels good to have him there. I shouldn't find comfort in a place like this, but gods… he makes it happen.

After a few hours, I change the blood-soaked clothes and wash the others the best I can. I lean back and wrap my hands around my midsection. My arm, my ribs, my womb—they all hurt.

When the hatch opens again, late afternoon greets me through it. Hibsej is there with a sneer on her face.

"You're still alive," she says simply, clearly disappointed.

My heart leaps at the sight of her. If she's returned, it likely means that I'll get to leave this cursed place and go and see the girls.

I'll make them something new. I'll kiss their faces and take every cursed beating from Griselda. When I move from my location on the ground, a rope is let down minutes later with a loop around it.

"Get over here," she calls down.

I grab on and then position it around my aching midsection. The knot is pulled, and it digs into my ribs and bottom. All of it hurts. It's so cursedly tight when it pulls me up, it feels like my ribs might pop. When I reach the surface, I'm greeted with the too-cold but mercifully fresh air. I inhale lungful after lungful while Hibsej watches me in disgust.

Little does she know that I would've died if it hadn't been for my ma—*for Ra'Sa.*

She doesn't say anything to me once the giants set me down. One of them gives a squeeze to my ass, and I don't even bother to look back. Instead, I stumble after the woman, following her through the trees and back to the house. When we reach the cabin, she heads inside, then pauses.

“No visiting your mother until you finish the clothes,” she quips and slams the door shut.

I watch the enormous wooden door for a minute, taking in the knots and veins of rich colors before I go back to my room.

No visits.

My heart lurches, and I try to comfort myself by saying that I am already late.

The second I walk in, I’m bombarded by laundry bags—more laundry than I knew the family was capable of dirtying.

I can't clean all of this tonight. It will freeze and ruin the cloth before the night is up.

A scream sits in my throat, choking me. Instead, I take a deep breath and start to sort through the masses of crudely woven sacks. It takes a minute to find them, but I grab my buckets for the well.

Outside, two warriors round the corner. I freeze.

"You," one says. "The king's summoned you. Come with us."

My mouth parts. Rholker?

"Now?" I thought he had gone with Eneko to the mines. Apparently not.

They nod.

I look at the buckets and drop them. I grab onto my still filthy skirt and inspect the stains, some of which are crusted while others look oily. The two guards start walking, and I follow after them without even going to grab my coat. As they guide me to the front of the house, I see Hibsej looking at me through one of the cloudy windows. The rough, bubbled texture distorts her face, but I can make out her frown.

When I look at the carriage, I see the royal insignia etched onto the sides.

Hostia puta.[2] *They weren't lying.*

It'll be nothing, I tell myself before the nerves can start to bunch up. The space between the ground and the step is significantly high, more so than the cart that Eneko uses. No one helps me climb in. When I get inside, I fall unceremoniously across the carpet.

I scramble to my feet and find a rough cloth has been laid across the seating. I sit, back straight, as the carriage starts to move. My gaze soaks in the fine fabrics lining the walls. Several of them are painted and stitched with golden threads. There's even a makeshift window made out of magical glass as clear as crystal. It keeps out most of the chill, but a frozen sort of stale air hangs around.

When we reach the palace, I am taken aback by how much of it is still rubble. I mark the completely destroyed hall, and the steps that look as if they've been ripped from the ground up. Slaves swarm the area, carrying lumber and stone as they patch the structure's skeleton.

Seconds later, the door to the carriage is yanked open.

"Out," one grumbles, and I stand carefully before hopping off the tall platform.

None of them help; they just begin to walk.

We ascend the stairs to the palace when Ra'Sa's voice returns.

Nearly finished. I will come to you soon.

I suck my teeth and say, *No. They let me out.*

There's a long pause, only filled with the sound of boots and slippers across polished floors as we head to the throne room.

Where are you?

I hesitate as the gilded wall adornments become increasingly elaborate. Precious metals glint, and the marble around me seems to glow from within. Hundreds of candles are lit in the chandeliers above us, and I savor the moment we begin crossing the plush carpet. It's soft on my aching feet.

We slow, and I see the entrance to the throne room.

The palace. I think they're taking me to see King Rholker?

What?

I don't answer.

Melisa. That's dangerous—he's a murderer. Get out.

I can't do that.

Two large gilded doors are pulled open. Rows of polished wooden pews line the way, each upholstered with patterned velveteen fabric.

The statues of Khuohr's brides holding up basins of fire have been lit and line the path to the throne where High King Rholker sits. He reclines against the gilded chair with a fresh, angry scar slashed across his eye. His oiled curls are arranged just so across his shoulders. A scepter is clutched proudly in one of his hands, and a golden, bejeweled crown rests upon his brow.

A woman stands behind him—a *Bruja*—lurking like a shadow. She almost sinks into the background, and my eyes cannot focus on her, try as I might.

To the left of Rholker sits the Elf King on the throne typically reserved for the queen. I also spot Lord Fektir, the new advisor to the king. He wears several Enduar diamonds on his doublet and scowls at me as I enter.

Elf King Arion is dressed for the high court in elaborate robes and silver details. I had informed Estela that the relationship between Rholker and the Elves was strong, but this is a united alliance like I've never seen.

I continue up the carpeted path. Upon reaching the end, I bow deeply enough for my head to touch the ground as the giant to my left announces me.

My muscles scream at the action, and gods, do I smell.

"Melisa, Formen Eneko's comfort woman, My King," the warrior belts out.

I stay there, looking at the short fibers of the hand-woven rug before Rholker's voice rumbles across the room.

"Rise."

I do. Slowly to account for my aches. Although I'm a stinking, ugly mess, I arm myself with my protective smile. The two kings look down at me. My empty stomach churns.

What am I doing here?

Tell me what's happening, Ra'Sa insists.

I sigh inwardly. *I can't talk to three men at once.*

Then let me in. Your mind is... strong. It resists me.

I hesitate for a minute.

Please, or I'll storm the castle.

You're insane, I retort.

Melisa, he growls.

Fine.

Carefully, I prod at that bond in the back of my head. I open it as much as I can, feeling him peer at the scene. His presence fills up the space in my mind and soul. I tell myself it's just easier than speaking to three men at once, but something about him being there eases my roiling belly. Ra'Sa growls at the sight of King Arion, and one word rings in my skull: *traitor*.

"You have been called here to answer questions about your fellow humans," King Rholker says at last.

I nod once, and he purses his lips.

"You assisted me with a slave. The one that recently escaped several weeks ago," he says.

A cold sweat beads on my back, and I swallow.

One of the king's bushy eyebrows pops up, and I realize he expects an answer, though that wasn't a question.

"Yes, Your Majesty," I say with a dip of my head.

"And now she is gone," he says with a frown. "Scurried through the cracks like a diseased rat."

More uncomfortable silence. That doesn't sound like a question, either. I push my shoulders back, fidgeting some of the tension out of my spine.

"Before Foremen Eneko left, he mentioned something to me in passing. Something that's caused me to ponder for many days." The king sits forward in his seat, looking at me with his shining, yellow eyes. "He said that he was grateful you had returned."

My breath stutters in my lungs. My mind races with the trek, Enduvida, the Enduares. How had a king taken note of a slave's location?

"Given the situation with the woman who escaped, I can't help but wonder where exactly you were," Rhoker's voice booms.

My breath continues, chopped up and shallow.

Breathe, Ruh'flor. *Lie.*

"The woman you speak of was insane," I say, voice steady.

King Arion smirks and leans over to whisper something to King Rholker. The two of them share a short laugh, but the giant's eyes snap back onto my face.

"Continue, girl."

You're doing well. Keep going, but don't mention being outside for a week.

"I tended to her for weeks, and she would ramble lies about the trolls. The night she escaped, she... did something to us. Used some sort of spell. I remember it hit me in the head, and then I fainted. I woke up when another slave found me in the yards and returned me to my master." The lies roll off my tongue, but they hang in the air for several minutes.

My head is bowed while King Rholker considers me, not daring to look back at his face and crack. I catch a slight movement as King Rholker looks at the Elf King. Slowly, King Arion nods.

"I detect no lie," he says.

I blink. Truly? Does he have some power where he can smell deception?

If so, it doesn't work. He is a horrid man, be careful, Ra'Sa says.

The giant king nods at the other king's words, but he doesn't seem satisfied.

"If you were beaten and left, why did all the other slaves go with her?" he demands. "She rarely had access to the outside world."

With the Elf King a few paces away, it's in my best interests to remain collected.

"It pains me to say I do not know, Your Majesty. I was busy preparing her for the coronation. Whatever happened, whatever spell she used with her strange magic, was something I simply cannot understand with my feeble mind," I say as innocently as possible.

The men before me accept this, but the *Bruja* behind them tilts her head to the side.

The Six are also human, so a part of me worries she will call out my deception. She does not.

The giant king turns to the Elf King. “Do you want her?"

Ra’Sa’s rage flows through me, watching intently.

The elf’s head turns to me, studying my face. He scans my filthy form from my feet to the top of my head.

"I think I'm still partial to the flame-haired girl," he says quickly, as unbothered as ever.

I relax, but then I begin to think of all the humans I'd ever known with red hair, and one comes to mind.

Is he talking about Arlet? The sweet-natured weaver in Enduvida? There aren't many humans with the vibrant red color that she sports on her head.

When did he meet her? I ask my mate.

He was in Enduvida for a time. We invited the elves in hopes of making an alliance, and he betrayed us to the giants. He is the reason Estela was taken.

Our conversation is interrupted with the giant king’s voice.

"Take her away. But be warned, human, I may have need of you again."

As the giants usher me out, I hear the Elf King say, "Do all humans in Zlosa tend to smell like rotten meat left in the sun?"

I clench my fists and walk through the door.

You did well, Ra'Sa declares.

I did? You don't disapprove of how easily I lied?

If I recall correctly, I was the one who told you to do it.

No matter. Most would probably wonder if they could ever trust me again if I openly showed such a conniving side.

You, Ruh'flor, *cannot hide from me. I trust you.*

You are sure of yourself.

Laughter rumbles through me, and I smile.

On the way out of the palace, the giants leave me at the steps. I notice that the carriage is gone. I look up at the guards, who stare ahead into the twilight. It illuminates the carefully curated gardens as the sun continues to dip down.

"Go home," one grunts, reaffirming my thoughts.

I take a deep breath and do just that, despite the chill. Resigned and grateful that the encounter with the kings went smoothly, I remember my daughters and what Hibsej told me. I will work hard tomorrow—for as long as it takes that I might see them again. Tonight, I will bathe. And then I will sleep.

Or perhaps, I should visit, Ra'Sa's voice returns.

I let out a long sigh.

Fine.

1. Shit.

2. Holy fuck.

Chapter 31
Ra'sa

It takes longer than usual for the giants to count the logs. We wait there, listening as they call out numbers and make notes. In the last week, nearly a hundred men have been executed in front of us. We've gritted our teeth and bore the back-breaking weight. Tonight, the air is tense as we wait for them to call out the ones who will be sent to die.

Instead, one of the warriors steps in front of us and cracks his neck.

“No racks. Now get back to the slave pens."

For a second, everyone stood there, frozen.

"Now!" he roared.

The men around me start to run, and I follow.

Melisa, I say excited.

I feel her listening.

No deaths tonight.

Melisa’s shock and pain skitter across my skin… Did she know how bad things were?

I… thought that would stop with Eneko gone. How many were killed? Her question is tentative as she braces herself.

I remain silent for a moment, opening the wound in my chest.

Perhaps a hundred.

And the poisonings, do they continue? she asks. I feel… anger on the other side of the bond. Hatred.

Yes, though not as frequently.

Melisa's presence slips away, leaving behind the metallic taste of her rage. I let her go, grieving the events of the last few days myself. As we pass the halfway point back to the den, Nicolás appears at my side.

"Can you believe it? They realized they still need men to chop," he says excitedly.

I nod, still feeling uneasy. After a long day of work, I can only think about Melisa. There's been so much death and loss, the only place I wish to be is at her side.

Nicolás seems to take the hint that I'm not very talkative because he starts to drift away. I didn't think it would take so little to sink into my old habits, but I am a sullen creature.

The night drags on, through dinner, and then as I wait for the others to sleep. When the snores begin to sound all around me, I rise and prepare to go to see my woman.

Stepping silently through the rows of men, I make it outside the door only to be restrained by a pair of hands.

My cry of surprise is silenced when a tall human wraps his hands around my head, covering my mouth. I break free, but four men latch on and hold tight.

One of the men at my side punches me in the gut. I bend forward. I thrash against them as they haul me behind the den and into the forest.

"Cálmate,"[1] Rodrigo commands, stepping out from behind one of the massive elms. His head tilts to the side as his lips pull back into a sneer. "Or do you not understand that word?"

I glare at him until they release their grip on my mouth.

"I know the human tongue fine," I spit back.

His long hair falls in his dark eyes as he searches my face. "Perhaps. But it was learned recently. I hear your accent in every syllable." He looks behind me. "Alberto, Felip, *ven*[2]."

The man at my back walks forward, and Rodrigo jerks his head toward me.

The one called Alberto cracks his knuckles and stretches his wrists. Then he pulls out a makeshift knife with a broken handle from inside his soiled shirt. It glints in the moonlight.

"You will start telling us the truth, or there will be consequences," Alberto says.

I open my mouth, but he holds out his hand and gives a firm shake of his head.

"No. I ask the questions. You answer," he continues in the common tongue.

I contemplate slaying the five of them right here. They aren't what I would call good men, but they know something about the rebellion. They might be my best chance to get humans out of Zlosa.

I decide against it just as Rodrigo asks, "I will ask you plainly: do you work for the giants?"

I grit my teeth. "No."

"I saw you visit the foreman's comfort woman while she was in the pit. Do you fuck her?"

I snarl. "No."

The men hold me back tighter, but Rodrigo smirks at my strong reaction.

He chuckles. "What are you?"

For a moment, I keep my lips sealed tight, refusing to dignify any of his crass words with an answer.

"I've come to help," I say at last.

Rodrigo continues to look at me with his shrewd expression. "You really have, haven't you?"

I nod firmly.

He bites his lip. "Rest assured, there is a spy among us. I was sure it was you. Your relationship with the slut would've solidified that for me—"

My muscles tense. I reach deep into my magic. A tremor rumbles underfoot. I break out of the mens' grasp. Alberto tumbles over, too, and I grab Rodrigo, pinning his arm behind his back.

"If you want me to let you all live, I suggest you stop saying cruel words. They've passed your lips too many times."

Rodrigo's tries to look back at me. "Protective over her? Why?"

"It doesn't matter. Does it?" I yank his arm up, almost to the point where his joint pops.

Rodrigo huffs. "*Hostia,*[3] no. Let me go, you crazy bastard!"

I do, roughly pushing him away.

Rodrigo looks up at me, angry but he doesn't attack.

"You started smelling poison when no others can. The giants can't do that. You don't have yellow eyes like them, nor do you have the large feet their half-breeds sport. I tried to write off your chopping as a giant trait. But it's something else, I know it. How many did you help cut today?"

I grit my teeth. "Ten."

Rodrigo lets out a soft whistle, rubbing his arm. "I think you should follow me."

He walks away, deeper into the trees. I continue after. There's a dipping feeling in my stomach, but I don't stop.

Rodrigo wanted to go drinking before, and now he's taking me into the woods to talk... He's a part of the rebellion.

Strange. He seems the most territorial, determined slave. The giants typically leave his gang alone. They are hard workers.

Was that all a front for something more?

Time passes slowly as we walk through a narrow path. One of Rodrigo's men brushes a long, feathery branch behind us, protecting our tracks from being left in the snow. Trees allow slivers of moonlight to slip through as we continue forward. When we reach a small, abandoned building, all of my suspicions are cemented.

As we walk inside, there are a few chairs scattered around the moldering cottage. Rodrigo pulls one out and points for me to sit down.

I do.

"Is your name really Rasa?" one of the men asks.

I chew on my lip.

"In a sense. But again, that's not important. What is important is what you are doing here?" I gesture broadly around me.

Rodrigo purses his lips. "You should've come drinking."

I raise my eyebrow, and he continues.

"If you would've joined us, you would've met groups like us all over Zlosa. All committed to one thing—the freedom of the slaves."

I let out a long breath.

"That is good news. I was starting to think you all were a myth," I say.

While it is a good thing to find the rebels, did it have to be *them*?

Rodrigo shakes his head and laughs bitterly. "We may as well be. It is not easy to get people interested in our cause."

"How long have you been working?"

"Years. Planning in the shadows and trying to find a way out. Admittedly, things have escalated since that human ran away with a breeding pen full of women. Her time here inspired lots of emotions among the slaves—confusion, anger, but most of all, the promise of some sort of sustainable life outside of Zlosa. I believe it was that firm, tangible vision that moved everyone to action. Especially after we saw how the elves panned out," another man says.

I adjust my sitting position and look out the broken window briefly before asking, "What happened with the elves?"

"We used to believe we could escape to their realm, but now we know. Since the giant and elf kings have allied themselves, I'm sure that any humans who made it to the elven kingdom were not saved."

I nod.

"You're one of *them*—the trolls—aren't you? I thought you were blue?" another man says.

"I am here to help. So, tell me your plan," I propose, ignoring the question.

The air is thick with tension, and the others go eerily silent. Rodrigo smiles.

"That's what I want to hear," he says. Then he stands.

"Where are you going?" I demand.

"To tell the others it's safe to come," Rodrigo starts.

As I wait there, Melisa's voice enters my head.

Are you well?

Half my mouth quirks up. So timid.

I caress the bond with my thoughts, encouraging her as gently as I can muster.

I've been called away to a meeting. I will come to you after.

There's a pause and then a strong burst, *A meeting? What meeting?*

At that moment, sound from outside the cottage filters in—the sound of footfalls on soft snow crunch and buzz in my ears. Not a few moments later, another head pops into the cottage before swiftly shutting the door.

Some men incline their heads to the newcomer. I can make out his thick, gray hair and stocky build. He has the same wiry strength that most men who work in the yards have, but he has a slight haunch. Not to mention, he limps when he walks.

He takes his place next to a few other men, not acknowledging us as the door opens again. Two more men filter in.

Still, we wait in silence.

It takes several more men entering the room—to the point of bursting—for someone to finally speak. Nine slaves are gathered around me when Rodrigo returns to the center of the building.

"You all asked to meet the new slave, so we've brought him," he says in the human tongue, voice low.

A flint stone sparks, lighting the end of a well-oiled rope. They hold up the simple lantern in front of me, trying to show my face.

I am still in my human form, but I tower over them.

"You're a godsdamned tree," one of the men says under his breath. "Are you sure you have no giant blood?"

"Yes," I grumble.

A few others nod, but the man with gray hair narrows his eyes.

“I’ve heard a lot about you, but I still don’t understand. Why do you want to help us?" he asks.

I purse my lips.

My father taught me about duty—that's a fine answer. But it runs deeper than that. These men don't need to know the sweetness of matehood and how I long for the songs that mine and Melisa’s crystals will sing back in Enduvida.

They also do not need to know what I feel when small hands wrap around my fingers, relying on me for food and comfort. Daughters that I’ve only met recently. The innocent beings who need me to get out of here and have a better life.

These things are more precious than all the gems and gold in Enduvida, but there is something that is the culmination of all—something invaluable. I have found a purpose.

They say you tend to solve your problems by helping others solve theirs. I supposed that was much of what it was like for me to move on from one attitude to another.

Looking at the men in front of me, I meet their eyes, hoping they see the determination behind my lack of words.

"I believe in the cause of the humans. Staying in Zlosa a second longer than necessary is a mistake for all of us. I also believe the giants should pay for everything they have done," I say at last.

A few of the men begin to murmur. I feel the weight of their judgment as they watch me.

"Yes, he's not one of us. He merely looks it," Rodrigo says, answering a comment I didn’t quite catch.

"Then you must be a troll, disguised somehow," the gray-haired man says.

I angle my body toward him. "A troll on giant land would be executed immediately."

"Rasa is your name, no?" he says, speaking in the common tongue with a thick accent.

I nod.

"They call me *El Lobo*,[4]" he continues. "Yes, that is my real name. When I use it in front of you, I trust you with my life. You could take such a name and blab it to the giants, and I'd be hoisted up in front of the slave pens with a pike up my ass."

I grit my teeth.

"The slaves in Zlosa are split. It wasn't that long ago that everyone started to whisper about troll caverns and some human queen who came to save us all. Those rumors became legends overnight when she succeeded at getting a few dozen women to escape."

The room around me is quiet, but a man to the left of El Lobo continues.

"I am called Tomás. And he's right. You see, against all reason and logic, when we heard about that human queen, many of us believed she would send someone to help. We think that someone is you."

I take a few deep breaths, considering. These men have proven their willingness to share themselves with me.

To this point, what has kept my mouth sealed has been the possibility that they will kill me, and Melisa will be left alone. There's no existence where I can let that happen.

But... Eneko returns soon. We need to leave, and the king and queen had tasked me with the challenge to bring back as many humans as possible.

Even more so, I want that. I want Abet and Nicolás to see Enduvida and feel freedom away from tall trees and endless chopping.

"I was born sixty-three summers ago, but my people age very differently from yours. I was young when my old king destroyed half of our lands, but I still managed to save my family from the lava that rushed through the valley. I come here now, knowing that Zlosa will soon be destroyed."

The silence that descends is felt in the depths of my bones.

"I've personally witnessed how they treat you, and I've worked until my bones ache to help as many survive as possible. I will help fight that all of you will break free from this life."

For a minute, the silence persists. And then one of the men shakes his hand.

"Then we agree. We riot."

Riot.

In my head, I see mattocks, axes, and whips turned against the giants. I see the mighty force of men capable of fighting back against a monstrous enemy.

"The stories about trolls were untrue, weren't they?" El Lobo asks hesitantly.

I huff a bitter laugh. "We are strong, but we are not needlessly cruel. Not anymore. And we never ate your kind."

Rodrigo comes forward and claps his hand on my shoulder as if we had somehow become friends. As if he'd never said any of the awful things I'd heard him say about Melisa.

"When exactly do you intend on rioting?" I ask.

The men look up at me, but Rodrigo pulls up one of the floorboards and pulls out a stained length of cloth. Slowly, he spreads it on the ground to reveal a map etched across the graying color with soot.

“The plan is next week. The giants have killed so many of us that they aren't watching as closely. They think our spirit has died."

One man snickers, then pulls out a bottle of something strong-smelling and takes a swig.

“Por la libertad,”[5] he whisper-shouts.

The others repeat the chant in hushed tones.

When the small bottle is passed to me, I smell it and take a drink, ignoring the uncomfortable burn in the back of my throat.

"How does this start?" I ask.

One of the men with a long, scrawny face grins, revealing several missing teeth. "With fire."

"For the last year, we've been storing animal fat and stealing cloth. In another location, we have two dozen barrels ready to be lit up. We can start putting them at the gates, holding them in the slave pens, but lately, we’ve had a new development.”

“Go on," I start.

Several of them glance between each other, but it is El Lobo who clears his throat.

“The giant lords don’t like the new king,” he says.

My ears perk up. This was one of the things Teo wanted us to uncover.

“Why not?” I ask.

El Lobo shrugs. “We don’t align ourselves with any giants, but Tomás has connections. Rholker’s own advisor, Fektir, is planning to jam a spear up his ass and put him on display.”

Gods.

“When?”

“Soon. Next week. The king hasn’t fled yet, but he might. That’s why it would be the perfect time to strike back, when he’s worried about dissent from within,” Tomás interjects.

I nod, listening as they explain how it will be the fastest way for everyone to escape from the dens, but they pause when I shake my head.

"If you put them in front of the gates, it will be too predictable. It won't take long for the giants to catch on and send reinforcements. It will be a massacre."

Rodrigo frowns. "I'll remind you that we've been working on this for some time. Our plan has been carefully considered."

I shake my head, placing my finger back on the soot-stained cloth. "What if... you put all the barrels in one location. Somewhere important. Make such a big fire so that everyone will go there. When all of the giants are there, they will leave the gates open. You won't get all the slaves out—only a few hundred to a thousand or more. You're going to need a plan with more longevity."

The men around me are silent, but El Lobo laughs. "You have a good head."

"I think you should put the barrels in the soldiers’ barracks. Do it at midnight, cause a huge stir."

"And then what?"

Everyone watches as I point to the map, as I gesture around. It's not dissimilar to the map that Melisa drew for me when I first came to Zlosa. I look at it with fascination.

"Get as many humans out as possible. Spread the word," I continue.

It sneaks up on me. I'm not a man prone to feeling a certain type of way about those who have passed on, but I know, deep in my bones, as sure as the moon shines on my face, that my brother would be proud of this choice. He would rejoice in how he's seen me work with humans, helping them, ushering them forward into a new era.

"What about those left behind?" they ask.

I look at them. "You're right. What if... before we start to light things on fire, we weaken them? Poison their food supply to make them ill, not dead."

Several pairs of eyes go wide.

"We harvest and butcher most of their food," Tomás says.

"Then it wouldn't be too hard," I reply. "Start in a few days."

"And for those who are still left behind after the fire?" Rodrigo chimes in.

"We'll run before they can catch us."

The men look at me with a ferocious hope shining.

"So?" I start. "In a few turns of the sun, you start to poison."

"And next week? We burn!" El Lobo dares to raise his voice.

A chill coats my skin as I consider their words. Eneko is meant to return around that time. If we do this, he'll never touch Melisa again.

The rest join in with a silent salute, lifting their fists.

As I study the plan before me, I think of the men I've come to know. I cannot wait to tell Melisa of everything—that we may also plan out the next few weeks. If all goes well, we'll be back in Enduvida soon.

The meeting draws to an end, and we all move out of the run-down cottage.

The thought of Melisa being safe and at home at last has my heart bursting with a sweet kind of calm.

We need to send a message to the king and queen, I murmur through the bond.

Melisa responds with a gentle hum, but says nothing more.

It takes me little time to sprint back to my hiding place to retrieve the speaking stones. A part of me is proud. We've worked hard this last month.

The rebellion's plan is neatly set, and I have a family. A lightness bubbles in my veins, and something akin to warm water washes over me.

My bond.

I look down.

It's… alive. My human form seems to interrupt our mating song, but right now, it blasts against my eardrums. I stumble against a tree when a new wave rolls through me. This time, I catch hold and identify the intense emotion.

Desire.

"Melisa," I growl, just quiet enough for the others not to hear.

For all her secrecy and talent at hiding herself from me, she couldn't hide the ripple of want heating my blood. I had planned to go to her tonight, but the need for her is as strong as the forces that hold the stars in the heavens.

I arrive at that small room at the back of the house of a giant I wish to slay—a pitiful room for what she deserves. It's merely a fraction of what I will give her and her daughters when we return to Enduvida.

I stop in my tracks when her voice enters my mind.

Ra'Sa, she moans through the bond.

I go still. But molten heat churns and flows through my body. my chest heaves. Her voice like that… that sound wakes something inside of me.

I want her to say my name like that again. I want to hold her, to strip away her clothes, and sink into her.

I hiss as a white-hot pain sears across my neck. It isn't midnight, and I haven't shifted, but I am almost sure if I were to look in the mirror, I would see two small, glowing dots.

Mating marks.

What on the gray, stony earth is she doing?

1. Calm down.

2. Come.

3. Fuck no.

4. The Wolf.

5. For freedom.

CHAPTER 32

MELISA

Ra'Sa moves over me again, kissing down my neck. Another cramp spasms in my lower belly, and I want to roll away from him, but he cups my cheek, holding me in place.

"Tell me what to do, Melisa," he murmurs.

I'm wet, that much I can feel despite the blood. I ache, too, but it's a delicious pain. One that borders on pleasure. Want.

My hips rise up to meet his, feeling the girth of his cock.

"Take me, Ra'Sa," I demand. Greedy.

His face is intense as he pushes into my entrance. Slow.

Too slow.

I push myself onto him, feeling the sharp pain that gives way to bliss.

His eyes go wide as he stays there, fully seated inside of me. Satisfaction blooms in my chest, as exquisite as the pressure and fullness he brings.

"Move, Ra'Sa," I murmur.

He groans as he pulls out, half way. The action is thrilling.

I've never talked during sex. Never told a man what to do.

"Come back."

He slams into me, and it's as if sparks ignite over my skin.

"Again, and move your hips from side to side," I beg.

A new pressure, wholly unique from his length, starts to build, like sparkling wine in a bottle.

Every direction I give him is taken with unfettered enthusiasm. Out of pure madness, my hand trails down my belly between us, reaching the spot he brushes against with his soft skin. He lacks hair, unlike giants or humans, but something about the tilt of his pelvis is enough to tease.

To coax.

When I rub through the mess I've made, the effect is instant. He moves inside again, and I cry out.

"Ra'Sa!"

It's impossible to hold back. Impossible not to climax when he moves so perfectly.

I pant and claw at his back.

"What is this?" he asks as my back arches off the bed.

"I'm coming for you," I say slowly, quietly, as the wave crashes.

I bolt upright. Sweat causes my nightgown to cling to my skin, and I press a hand to my forehead.

My cheeks are flushed, as are my neck and chest. My breasts are sensitive and heavy.

Gods. I fell asleep.

This attraction to Ra'Sa is seeping out of my sleeping moments and into the real world. They've plagued me, waking moments that only began to peek back after kissing Ra'Sa in the woods.

After lighting one of the small lamps near my bed, I smooth my hands across my hair. There's still laundry everywhere, but at least I found space to bathe.

When I stand, preparing to go for water, my night dress scratches over my skin. The heat—the dryness in my throat—intensifies.

The scrape against my nipples feels like torture, and I gasp.

I know what I like. Years of pleasing men have left me an expert in my own body. Wanting someone else, man or woman is rare, and these emotions have only grasped me a few times since the twins were born.

Before the girls, my short affair with Seranya was nothing more than kisses, but she would say such delicious things. She taught me the art of self-love, and I was grateful for that.

It helped me make the rules.

But Ra'Sa… I'm not supposed to feel like I could unravel at any second.

An abdominal cramp has me doubling over, and all I can think is how good I imagined Ra'Sa to feel.

I see him so clearly that I can almost feel his touch. Everything is tender. Ready.

The deep wanting mingles with the throbbing pain.

My tentative grasp on reality fades, and a wave of longing washes over me.

It wasn't the first time I'd wanted sex during my courses. Nothing quite eases the pain of menstruation like a release. An unhelpful part of my brain supplies that everything would feel better if I could just be filled to the point of breaking. I ignore it, waiting for the raging want to pass along with another cramp.

Godsdamnit.

Giant men don't touch women in this state. I've heard human men are generally the same. Why would Enduares be any different?

But… he held me when I was sick and gave me his shirt when I bled.

The thought makes my eyes burn.

He doesn't seem afraid of anything, and that makes me want him more. I want his soft blue skin sliding between my thighs.

But not yet. And not *here*.

I lean over the side of my bed, breathing through the disappointment.

Just lay back down.

It'll pass.

Instead, a soft knock comes at my door.

I leap to my feet, heart racing, looking at the wooden entrance. Eneko hasn't returned, and Hibsej is decidedly ignoring me, especially after sending me out to meet with the king.

Wrapping a thin blanket around my body, I creep to the door. My hand presses to the wood just as another knock hits.

I suck in a sharp breath when the smell of Ra'Sa reaches my nose. I inhale deeply, savoring the smell of the underground mixed with freshly cut wood. Even with my human senses, I would know him anywhere.

My body rejoices while I debate opening the door.

Melisa, Ra'Sa's voice purrs through my head. It is softer than velvet and decadent as the wine in the king's castle.

I take another deep breath.

You let me into your head so easily now, he continues.

My cheeks heat. My dream. How much did he see?

Fuck.

Go away, I retort.

Melisa, please.

My eyes flutter closed. I could say goodbye, let this end.

But there's something about the way he says my name.

I can smell your need. Feel your want. Let me in.

The way he speaks compels me, like those rumors and myths of trolls luring humans away with something akin to a siren's song.

If he wanted to, he could enter. The lock to my room is on the outside. But he *asks*.

My hand reaches for the handle, and I pull it open slowly.

I could imagine him standing before the door—could picture him leaning against the wood, looming over me like a starved man coveting a feast. But seeing it with my own eyes makes my skin flush with heat. The shadows on his face make him seem more feral than I pictured, and his eyes practically glow.

"W-why are you here? You should go," I stumble through my breathy, husky words.

He cocks an eyebrow. "You called me here."

I blink. "I did not."

"Melisa, I heard you say my name," he insists.

A bolt of pleasure shoots across me, and I step out of the way.

His movements are calculated and swift. He takes up every inch of the room, sucking all of the air out of my lungs. His presence pulls me into the space between 'yes' and 'wait.'

Instead, I say, "It's a mess in here. I was given chores."

I give myself a moment to stand there waiting for whatever sweet surprise he has waiting in that purposeful look.

He falls to his knees. Those eyes haunt me, swallowing all of the surroundings and refusing to let me look away.

My chest rises. His jaw flexes, and his nostrils widen.

"You're still bleeding."

I nod, even though every man I've ever known is disgusted by such things.

“And you ache for me. I can feel it through our bond." His eyes flutter closed. Then they open and lock back onto my face. "Won't this hurt?"

My mouth parts at his boldness, and his eyes snap down to watch my lips.

“I—”

My neck goes hot.

All of the dreams, the attempts at seduction. Is this really going to be the moment when I turn shy?

"Giants and humans don't touch women when they bleed. They think us unclean."

"I'm not a giant, and I know of no hunter deterred by a bit of blood," he retorts.

"You are a stone bender."

"I can be whatever you need tonight," he says. "We have been through this—I see you. I know your thoughts. You cannot hide from me as you wish. I came because you need me."

My breath hitches, and my core hums. When he says it like this, the sense of fighting flows away. This was what I wanted—to have him so thoroughly wrapped around my finger that he'd never leave.

Reason and want war within me, but instead, I reach up and pull at the string that cinches the gown around my shoulders and keeps it from falling. As the fabric loosens and slips off of my skin, I take a deep breath.

His hand moves before his thoughts, pausing a mere second before touching me.

"May I?"

I grasp onto his hand with both of mine and press it to my breast, gasping. My skin breaks out in flames.

He growls and pulls me onto his lap, burying his nose into the side of my neck. He inhales deeply and then lets out a satisfied noise.

“Will you let your mate claim you?” his voice thrums.

I freeze. Will I?

All the time I spent fighting for this moment, and now I'm unsure? Men don't like rejection.

"Y-yes."

"I hear the doubt in your voice. You cannot pretend for me as you have for others," he murmurs, his lips tracing maddening shapes across my throat. "Tell me your thoughts since you refuse to speak them to my mind."

This time, my words come quickly.

"You rejected me before. And now you want me because I am your mate. But I worry... you don't understand what it is to take on someone like me."

He pulls back, fingers skimming across my waist.

"That's not true. I was called to you before the bond opened between us," he says gently.

I cup his face. "I pursued you, not the other way around."

His brown eyes slowly shift into the blue ones I've come to adore. He places his hand over mine.

"Perhaps you pursued me, but I followed. I followed you into enemy territory and have thought of you every day. When I heard you in my head, it was as natural as breathing. I'm not one to give speeches, but I will speak for as long as it takes to convince you."

My breath catches. Did he know how desperately I wanted to hear something like that? If he were to take me now, I don't even know what it would be like.

I've never been so ready for sex, never wanted my partner as much as I desire him. But… when he fills me with his cock, and kisses me with his eager mouth, will I resist the divine magic between us?

"You told me that you felt stupid for saying you wouldn't care for a woman's previous daughters, but my secrets don't end there," I start.

His brows furrow, but he waits.

"I don't want to be pregnant again," I say, letting the words out into the world. It had been so difficult, so painful. "It was… the hardest thing I'd ever done. I almost died. By some miracle, I didn't. And by another miracle, I went back to work."

He still doesn't say anything.

I bite my lip, uncomfortable by the silence.

"I take a brew for being with Eneko, and I don't have any illnesses, but if you make love to me, you can't ever expect another child," I say, ears ringing.

My heart pounds, and I look away from his face, not being able to bear what comes next.

His fingers stroke my hand, coaxing me to look back up at him. "*Ruh'flor*, when I said what I said in the tent, I did not know what I was talking about."

"And now you do?" I say bitterly.

He brings my gaze to his.

"Yes. What you say… it does not bother me. It does not hurt me."

"But how?" I insistent.

He sighs. “As living beings, we have this tendency to trade our unseen injuries—the pain of loss, regret, harm—for wisdom. Some pains are too sweet to remove because... because of all that they represent. Years went by. Decades. I carried my abrasions just beneath the surface of my skin in sacred vigil for my sisters. My father. My brother. I went against my king and shut myself off from all, save my mother."

Ra'Sa drops his hand and trails his fingers up my bare arm, pushing my fingers out of my clenched fists and spreading them wide. They barely come up past his palm.

He continues reverently. "I fought it for a time, but when I held you in my arms while you panicked, something changed. I had this... uncontrollable desire to be better. Moreso when I met Thea and Wren. You are more than enough.”

I pause. “Why?”

He strokes my hand. “The walls around my heart tumbled down by the force of our song. It was as if my soul woke up and told me to make space for something new. For you and all the glorious newness that comes with you and your people."

He leans forward and kisses me.

"Your ingenuity."

His lips press to my forehead.

"Your daughters."

His mouth drops to my heart.

"Your strength."

That same wicked mouth trails along my collarbone to my shoulder before speaking into my skin. Speaking to my soul. This level of intimacy doesn't exist for whores.

"Some people require long periods of time to change. I didn't. I will be your mate and their father. Please, accept it. Accept me."

My heart flutters furiously. Don't fall. Do not fall for him.

"But what if we get caught?" I don't mention that Eneko will be back from the mines soon with information I need to get. I don't think about my one resource in excavating it from the foreman's thoughts. "They'll kill you. They'll kill me."

"I'll kill them faster."

I think of the giant that he murdered in the pit. He did it mercilessly, as he had with the other giants trying to slay us upon escape. There's a brutality to him that is untempered by right and wrong. His mind is clear, determined. He feels no remorse for the deaths because he sees a need to eliminate anything that threatens someone in need.

Don't fall—

My words are snatched away when he leans forward and kisses me, bringing me to the edge of the bed.

"If we continue," he starts, "I'm afraid you'll have to tell me how this goes. I fear hurting you."

I press a hand to my forehead, looking at him. Unexperienced. Eager. There are things I want to teach him. To take him into my mouth, to show him just how pleasurable this next part can be. That ache inside of me is insistent.

"Remove your clothes," I say firmly.

"Now?" he asks.

"Yes. Hurry."

He does, starting with his coat and then his shirt. My mouth goes dry as his muscles are revealed, and then, I watch hungrily as his pants fall away, letting his cock free. It's different than my dream—somehow wider.

I lean forward and grasp his length with both hands. A bead of glistening seed has already appeared on the head of his member. My hands move up and down, and I luxuriate in the responding gasps from this man seemingly unmoved by anything.

"Shh," I coax as he melts in my hands. "You must be quiet."

He seals his lips together as I work him. Then he grabs my hands.

"Enough," he demands.

His voice thrums through me. Powerful, demanding.

"I wish to touch you as well," he says.

Gods yes.

He looks around the room, grabbing onto one of the towels I use for bathing. He places it on the bed, after tenderly lifting my legs. Then he grabs my bucket of water and another strip of cloth.

"Tonight, I am your student," he murmurs as he peels off the rest of my clothing. He sees the scars always covered by a nightgown. He strokes across them and pauses.

"I asked you what these were once," he says.

The scratch of his calloused hands against my soft skin is delicious, but I find it in me to nod.

"I understand now. These were from carrying your daughters."

I swallow, then say, "Yes."

"You are my strong warrior."

He dips his head down and brushes his lips over each mark, and I swallow back unexpected emotion.

Then he wets a rag and removes the ties that keep the bloody padding in place. He sets the rags in the washing bucket and begins to clean me.

Once finished, he looks at my sex. I feel exposed in a way that makes me want to curl up.

"What're you doing?" I gasp when his finger traces me.

“Is this not all right?” his eyes meet mine, panicked.

“It is. I just… most men are disgusted by this.”

His eyes return to me. “I am not.”

I ease against my forearms. He touches the bundle of nerves that no man has ever attempted to touch. In my sensitive state, I arch off the bed.

“Are you in pain?”

I shake my head. “This is good. Do it again.”

He does, watching me with burning eyes. And... he moves toward my aching entrance.

“Ra’Sa,” I beg when his thumb reaches for that spot again.

His hand moves against me with extra pressure.

“Say that again.”

I glare at him.

“Be quiet,” I hiss.

One of his fingers slips into my entrance, and I choke.

I’m ready, but that doesn't lessen the torture.

“Ra’Sa,” I say anyway, and he groans. “Enough. I want you inside of me. Now.”

I watch him wipe his hands clean, and then I grasp onto him, pulling him over me until his length is lined up with my entrance.

I blink at the ease of it all, confused.

My mouth parts as he moves.

A slow smile spreads over his face. "That's right. As if we were made for each other."

Every part of my body thrums with pleasure. I lean into the stretch as he fills me so beautifully, mesmerized by the feel of something I've craved for so long.

It isn't the same as my dream. No, when he fills me, he reaches places deeper inside of me that sing. And his hips don't merely graze the sweet spot between my thighs, they stroke it, as sure as his hand.

The pain mingles with the sweetest ecstasy, blooming through my mind. All the aches that come with bleeding ebb away.

I let out a quiet moan of relief.

He tenses at the sound and moves faster.

"Yes," I breathe. "Harder."

He obliges. Working until the same delight from before starts to bundle up my nerves, until I feel myself start to press against that edge and freeze.

The pain of stopping just before release is something akin to torture, but coming for a dream was one thing.

Having him before me, inside of me, is another.

I can't do this. I can't break my one rule. The fear returns, and I tense up.

Ra'Sa strokes my face. I can't keep him out, and his brow relaxes as he understands.

"Ruh'flor, it's okay. Unravel for me. I am here."

The words sink into my heart. Curse every inch of my being, but I believe him. His fingers move to my jaw, and then he pumps in and out once more. This time, he is desperate and his face slowly twists as he loses himself to the feeling.

I hold his wrist, watching his face as I walk over that edge and fall. Fall in more ways than one, down to a sweet, small death.

It shocks me. It delights me.

As the shudder starts, I arch into him, and he holds me through the act. The sweetest of all feelings grips me—one that I never thought would touch me.

Love.

The words are sealed behind my lips. I don't say them, though they threaten to break free. When his eyes meet mine, he sees. I plead for him to leave me be. It wouldn't take much for him to coax them from my soul, but he understands.

I did it. I fell in love.

Surprisingly, it doesn't hurt.

He kisses me, still buried deep, and says, "Melisa. I am yours."

My eyes widen at the sound of the words. How could I have ever expected to be strong enough to fight against this man?

Instead of returning his words, I kiss him back. Hungry. Helpless.

He thrusts again and again, his gentle presence easing past all the walls around my heart until, finally, they are all gone. I come again, and he presses his hand to my mouth and follows.

The act is quiet, feral, lost, and tense. I hold him back, letting him lay atop me.

In and out.

He exits, and moves to hold me on his side. For a long while, we lie there, suspended in heaven.

I don’t dare move and shatter whatever just happened between us.

Then he stands, hand grazing up my curves, and says, “I will return.”

Before I have time to turn, he is back at my side with the rag. He cleans me and himself and starts to dress.

I roll over, sated, but slowly becoming anything but.

Watching him dress makes me bite my lip.

What we had done was dangerous. It was wrong—especially in this house. He should run, and yet, he kneels next to the bed and covers me with a blanket.

“Gods, you are the most beautiful thing I have ever beheld.”

My mouth parts. “I—thank you.”

Then he brushes my hair, rubbing the strands between his fingers, and says, "Did you visit the girls?"

I shake my head.

"I can’t—not until I finish all the laundry.”

He looks confused. “How would she know?”

“She probably asked one of the guards to watch me. If I leave before finishing, I risk returning to the pit.”

Ra’Sa bristles. “Never.”

I reach out and take his hand.

“I will work hard and finish fast. It should only take a few days. Though, I am worried. Hibsej took the gem I was going to give them."

He strokes my back. "Wait for me to go with you. I will bring them gifts."

I look up at him. "Really?"

He nods.

My head spins. I want to let this happiness swallow me up, but something holds me back. A very big complication.

"What happens when Eneko comes back?" I blurt out. "He's where we get most of our information."

"I know."

"Ra'Sa, you can't keep wanting me like this. I am… I'm not someone for you to love."

"I disagree, especially after what we just did."

"I worry I'll break your heart. And shatter my own along the way."

"Perhaps as a young boy, I would've made such a mistake. But I have seen the world as black and white and everything in between. I would be a fool to think I could want you so and not accept the parts of you that have formed your soul. This is the mission. One day, it will end. What I feel for you will not."

His eyes, those damned blue eyes that have haunted my dreams, stare straight into my soul. His perception is too intense. Too wholly consuming.

I don't like it.

I made a mistake when I picked him for his sculpted arms and gentle tongue. This was supposed to be for the twins.

Between us, our breaths mix. My hand rests on his strong, beating heart.

I swallow, trying to bring moisture back into my suddenly parched mouth, all the while knowing that his heart beats in time with my own.

I bite my lip. "I still don't understand… this."

"We will have a lifetime to learn."

His hand moves under the blanket and strokes my thigh, "Can we do it again?"

I bite my lip, but something pops into my head. "I thought you needed to send a message to the king and queen?"

He groans. “Damnit. You are right.”

“What happened at the meeting you were at?” I ask, rolling over.

There’s nothing calculated about this, not as he holds me. We are just existing. It feels nice.

“There is a rebellion brewing amongst the slaves, and they have a plan to burn the giants’ barracks. They want to start soon because the giant lords are turning on the king,” Ra’Sa says gently.

My eyes go wide. “Really? I’d only ever heard rumblings.”

He nods.

“You need to tell Estela that,” I say.

His head tilts to the side. “You really like her, don’t you?”

“She’s one of my… friends,” I say, eyebrows furrowed. “The gem I want to give to the girls came from her. She’s the first person who ever gave me a gift. It was a necklace.”

Ra’Sa considers this. “Then I will need to work on finding you some trinkets.”

I grin, and inch closer to his warmth.

His hand goes back to my ass. “I will send the message in a minute.”

That mischievous hand ventures lower.

I sigh, but my heartbeat picks up.

“If you make a sound, we are dead."

He reaches for the closure of his pants and huffs. “Is that a yes?”

I meet his eye and say, “Only if you make me come on your cock again.”

His eyes look like blue flame, and he shifts completely as he removes his clothes a second time. Two bright marks glow on the side of his neck. I’d seen them before in Enduvida.

Mating marks.

Oh my.

My thoughts are silenced when his tail reaches towards me and rips off the blanket.

For a second, I marvel at him, not as a man any longer, but an Enduar.

Terrifying.

Enticing.

He wraps his tail around one of my legs, pulls it away from the other, and then sinks into me.

"In a week, we could be home. I'm going to give our family everything."

I cover his mouth. "Shh."

He nips against my fingers and then covers my mouth.

I smile as we start to move.

And gods, I swear I see the stars in the heavens as if they danced in this very room.

PART 3

CHAPTER 33

MELISA

Five Days Later,

"You're practically glowing," Alisa teases in the human tongue.

I pour another bag of laundry into the swirling *cesto de lavado*. [1]The unfrozen river beats through a spout into a conical pool. As the clothes spin around in the water, I bite my lip and unceremoniously dump another bag of grated animal fat soap into the whirlpool.

"I'm merely well rested," I say at last. It's a lie—I'd been working hard mending, washing, and drying from morning until dusk. When I get close to the end of my chores, a new bag seems to magically appear.

But not today.

Tonight, I will be finished, and I will finally be able to celebrate Thea and Wren's birthday. It's lightened my mood.

Alisa and Daria are still laughing when they pass me one of the long staffs to beat the grime out of the clothes. This is the first day I've been able to wash with them since I returned.

At the feast weeks ago, Alisa and I had danced around the subject of my departure. Today feels like a continuation of that.

"Well-fucked is more like it," Daria says then glances around for any newcomers before leaning close. "Except the great bear of a man who leads your house is far, far away from Zlosa."

"A lady never kisses and tells," I say quickly.

Both of them chortle. But then, when Alisa looks at me, her face grows serious.

"I'm happy for you. I hope you know that," she says.

I swallow, then turn back. "Please, don't tell anyone. I beg you both."

The women exchange glances, then nod. They seem different—closer than before.

"I swear it," Alisa says.

"On my life," Daria continues.

I go back to washing. For a time, the only sound in my ears is water rushing. It drowns out everything else, and it almost chases away the dark thoughts lingering in my mind.

Ra'Sa has been silent today, but I can't stop thinking of our nightly trysts. I see him over me, feel him fill me up, and the ache turns into ecstasy. Reliving the moment when I fell apart in his arms has me blushing.

Fucking. *Blushing*.

I had been careful—very careful for quite a while. I just want to know how I ended up in this place.

And how I agreed to let him come with me to visit the girls tonight. I'll apologize for missing their birthday. I'll make it right. But... he'll see it all.

"Did you hear they stopped killing the lumber yard slaves?" Alisa says, almost out of nowhere.

I pause, looking back at the two women as they set in on another batch of brown and white cloth. I find they are waiting for me to respond.

"Yes," I say, wiping the sweat collecting on my brow. I don't know what more to say. The amount of death feels surreal. Colossal. It's hard to tell if this is an end to the pain, or merely a pause.

I hope it is the former.

Alisa's head tilts to the side. "We've had such little rebellion in this region. I think that they couldn't afford to lose more workers."

Daria laughs bitterly. "There are so few of us left. They're content to breed us like cattle and work us to death. What a nightmare."

I nod. "I agree."

Silence falls again as we beat dirty stains from the clothing. I measure the seconds, trying to find the right time to continue the conversation.

"Have either of you heard anything more about the rebellion?"

Everything is silent between us, and I use the other end of the staff, the one with a hook, to start dragging out all the remaining cloth.

Daria speaks first.

"I don't know about any of that."

I straighten, going over to hang up some of the heavier pants and coats that will need extra time to dry before being brought back inside.

"Are you sure? Just a few months ago, you were whispering to me and—"

"That was before the women escaped," Alisa interjects.

I swallow. Time to stop dancing around this.

"You were conspiring with Paoli and Abi; now they are gone. You were gone for a week or so," Alisa says, balancing a woven basket on her hip. She smiles, ensuring that any onlookers wouldn't know what a heavy subject was passing between us.

"I was unwell," I say quickly when a giant guard walks out of the forest to watch us. I throw more clothes into the water.

“Meli, don’t take me for a fool. I think you escaped, too," she accuses. "I've been watching you since you came back. I can see it in your eyes. You have a new lover, new confidence, new purpose."

I bite my lip, thinking of our task to bring back humans. I know that Ra’Sa has been working hard, but I did my best work when I escaped with Estela. This time around, most of my days have been consumed with survival.

Taking a deep breath, I face my two allies. "Yes. You are right."

They both go utterly still, letting their clothes spin free.

It’s Daria who responds first. "Why didn't you tell us? Have we not been friends for years?"

My hands are still on my staff as it swishes around the clothing in the vat.

Friends?

"Well?" Daria pushes.

I think through my answer carefully, rehearsing each possible turn of phrase and how I could make it into my favor. I didn't want these women to turn against me, but I didn't want them to get angry at me for not answering.

"Abi and Paoli did escape," I say at last. It's not a direct answer to their question, but perhaps offering up this information would pacify them.

"Fuck. I knew it!" Daria shouts. She lets out a whoop and throws her arm around Alisa and me.

"Settle down," I hiss, pulling away. "They'll hear us."

She grins.

"So you'll help us escape, too," she says. "You came back to help us all. No one knows how, but half the giant warriors have fallen ill. Wintertime coughing sickness, they say. We're preparing to escape, aren't we?"

My heart stutters.

"Just… be alert," I murmur. "Someone may come."

Both of them smile, trying to keep a reign on their excitement.

Friends.

The word dances through my mind again. Maybe, when I go back to Zlosa we would be true friends.

Alisa's hand reaches out and brushes over Daria's arm. I blink at the affectionate touch. A look passes between them, and something clicks into place. Perhaps I hadn't cared enough to look before, perhaps I merely didn't understand the emotion. But now, after Ra'Sa, I know what I see.

Love.

Daria looks up at me, still smiling. "I'll tell you if I hear anything more from the rebellion."

"Use the common tongue!" the new giant guard bellows from nearby.

We all look up at the red-faced being as he arrives to his station.

We murmur our apologies and switch back, but when he looks away, I nod to Daria, grateful.

Then I start to gather the hanging clothing, replacing it with the newly washed pieces. We are quiet as the sun makes its path through the sky.

When dusk approaches, I look at the two women and bid my farewells.

At last, as I walk down the beaten path away from the river and to the cabin, Ra'Sa prods at me. My heart quickens.

Soon... he whispers.

A smile tugs at the corners of my mouth.

I knock on the door, leaving the baskets of folded shirts and pants on the steps. Then, I return for a second trip. Hibsej doesn't retrieve the laundry immediately, which forces me to knock again on the door to the main house and wait.

I need to see my girls, but I can't go without her permission.

The door cracks open, and she stands there frowning.

I wait for her to address me, which she doesn't do, before saying, "My Lady, all of the laundry has been washed. I would like to take leave to visit my family."

She still doesn't respond.

I stand there, waiting. Uncomfortable.

At last, one of the boys makes a noise behind her, and she sighs.

"Fine. Begone," she commands before the door shuts.

A lightness picks up in my chest. I don't just smile. I grin and hurry back to my room.

I bathe, clean myself, and toil away, grabbing the two dolls I made from scrap cloth. Once finished, I grab a bone from the discard pile for Coco and leave the cabin.

I am on my way, I say through my bond.

Meet you there, Ra'Sa returns.

A part of me is sad that he will not walk with me, but it would be foolish to be seen traveling together.

As I reach Griselda's door, there's a whistle from the far side of the road. I whip around, and the hair on my neck stands up.

Several buildings down, there's a group of men. They've all come from the lumber yard, but I don't see Ra'Sa around. One of them waves his hands to make the shape of a woman, and another makes a crude gesture.

"¡Mujer tan bella!"[2]

I turn back around, only for one of them to yell, *"¡Puta!"*[3]

My fists clench, and I bang on the door. Coco lets out a howl, and the men behind me laugh.

The door opens a second later, revealing Griselda. She looks at me with a stern expression.

"What are you doing here?"

"I came to give the girls gifts for their birthday," I say quickly.

The men behind me continue yelling, and I keep my mouth shut. They'll stop if I ignore them.

Her eyes narrow. "That was days ago."

I fidget with the dolls behind my back. "I know."

"That's it?" she scoffs. "'I know'. Care to expand on that thought?"

I purse my lips. "I was... detained."

She lets out a mirthless laugh. "I see some of your admirers have come to chase you around. Go with them, and leave us be."

My mouth falls open. I knew she hated me but this...

"Please. I'm asking kindly. I just want to see them."

"They aren't interested in seeing you. You missed a special day. Go back to your master." she spits.

I hear the girls behind her, and Coco howls once again.

"Mamá!"

My heart swells. They want me near. That gives me strength.

"Griselda," I start. "Let me in now."

She casts me an unkind glare, but steps aside and lets me in. Once past the door, I smile and begin to sing.

"Un cumpleaños feliz…"[4]

"Mamá!" they cry again and wrap around my legs.

I smile and pet their backs gently before rubbing the top of Coco's head. I hug each Wren and Thea tightly before giving them their dolls. I savor their nearness as they chatter about how much they've missed me.

A sound from the back room turns my blood ice cold.

"Melisa," Griselda starts, voice stern.

My head snaps up, but she abruptly stops. Ra'Sa stands there, in the home where I was raised. A home where I was hurt and lonely. He fills the space, somehow chasing away all the bad memories with his presence.

My heart thumps in my chest. He wears a smile that he didn't use to wear when I first met him, and he looks down at me with that intense look that burns straight into my bones. His clothes are dirty from work, and he still wears the face of a human, but I can feel how big his hands are as I remember them around my midsection.

I open my mouth to say something, but then.... the girls look up at him.

They squeal, and I am helpless to do nothing more than marvel at the joy pouring out from my little girls as they clamber over to him. This was what I had wanted.

Somehow… it is better than I expected.

"You know him?" Thea asks me.

I smile, looking up at him. "I do."

Then he pulls out two huge red gems from behind his back. One is the one that Hibsej took from me, but the other is new.

My gods.

The commotion through the room is chaotic. The girls latch onto them, but Thea holds one close to her face, as if she could pick out every detail in the crystal.

Something sour coats my tongue, and my heart cracks. Tears spring to my eyes.

Ruh'flor, *you wanted the gems back from Hibsej, no?*

I bite my lip and pull my mouth into my smile.

Yes. It was thoughtful of you to do that.

But...

I feel a prodding at my mind, and I frantically try to hide the image of the dolls.

He sees anyway... of course, he does.

Abashment at my gift floods through me, and I keep the gifts hidden in the folds of my gown. But Ra'Sa watches me.

My cheeks heat. What would he think about someone like me? My poor attempts to be a mother would've made anyone laugh.

Instead, his eyes soften.

"Wren, Thea," he says. "Your *mamá* brought you something too."

I feel Griselda sneer from the corner, but I slowly pull out the handmade toys. I wait for the disappointment and fear the flames creeping over my skin and causing my stomach to roil.

But then Wren hands the gem back to Ra'Sa and rushes over. Thea keeps her crystal, but approaches as well. Curious.

I hand them both one.

"One for you, with a blue dress because I know it is your favorite color," I say to Wren.

She smiles and looks up at me. "I like red. Like you."

My mouth parts, and my eyes burn. They… they don't understand.

I look at Thea and say, "And green for you. As I know you love plants."

Thea grins, takes the toy, and then immediately ties her gem around the neck of her dolly.

"Now she's got a necklace. Like a queen," she says.

"Like mamá," Wren corrects.

Ra'Sa laughs, "That she does. And they are both beautiful."

My throat aches, and I swallow thickly. Ra'Sa comes to my side and kneels down. As he does, he takes my hand.

Coco winds her way between us, pressing her face into the space where mine and Ra'Sa's arms meet. She watches the girls, as does my mate, but I don't miss the disgruntled woman in the corner.

Griselda sucks her teeth. Too low for the girls to hear, then she stands up and approaches. "I didn't realize you were seducing him, too. Do you know no better way to improve yourself?"

Ra'Sa goes preternaturally still. His head turns slowly, like the predator he is perfectly capable of being.

"What did you say?" he grits out.

I squeeze his hand. He'd killed the guard for me, hell, I'd even seen him shut the men up when Eneko paraded me through the yards.

But this... to the woman who's made me feel small my entire life.

I should tell him to stop.

Griselda sticks her chin out. "This is between me and Melisa. She knows what she is. She's not even ashamed."

Ra'Sa stands, and the girls stop playing. "How dare you say that?"

I scramble to get up to my feet. "Ra'Sa," I whisper, grabbing at his arm only to find it completely tense.

"You use the same cruel words that the scum in the yards use to describe your own daughter?"

My throat closes.

Griselda sneers. "I merely speak the truth."

Ra'Sa lets out a bitter laugh, and the girls watch, confused and slightly nervous. Coco leaves my side to corral them.

"Truth, you say. I think the truth is that your daughter has done everything she could for you to be safe. Does that mean nothing, you heartless woman?" Ra'Sa grits out.

Griselda's eyes go wide for the shortest moment before her face hardens over.

"You won't come in my house and lecture me—"

"When it involves Melisa, I will."

I suck in a stuttering breath. My fingers dig into his arm, and his other hand comes up to brush over my fingers.

Are you well, Ruh'flor?

I look up at him, eyes wide, and nod.

His attention remains fixed on my mother.

"You will never speak to Melisa like that again. If either Wren or Thea tell me that you've said something against her, then you will regret it. Hurt the girls, and I will leave you in the middle of the woods with the wolves. Do you understand?"

I swallow hard.

Griselda's sneering expression melts away into fear.

"Say you understand," Ra'sa repeats.

Slowly, Griselda opens her mouth. First, she huffs, but then she says, "Fine—I understand."

Ra'Sa's expression changes in an instant.

"Perfect. If that's all settled, there's no reason to miss a celebration. I brought more gifts!"

The girls are grinning and laughing in a second when Ra'Sa pulls out a few more stones and starts to sing. I should be more worried that the others outside would hear, but Ra'Sa tends to comfort all my worries.

I let myself listen as a happy tune pours out of him. I'd forgotten that he could sing so well—his voice is rich and layered as it hits the gems the girls hold in their hands. We continue to laugh, and then we start to dance.

When I do, I feel Ra'Sa's eyes on me. Heat sparks. I realize I want him.

His softness, his joy.

His kindness.

After Wren and Thea fall asleep in his arms, and he puts them to bed, we leave.

But, instead parting ways, I take him by the hand and sneak him back to the cabin. The fire grows hotter.

I want to show him how much pleasure he can feel. I want to fall apart for him again.

And again.

I'm delighted that the lights are out, and I have no trouble drawing him into the room at the back. He growls once the door is shut and grabs onto the skirts of my dress.

I gasp, but he puts a finger to my lips.

We can't have anyone waking up and finding me buried balls deep in you, now can we?

My mouth parts, but I can feel the rush of wet warmth between my legs. There was something so delicious about the thought of him taking me here again. On my terms.

Willing, but utterly helpless against him. Against enjoying what he wanted to give me.

You're all talk, I say back, breathless even in my thoughts.

He pulls up the skirts of my dress, and I fall back onto the bed.

Are you sure you want this now?

From this angle, I see him straining against his pants.

Yes, I say desperately before I reach forward and unlace his britches. When he springs out of the restrictive clothing, I take him into my mouth. He practically chokes, and it's like music to my ears.

I'd pictured taking him like this when I'd wanted to seduce him, but I'd never thought that it would be this... pleasurable.

He thrusts shallowly while I continue to move up and down. When I brush my tongue against him, he shudders.

"Stop," he pants.

I pull back, confused for a second before I see the flames burning in his eyes. He covers me with his large body, the both of us still mostly clothed. Then he presses his hand over my mouth.

Quiet, Ruh'flor.

In a second, he lines up his pink, human-glamoured cock with my entrance and pushes straight in. I gasp against his fingers, biting down lightly. He smiles and replaces his hand with his mouth as he works his way in and out of me. It's too much.

It's a sweet existence.

The things I'll do to you when I can finally hear your screams, he murmurs against me.

I smile, only for the action to be broken by a moan.

What do you even know of experimenting?

Enough, he purrs and I shudder.

I had not known a woman, that does not mean I know nothing.

Whatever instincts and imaginations pull him along, he does it all very well. And when we fall over the cusp of finishing, spiraling down together, I feel safe.

I feel the way he did every time he cared for me. No one had ever cared for me before.

After we finish, I draw him into the bed and wrap him around me. Slowly, he works off my dress until we are skin-to-skin.

It's heavenly.

For a few hours, I can pretend this is all that we are. Free. Blissfully happy despite the sadness that swirls around us. The feeling is like a bubble. Happy. Contented.

I don't want it to go anywhere.

1. Washing basket.

2. Beautiful woman!

3. Bitch!

4. Happy birthday…

CHAPTER 34

RA'SA

The smell of ice and pine blankets the air as I walk through the dense underbrush with my boots sinking into the snow. The derelict cabin, a sanctuary for the rebellion's clandestine nighttime gatherings, comes into view. I grasp the leather straps of the heavy sack slung over my shoulder and quicken my pace.

A soft glow breaks free from beneath the door as I approach, signaling the presence of the rebels already assembled within. With a cautious hand, I rap on the weathered wood in the coded rhythm we've all committed to memory. Three short taps, a pause, then two longer, heavier knocks. The door creaked open, revealing Rodrigo's stern features, softened momentarily by relief upon recognizing me.

"Ra'Sa, good," he murmurs, ushering me inside. "We were about to begin."

The cabin's single room was cloaked in shadows, save for the flickering dance of candlelight across the faces of the gathered. Some men perch on makeshift stools; others stand, their expressions etched with determination. I nod to each person before setting down the sack with a muted thud.

Rodrigo has his dirty fabric map spread across the floor. He reviews the plan we had begun to form the last time we met. I know it all by heart—had thought about it while chopping and working. Burn, liberate, escape.

It sounds so simple.

I'd fought before and studied the art of war, but my confidence wanes as I consider the task before us. My king had sent me here for this exact purpose—Melisa had gotten information from Eneko. She'd met with a king. I'd learned all that I could while living and working with the slaves. I'd found and joined the rebellion, and now, there was a real possibility for thousands of slaves to be freed.

If I think about it all too much, pressure sits heavy on my chest.

A lull in the conversation has me swallowing hard. I look up, catching Tomás' face. I recognize him from the last meeting.

"The poisonings have been working, yes?"

Tomás nods. "They write it off as seasonal sickness. They have no idea." Then he pulls out a small note. "I have some good news. It seems Eneko has already departed and will be arriving tomorrow. He brings important papers for King Rholker."

My heart swells. Papers.

Not just his memories. Papers could be stolen.

"Are you sure?" I ask, trying not to betray just how hopeful I am.

He nods. "My contact confirmed it."

I feel like I could fly away from here. If we just need to steal that information, then I've finally figured out how to spare Melisa from joining him in his room.

"Well then, our time here draws short. What else do you need from me?" I say, skin still buzzing with excitement.

El Lobo, who has been silent to this point, shifts. “Let’s see what you’ve brought.”

With deliberate movements, I unpack loaves of bread, bundles of dried meats, and containers of fresh water. We’d decided to send the women, children and elderly to this meeting house, and these provisions will help sustain those not fighting.

“Well done,” Rodrigo says. “Where did you steal this from?”

I cast him a wary look. He doesn’t need to know that I was rifling through Eneko’s house when Hibsej stepped out. They also don’t need to know that I was looking for any information Eneko could’ve left behind.

Everything was empty, but I saw the room where he slept. Ever since then, that visual has weighed upon my heart. Melisa was ready to go to him.

I can’t wait to tell her she doesn’t have to.

“I am good at finding things,” I murmur.

El Lobo laughs, and the cabin grows still, save for the rustle of fabric.

“Every day, I am more grateful that you are on our side.”

I smirk and finish removing the last supplies.

“Tomorrow,” I finally say, my voice firm. The word hangs between us like a sacred vow. "We begin our escape."

Heads lift, and eyes that held sparks of their own meet mine. We risk discovery. We’ve used our precious time debating strategies and anticipating obstacles. It’s time our meticulous schemes now be put to the test.

“Tomorrow, we will reclaim what has been taken from us," I continue. "Our freedom and our dignity."

A murmur of agreement ripples through the group.

“Do your part, my friend,” El Lobo says. “Call on me when it is time.”

I nod, but the pressure in my chest intensifies. I can only think of one thing: Melisa.

The need to see and touch her prickles along my skin. I need to kiss her, to ask her something important.

CHAPTER 35

MELISA

Each day, we get closer and closer to our departure. All that is left to do is to see what Eneko brings back from his trip. Through the speaking stones, we will tell the King and Queen that Rholker still resides in Zlosa, reveal all his secret plans, and leave.

Soon, I will see Enduvida. The crystals and the jewels. I'll hear the sweet songs my mate loves so much.

I sit on the bed, sorting through my dresses. As I look at the clothes hanging in my closet, the clamminess of my skin and unsteady beats of my heart take over.

Tomorrow.

I'd been dreading the day that Eneko would return for the last week, and now here we are.

I take a deep breath through my nose, the words sitting in the back of my mind.

We need information… but I don't want him to come back.

When the sound of feet walking up the steps to my door filters into my room, I startle, but then close my eyes.

Ra'Sa.

Fuck.

He's weary. He spends so much time planning with the other humans, organizing supplies. I should cast him away, and yet, I open the bond between us.

Come in.

The door swings open, and he stands there, looming in the doorframe. Chest heaving. Eyes glinting in the firelight. He slips inside and shuts the door behind him quietly.

"Ruh'flor," he exhales, seconds before he wraps me up in his arms. Instinct has me wrapping my arms around him, too. I breathe in the scent of stone and wood and let my eyes flutter closed.

I once thought I had a heart of stone, and yet, all I needed was a stone bender to work it to life. To force the organ to beat, to pump blood, and to feel anything other than anger, survival, or terror.

"Is everything all right?" I ask quietly, acutely aware that he still refuses to pull away.

He nods, his chin digging into the top of my head.

Yes. Everything is ready for tomorrow, he replies to my mind.

I let out a long breath.

It's really happening.

It is.

His fingers thread through mine.

Melisa. I have good news.

Oh? I say, not letting on how much that makes my gut churn.

Eneko will return with a caravan tomorrow. There will be a small reception, and while everyone is out, we will set fire to the barracks.

I pause.

They'll massacre the guards and give as many people as possible enough time to get out. But Eneko... well, he's bringing home papers. Plans in writing.

My heart skips a beat.

If the rebellion starts tomorrow, Eneko will come home to chaos. We can hopefully learn what he has brought back with him and then flee.

We will be free of him before I ever have to touch his bed again.

Suddenly, my heart lights on fire. I pull back and look into Ra'Sa's eyes. My chest goes concave, and a mangled sound passes my lips.

He looks down at me, almost... lovingly.

Fuck.

Then he cups my cheek.

Melisa, I know how you hurt. How you tear yourself up over what you believe you must do—but you won't have to touch him. Not ever again.

My mouth parts. For all I have shared with him, all I have given him, I didn't think he would ever say such words to me. He was a plan. He wasn't supposed to be... this.

"Now that we have eliminated that particular problem, there is something I have to ask you." He brushes his finger over my cheek.

I swallow. "Yes?"

"Would you be my wife, Melisa?"

My hand comes up to brush my fingers against his. "I—"

A wife. I never expected to be anyone's wife. Who would've wanted me after having two hidden daughters and most of my adulthood spent in Eneko's room?

I want you, Ra'Sa murmurs.

I take a deep breath, swallow, and ask, "You would be my husband?"

A smile spreads over his face. He gives me one of those devastating looks that makes my stomach flip and my heart pound from something very different from fear.

"I would, *Ruh'flor.*"

The tears come faster than I can count. They well up in my eyes and spill over.

"You love me," I say quickly. Not asking a question.

His hand drops to my heart. "I love you."

A tear slides down my cheek. “I—“

He saves me from having to finish the sentence and kisses me. His taste is husky. When he parts my mouth with his tongue, it makes my core light on fire. I think of him thrusting, of every time he's made me come with a hand over my mouth so we don't get caught. I think of his sweetness, the way he's defended me against my mother, Eneko, Hibsej, and even the other slaves.

The tear is burned away on my hot cheeks, and I throw my arms around his neck, pushing up onto my toes as I meet his ferocity.

I pull back, breaking the kiss.

I fucking love you.

He grins and gently lifts me onto the wall not touching the cabin. My legs wrap around his waist, and I grind against his stomach. Between the friction of my dress and his solid form, I let out a quiet gasp. My neck knocks back into the wall, baring my throat. His chest begins to rumble, and I look back at him just in time to see him shift.

From brown to blue, he goes back into the form that he was always meant to have. He grins, blue eyes sparkling back at me then he nuzzles into my neck.

"My bride."

His lips skim across the column of my throat, kissing and sucking.

You're a little too good at that for me to believe you've never done this with anyone else, I say back to him.

I feel him chuckle.

I can't help but to taste you.

A sharp sting comes at the side of my neck, and I flinch. My hand leaves his neck and presses to my throat. When I pull back my fingers, there is no red.

Shit, forgive me. I got carried away, Ra'Sa pants.

My brows furrow. When he shifts into his Enduar form, Ra'Sa has two glowing dots on his throat. When I tended to Estela, she had these marks we would cover.

This is something they do.

Biting my lip, I look back at him. So much time has been spent with me belonging to someone else. Did I want such a blatant show of belonging to someone else?

Not yet.

"Hush, it is all right. Help me with my dress," I say hurriedly.

His expression goes hot again. His hands clench into the fabric of my nightgown, and he starts pulling. As the fabric slides over my head, my hands drop back to the hem of his shirt. I yank until I hear something tear. He chortles and returns to my neck before helping to ease off the cloth.

My nipples scrape against his soft chest. A short, velvety layer of fur covers his skin, making him feel like one of the finest fabrics I've ever had the pleasure of touching. I arch into him, craving the action again, just as one of his hands comes up to palm my breast. He squeezes, and I whimper.

A small barrier of clothing still separates my entrance from rubbing against his bare skin, but I'm dying of simple friction.

For a second, I think about how many firsts have happened with this man. The first time to orgasm with a man. The first time to sleep an entire night together.

The first time to fall in love.

His hand shifts, situating his thumb and pointer finger to pinch my nipple. He watches my eyes.

"Do you like this?"

I smile and groan as he does it again.

"Yes."

"Shh," he eases. "Careful, my little love. Do you trust me?"

"I think I've more than proven I do," I retort.

He smiles. "You've given me a gift with your body; let me show you how grateful I am."

I sink into the sound of his voice, but frown when his hand slides away from my breast. It passes over the stretch marks on my belly, over the scar I gave myself, and to the small loincloth. He tugs at the ties, until they come undone. His hand moves slowly from one side to the other.

He hums.

I feel every brush of his fingers, but remain watching his face as he explores me. The same fascination that he's always held forefront while making love with me is there on his face now. A pure heart, but the passion of a man.

The fabric slides away, and I suck in another sharp breath at the delicious sensation. His fingers move through the curls above my folds and then he brushes his finger against that small bundle of nerves. He works it again and again, moving over me until I am panting and pushing into the cold wall.

While he does, something coils around my calf. Something soft and playful.

I look down and see his... tail.

The thought is long gone when he inserts a finger inside. Working me harder. I am sucked back into the moment and smile brightly at him. I open my mouth, ready to tell him to get inside of me with the fury of a woman possessed, but instead, the edge of my orgasm races through me at lightning speed.

A hand covers my mouth as I come. It ripples through me, waves crashing over and over my body as I see the starlit skies before my eyes. He kisses me, and the feeling lasts even longer.

When it finally subsides, I slump against him, skin to skin. Sweat makes my body slide against Ra'Sa.

"You're beautiful, *Ruh'flor*," he says, brushing his lips against my head.

“What exactly does that word mean?” I finally ask. He uses it with increasing frequency every time we meet.

He smiles, bright and handsome in his blue skin.

“Cave flower. For the first time I saw you in Enduvida, you looked out of place amongst the stone, and yet I desperately wanted you to stay and share your beauty with my home,” he says.

I swallow. He flatters me too much.

"Get on the bed," I say.

His head tilts to the side. “Why, my demanding mate?”

I dip my chin down, wiggling out of his grip, and standing in the cold cottage, naked and panting.

"Remove your pants and get on the bed," I demand again.

He grins and then follows my command. He works quickly, almost not giving me enough time to enjoy the sight of his long, bulky body, nor worry over the dips and hollows that have started to show from the cruel conditions of the lumber yards. Markings that certainly weren't there before.

I walk over, sauntering before finally joining him.

I press a kiss to his lips, pinning him to my pillow. I don't care that his feet hang over the edge or that his hip bones dig into my thighs. I'm just happy to be here.

Happy to know that everything won't end tomorrow. That we will be free.

A wife.

I climb atop him and then lower myself. He pulls us to the side so each of us is half lying down as he moves in and out. We watch each other, moving toward another great emotional cliff.

Not to fall, but to jump, hand in hand.

Just as I reach over to intertwine my fingers with his, there's a sound outside our door. A shouting. We both freeze and then he pulls away from me. The sweat that had felt so comforting, so intimate, turns to ice upon my skin.

"Where is Melisa?!" Eneko shouts.

I barely have time to blink before the door to my room is yanked open. The force is hard enough to splinter. The two of us are there, naked. Ra'Sa in his Enduar form, and me, hair unbound.

Eneko stands in the door, home even earlier than expected. It's clear he's spent the last several days on a cart.

His wild eyes take us in. Already red cheeks turn deep scarlet. His nostrils flare, and his hair sticks out around his face.

“Eneko, wait!” Hibsej yells from the outside.

"You dirty, traitorous slut," he seethes and then he points at Ra'Sa, "And you! *I’m going to kill you.*”

He charges into the room, grabbing Ra'Sa.

My mate snarls and breaks free. His back curves as he adjusts into the defensive stance he taught me. I can feel the movement of the stones underfoot. “Weak, pathetic man.”

Hibsej’s head pokes into the gaping hole. When she sees Ra’Sa, she screeches, "Troll!” and then runs.

“Help!” Her shrieking voice pierces the air.

I kick Eneko to get him away from my mate, but he shoves me across the room. Splinters slide into my thighs as I slam into the wall. More shouting comes from the outside.

My chest tightens. The pair of guards who watch over the path to the slave pens are here.

Ra’Sa seethes, his eyes glowing in time with the stone glowing in his chest. He removes himself from Eneko’s grip with ease. His fist slams into Eneko’s jaw.

The foreman grabs him, pulling my mate’s arms behind his back.

Ra’Sa cries out as the guards arrive. They thrust spears in his face. I see the rage boiling there, but naked and exposed, he pauses. Then he looks over at me.

I’m going to kill them. Nothing will happen to you. Please, trust me.

And he surrenders.

I suck in a sharp breath.

"Take him to the slave pens,” Eneko fumes, wiping blood from the corner of his mouth. “Scare the slaves shitless, and then kill him.”

He turns back to me, "You'll pay for this, human bitch."

CHAPTER 36
MELISA

NOTE: There is a serious trigger warning in this chapter. It begins immediately and you will see a ** when it ends.

"Please Eneko," I beg, shaking with the cold as he stomps over to where I am curled up against the wall.

Ra'Sa bellows outside.

The sound slices through me, tearing apart my heart.

It was too soon. Finally, I had tasted love. I'd found exactly what I was looking for. I almost got it all.

Eneko rips me away from the wall. I scratch at his skin with my fingernails. Flesh tears, and blood pools across his shoulders and neck, but he laughs.

"I've spent weeks waiting for you. I wet my cock on some whore in the mines. The whole time, I was waiting to be back to this room. I return and find you betraying me. You'll regret this every day that I let you draw breath into your lungs."

His spittle rains over my face and then he throws me onto the bed, hard enough for my head to crack against the wall. I cry out as I'm laid bare before him. I grasp for anything, wishing I had the stone knife that Hibsej stole from me. There is nothing within reach.

Eneko's hand hits the mattress next to my head. Some of his blood drips on my unclad shoulder, and I flinch as his other hand presses my other shoulder down into the bed.

I kick, ramming my foot into his balls.

He grunts, pressing down harder. Too hard. My body bends under his weight, and something pops near my collarbone. A flood of pain rushes through me.

"Ra'Sa!" I scream.

Eneko slaps me, then covers my mouth with his hand.

"Enough. Be still, or I will kill your family."

Every attack halts in place, and I lie there, helpless.

He reaches for his pants.

"Fucking whores," he mutters as he pulls on his ties.

My mouth opens, and I prepare to scream. Only a sob comes out.

I close my eyes, thinking of all the times that Ra'Sa told me to look away. Damn him. Damn him for sparing me pain for a short while.

Damn him for making me love him.

The pressure on the bed around me shifts, and I squeeze my eyes tighter.

A whirring sound cuts through everything, and the pressure is lifted.

My eyes open at the exact second that Eneko turns back to the door. Something large and jagged crashes through the front part of my room. Wood splinters and sprays, and I duck into the bed, rolling over and grabbing a pillow as pieces spray all around. Something cuts across my back. I cry out.

Then, a meaty thud rattles the room.

****End of Trigger Warning****

I look up to see Ra'Sa bathed in silver moonlight. It shines down on him in thick beams. It's almost unnatural, with his hands stretched forward and palms up as he commands a flurry of stones. They swirl around him like the whirlpool we use to clean clothes. The wind whips his short, silver hair against his face, and the stone in his chest glows bright like a fire.

Nudity equates to vulnerability, but for a god like Ra'Sa, I don't think the rules apply.

My head turns to the side. I behold a giant ripped apart by the wood and stone. He's covered in blood, and parts of him have been reduced to a gory pulp. I gasp, and his chest rises.

Eneko lives.

"Ra'Sa," I sob, pulling the blanket over me. Stings and cuts cover my body, and it hurts when I step off the bed, but I don't stop.

Stay there, he commands through our bond.

He cast his hands to the side. The stones fall, thudding in the snow, and he walks towards me.

Hewn from stone himself, beautiful as the finest sculpture, he walks right in front of Eneko.

Ra'Sa looks directly into the eyes of the foreman.

"You are pathetic," Ra'Sa says, voice full of venom.

Eneko wheezes and then chokes on his own blood. I watch, shaking, as he says, "I should have killed you when you brought her back to me."

My mate sneers. “I should’ve killed you the second I saw your ugly face.”

Eneko spits blood. “The cause of the humans will fail, troll, and the giants will reign for a thousand years.”

"You're wrong," Ra'Sa says. "You will fail. You were born of the god of war and will die by his fiery blade. Only this time, you will not rise from the ashes."

His words ring like a prophetic song etched in rock.

Then he hesitates.

"Melisa," Ra’Sa coaxes, breaking me out of my shuddering revelry.

I meet his eye, terrified and shaken from everything that happened. His hand reaches out again—the stones on the ground stir.

“It is your right to kill him if you wish," he says.

My heart stutters in my chest.

"What? You won’t do it?”

Ra'Sa shakes his head. “I would if you ask me. But I have tasted your anger and felt your fear. I think… you deserve revenge.”

I look at the blade, then look at the dead guards just outside before returning my gaze to Eneko.

Kill him.

Kill the man who plucked me out of the yards and forced me on my back. Kill the man who hurt and tore at me, subjecting me to a life of ridicule and humiliation.

The words swirl around me, and then, adrenaline rushing through my veins, I take the blade.

“I’ve never killed… anything,” I say.

My mate straightens. “Then you will take this blade and free yourself forever. No more anger, no more fear. Let his death herald your future."

I blink, step forward, and take the weapon.

Ra'Sa makes a deep, rumbling sound, and the stones around us quake.

As he had that first night in Enduvida, Ra’Sa begins to sing. His chest puffs out, and he lets out one long, sustained note. It bounces off the rocks around him, a rough, guttural cry. It is like the strike of a drum.

Freedom.

I raise the blade. I think of everything he taught me. To slash and swipe. To plunge deep through the ribs. I think of every time Eneko had used me. Each memory flies before me in rapid-fire succession. I'd done it all to save my family, but let the pain and anger mount.

And now... freedom lies before me.

"Melisa…" Eneko wheezes.

My hand strikes quick and true, plunging the stone blade straight into his throat.

He makes a gurgling noise, and I push away from him with a loud cry. Eneko slumps forward. I watch the life drain from his body as his blood flows from his wounds.

Ra’Sa’s hand pulls the knife from his throat and hands it to me as he wraps his arm around me. I hiss as the cuts along my body burn.

"You're hurt," Ra'Sa comments, tearing off the blanket, keeping my body free of the chill settling in my bones. I shake in the intense heat, fueled further by the spiraling adrenaline.

He looks furious at each wound, but I shake my head and push away from him and toward the closet. I start pulling on my warmest clothing.

"Where is Hibsej?" I ask.

He looks at me grimly, and I see her sons' faces. "Did you kill her?"

He shakes his head. "I don't think so."

Fear spikes in my heart, and I pull on the clothes, burning cuts and splinters be damned.

"Dress and take me to her," I demand.

Once clothed, we sprint around the side of the house. A rasping breath breaks through the still night.

I see a giant woman lying near a tree. Hibsej. Her chest rises and falls, and I dash to her side. The front door of the house is open, and soft sobs are coming from inside.

"Fuck," I curse. I turn back to Ra'Sa, "Get them to stop crying. And ensure they don't wander to the backyard. I will deal with Hibsej."

Ra'Sa frowns but follows my instructions.

Alone in the snow, I cross to Eneko's widow. I kneel next to her, rubbing feeling into my now gloved hands just as snow begins to drift down from the heavens. My breath clouds in front of me, as does hers. I shake her arm roughly.

No wounds, but she doesn't move.

"Come on, you stubborn bitch," I say, shaking her more vigorously this time.

At last, she stirs, and her eyes flutter open with a start.

I press my knife to her throat as she looks at me with unnerving precision. She snarls, and I position the blade at her chest.

"Easy," I say. "Don't move too fast, or you'll hurt yourself."

She snarls, but eases back. Her eyes frantically scan the house—the open door, the scattered wood visible at the back of her home.

"What have you done? Where is the troll?" she rages.

I consider answering her questions, then bite my lip. I could kill her. Leave her sons orphaned, as so many humans have been wretched away from their parents and families.

She watches me with the same hatred I feel. It melds and sears together within me.

"You killed Eneko," she says at last, her brow softening.

"Yes, I did," I say.

She lets out a bitter laugh. "Let me guess, I'm next."

My throat aches.

Her eyes close, cutting me off from the conduit of pure agony. "Very well. What does it matter? My husband is dead."

In that moment, I know I can't be like the giants. I had been so sure I was always willing to do what was necessary for my family. For my future. But I've changed.

"Enough mourning," I hiss. "We both know you were married to a devil. You need to take your sons and leave Zlosa."

Hibsej's eyes blink open.

"Eneko gave us food and a house. What will we do now?" Her chest moves quickly.

I think of how I felt the day the twins were born. How lonely and awful I felt looking down at the two wrinkly infants in my arms. The path ahead for me had been murky, riddled with mistakes, shame, and pain.

"You will do what you must," I say to her, removing the knife.

For a second, she looks like she might kill me. Then her anger and ire drain from her, seemingly all at once.

She shoves me off her, and I fall back onto my stinging cuts. The chill shocks me.

Hibsej stands tall.

"Urdort. Relmos," she calls and charges into her house.

I clamber to my feet and approach. My face burns from the cold as she grabs and packs what she can.

Ra'Sa stands in the sitting room, watching her as well.

It doesn't take long for her to drag the two boys out. Relmos holds a large sack, and she carries Urdort in her arms.

She sneers at my mate, but then she looks at me and her face softens.

I almost expect her to say something, but her mouth remains shut.

Ra'Sa growls at her, and she hurries away into the woods.

I watch her go. The emotion that greets me is… relief—relief like water after days without drinking. Relief like night after a day of burning heat.

Ra'Sa comes to my side and folds me into his arms.

"I didn't realize just how soft your heart could be," he murmurs.

Flakes still fall from the sky, glittering in moonbeams and catching on the evergreen needles.

"Neither did I."

We are silent for a time, but my mind races. Eneko is dead. The realization sinks in, and then sours.

"Fuck, the papers Eneko brought back from the mines," I all but shout.

Ra'Sa rubs my uninjured arm. "Peace, *Ruh'flor*. They are inside. Scattered across every surface."

This is good news. I look up at him, then stare at the house. So many memories. We're so close.

But my chest tightens and my eyes burn. Perhaps it's the fact that Eneko's dead, but I can't seem to move my feet.

"I… can't go in there. Never again."

Ra'Sa nods. "You must, for a little while. It is too cold for you to be outside. Give me a little time, and I will take you to a hiding place we've been preparing so I can tend to your wounds."

I watch the snowfall and look back at the cabin.

"What if someone else finds us?" I say.

Eneko's cabin was far enough away from the slave pens that we would have time.

Ra'Sa shakes his head. "There will be no more guards for a while. I know their patterns. Just let me send a message to King Teo, then we may leave. Tomorrow, the slaves will riot. And we will begin our trek home. It will not matter."

I look up at him. "Take me with you."

His brows furrow, so I don't allow him to respond.

"We need to get my family. And I need to warn the comfort women."

He looks down at me, wary. "Very well, but we must run."

"I can run well enough."

CHAPTER 37

RA'SA

We run toward the slave pens as fast as my legs can carry me. The air is charged with electricity as I whip past trees. Some of the branches hit me in the face, scraping against my little Melisa's skin, almost demanding that I slow down and reach some common sense.

But I can't stop.

Not until I warn my king. Not until we get Thea and Wren.

Ra'Sa, Melisa says to my mind. *I can't keep running. I'll stop back here. Come and get me when you are ready to go for the girls.*

I swallow hard. My skin burns against the onslaught of cold. I'm comforted to know she's not far behind.

Stay hidden. I'll only be a moment.

When I draw close to the slave pens, my chest constricts. I stop, gasping for breath near one of the trees, and lean against it.

It's Melisa's presence in my thoughts and the need to return to her that makes me push off of the bark and head to the fence. Once easing through the hole, I find the new hollowed out rock where I'd hidden the stones.

Through my magic, I can feel the weight of hundreds of humans in this place, and the guards moving through the area. My brows furrow. There are two more than usual.

Did they find the men I killed?

No. All hell would be boiling over if they did. It must be a change of the guards.

Rolling my shoulders, I command calmness to settle over me like a blanket. We're so close.

I remove the snow-covered rock with my magic and reveal the small bag of magical stones. My hand brushes rough fabric as new vibrations skitter over the ground.

Steps.

My head snaps up, trying to make out the figure that waits for me in the shadows.

I stuff the speaking stones into my pocket as Abet appears. The tension that had been coiling inside of me eases like a serpent unraveling.

"Amigo,"[1] I say, straightening and brushing my hands over the front of my dirty, threadbare shirt. Grateful I had reapplied the glamour.

"Rasa," he says gently. "I thought that was you."

I let out a long breath, allowing the air to cloud in front of me. An invisible thread tugs me backward toward the trees where I left Melisa.

Make this quick, I urge silently. My soul longs for the comfort of my family, small and fragile, safe in my embrace before all hell breaks loose.

"What are you doing out so late?" Abet asks.

I cast him a strange look. "I needed to relieve myself."

Abet nods thoughtfully. "That's strange because you never came to bed."

The chill from the ground spreads up my legs, freezing my muscles.

"Why do you care?" I ask.

He shakes his head.

"Things aren't safe tonight. I've been hearing all manner of strange things. You should go inside and sleep."

I look at him, watching the way he shifts his weight from one foot to the other.

"I'll be in soon," I say uneasily.

Something cracks in Abet's face. He swallows thickly. Then he opens his mouth and lets out a yell.

"HE'S HERE!"

Time stops.

Half a dozen pairs of feet I didn't sense pour out from around the men's sleeping quarters. My head whips left and right before settling back on Abet. He backs away toward the building.

The betrayal is swift like a dagger. The truth unfurls before me, each revelation mocking the friendship I'd believed in. Realizing that I have been a fool is almost more unbearable than the act itself. Nothing is left but a hollow ache where trust used to live.

"What the fuck is going on over here?" one of the giant guards shouts.

Melisa. Thea. Wren. Must protect.

My eyes lock with the shortest of the group. His lips curl back, and he charges.

Magic sizzles in my veins, still hungry after what happened at the cabin. It beats to the aching of my Enduar heart. Eagerness has the ground fracturing and cracking into large, icy chunks. They lift, ready to destroy.

The wind of the movement almost blows me back, but shoots of earth come up to brace my legs.

Once steadied, I cast it all forward.

The boulders crash into trees, knocking down the enormous ancient elms. The giants tumble. Bones crush and flatten against the ground.

The fence falls.

New stones, much smaller and more precise, wait for my command. My head throbs. The rush from using the magic is wearing thin, but the gem in my chest glows brightly.

Dozens of fractured shards slash at flesh, cutting and slicing to the bone. Blood sprays out of the wound at a giant's neck.

I watch with grim satisfaction as giant after giant dies before ever hitting the ground.

Another throb wracks my skull, and pain flashes hot over my skin. The brightness of my Fuegorra makes me close my eyes as another wave of dizziness crashes into me, and I sag to the ground.

As I shift, my skin burns and prickles like being scraped with dozens of pine needles. I stare into the snow, gulping as much air as my lungs can hold. The Fuegorra emits a long, sustained glow as the gossamer threads of my power weave together.

Songs are spun from thin air, reverberating off snow crystals and boulders alike.

I am a beast let free.

Two more giant warriors try to approach, but they are sliced and dying on the ground in mere moments.

For a second, all is quiet.

My chest rises and falls as the world spins around me.

And then, from beyond the now broken barrier of the fence, Melisa approaches. Her light steps mix with the music.

Worry spears my heart.

The slave pens are far from the palace and soldier barracks in the upper city, but soon, a new shift of giant warriors will come and find the carnage.

We will not have long.

The stones I bend tell me that more humans are approaching. Turning to look at the large den behind me, I see them peering at me from behind the corner of the building, and then—emboldened when I do not move—they step out.

"You... you are one of them," a woman exclaims. Murmurs break out.

"Troll!",

"Enduar!"

"The human queen! She told us someone would come."

"¡Por la libertad!"[2] someone else shouts.

Fragments of the common and human tongues fill the air, each person speaking too quickly for me to understand. People move and rush around the bodies of the massacre.

My head spins as dozens of voices fill my ears and mix with the rush of battle. My mate surprises me with her yell.

"¡Callense!"[3] she shouts, pushing up to a sitting position.

The crowd begins to go silent, but I don't miss how some sneer at Melisa. One woman lifts her chin, spitting toward my mate.

I'm too hot, too volatile, for this right now. I cross the distance and stop before the woman, towering above her. Most shrink back at my approach.

"Do that again, and you will be cast out," I growl.

The woman's throat bobs. She opens her mouth and then closes it, clearly trembling.

"For-forgive me," she stammers.

"Say it to her," I command, gesturing back to Melisa. She stands in the breeze, cheeks red and hair unbound.

Everyone holds their breath, watching as the woman grits her teeth.

"My apologies," she says, dipping her head.

"Use her name," I growl. "Melisa."

My mate casts her displeasure through the bond but the woman lets out a long breath.

"Melisa, forgive me. I will never spit on you again."

I nod, satisfied. Melisa however frowns. She is oddly quiet.

One of Rodrigo's men steps forward. Felip. He had accompanied me to the meeting. His mouth is downturned as he takes a deep breath.

"Ra'Sa," he calls.

"Where is Rodrigo?" I ask, scanning the crowd.

"He was murdered in his sleep," Felip says.

I suck in a breath.

I think of Abet, and the scenes from earlier in the night make sense. He waited for everyone to return from the meeting and killed each one. He would've killed me had I given him the chance.

Another traitor.

"Then you will stay with me." I have questions, but there is another human I search for. I turn back to the broader group, my stomach dropping. "Nicolás?"

My blond haired companion pushes out from the group.

“Rasa!” he calls, slightly horrified.

I breathe a sigh of relief. “You live!”

He grins. “Unfortunately.” Then his smile drops at my blue skin. I see him survey my Enduar form, eyes still full of disbelief.

“You come, too. The rest: go to the gates leading into the slave pens and begin to construct a barricade. It will not keep the giants out for long, but it will alert us to their arrival. Those too young or feeble to fight should gather anything that could be used as a weapon.”

Most scramble, moving through the area and bustling over the bodies of their slavers. Melisa joins my side, sliding her arms around mine. I pull her close, embracing her.

Felip clears his throat, and I pull away.

"What would you have me do?" the man asks.

"Find the others of your group in these pens. Any others dead?"

“Everyone who attended the meeting save you and me,” he admits, and I take a deep breath.

“Why weren’t you harmed?” I ask.

“I left to visit my partner,” he says.

I search his face for signs of deception and see none. But I had been foolish before…

“Are you lying?” I demand.

“No.”

“Where is your partner?”

He turns back and points to one of the women sprinting across the way.

“I can get her if you’d like,” Felip says.

Time is not my friend, and I have little choice but to ask for help. Hell is coming either way, let’s hope Felip doesn’t herald it.

"No, that's fine," I grit out. "I need you to find El Lobo. Take him to burn the giants' barracks."

He nods but lingers, looking at Melisa. I remember the things he whispered with Rodrigo and their cutting team. My blood heats.

After a minute, he says, "I didn't know she was yours. " It sounds like an apology.

Melisa, however, is not impressed.

"It shouldn't fucking matter if I was his or not," she snarls at him, gripping my arm tighter.

He tightens his lips, nods, and then turns and leaves.

"Forgive me again, Ra'Sa… and Melisa," Felip says before hurrying away.

Nicolás remains, and I give him a sad look. "Melisa, this is Nicolás. We worked to gether in the lumber yards."

She nods. "Hello."

"Hello," Nicolás nods back, but his eyes scan the carnage behind the den. I wonder if he looks for Abet.

"I didn't know about Abet. I swear," he says softly, still not looking at me.

I frown. "I didn't either."

Nicolás's eyes meet mine, and I find them full of determination. "What do you need?"

"Deep in the woods, past the bodies, there is a cabin. We will send the women there. Go, prepare the space. I will meet you soon," I say.

Nicolás nods and then makes his way into the forest. He steps carefully over the remnants of the fence, past the bodies and the blood.

I wonder what he thinks.

"Ra'Sa," Melisa whispers, pulling me away from my thoughts. "I am sorry about your friend, too."

When I look at her, the song hums between us. Insistent and strong.

"Thank you," I say, holding her close. I stroke her soft hair. She folds into me. It eases the strain on my body.

When I look up at the horizon, it has already started to turn pink and bright. Dawn approaches.

It brings danger—a colossal task.

Her hand strokes my arm.

I take a deep breath of her scent. Then another.

The song increases. It sings of our matehood—our divine blessing long since repressed by the magic that molded my face into a human's. From loss, abundance will emerge.

"Do you hear that?" I ask.

She looks up at me and nods, almost smiling. I kiss her softly, savoring the feel of her lips.

I take another deep breath, taking in the moment, and then let go.

I will fight, and I will win. For her, for Thea and Wren, for Tirin. My mother. My sisters. My father's legacy.

"Let us go and get the girls."

The walk to Griselda's house is filled with the bustle of people scavenging, tearing, and moving. A lump forms in my throat when we reach that small house on the corner next to the elm.

It unexpectedly reminds me of the day we left Ruhsavida.

Melisa notices and looks up at me. "What is it?"

I take a deep breath. "I was alive the day the volcano started to smoke. My father worked for the king; he told us to leave. My mother, brother, and I ran, and we survived. But… I do not know if I can see Thea and Wren and then stay behind to help the humans."

Melisa holds my hand. "This isn't goodbye."

I nod, eyes burning. "I will make sure it is not."

She smiles, kissing my hand before she pushes open the door.

1. Friend.
2. For freedom!
3. Shut up!

CHAPTER 38

MELISA

The small, two-room den is dark, but I can see the girls huddled around Coco in the corner. What surprises me is seeing Griselda sitting behind them, holding them close. No sooner than Ra'Sa casting a spell light into the air that I see my mother's face, haunted with worry and fear.

She looks so frail, so fragile. But then, Griselda looks up at us, and her gaze heats.

"You have brought death, outsider," she spits out as Coco and the girls head straight to their mother.

"I have come to help you find freedom," Ra'Sa retorts.

Griselda says nothing for a long minute. "You speak of freedom, but you know little about being enslaved. I see you are not one of us. You are a monster."

"Quiet," I cut out.

Griselda bites her tongue, but lets out an indignant huff.

"We need to leave the pens," Ra'Sa continues. "You can go with Melisa and the girls, or stay here. But be warned, the dawn heralds a new day, and it will be a bloody, harsh day indeed."

I look up at my Enduar, feeling the tension thicken in the room. Every second that my mother doesn't respond makes my hands grow more clammy.

“Griselda, you can't stay here," I plead, voice cracking on the last word.

A part of me is surprised at my reaction. My mind was firmly against her… but my heart? Some part of my heart still belongs to the young girl who wanted a mother and prayed that one day, Griselda would wake up and change.

But watching her not choose me *again* makes my skin crawl.

"I will do whatever I want," Griselda responds, chin high.

It’s like a punch to my gut.

I step forward. "You hate me so much that you don't even wish to come to a new life? A better life?"

Griselda tracks my movements carefully but doesn’t speak.

Silence.

This is a wound that has been poorly stitched up time after time. Ra’Sa nudges me through our bond—he wants to step in, to smooth over the hurt so clearly radiating between us, but I push him back.

"A better life?" Griselda starts, standing. "There is no place on this earth that would offer peace to a human. I will not lay on my back for the Enduares in exchange for food and shelter. I would rather die here than suffer in the depths of hell."

I’m shocked.

You don't need to hear this, Ra’Sa tells me.

Except I do. Because maybe then, I can let go. All the years of neglect. It was as if I’d been hollowed out, taking the warmth I’d had once known. A million memories tumble through the cracks in my thoughts.

“Do you despise me that much? For so long, you told me that I shouldn’t be a mother because I wasn’t cut out for it. But I tore myself apart, brick by brick, and crossed the land to come back for my girls," I grieve. "It's made me realize, maybe I'm not the unfit one."

I remember all the years wanting my mother's approval, only to be given insults. Each image is filled with shame. Heartache. Despair. I thought it was my fault.

But now I know she was responsible for her actions. I can't fix her. I can't make her understand me.

It kills me.

Griselda's eyes glisten in the light.

"So that's it. I helped you, and now you paint me as some awful person?" she rants.

A part of me cringes away from the rage in her voice, but another part, one supported by my mate stands tall.

"You gave me food, brushed my hair, and told me stories, but you refused the one thing I ever truly wanted." My eyes burn as tears well up.

"And what was that?" Griselda sneers.

"*Love*. Your voice is the voice in my head that calls me a whore, that endlessly berates me, that has made me believe I deserved the broken life I was given," I grit out.

"Where is this coming from? Does the monster poison your thoughts? I loved you well enough." Griselda glares at Ra'Sa.

"But you didn't! Love doesn't look like this—this is hatred. Resentment. I don't believe you ever even wanted me," I sob.

Griselda looks like she would burn me to the ground if she could.

"How dare you say that to me. If I was so awful—so severe with my words that they turned into the cruel voice in your head—why couldn't I prevent you from coming home with two babies mere months before you left my house to become a whore? If I governed your life with such an iron fist, why are you in such chaos?" Griselda spits as if she were a viper spewing venom.

I open my mouth and let out a long, disconnected breath as each of my mother's daggered words pierce the last remnants of my hope.

"I have loved my daughters since the moment they were born. I stayed away because I was desperate. Now, I regret it." I say through the tears on my cheeks.

Griselda remains sitting, grinding her teeth. "If I am so horrid, then go. Take them, and let me properly mourn the loss of my family," Griselda says.

Even after everything, her words hurt.

They shouldn't.

But they strike true, knocking all the breath from my lungs.

Ra'Sa touches my back, and I see the girls tucked against Coco.

It strikes me that Ra'Sa had been willing and ready to take on the daughters with which he shared no blood. And yet, the woman before me, who had given me her own blood, casts me out as if I were nothing.

"Lita?" Wren says, and Griselda shakes her head.

"Let me die peacefully in my own home, away from those who would accuse me."

The word 'please' sits on my tongue. Instead, I burn the bridge between us. I turn around, wiping my face and gesturing for my daughters.

Together, we walk out. The girls are confused by the quiet. I don't know if I'll ever be able to explain what happened.

The door closes behind us, and more rays of pink appear over the horizon. Ra'Sa pulls me close.

"Lita no viene?"[1] Wren asks.

I shake my head.

"Mamá—"

"Did you see that bird?" Ra'Sa interjects, drawing the questions away from me. I feel his worry but have little to offer in terms of comfort.

Since I've known him, so much tragedy and goodness have entered my life. He walks alongside me, putting Thea and Wren down so they can hug my legs. Coco trots next to us, curious but unaffected.

It is only me who mourns silently. Perhaps it is madness to grieve a mother who was never truly mine.

But I'd sooner tame a bear than control my own heart. I let the feelings come, watching them pass like clouds in the sky.

Snow falls quietly as we walk across the yards, and Ra'Sa guides us from the carnage to another part of the broken fence. We hike past trees and parts of the unfrozen river before we reach a dilapidated cabin.

A young man appears. He is tall and toned like a worker from the lumber yards. He grins as we approach.

"Gods, it's strange to see you like this," he says to my mate.

He smiles as Ra'Sa says, "I need you to watch over my family. They need to eat and rest."

He looks at me and the twins, and his eyes widen. Then he nods and races off into the house to find something.

Ra'Sa turns to look at me. "Are you all right?"

I glance between him and the young man with light brown hair.

"I am well enough to do what needs to be done," I respond.

He nods. "Stay here, Nicolás will care for you."

I swallow thickly. "You sure you cannot stay?"

Ra'Sa shakes his head. "No, but I will return later."

Then he hesitates. "Melisa, I swear upon our matehood that I will do everything in my power to return."

My throat closes, and I barely manage to choke out, "But…"

"But if you don't hear from me within three turns of the sun, you must leave."

I let out a long breath, stopping the tears before they can start. "You will come back to us as soon as you can."

Grabbing his shirt, I pull him down and kiss him again. I savor him—beg him to return.

Once finished, I kneel to scoop up Thea and Wren. So much of them is still new to me, but they lean into me. And they reach for Ra'Sa, as if eager for the connection that flows between us all.

Starlings, he murmurs in my mind.

"Papá Rasa," Thea says. She reaches into her dress and pulls out the red stone that Ra'Sa gave her for her birthday. She holds it out to him.

"For you," she says in the human tongue.

He shakes his head, eyes wide.

"That is yours."

She waits. "It will help."

"Mine, too," Wren says quickly, also handing her stone.

His throat bobs, letting a few tears run down his cheeks.

"Gracias," [2]he says quietly.

Then he kisses.

"Goodbye," I choke.

For now, he promises.

Dawn is coming. Fighting is coming. Blood, carnage, and death.

"Strength, friend," the one called Nicolás calls to my mate.

Then Ra'Sa walks away, carrying half my heart with him.

1. Grandma isn't coming?

2. Thank you.

CHAPTER 39

RA'SA

My soul feels more cracked than whole.

So many... so many gone forever.

Today, as I walk away from my family and into the fight, I am flanked by an army of the fallen. I will wage a rebellion bloody enough to yank the gaze of the gods from their cosmic toils and focus on our wretched souls. They will watch today, and with luck, some will heed our plight. The stones of fate may sing again, a song of triumph. Those who rise from the ashes will walk into the light as free men and women.

My face turns to the sky, where a thick pillar of smoke billows.

A bitter taste coats my tongue, and my palms grow clammy.

The rebellion has begun.

I take a deep breath, taking the chill deep into my lungs.

Our entrance to Zlosa was accompanied by smoke and the burning of the slave pens. The same sign will mark our departure.

The high of killing, the anticipation and worry of what is to come is something that is nearly too much for me.

Instinct takes me to the dead giants scattered throughout the forest.

When I arrive, I halt.

This is a wasteland.

I had watched it happen, *made it happen,* but walking through it felt like being thrust into ice water. It looks like some great drake had ravaged the land.

The crushed bodies of giants are grotesque. Limbs twist at odd angles, and entrails scattered across the snow. Some must've died instantly from the blast, with one of the boulders crushing skull and face at once, while others suffered under the weight of the rock.

The sun paints them all a gruesome picture, but something stirs—something small and distinctly non-giant. It calls to me from the other end of the clearing, and I follow, stepping lightly over the carnage.

Half a dozen paces take me to the middle of the area, and I look to find one of the trees and a small human leg sticking out.

I freeze, knowing instantly whom that leg belongs to.

My jaw clenches, and I let out a huff.

Abet. He killed those who went to the meeting with me and tried to kill me. He threatened my bride. A man I had worked alongside for weeks. I had been so sure that he was a man worthy of trusting.

I had been wrong. Stupidly so.

A part of me wants to keep walking, to let him lie there.

But I hear a feeble cry for help.

It agitates my soul, which answers before my mind can object. I walk forward and drop to my knees. My hands shake from the anger and frustration, and I lift the tree.

Beneath it, Abet cries out. The sound pricks at my ears.

"I can't move," he moans.

Begrudgingly, I use my tail to wrap around his non-crushed leg and pull him out. He barks in pain, and I drop the tree and turn to him. His graying hair is caked with snow and blood, and when I kneel to grab his face, he lets out a grunt. His skin is cold to the touch.

Too cold to survive for much longer.

His lips have already gone half purple, and the bottom half of his body is entirely soaked in blood.

I look down at him, and he stares up at me, not full of ire and spite... but sadness.

"I should leave you to die," I seethe.

He stares at me, a wheezing sound coming with each breath.

"It would be the right thing to do," he responds.

I tighten my fists. "You killed men in cold blood. You tried to kill me!"

If his body weren't already so broken, I would've shaken his shoulder. Thrown him to the ground and stomped on his throat. But he continues to look up toward me, pitiful and wholly at my mercy.

All the fury and bitter words melt off of my tongue, and as I look down at him, I can only think of one single, solitary word.

"Why?"

He looks up at me and struggles to breathe. "My woman was taken by the giants a month ago. They told me that she would be questioned. They told me that if I wanted to see her alive again, then I would do as they wished."

For a second, it is just us. The breeze, the blooming morning, and two men, once friends, now enemies.

And then I think of myself. What I would do for the woman I hid in a cabin. I let the air push out of my body and swallow thickly.

I think of what the giants did to Queen Estela. How she skirted around the camp, eying the water with mistrust. I think of what they did to my sweet Melisa, how they cut her and threw her in a pit to starve. What things must they have done to this man's partner?

He leans forward and lets out a hacking cough. Blood sprays over his shirt, my pants, and the snow.

"You were a strange-looking human, but you look... right, as one of those trolls," he says a second later. "I always knew you were keeping secrets."

"I didn't think you kept secrets. I thought you were a good man when we worked together," I say.

"Good, bad, what does it matter? We all die in the end. No god is waiting to receive me in the afterlife," he labored bitterly.

"I do not relate to someone who would betray his friends," I reply.

"The giants believe they do good by their family. I did good by my family, too. She was all I had," he says after a minute.

I take a deep breath. "You did good by trying to ruin your people's chance at freedom. For what? To keep her serving under the giant's thumb?"

"To keep her living. You delude yourself into thinking that there is a life after this. We will never break free from Zlosa, troll. You should know that," he says.

I step back. "We're already breaking free."

"Lies. We may be free in the physical, but we will never escape the constant thoughts of what it was like to be here. What has happened to us will decide every action we take for the rest of our lives. And to go from one master to another sounds as good as cutting off my own toes. I stayed, and I kept my woman alive a little longer," he confesses. Each word is slower and slower to fall out of his mouth.

"I will die. And you all will die, too," he adds after a moment.

His words cut deep.

"No, I won't."

He coughs again, and more blood sprays over his dirt-crusted shirt.

I could end his suffering right here and let the ghost of his words linger in this cursed grave.

But instead, his voice sounds in my head. *You saved those men—let it be enough.*

Then compassion moves me again.

"Kill me," he requests. "It would be a kindness."

I look down at him and wonder what my father would do. Would he show mercy upon those who betrayed him? Especially one who had acted out of reasons he deemed noble?

I didn't know.

"I never told them I was suspicious of you," he says a moment later. "Most bought your story, but I knew when I looked at you. You looked like a man with a purpose, not some half-breed. Not something common in this place."

For a moment, I take in the words, and then I let out a long breath.

"Where is your woman?" I ask at last.

He coughs again, and his wheezing intensifies. "She'll be dead now."

My mouth parts. "But I thought—"

"I was meant to bring your head by midnight. They had her ready to hang."

I suck in a sharp breath. “But maybe…”

“She’s dead. I can feel it,” he chokes. “And now, I wish to follow.”

I nod, then kneel before him. "I will help you.”

The only response is another cough. The man before me is broken beyond repair. Not forgiven, but understood.

For the consideration he gave me, I would grant him compassion with the cold embrace of death.

I form a blade from the ground. The stones come slowly to my palm, pulling past the snow and causing small mounds of white ice crystals to form around my legs, burrowing me in the chill. My hand wraps around the makeshift handle with ease, one that has come to me as I trained over a lifetime of stone bending, and then I plunge it into his heart. There is one last gurgle as the light leaves his eyes.

All that is left is a mangled vessel.

Pushing back to my feet, a bittersweet emotion takes over my senses. I look around at the dead bodies of giants scattered around him.

Being left out to rot among enemies would be a disgraceful end. I am unsettled. Though Abet betrayed me, leaving him out here would speak more of me than him. He acted in cruelty. I do not wish to—not like this.

So I step back and call upon my power once more. The sluggishness is concerning, but I dig and push him into a shallow grave. Once he is covered, I let out a long breath.

My eyes return to the vast sky, where Grutabela lives in the distance. I don't know if I have enough strength to hope that he goes to a place of peace, but I ask the goddess to guide him where he belongs.

My love, are you well? Melisa's voice emerges from the depths of my mind.

Hearing her voice tugs at something fragile inside of me.

Well enough, I say back. *Has anyone turned up on your doorstep?*

A few women. We are making do with the space we have, but I worry.

I take a deep breath and close my eyes.

I worry, too.

Ra'Sa, Melisa starts.

Yes?

There are two comfort women. They didn't come with us when we escaped last time. Daria is a comfort woman in the northern lumber yards. Alisa lives near her. Will you get them?

Yes, Ruh'flor. *Take care of our little Thea and Wren. Please, be well, and remember what I told you. If you don't hear from me in three days…*

A kind hand brushes through the bond in acknowledgment, and then she leaves me. The loss of her sweet voice in my head is unwanted, but it is for the best. I must focus. A little time apart now will soon be rewarded with a life together.

Weary and tired, I walk toward the slave pens. Crossing the fence, I walk inside and find humans everywhere. A group of men are huddled in the middle, and I ask, "Report. Who knows anything about the smoke?"

A few turn back, but I'm surprised to see Felip guzzling water. He is utterly winded, probably from running.

"Rasa," he says, standing. "El Lobo sends word. They are burning the barracks."

"Good. Keep evacuating to ensure we can all leave."

We have few supplies and even fewer people who can be spared to help.

Still, those available nod and get to work. Men and women hurry through the structures, yelling for others to come.

Humans pour out of houses and follow the small group of men. I let them go and start preparing for the upcoming conflict.

Those who stay behind sharpen the dull tools upon rocks and boulders that I conjure. I lay out our old plan and even run exercises to show them how to defend against an enemy.

We gather and scavenge and plunder and train for hours until the sun passes the midpoint in the sky.

And then, someone arrives at the other side of the barricade.

"Blue one!" a human voice yells.

I move through the horde of men and supplies toward the wooden structure made of tables, chairs, benches, and parts of roofs.

I climb to the top to see El Lobo.

My eyes go wide.

"Friend! You live!" I call down.

"Not for long," he retorts with a chuckle.

Blood covers his face and hands, and he doesn't even try to wipe it off. He stands there, some giant warrior's spear in hand, and looks me over, from my head to my feet.

"It looks like you've also fought hard, no?" he calls up.

I look behind him at the four men accompanying him. They all are equally bloody, but some are burned.

"There are a few materials for healing inside here. Come," I reassure.

He sucks his teeth. "Thank you."

They make quick work of climbing.

“The fires still burn, reducing what is left of those damned quarters to ash,” El Lobo begins. “Many were lost in the attack on the barracks. But many more giants are gone, thanks to your idea."

We climb back down, and I brush the snow and splinters from my pants.

When I turn, El Lobo shakes his fist to the sky. "The bastards thought they would squash us like a bug, and we went straight for their throat. May Khuohr forsake them in the afterlife for their weakness!"

I laugh at his exuberance. My own gods are a pair of powerful, righteous deities. I couldn't imagine what it would be like to be cast out of our afterlife, Vidalena, for the ache would be too great to tell. To be separated from my Enduar family would be a fate worse than death.

After a moment, I change the subject and ask, “Do you need help in the city?”

“No. Even after the purges, we are still outnumbered by the giant warriors, three to one. This is not a battle that will be easily won, and we need to start mobilizing to escape.”

“Right you are,” I respond.

He walks at my side, closer to the groups of men practicing their knife skills.

“Otherwise, we will be a bunch of humans lost in the forests, waiting for the giants, wolves, and whatever creatures lurk between the trees to pick us off,” he says with a laugh.

I hum in agreement as we walk back to the pile of supplies that the humans had gathered before sending the women off with my Melisa.

“We have already sent humans to the old meeting place. They won’t be safe there for long.”

El Lobo shakes his head. "No, they won't."

"However, we could spare a few men, they could start the journey to the Enduar Mountains early," I say. I observe his expression—no one save Melisa has explicitly told me they wanted to go there. Their eagerness for a human queen has caused me to assume it, but I do not wish to take anyone who does not want to go.

The men before me are silent for a long moment. El Lobo's jaw tenses and releases several times. I take a deep breath, counting the seconds before he opens his mouth.

"That is wise. We will consider such things—but we won't be able to get them out for a few days," he says decidedly.

"Excellent," I say measuredly. "Thank you for the barracks. No giants came to change guard this morning, and we spent the time gathering anything we could find. Food, tools, supplies, and the like. Some of it is piled up there, where you'll find herbs and bandages." I gesture to a large pile of tools.

Honestly, I don't know how the men found so much since the tools I used in the lumber yards were always carefully monitored.

The one with the burns thanks me and rummages through for bandages to bind his wounds.

"Any new clothes?" one of the men with El Lobo asks.

I point at one of the men passing by, a few blankets in his arms.

"You!" I call. "Where are the other supplies?"

The man visibly flinches as I call to him. He nods meekly and then points to a house on the far wall. I thank him and take the rebellion leader over with me.

El Lobo is silent as he inspects everything.

I look at the pitiful piles of things stacked up—holed blankets, meager clothes, buckets, and large stretches of oiled fabric. Tent canvas, I realize.

No food, but hollowed gourds for water. My heart races. How the hell will we survive a week of walking and camping with this?

The men at my side aren't so easily discouraged.

"This is an excellent start," El Lobo says. Then he turns to me, graying hair looking like strands of silver in the weak light. The curve of his spine looks less noticeable, but there is still a slight limp to his step.

I meet his eyes, trying to ignore the twinge of dread in my gut. These men aren't warriors, or hunters, or fighters. They are strong, but their bodies have been broken repeatedly, and they lack technique.

"I think we should use these slave pens as stockpiles. We'll be heading to the other dozen pens that remain. We will liberate them, take their supplies, and bring them here."

Unease stirs inside me.

"Each will be harder than the last. This one was easy because they did not know we were coming. The same grace won't be extended to us twice. It will be a bloody way ahead," I say grimly.

El Lobo and the men around him shift their weight uneasily. Then, a young one in the back speaks up.

"You are right, but the life our kind has been forced to live for over a century must stop. The simpering half-life of serving others must stop."

My heart clenches. "I agree."

"So we fight," El Lobo states firmly.

I nod.

"Everything is in chaos right now. We should go to the next pen while the giants are still reeling," I suggest.

The men behind him nod in unison.

"It will help spread the word of our cause to the other humans, too," another man chimes in.

I agree, "Let us gather the men."

Chapter 40

Melisa

Nine Days Later,

Smoke continues to billow up around Zlosa, far worse than when we arrived. Hundreds of women have been gathering in our secluded area, spilling out from the small, broken cabin and into the surrounding forest.

Mercifully, Ra'Sa sent word before his three day mark.

The rebellion must be going well, for we are mostly left alone. I try not to think about the worst while I spend my days watching Wren and Thea and tending to more wounded with melted snow and all the leaves we can forage.

By day five, the hundreds had turned into around two thousand. Worry pierced my heart over the increasing numbers and limited resources, but then an army of human men appeared, weary and armed, and said they would begin the trek to Enduvida.

Small mercies. And within a day, the forest was mostly empty of people.

They asked me to go with them—said their leader requested that I leave with the girls.

I didn't need to ask to know who they meant.

Ra'Sa.

I couldn't. Not yet. Not when no one would make me feel as safe as Ra'Sa.

So, even as our camps slowly fill up again with women and children, I work hard to help feed them with what we scavenge and the men hunt. We make *sopa de carne*[1] and *bola de hoja*[2] until I can't see straight. Then, just like the first group, they leave.

However, Daria and Alisa are still missing. Ra'Sa's voice is quiet, and his absense drenches me in unease.

This morning, the girls act like little fleas, clinging to my legs as I help to tend to a woman who arrived with cuts up and down her back. Another comes in with one of her arms half gone, and I send the girls away so I can stitch her up with a makeshift needle.

The blood makes me nauseous, but I try to remember the animals that I cared for in my old life. Blood doesn't mean death. I can help them with the few skills I know.

Luckily, a woman named Maria arrived yesterday, and she knows all about the medicinal herbs the forest provides. She brings leaves that help to ease the pain and moss covered in sap to bandage the wounds.

After cleaning the blood from my hands and apron, I go over to a woman who looks too sick or weak to walk. Maria and I try to feed her, but she is old. Her eyes sink into their sockets, and several teeth are missing.

I fear she will die.

It hits me in an unexpected way. The sudden, bloody deaths that the giants dole out are horrible. They tear at my heartstrings. But… watching someone slowly fade away, utterly helpless against the call of death, prolongs my pain. Perhaps some part of her reminds me of my mother.

Does Griselda still live?

Over my lifetime, I'd had a thousand different emotions toward this woman. Fear, love, jealousy, anger, desperation to be loved… to be accepted. I'm still raw from the rejection.

And at the end of the day, it doesn't matter. She made her choice. I should feel guilty for not grieving her more, but those words she spoke still echo in my mind.

I don't hate her. I just… hope she finds the peace she never found as my mother.

I hurry back outside to find some of the herbs Maria was cutting on an old stump. Thea and Wren play with Coco in the snow, tossing loose balls of snowflakes and giggling with delight. Seeing it gives me pause, for I'd observed their playtimes so infrequently.

"*¿Tienen hambre?*"[3] I call.

They look up and shake their heads. The light-haired young man, Nicolás, leans against the tree and watches them.

I nod to him and return to the cabin. When I reach the door, I sway.

"Gods, I didn't realize how tired you are," Maria comments, coming up to steady me.

"I'm fine," I start.

"Go—sleep."

"Call if you need me," I respond reluctantly.

Maria walks away, and I find a spot next to the dying woman. It isn't ideal, but it is calm. I sit, and somehow the girls also find their way to my side. I smile, letting them curl up on my lap. Once settled, I begin braiding their now-sweaty hair.

Once finished, I press their heads to my shoulders, holding them as I had ached to do many times in the last three years. They aren't babies anymore, but I will take every second I could get.

"Mamá," Wren says. "When is Papá Rasa coming back?"

My heart squeezes. I didn't know. He'd been gone for over a week now, and I could see the distant effects of the war he waged against the giants. I loved and hated him for being as powerful as he was. I wished that he could be here with me.

"I don't know," I say back to them in the human tongue.

Then Thea announces, "He's all right."

I look down at her, my heart full of tenderness.

"Oh? How do you know that?"

She confidently looks to me, "He promised us he would come back."

The trust on her face is a blade cleaving my heart in half.

"He did promise that," I say softly.

Then Wren holds me tighter. "Is he our papá?"

My throat closes. Then I hear his words, *"Your daughters will be my daughters, my starling children promised to me by the stones of fate."*

"He… is," I say softly.

They both smile, snuggling further into my arms.

"You are so soft," Thea continues.

I brush back loose strands of her straight black hair and kiss her head. I feel like a woman fraudulently playing a part, yet I am filled with gratitude.

Being with them hurts and heals me all at once.

I close my eyes, ignoring the places where my body begins to tingle and prickle from their weight, and let myself doze.

Melisa?

I bolt upright to noise outside our camp. The girls wake up disoriented, their hair messy, and then ask me what's happening.

Ra'Sa? I ask.

Yes. I've been trying to speak to you for a while—

I cut him off before he can finish.

You're back?

Something in my chest stirs. Yearning, beckoning me in the distance. I stand, holding them as I make my way out of the cabin.

The sight nearly brings me to my knees.

An entire group of men and women stand outside, led by Ra'Sa. Wren and Thea see him at the same time because they both scream, "Papá Rasa!"

I let them down as they run to him.

His head snaps up, looking at them with the most beautiful, open expression. Soul-splitting joy blossoms on his face as he kneels, ready to catch them in his arms. He's glamoured and covered in soot and blood, but they don't care. He holds them close, eyebrows drawn together as they throw their arms around his neck.

Behind him, I see an array of brightly colored dresses among the slave clothing. My heart lurches as I realize they are comfort women.

Chestnut, black, and deep red hair flow over their shoulders—half tangles, half waves. I recognize many of them from washing. Each face passes quickly as I look for my two friends whom I couldn't help the last time I was in Zlosa.

And then I see them: Alisa and Daria. I smile, waving in their direction, as they nod and make their over. Holding hands, though Alisa carries a sack.

I smile, grinning to see them together again.

Ra'Sa and the girls catch up to me first. Somehow, the tall man finds a way to sweep a hand behind my back despite holding Thea and Wren. I barely have a chance to gasp when he catches my mouth in a kiss.

I let myself fall into him, working through the layers of fierce longing I'd had over the last week. Even when his mouth pulls away, he keeps me close to his body, between the girls.

They begin to chatter along in the human tongue, telling Ra'Sa about the women we helped and the things they found.

He's exhausted. That much is easy to see. But he smiles and nods along to Thea and Wren.

"I told you it wouldn't be goodbye," I say.

Finally, he looks back at me and gives me a slow smile. One that is as sturdy as him.

"Forgive me, I couldn't return sooner," he says softly. "But I promise not to leave again."

My heart picks up speed. "Really?"

He nods. "Melisa, I've brought the women back with me," Ra'Sa says.

I push up on my toes to kiss him.

"Daria and Alisa. Thank you—truly." My head automatically turns, looking to watch as Alisa drops the heavy sacks on the ground with a grunt as the weight eases off her body.

"What's this?" I ask.

"Food. For the voyage to Enduvida," she says gently.

I don't miss the way that their gazes travel to Ra'Sa. Wary. Biting both lips, I bend over and open one of the sacks.

The sound of women settling around us fills my ears as I uncover vegetables, loaves of bread from gods knows where, and hard cheeses. The round, partially carved wedges are glossy in the afternoon light.

Cheese is a delicacy. Slowly, my head rises.

"Where did you get this?" I ask.

Alisa smirks before walking past me. "Forik won't miss it."

I grin and throw my arms around her.

It's awkward—we've never hugged—but she doesn't pull away. In fact, Daria joins us.

"I'm so glad you both made it out," I say, still smiling.

Once we break away, I turn back to Ra'Sa.

"We will find you later," Daria says quickly, before going with the other women to set up a place to sleep.

I toss a quick, 'see you then' over my shouldber but stay frozen, entranced by the scene before me. The girls have been let down from my mate's shoulders and arms and now play with the two crystals they had given him before leaving.

My heart burns as I watch the display. They whisper words into the gems as if they could imbue them with blessings.

Strange girls, we humans are not ones protected by some patron god or icon. I almost tell them that.

But something holds me back.

The world they will grow up in is a world I have never known.

When Coco arrives and snuggles into the girls, Ra'Sa pulls me to the side of the house and wraps me in his arms again as he sits on one of the makeshift chairs. I'm sure it will snap under the weight of both of us, but it stays strong as he holds me.

Beneath me, he relaxes as if I were his safe place, too.

All of this is new. Both intrinsically right and terrifyingly unknown. Every path I could take would end up with him, with us as a family.

I ease back, resting my head in the space between shoulder and chin.

"I've missed you," I admit.

Ruh'flor, *smelling your scent is a joy as sweet as a feast after weeks of boiled grains,* he murmurs into my mind.

The weariness in his voice, even through our minds, worries me.

How is the rebellion progressing? I venture to ask at last.

I feel him groan at the question.

We gain a little and then lose… too much. We've visited eleven of the twelve remaining slave pens across Zlosa. The slaves are mostly prepared when we arrive, but that means the giants are as well.

My throat goes dry.

You aren't hurt, are you?

He hums, and I feel the sound reverberate through his throat and into the side of my face.

No, my love.

I pause at the title but then ease. Love. We'd already said that to each other. I could grow used to such names.

Others are far worse off than I will ever be. So much slaughter. This morning…

His words trail off, and images pass through our bond. I see the smoke, the blackened bodies of women and men alike. I see the cleaved limbs and blood-soaked ground. A part of me wants to look away, but I can't.

You've saved so many. I hope you think of that just as much as you think of those left behind. Perhaps death is a kinder place for them than life right now.

Ra'Sa's disagreement is palpable through the bond.

Then he lets out a long breath. The warm air tickles my throat, and his hand tightens around my midsection.

We sink back into silence, but small flickers of what he's seen continue to pass through our bond as he just sits there. I can feel that he doesn't sleep.

The berserker's fury displayed across the painted face of a giant slips through, as do the bodies that fall to the earth. Some of the visions are cloudy. I see women, the *Brujas*, I think, arriving at the pens. I see the dead rise from the ground, but the vision clouds and fades too fast.

The sight of dead men walking once more makes my skin prickle, but I let it all come through, not wanting Ra'Sa to hold back or protect me. He does that enough.

I can share some of the weight of his burden.

"You need to sleep," I say.

He sighs.

"There is a tent in the forest. Take the girls. They didn't nap today. I will finish my chores and join you."

He smiles weakly. "Are you sure?"

"Rest now," I reply firmly.

"Thea, Wren!" I beckon the girls. They bound over obediently. "Show Ra'Sa to the tent. I need to help get the meal started."

They grin and do just that.

1. Meat stew.

2. An edible leaf ball.

3. Are you hungry?

CHAPTER 41

RA'SA

R*A'SALORE,* Melisa's voice fills my mind. *Come!* Already shifted and mind hazy, I bolt up. The two girls nestled next to me, and I growl at the furry addition when I find the wolf has joined us.

Then I hear a scream.

Thea wakes up first and starts to cry.

Fuck, I think as I lunge forward and pull them close.

"Shh, it's all right. I'm here," I tell them, trying to quiet them as the wolf goes on high alert. She paws at each girl, nudging them with her nose. Red light shines outside the tent.

No. No, no, no.

Melisa. The women. The men.

I haul Thea and Wren out of the tent with me and immediately see burning torches and spears. The air smells of blood.

Melisa! I call out.

I'm here. In the cabin, she responds. *Get the girls to me. They'll be safe inside.*

The girls cling to me, and the wolf circles in front of us, protective and alert. We leave behind all the belongings in the tent, and I take off sprinting toward the structure.

"We're going to your mother," I say soothingly as the girls hang cling to my neck. "I'm going to leave you with her, and then I'll get rid of the bad people."

When I reach the back of the cabin, the screams undercut the goodbye as I set them both down. They cry, but the wolf comes between us. She nuzzles them away from me, away from the fighting, and up to the back door.

"Stay down. I will return," I promise as someone opens the door, but I run back to the fighting.

Ra'Sa, the girls are here. Are you okay? Melisa asks. An ugly lick of fear paints her voice. It shreds my insides into ribbons.

Just let me take care of this. It will be fine.

People are dying, is her only response.

The words gut me, and I sprint toward the fighting. Even though interrupted, sleep did me good. I can feel it in the quick return of my magic. I feel the feet pound against the ground, the way the giants beat against the rock with more force than the humans.

I count, finding an entire squadron of forty giants racing across the ground. I also feel the fire heat the stone in the ground.

When I burst through the trees and into the light, the ground beneath us is already covered with oil. They mean to burn us, just as we have done to them time and time again in the last week.

Several men run to me, including Nicolás and Felip. Felip has already helped me with several raids, so I give him simple instructions.

"Spread out, don't allow yourself to be caged in. Stab just as quickly as you dodge." Then I add, "Ignore the fallen. There will be time to mourn them after—right now is for the surviving."

Nicolás nods alongside Felip with a sharpened ax.

I draw up a new weapon from the stony earth and lift it high.

I let out a bellow, wishing for a proper battle song.

Memories sing the beats back to me as I jump into the bloodbath. As I hack and slice, men fall, and the closer I get to the cabin where Melisa is hiding with the weapon.

I'm coming soon, I reassure repeatedly, despite the fear I feel flooding through her.

Using my stone bending, I blow back the oil barrels and clear heads off shoulders. It's all become so awfully normal. With each death, I don't feel regret or joy. I feel relief that one less threat exists for my people and me.

After the first wave of giants are slaughtered, another pours out of the trees. This time, my men start to fall. Each life slips through my fingers, part shock and part rage. When I look up, I see my mate watching me through the cracks in the door.

Get out of sight! I yell down the bond.

Ra'Sa, behind you!

Three giants come near me, cornering me in a copse of trees. I look up to them and slash just as one of them runs and crashes atop me. He flattens me to the ground, and I gasp as the air is knocked out of me. I can hardly fight back as he drags me by the hair through the snow to the center of the fighting. Around me, there are bodies stacked atop each other and men bound with ropes.

The ground beneath us is wet with snow, oil, and blood.

It's not a good combination for burning, but the giants don't care. They look at me with their fury-raged eyes. Multiple sets of hands hold me down as they press spears into my back and bind me with ropes to other men.

It's an ugly, gruesome sight.

When I try to stand, one of the warriors kicks me in the legs hard enough to fall. My bones crack, and the Fuegorra in my chest bursts into light.

"Fucking cave rat!" one of the giant's roars and signals to another giant as I writhe and pant through the pain. "Over here! Burn him first! And you get inside that godsdamned shed! There are more hiding in there!"

I start to panic through the agony and throbbing from the Fuegorra's healing. The slick, chilled oil splashes over me as I thrash against the bindings.

When I look up, I see Melisa's moved and is now standing outside the doorway.

My heart lurches, and I want to throw myself in front of her, hide her from the men who threaten to kill us all.

Run, I cry through the bond.

CHAPTER 42

MELISA

He told me to stay hidden.

When Thea and Wren arrived at the cabin, I was relieved. But something tugs me outward, toward the fighting.

Maria comes to my side, drawing the girls away. Her mouth opens, but press my finger to my mouth.

Some of Ra'Sa's men are at the back of the cabin, carrying the wounded out. Maria leaves me and watches as the girls huddle in the corner with Coco.

I'm tugged to the outside again.

Ra'Sa? I ask.

No response.

I cross from the door to Thea and Wren. I kiss them both and say, "Don't move from here. You understand? Stay with Maria."

Maria starts to protest, but I hear another scream.

"I'll be right back," I promise and let go.

Please, I pray to any god who will listen. *Keep them safe.*

I return to the other side of the cabin. From the cracks in the crudely covered windows, I see the men surrounded in the center of the field in front of us. The giants hoist spears towards them while others pour vats of what looks like water over them.

The iridescent sheen glints in the light from torches.

Fuck. Not water, I realize. *Oil.*

My hands go cold. They're going to burn them alive.

"They're going to kill them!" I panic, my voice tinging on hysterical.

Some of the people in the room spare me a look, but most continue to move more bodies out the back door, away from the massacre.

"Do something," I beg, rushing to two men carrying a woman out.

"I am sorry," one of them says. "We have to escape."

My heart races.

So what? I'm just supposed to be in this room, watching as they burn my mate to death?

It would... Gods, it would destroy me. It would destroy my body and soul.

"Melisa," Maria's voice sounds behind me. She grabs my hand.

"Come sit."

Shaking my head, I yank out of her grip, and then push to the door. A new warrior almost cuts my mate in half.

My gaze meets Ra'Sa's, and he shouts, *Get out of sight!*

Ra'Sa, behind you! I cry.

He heeds me, but not fast enough, and I'm forced to watch as they bind him.

For the last three years, I've been humiliated, treated and used like a thing rather a person. Degraded so many fucking times.

Then, they pour the oil on Ra'Sa.

This stops here.

I want a future. This is my choice. My plan.

I grab the knife we've been using for cooking and step outside into the cold. The snow burns through my boots, and I trudge forward into the blood bath.

Ra'Sa sees me. He always does.

Run! he shouts.

I ignore him.

The waking nightmare starts slowly, with a tingling in my hands. If I could, I would run. But I can't.

"Warriors!" I call out with the last bits of breath that fill my lungs, fixing a smile on my lips.

This is insane. You're insane. What is wrong with you?

I'm saving the ones I love, I bark to the harsh voice in my head.

I take it all in: the light of the deadly flames they hold, ready to be dropped atop the oil split across the men, the humans, and my mate.

"Oh, mighty warriors!" I shout again while stepping into the light.

More than half the warriors lie dead but the remaining giants turn toward me, one by one.

Some recognize me. One even whistles.

Time slows, yet my heart thunders in my chest.

You are strong. You are fierce. You are capable.

Yes.

I fucking am.

Melisa, RUN! Ra'Sa's voice shouts through the bond again, but my hand is already raised, dagger poised at the neckline of my dress.

"You fight so well. You all deserve a treat," I call as I bring the blade down, slicing through cloth and thread. The bodice opens up, my breasts spilling out and the cold stinging every inch of my now exposed flesh.

Mi amor,[1] *you have two seconds to kill every last one,* I say as they all stare at me, thoroughly engrossed in how the fabric flutters open.

I don't shrink away or try to cover myself.

Ra'Sa doesn't make me wait. Hardly a blink of an eye passes before he manages to stand. His hands snap out to either side of his body, breaking his bindings with his palms facing straight up.

The ground around us lurches, the top layer roiling into a wave. I lose my balance as it passes under me, rending the ground, and we all fall like dominoes, all, that is, save Ra'Sa.

He limps, and yet, his magic is stronger than ever. As he commands the stone beneath us, it bursts out of the ground, spraying snow and extinguishing the flames. Rock parts, splits, and cracks. Those jagged bits, broken as I once had been, form themselves into weapons that pierce and shred.

It all starts to rotate around him in a lethal tornado.

I watch in awe as the broken shards prove more effective than blades crafted by weapon masters.

The giants who still stand, a measly six in total, try to scatter. But every jagged piece of rock finds a home in the body of a warrior.

The giants drop like falling leaves in autumn.

Once the screams fade, I let out a long breath, finally covering my exposed chest.

Ra'Sa's arms are around me in a second, scooping me off the ground, pulling his coat over my bare chest and pressing my face to his.

"I'm so sorry, *Ruh'flor*," he says into the side of my head. He doesn't approach me tenderly in grief. He loves so fiercely, so thoroughly that it puts a blanket around my fragile heart.

All of my emotions continue to spiral and storm inside of me, but I don't get swept out to sea; I remain right there in my mate's arms.

"You shouldn't have done that," he says. His words aren't accusations; they are cracking with pain as if he could only seem to see the alternate universe where I am lying on the ground and not Maria.

"They were going to kill you," I weep. "I couldn't let that happen. Not for me, and not for the girls. We depend on you."

He cries out, and I grab his face, pressing his lips to mine. Just to know what he tastes like once again. He kisses me deeply, ravaging my lips with his need to have me close.

I'm the first to pull back to look at the men around us.

"I love you," I pant.

Ra'Sa brushes my back.

"I will not leave your side again," I say firmly.

He sighs, then helps me stand. "Fine, stubborn woman." His hand lingers on my back a second longer.

Humans have already started to search the makeshift battlefield, helping to carry the wounded and bury the dead.

Ra'Sa holds his hands out in front of him, using his magic to create an impression deep in the ground.

Afterwards, we make our way through the chaos. Ra'Sa is ever watchful, his gaze darting back and forth, his senses attuned to the slightest hint of danger.

Nicolás comes running a second later. "Rasa!"

My mate's body tenses. "What's happened?"

“We found this on one of the giants," he says, handing a ragged parchment to Ra'Sa.

Ra'Sa takes the note, his eyes scanning the words, his lips tightening into a grim line.

"The king has left Zlosa," Ra'Sa reads aloud, his voice low. “Fektir tried to kill him.”

I look at him, my heart pounding in my chest. “Really?”

“We must move quickly," Ra'Sa says, his gaze locked on the note. “Rholker’s departure is crucial for King Teo. I must send another message to let him know."

I nod, swallowing hard. "What should I do?"

Ra'Sa turns to me, his eyes filled with determination. "Help the others pack. We leave Zlosa as soon as possible. Without the king, this war is done. We won.”

Nicolás catches onto the words and lets out a whoop. He runs back through the crowd, thrusting his fist.

“*¡Por la libertad!*”[2] he screams.

Humans stop their jobs while others come out of hiding. They all start to shout alongside us.

My mouth parts, scarcely believing it all. I’d come here with a plan… nothing had turned out how I’d imagined.

It was better.

And now we were going home. All of us.

My eyes scan the forests, the blood, the burning torches, and broken boulders.

Ra’Sa takes my hand and pulls me along.

We raise our hands together, screaming the phrase with the other humans.

“¡Por la libertad! ¡Por la libertad!”

For freedom.

My heart sings as I look back at the capital. It seems so far away from here. Barely visible.

Coco leads Thea and Wren to us before we can seek them out. They are shaken and pale, but I don't fear when I hold them close. I know I'm exactly where I am meant to be.

It is time to leave this all behind for a fresh start.

Finally.

1. My love.

2. For freedom!

1ST EPILOGUE

RA'SA

Travel is slow but graciously uneventful. Days pass, and more humans join us along the way.

Every night, we stop for camp and leave messages for others still traveling behind us.

With thousands of humans scattered and traveling along the way to the mountain, I feel the pressure of responsibility and the shame of falling short.

It keeps me focused.

I refuse to allow myself peace even when the black mountains come clear into view. Even when we pass through the ice passage and the frozen sea, I don't let my alert drop.

Melisa, the girls, and I walk alongside each other at the front of the group. Guiding us into a new life.

Feelings from long ago return.

I had once brought my mother and brother to this cave, knowing that once I stepped inside, nothing would be the same. The same is true again tonight. Once we cross that barrier, our futures will be irrevocably changed.

There is no question whether or not I will accept this new fate.

It happened the moment I laid eyes on the beauty at my side, my cave flower—meant to blossom below ground. I did not even know it then, as it manifested into protectiveness.

Melisa, somehow sensing my thoughts, looks up at me. She gives me a knowing smile, but I look away, concealing the curve of my own lips.

When we are near enough for the humans to see the red veins swirling and the carved golden metal of the door, I halt.

Melisa sighs, and I feel the potent relief flow freely between us. But the girls draw close, intimidated by such a massive sight.

For the first time, observing the children at my side, I understood how the Enduar mountains could be a thing of terrifying stories.

Showing Enduvida's majesties excites me.

I cannot wait for Thea and Wren to see the Ardorflame Temple, to behold the crystals, and to hear their song. They love that simple red beryl I gave them. How much will they love to see mushrooms the size of me?

I turn back to the humans, letting the essence of the mountain seep into my pores. I feel the thrum of the magic—of my home.

"Humans, friends, brothers and sisters," I call, using the stones of the mountain to project my voice so that the thousands traveling behind will hear.

"My family and I will enter this cave. We intend to stay, but you are not obligated to do so. I know what you have heard in the past about my people, and I know some of you still believe it. Rest assured that your first act will be one of choice. Choose to join us—it matters not if just for a few nights or forever—or choose to go your own way. I will not sway your decision."

I don't wait for them to respond; I merely turn around and walk to the massive, golden entrance.

The girls run up to me.

"Papá Ra'Sa," Wren says, pronouncing my name correctly for the first time. I grin down at her. "Is it safe here?"

My eyes burn. "Very safe, my starling girl."

She looks unsure, so I say, "Would it help if I carried you in?"

Both she and Thea nod, and I scoop them up into my arms as the door opens, revealing the tunnel down to the main cavern. A girl on each arm, I begin down the walkway.

It feels like the gods themselves bless my steps. I savor the feeling, letting my eyes grow misty as Melisa walks next to us.

The faint pumping noise, the sulphuric smell, the song, the warmth; it all comes back to me in an instant.

When we reach the lights of the open cavern, it is somehow more majestic and brighter than I remember. The reds and blues dotted the ceiling, the gleam of the Enduar Palace, the glow.

It is... beautiful.

Thea lets out an excited squeal, and she grabs onto my head, using it to stabilize herself as she points at the enormous focusing crystal near the Enduar Palace.

Being home makes old feelings swirl. I wonder if my family smiles down upon me, proud of all I have accomplished in the last few months.

A part of me can't believe how much I have changed. Grown. My heart, I believe, has grown the most.

We barely reach the first main bridge before we are met by King Teo and Queen Estela.

The king looks tired, but wears all the finery of a festive meal. The queen glows.

I blink, expecting the sight to be a simple trick of my eyes. It isn't.

My gaze drops from her luminous aura to the enormous babe in her arms. It looks like a giant.

Though I tense at the sight, Estela opens her free arm wide and embraces Melisa.

"My friend. You made it home!" the queen says excitedly.

New emotions flood through our bond from Melisa. Nervousness, shyness, gratitude, relief, affection.

She doesn't trust others easily. Their display softens something inside of me. If my wife cares for the sovereigns, perhaps I could make more of an effort to tolerate them.

"We escaped," Melisa starts. "We took as many as could walk, but there are more on the road."

The queen begins inspecting Melisa, glancing at me between her and ensuring she has no cuts or bruises.

"How long were you walking for?" Queen Estela asks.

At that moment, the girls start to squirm on my shoulders, and I move to put them down. It's then that King Teo's eyes find mine.

A part of me recoils, but another part of me is just... cautious.

I nod, and he nods back.

"Well done, Lord Ra'Salore," he says quietly.

I straighten my shoulders as the women continue to talk about the journey, but then, behind the king and queen, other Enduares begin to congregate.

My mother's face catches my eye. Strange that she would be out of her home for a festival without me.

And then...

Oh gods.

A tall, angular troll stands next to my mother. His hair has faded from gray to pure white, and his body is sinewed, with some darker blue spots scattered over his face and arms. He wears crystal spectacles, and his face has deep lines.

"Pater," I gasp.

My father, flesh and bone, yet a ghost as far as I had known.

I leave the girls to stand next to Melisa, but I push forward, eyes burning, until I force myself to stop two paces before him.

"You are a phantom," I choke out.

My mother looks at me with tears in her eyes.

"Salore," she starts. "They found your father under the sea."

"But how?" I ask, confused by his smile, which is familiar yet different with age and harsh living. Guilt strikes true. "I left you to die along with Sera, Orena, and Anina."

My father shakes his head, a sadness morphing his soft expression.

"No, you didn't. Your sisters... there was no way to save them. But they called on me to guard the king. It was a futile mission. We sunk into the ocean with the rest of the cities. The Ardorflames kept us alive."

Ragged breaths are torn from my chest. "And you survived."

His smile brightens. "While you have been gone, your new king, a fine man, has started to bring the battalions up from the depths."

My eyes burn, and I reach across the distance, embracing him tightly. His hands clap against my back.

"I did the best I could, but I failed. I failed Tirin," I recall through tears.

He shakes his head, and the movement rustles my ragged slave clothes.

"Please. Your mother has told me of all you have accomplished—how you have led. I am sorry you have been forced to live with such loss," he says. "I am proud of you, my son."

Over the last five decades, I have imagined what words my father would say to me. These exceed each invented scenario. My attempts to recreate him in my mind never compared to the goodness of his vibrant, loving soul.

At last, I pull away and turn behind me. There, standing a ways back, is Melisa. She watches, unsure.

Come, I beckon with both mind and hand.

"*Mater, Pater,* this is Melisa. My human mate. These are her daughters, Thea and Wren," I say joyfully.

Melisa shifts her position, but the girls hide behind her. "I know your mother. We met while she was tending to her mushrooms."

My father laughs, the sound rich and warm.

"She loves her garden. The cook Ulla has already started to use hers over the royal garden's mushrooms."

My mother preens.

"I am a woman of many talents," Mer'Leuel glows.

A part of me marvels at the sight of her. Without my father, she had shriveled with grief. Just as I had shriveled without family. Love changes people. Children. Brothers. Fathers. Mates.

Wren peeks out from behind Melisa, and my father notices. He crouches.

"My name is Ra'Tirsa," he starts in the common tongue.

Thea appears.

Then my mother kneels at his side, making herself less tall for the little ones, and says, "And I am Mer'Leuel."

The girls stare, unmoving.

"We are... Ra'Sa's parents," my father continues. "We would be your grandparents."

Wren looks up at her mother, confused by the word.

"Granparnt?" she says, tripping over the word.

My heart squeezes. Humans are pouring all around us, people getting to work, shouting for food, for houses, but I wouldn't move from this spot for the whole world.

"Abuelos," [1]Melisa clarifies in her tongue. *"Es tu abuelo, y ahí está tu nueva abuelita."*[2]

Thea and Wren grin like I've never seen them smile before.

Wren squeals, *"Lita!"*

She throws her hands around my mother's neck, and my father laughs as Thea hugs him, too.

My parents stand, holding the little ones, and I wrap Melisa in my arms.

"Come," my father says. "Let's find you a new home."

A part of me relaxes. Leaving my mother alone in her home no longer worries me. "One near yours."

"Obviously," my mother starts. Then makes a funny noise. "We'll need all the time we can with these little ones."

Wren giggles, and they join the sea of humans and Enduares.

Melisa hangs back. I turn to look at her.

"What is it, my love?" I ask.

"You have… parents," she breathes.

I nod, a smile playing on my lips.

“Will they like me?” she asks. “I don’t know how to act around them.”

A grin spreads over my face. “I will tell you what you know about my customs until I have no breath left in my body, but perhaps I should consult with the king and queen."

She tilts her head to the side. "Oh? Why?"

I smirk. "We could have classes on each other's culture."

For some reason, this makes her grin. "Do you fancy yourself a professor?"

I raise one eyebrow. "Would you like that?"

"I find your intelligence quite attractive. So yes."

The conversation feels good. Normal, after so much time of pain and uncertainty.

"Well, now I must ensure this matter is raised to the highest levels of Enduar government," I tease.

A small laugh escapes my mate’s mouth, and it turns into yet another sigh of relief.

The emotion bubbles up suddenly, moving me to speak.

"I love you," I say, marveling at the words.

"I love you, too.” Melisa grabs my hands and turns.

From here, I can see more children join Thea, Wren, and my parents.

“They didn’t make it far, did they?” Melisa says.

I laugh. “No.”

Though their play seems chaotic, it brings peace to my heart. To play out in the open, safe.

This is joy. This is freedom.

Once again, my heart… stirs.

1. Grandparents.

2. This is your grandpa and your new grandma.

2ND EPILOGUE
MELISA

One Month Later,

The *dual'moraan* and *grutaliah bondyr* ceremonies have never been performed for one person on the same day.

But today, we make history. I finally join the Enduares, along with my daughters. With Ra'Sa, we will bind ourselves to the mountain and each other for the rest of time.

The Fuegorra cavern glows red, just as it had during the *dual'moraan* ceremony I attended months ago. My daughters wear deep purple dresses that match my gown. Coco trails at my side, already sporting her own Fuegorra, while my mate holds my hand.

Ra'Sa is stunning in his deep purple clothes. He even wears a bracelet with four little charms, one for each of us, save him.

It was a gift from one of his stone benders.

We walk in procession with hundreds of others, but we are put at the front of the line, just behind Mother Liana and Estela.

King Teo, Ra'Sa's parents, Lord Vann, Mikal, and all the women who had joined me in my house this morning are following.

When we finally enter the cave, a song that I knew well, one that had called to me before I left for Zlosa, sings to me.

My eyes fill with tears. Before I left, that moment had been sad. It had reminded me of heartache and how much I missed my daughters. Now, it sings of joy, and the intricate tapestry of my life.

The rest of the procession stops just outside the cave, and all, save our witnesses, family, and friends, enter. Lord Vann hands hammers to me, Thea, and Wren. I show the girls how to hold them as Mother Liana reminds me of the instructions.

"Be very still, my children. Listen for the song that will be sung only for you. Remember that the pain of the stone will last only a moment," she says.

Thea looks up at me. "It will hurt?"

"Hardly," Ra'Sa interjects before she has a chance to grow afraid. "And I will be here the whole time. It will help you feel like you have magical powers."

Perhaps she will, I say teasingly through the bond.

Ra'Sa grins. *I would love nothing more.*

"Listen closely," I say again in the human tongue. "This is the stone of your *mamá*."

I point to the gem, almost like an old friend. And then I strike with my hammer. The jewel comes loose immediately, but the second it falls into my palm, the song blows back my hair. It glows bright as its music and rhythm blow over me with the force of autumn winds.

Thea and Wren, delighted, run away from me and deeper into the cavern. Ra'Sa and I watch, corralling when necessary until both stand near their Fuegorras.

Once all the stones are selected, Ra'Sa and I help our children break them off the wall, and then, at last, the moment we have been waiting for comes.

"Approach, friends," Estela says, her face beaming in the red light.

We do.

I present myself first, waiting with sweaty palms as the gem is placed in my chest. A flash of light pain skitters across my skin as it bonds with my soul, and then... everything blacks out. I feel myself stumble into solid arms. And then, the world comes back into focus with dazzling light and sound.

The cave looks less dark, and the song between my mate and me makes tears well in my eyes. I look at him, utterly helpless as a world of magic blooms across all five of my senses.

He smiles at me with such love.

"Look at you, blossoming like the prettiest of cave flowers," he says softly. I push onto my toes and kiss him before ushering the children forward.

Neither of them cry; they are strong and brave. Much more so than I would've been at their age.

For a second, we take in the new world.

And then Liana raises her hands again.

"Now, it is time to bind this fine family together!" she calls.

King Teo has retrieved a small, cushioned bench from gods know where and places it in front of her.

"Approach, Lady Melisa and Lord Ra'Salore. Kneel before your gods," she commands.

We move slowly, but we kneel. My heart races as Ra'Sa squeezes my hand.

"Do you accept your matehood?" Liana asks me directly. Her voice echoes through the cavern, and the words sink into my skin.

A choice.

I swallow hard, looking at Ra'Sa, and then nod. "Yes."

A knife is produced and then handed to me.

"You'll need to cut my palm," my mate explains gently.

My heart races. I think of the last time I used the knife. It had been the right choice then, too. But for a very different reason.

"I don't think I can," I say breathlessly.

Ra'Sa smiles and nods encouragingly. "You can. You are fierce, *Ruh'flor.*"

He's right. I am.

I can make new memories. New meanings.

Bravely, I press the blade to his palm. I suck in a sharp breath and slice shallowly.

Perfect, my love, Ra'Sa purrs.

I smile, and he cradles my hand, only pricking my palm instead of slicing. My blood wells.

"Join hands, my children," Mother Liana says.

We do, and then the girls join us on either side, and we hold their hands as well. Estela produces stone silk ribbons dripping with gems on both ends and wraps them around our wrists.

I watch, mesmerized. I like seeing us tied together by magic.

Then the singing starts again. The red stones around us pulse in time to the melody, twinkling like stars in a cloudless night.

"Our gods bless your union!" Liana cries. "From this day forward, you are a family blessed by the earth and the stars."

A smile spreads across my face, wide enough to hurt my cheeks. I glance at the girls and find them beaming, too.

But the ceremony isn't over.

No, it isn't my love.

Ra'Sa takes a deep breath, drawing my gaze to him.

"My beautiful, brilliant Melisa. I give myself to you in life and death. As I have in the past, I will continue to defend and protect you against all that seeks to hurt you. I will help you build and heal this family, bit by bit, until the end of my days. I love you. I promise you will never regret binding yourself to me."

His words pierce straight to my heart.

"Ra'Sa," I begin. "I love you. When I was weak, you taught me to fight. When I was afraid, you calmed my heart. I will spend the rest of my days at your side. I will give you everything I can because you are the person I choose. You are mine, and… I am yours."

Tears well up, and then the singing starts.

The crystals reverberate around us, singing of joy, life, and celebration of love. I let it all cascade around me.

I kiss my mate once again, and then, the ceremony is complete, and we stand. Coco nudges my knee and Estela helps us unwrap our hands before hugging the girls.

Somewhere along the way, Ra'Sa's parents join us on both sides. I see Mer'Leuel looking at me, weeping.

I smile at her tender heart. My mother's heart was never so soft.

She wraps an arm around my shoulder.

"Welcome to my family," she says loudly, over the singing. "You know I lost my daughters long ago."

My throat tightens.

"I am just glad to have gained another."

I grin and pull her close.

“I am honored,” I say, loud as I can through the emotion clogging my throat.

She squeezes my shoulder and then pulls away, joining her mate.

The moment swells and shifts, and then, I find myself back in Ra’Sa’s arms. Thea and Wren have gone with Arlet, while Coco stands at Estela’s brother Mikal’s side.

My eyes turn back to my mate just as cheers echo from the outside.

I don't know if I've ever believed in omens, but this one seems like a good one.

Ra’Sa picks me up and spins me around.

"You are my husband!" I say, letting the laughter bubble up. Words that I never thought could be true.

"I am your mate," Ra'Sa says. "And you, my sweet love, have given me everything I've ever wanted."

"You have done the same for me.”

The music continues to swell, and then we walk out of the cave and into our new life.

"We should get the girls," he says, looking back to find them with his parents.

I hesitate. I’d made arrangements to have the evening to ourselves.

“Later. Your mother will watch over them at the feast,” I say brightly.

Ra’Sa focuses on me, and my heart skips a beat.

It has been a while since we’ve been alone, and while I don't begrudge my new life, I want to have him all to my self.

His eyes blazed. "Your wish is my command, *Ruh’flor*."

From that moment, it takes a small eternity to thank and hug the well-wishes from our guests.

Once out of the caverns, we break from the group, heading to a little home three houses down from his mother's dwelling. He picks me up, carrying me in his arms as he opens the door.

I laugh at the silliness of it all.

The simple bliss.

My laughter stops when I look at the ground and find the sticks and stones the girls and I arranged a few days earlier. Usually, he picks up our messages when he returns.

But this one was simple and sweet…

Ra'Sa meets my eye and gives me a shy smile.

My heart almost explodes as he takes me through the threshold.

And then the door shuts and I hear nothing of the outside world.

Everything smells like us. Gems the girls have already started hoarding and gifts from others are strewn about, and we walk past the living room and into the largest bedroom with a deliciously large bed—one that has had far, far too few uses.

Ra'Sa lets out a feral sound that emboldens me as we walk in. He closes the door behind him and walks to the bed, sitting down.

"Well, wife. We have arrived," he all but purrs.

I grin. "We have, husband."

He takes his time looking around the room and then setting his sights on me.

"What now?"

Heat flashes over my body.

"Take off your clothes," I say slowly. My heart races, and my breath mimics a stacatto. I want to enjoy this. I want both of us to love this.

Ra'Sa follows my directions perfectly. He starts with the fabric around his neck and then unbuttons the shirt that wraps across his body. He neatly places each article on a chair near the wardrobe. I watch the flex of his muscles, admire the jewels glinting in his ears, and admire the length of his hair. It has already grown long again, and he wears it in a low bun on the nap of his neck.

"May I approach?" he asks slowly.

I fight the smile that tugs at my lips. Not because his words are funny but because I deeply enjoy this part.

"Only if you help me with my dress," I say.

He does. He crosses the room in a second but doesn't envelop me. Instead, he hums and the stones around our room light and glow. He's so talented with his song, and it reaches deep inside of me. It coaxes out new depths that make my skin burn and my core tighten. My toes curl as the friction of fabric sliding against my skin makes my nipples harden and cheeks flush.

Once he's finished, and I sit there on the bed, I continue.

"Lay down," I say softly. Breathlessly.

He does. His long blue tail, splaying out to the side.

I look at it. Thinking of how it wrapped around me. Holding me tight.

What other wonders could it be used for?

My cheeks flush.

"What are you thinking of?" Ra'Sa demands.

I blink, and I feel my skin grow hotter.

"I think I would enjoy it if you bound my hands and held me tight today," I say.

A predatory smile spreads across his face. He sits up and reaches for me.

"Whatever you'd like," he says, and then wraps me up and pulls me close to him.

The feel of our skin pressed together heightens my arousal. Gods, he envelops me. Safe. So safe. So held together.

The soft, suede tail binds my hands around my back as he kisses me. I grind against his hips, feeling the slickness there. He growls into my mouth. He kisses my jaw, my earlobe, my neck, and then my collarbone.

When he returns to my neck, I feel half insane with desire.

"I'm ready, Ra'Sa. Fill me," I command. He smiles and then does that as well.

The sensation is sweet, but it is not quite as sweet as the knowledge that he complies to my wishes so eagerly.

The pressure at my entrance gives way to such exquisite fullness. It is beautiful.

"Yes," I sigh.

His lips return to mine as he moves. And then, slowly, I find them back at my throat. He presses on my tender skin in the exact location where his own mating marks show.

May I?

How could I have bound my life with his in every way while my neck remains unmarked?

I wanted it all.

"You may," I say softly.

I can feel the way his heartbeat races, pressed against my chest. When he returns to the spot, his movements are more frantic, more desperate. He moves too fast. This will be over before I finish. The thought makes me want to cry. The pressure, the fullness, the closeness, I can't let it end yet.

"Ra'Sa," I say, breathless at the pressure at the side of my throat increases. "This feels good. Don't come yet."

He grunts his acknowledgment as the pressure gives way to sharp pain in my neck. His movements slow, becoming more even as he licks the hurt. When he removes his mouth from my skin, I see his lips are slightly purple.

"Like this?" he asks.

"Yes," I pant.

He groans and presses further into me. The slide of his skin against mine is beautiful.

"Gods, I haven't ever had it this good. Don't let it end," I moan.

So he doesn't. He works and waits, sweating, desperate for me as we work ourselves back to the precipice of my climax.

When we reach it, and I start to fall, it comes with a cry.

"Melisa," he begs, "now?"

I grab his face and pull him back down.

"Yes, *please*."

And then he releases my bindings and finishes with me.

I will never tire of the sweet, heart-stopping moments like this.

I will never tire of *him*—the stony-faced troll who cut his hair and became a human because I asked him. The one who crossed the world to protect me. The man who became a father to my daughters.

"Ra'Sa, thank you—for everything."

He smiles, studying my face and only letting his eyes drop to the new mating marks on my neck for a second. "I would do it all again for a moment in your arms, *Ruh'flor*."

My heart flutters with an emotion I never thought I'd feel.

"I love you," I whisper.

He draws me close to him, stroking my skin.

"I love you, too."

And what a miraculous thing that is.

The end… for now.

If you enjoyed To Defend a Bride*, please take a moment to leave a rating or review—it really makes a difference! Book four,* To Beguile a Bride*, will be releasing in March, 2025! Join me for the start to Arlet and Vann's duet.*

MORE BY DANIELA A. MERA

I have a lot of different works! Check them out below:

Legends of Love

New Adult Urban Fantasy Romance

(co-authored by Daniela A. Mera and Elayna R. Gallea)

Entangled with the Enduar

New Adult Fantasy Romance

The Stones of Fate

(In the Enduar World—Liana's Love Story)

New Adult Fantasy Romance

The Blood Tournaments

Young Adult Dystopian Fantasy Romance

ACKNOWLEDGMENTS

The greatest thanks will always go to my husband, Josué. Writing this book had me digging deep into the dark corners of my soul. No one could see how you supported, held, and cheered me on as I Did The Hard Thing, but I will tell them. I will always shout from the rooftops that you are my greatest love.

As always, to my dog, Biyuel.

My mother, my sister, and my brother and his wife, whom I love deeply. Each book come with memories of what happens in our personal life, and this one will have big ones.

To Margie, for supporting me through another book and a Kickstarter. Thank you for taking all my wild messages in stride. You are one of my best business decisions.

Kourtney, thank you for reading this book and providing me with invaluable comments. This book was very rough in its first drafts and wouldn't have made it forward without you.

Sydney and Chelsea, thank you for editing my book. I appreciate your comments, support, and critique. This book was hard to write and had to go through many rewrites—thank you for carrying me through that.

Elayna, thank you for being my work wife. For all our years alongside each other. Thank you for checking in on me while I am in the trenches.

To Nisha J. Tuli, for being a generous friend. Thank you for helping me with artwork, critiques, blurbs, and transitioning into authoring life. Thank you for sprinting with me. You helped me get this book written.

To Demi Winters, for sprinting with me and killing many a crab dragon in the name of daily word count. You are a lovely, kind soul.

Cassie, my plot muse. Another book was finalized and saved by your brilliant mind. Thank you for being someone who said, *"Actually you CAN"* when I was decidedly talking myself out of it.

To Ophelia Langsley Wells and Fleur DeVillainy for being such a strong source of support in my life. Thank you for sprinting and tackling monsters together. Thank you for holding my hand when I fell apart.

To the artists who brought Meli and Ra'Sa to life. Jaqueline Florencio, Covalienne, Agnieszka Gromulska, Teviense, Lia on Fiverr, E. Kathrin, Nebraska JC, Surya Dextor, and Artscandre—thank you. Your art is the perfect harmony to my writing and I feel so honored to show off your stunning skills.

And finally, to my readers. As time goes on, I find it increasingly humbling to have your support. Thank you for trusting me to write stories you love. While it would still be impossible to list all of you, but I want to say a special thank you to a few IG handles in particular. Namely, reesiecup08, polvodeletras, evenromanceisnerdy, tempest_reign_book_reviewer, noribooreads, _bethsbookcollection_, kiaras_booknook, kels.lovesbooks, bookish_selenovert, karmengallucci, tairen_soul, badwitchesbookcoven, de_boekenplank_van_floor, arielrosereadsandwrites, emeph.writes, balancing_books_and_beauties, spookymess_, taylor.bilyeu, danii_ramage, readingtomyplants, emvz.woodandbooks, spaghootlesreads, thenarnianreader_, zelspov, reading_isa, greeneggsandsambooks, tasha2205s, and countless others.

It took a village to write this novel. I am so grateful I had you all.

No thanks go to: insomnia and occular migraines.

ABOUT THE AUTHOR

Daniela A. Mera was born into a royal Fae family in California. She was a free spirit who loved traveling and cloud watching while laying velvet-soft grass. When she came of age, her mother forced her to travel to Las Vegas in order to kill a dragon and conquer a neighboring kingdom.

The dragon turned out to be a man, whom she fell wildly in love with. The couple ran away to the gentle hills of Mexico where Daniela ate lots of tacos and fruits the size of her head.

Something along those lines, anyway.

She writes whimsical tales full of lore all around the world, full of emotionally available men and women who run the world. She can be found listening to sappy romance ballads while writing scenes meant to emotionally damage her readers.

When not writing, Daniela can be found doing yoga and playing video games. Join her newsletter for freebies!

Visit: http://danielaamera.com/